Lucky Santangelo Novels by Jackie Collins

Dangerous Kiss
Vendetta: Lucky's Revenge
Lady Boss
Lucky
Chances

Also by Jackie Collins

Deadly Embrace
Hollywood Wives—The New Generation
Lethal Seduction
L.A. Connections—Power, Obsession, Murder, Revenge
Thrill!
Hollywood Kids
American Star
Rock Star
Hollywood Husbands
Lovers & Gamblers
Hollywood Wives
The World Is Full of Divorced Women
The Love Killers
Sinners
The Bitch
The Stud
The World Is Full of Married Men

HOLLYWOOD

DIVORCES

JACKIE COLLINS

DOUBLEDAY LARGE PRINT HOME LIBRARY EDITION

SIMON & SCHUSTER

New York London Toronto Sydney Singapore

This Large Print Edition, prepared especially for Doubleday Large Print Home Library, contains the complete, unabridged text of the original Publisher's Edition.

Simon & Schuster
Rockefeller Center
1230 Avenue of the Americas
New York, NY 10020

SIMON & SCHUSTER and colophon are registered trademarks of Simon & Schuster, Inc.

Manufactured in the United States of America

ISBN 0-7394-4009-8

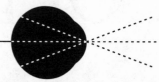

This Large Print Book carries the
Seal of Approval of N.A.V.H.

For
Tracy, Tiffany, and Rory
Didn't I say—girls can do anything.

And for
India, Dylan, Ben, Chloe, Jordan, and Austin
You are the sunshine of my life.

And for
Oscar and Frank
You have my heart forever.

HOLLYWOOD

DIVORCES

CHAPTER

1

Shelby Cheney took a long, deep breath and prepared to make her entrance. Head up. Shoulders back. Superwatt smile. Artfully windswept shoulder-length raven hair. Dazzling Badgley Mishka lace gown cut down to Cuba. Diamonds at her throat and ears. Movie star husband by her side.

Shelby Cheney had it all. Or did she?

Tonight she was at the Cannes Film Festival with her husband, Linc Blackwood. Each had a movie to promote.

Hers: an edgy drama about a woman

on the brink of a total collapse—a thirty-something sex addict who reveals more than her mental breakdown on-screen, with nobody around to help her. And of course, one blistering sex scene, because Shelby had all the attributes; and since this movie smelled of an Oscar nomination, she hadn't minded showing them.

His: a tough-guy superhero movie. Hard-boiled cop. Sexy. Sardonic. A sequel to his two previous blockbuster hits playing the same character. Linc Blackwood, once one of the highest-paid box office stars in the world, was still up there.

Tonight Linc wore a midnight blue Armani tuxedo with a dark blue silk shirt. No tie. Muscular body. Clouded green eyes. Longish dark hair. Stubbled chin. Crooked nose—broken in a fight or two before he was famous and powerful enough to insist on a double for his more dangerous stunts.

Shelby and Linc. A movie star couple set to thrill the throngs of fans who eagerly watched them as they made their way—flanked by various publicity people and assorted flacks—into the Palais des Festivals, where Shelby's film, *Rapture,* was about to be shown.

"Shit," Linc mumbled under his breath, waving at the paparazzi while flashing his trademark grin. "I need a fuckin' drink."

"No you don't," Shelby managed to reply, as she smiled for the assorted cameras and TV crews lined up three deep, all shoving and struggling for the best shots.

Linc's drinking was a big bone of contention between them. He'd been in rehab twice. It hadn't done him much good—he was still a hard boozer whenever the mood took him. And tonight the mood was *definitely* taking him.

Shelby knew he'd had a couple of shots at the hotel, and now he was muttering that he wanted more. This was not a good sign. She had hoped to relax and enjoy the night, but if Linc was on the prowl, she'd have to spend the evening watching him to make sure he didn't embarrass them both— something he was quite capable of doing. When Linc got drunk it was disaster time. He either became belligerent and ready to pick a fight, or got compulsively amorous, flirting outrageously with every woman in sight. Both were equally unappealing traits.

Damn! Why couldn't she simply revel in her triumph? Because everyone had assured her that her performance in *Rapture* *was* a triumph—everyone except Linc, who'd seen a rough cut of her movie and immediately remarked that she looked tired and drawn and that the cinematographer hadn't lit her well.

Didn't he *get* it? She was playing a woman on the verge; she wasn't *supposed* to look her usual, gorgeous self.

The truth was that even though he'd never admit it, Linc was jealous, eaten up with envy that she was starring in a movie that was destined to receive critical acclaim *and* box office success—a combination he'd never quite managed to achieve.

The one thing Linc craved was respect and acknowledgment for his acting talent, not merely his physical antics. His movies still made megamillions, but his reviews were abysmal. This drove him slightly crazy—especially now that Shelby was about to make a major impact as a serious actress. She had no doubt he loved her, but things were about to change for her career-wise, and she wasn't sure how Linc would take it.

Sometimes she worried that maybe she should give it all up, stay home, and do nothing but look after Linc, because even after four years of a somewhat turbulent marriage, she still loved him, in spite of his drinking and womanizing and going off on binges with his gang of asshole buddies, whom she'd never been able to persuade him to get rid of. Lurking within the macho movie star was a little boy lost, and the little boy was always there, sweet and needy and—most important—all hers. Especially at night when they were in bed together and she snuggled up behind him and fell asleep breathing his smell, feeling his warmth, loving every inch of him. It wasn't all about sex, and Shelby liked that. Linc was her man, and she desperately hoped that he always would be.

Nobody knew the real Linc except her. Nobody had any clue about his abusive childhood, with a father who'd beaten him daily when the old man wasn't busy battering Linc's mother, a gentle woman who was simply not capable of protecting her only son from a man who victimized them both.

Linc had one sister, Connie, who, at forty-eight, was six years older than her brother. They shared a tough family history. When Linc was twelve his dad had beaten his

mom to death, then turned the gun on himself—blowing his brains out all over the
kitchen walls, leaving Connie and Linc to
fend for themselves.

To her credit, Connie had never let her
brother down. She'd taken a job as a waitress, managing to keep him out of foster
homes until he'd run off to L.A. at the age of
seventeen and started on the long and
sometimes treacherous road to success.
Connie was a dedicated lesbian who refused to have anything to do with men. She
lived with her girlfriend, Suki, on a ranch in
Montana—bought for her by Linc. The two
of them rarely left it.

On his own, Linc had achieved phenomenal success, and Shelby loved and admired him for it. On the other hand, Linc
Blackwood was a handful, and Shelby
wasn't sure how long she could continue
putting up with all his games.

She wanted a baby.

He didn't.

She wanted to lead a less public life.

He didn't.

She wanted him not to flirt with every
woman who gave him the "available" signal.
And they *all* did. Linc was a movie star; he

might as well have FUCK ME emblazoned on his forehead.

Shelby, however, was completely loyal to him. It wasn't part of her moral code to even contemplate having an affair. Her parents had been together forty years, and they *still* held hands, exchanged loving looks, and indulged in secret conversations. She often dreamed of a marriage as good as theirs.

"Shelby!" screamed the photographers. "Over here! Look over here! Shelby! *Shelby! Shelby!*"

As their pleas grew more frantic, Shelby obliged, turning her head this way and that, holding everything in, making sure she didn't fall out of her daringly low-cut gown. She tossed back her mane of raven hair, her hazel eyes wide and appealing. Image was incredibly important, and even though Shelby was only thirty-two, she was well aware of the hordes of up-and-coming actresses *rabid* for their chance at stardom. They all wanted to be her. They all wanted to have her career, be married to a movie star, and live in a magnificent Beverly Hills mansion.

Tough luck, girls, she thought, smile fixed firmly in place. *Linc Blackwood is mine.* All *mine. And in spite of his many shortcomings, I definitely intend to hold on to him. So back off. Linc Blackwood is taken.*

"I *want* Linc Blackwood," Lola Sanchez said in her low-down, husky voice, not looking at Elliott Finerman, the producer of her upcoming movie, who sat in the back of the limo next to her, while her husband, Matt Seel, a former professional tennis player, perched opposite them, sitting beside her publicist, Faye Margolis.

"We've gone over this a dozen times," Elliott said, barely able to contain his annoyance. "I was thinking Ben Affleck or Matthew Mc—"

"No!" Lola interrupted sharply. "I *want* Linc Blackwood. And if you *can't* or *won't* get him, then I suggest you find yourself another leading lady."

Bitch! Elliott thought. *Who do you think you are? Four years ago you were a waitress at Denny's, now you're telling me what to do. Me, Elliott Finerman, producer of over thirty successful movies.*

"Well?" Lola demanded imperiously, tilting her pointed chin.

"If you insist, sweetie," Elliott said, forcing himself to sound calm. "However, I do think—"

"Fine," she said, cutting him off again. "Then if Linc says yes, we're all set."

Elliott stared out the car window. It was glaringly obvious that this diva couldn't care less *what* he thought. It was all Anna Cameron's fault. Anna, head honcho at Live Studios, had agreed to green-light his latest movie, *New York State of Mind,* only if he signed Lola Sanchez. And Lola had agreed to sign only if she had leading-man approval.

"Give it to her," Anna had said. "You and I will steer her in the right direction."

Sure, Elliott thought bitterly. *Some right direction.*

From the get-go Lola had started mentioning Linc Blackwood. He'd honestly believed that he could sweet-talk her out of her choice, but no, Lola wanted Linc, and she was one determined, spoiled, full-of-her-own-importance movie star.

Elliott couldn't understand why she was so insistent. She didn't even *know* Linc, and when she did get to meet him, she'd be sorry. Linc Blackwood was trouble, making outrageous demands on the set and screwing other men's wives when he thought he could get away with it. Elliott had personal experience with the way Linc operated. He used some of the oldest lines going, and yet women still fell for them. Not that they needed much pushing—when it came to movie stars, women were open-leg city, ready to give it up for a glance, a smile. Elliott should know; his ex had been no exception. Lynsey Fraser, a pretty but easily influenced young actress. Three months after marrying her he'd foolishly given her a minor role in one of his movies that starred Linc Blackwood. A week of location later he'd caught her servicing Linc with a blow job in his trailer.

That had been ten years and one divorce ago. Needless to say, Elliott had chosen not to work with Linc since.

Elliott felt sorry for Shelby Cheney. She was a very talented actress and an extremely desirable woman, although obviously not too smart, because apparently she was completely unaware of what a cheating piece of crap her husband really was.

"If you're absolutely sure—," Elliott began, in an uptight voice.

"Yes!" Lola snapped, not giving him time to finish his sentence. "I'm sure."

Elliott fumed. *Diva cunt!* America thought she was such a sweet and sexy piece, when in fact she was a twenty-four-year-old killer bitch who happened to have been blessed with long legs, big breasts, full sensual lips, glowing skin, and a stone-cold heart. America was in love with her legs, her lips, and her wide, appealing smile. They remained unaware of her failings as a human being.

On second thought, Elliott mused, maybe Lola and Linc deserved each other. Between the two of them they could self-destruct their way out of the business. As long as *New York State of Mind* was a box office smash, what did he care? Let them create chaos and garner major publicity. After the movie was launched they could ruin each other's miserable lives.

Movie stars! A bunch of overinflated assholes with a short shelf life. Five years down the line people would be saying, "Lola who?"

Unfortunately, Linc Blackwood would probably always be around. Like Stallone, Willis, and Schwarzenegger, he was a survivor in a tough business. Plus his movies still made money, especially in foreign and video and DVD sales.

"We're almost there," Faye Margolis announced. Faye was a formidable woman in her late forties, with iron gray bobbed hair and an unbeatable knowledge of the P.R. business. Any celebrity in Faye's care was guaranteed maximum exposure *and* copy approval. Faye protected her select list of clients with a fierce loyalty.

"How do I look?" Lola asked, exhibiting a rare flash of insecurity.

"Hot!" enthused Matt, who was quite hot himself, with his athlete's body, long dirty-blond hair, and small Vandyke beard.

Lola ignored him. "Faye?" she asked tentatively.

"Make sure you stand up straight," Faye ordered in her smoke-enhanced voice. "That dress is a walking hazard, and don't you forget it, or your breast'll fall out."

Lola giggled. Only Faye could get away with speaking to her in such a fashion. Now that she was a big star she demanded respect from all who came in contact with her.

"If her tits fall out she'll make every front page in France," Matt sniggered.

"Don't you mean *the world?*" Lola corrected, throwing him a withering glance.

"If you say so, honey," Matt agreed, suitably abashed.

They had been married for five months. As far as Lola was concerned the honeymoon phase was way over, although Matt had yet to realize it.

They'd gotten married on a billionaire's Malibu estate in a blaze of publicity, with helicopters hovering overhead, paparazzi hanging out of trees, and a star-studded guest list of people they hardly knew. An English magazine paid two million dollars for exclusive pictures of the happy couple, and Faye had made sure that everything happened exactly the way she planned it. "No mistakes" was Faye's motto, and anyone who made one was permanently off Faye's extensive payroll.

Lola wasn't quite so thrilled anymore. She got bored easily, and apart from beachboy looks and a buff body, Matt did not bring a lot to the party. He'd given up professional tennis, preferring to leech off her. When she'd complained about his lack of activity, he'd assured her that he was writing a screenplay, and also planning to take acting classes.

Great! Why hadn't he confided that he had aspirations to be in show business *before* she'd married him?

Here's what *he* didn't know. She married him only to preserve her public image as *the* sexy superstar of the new millennium. Forget about Halle Berry, Jennifer Lopez, and Angelina Jolie. Lola Sanchez was *it,* and she had to keep her credibility level right up there. Before her marriage to Matt, she'd been indulging in a high-profile romance with Tony Alvarez, a brilliant Latino movie director who some considered to be the Pedro Almodóvar of his generation, except Tony was a product of the Bronx, so the three movies he'd directed were pure Americana with an edge.

Tony's problem was that he had an ongoing drug habit, and in spite of a couple of well-publicized arrests for possession, and a lengthy probation, he still managed to get into trouble. Once his bad-boy ways began reflecting negatively on Lola's image, her advisers had warned her that she'd better distance herself from him, as it was becoming increasingly possible that he might have to serve a few months in jail for supposedly dealing—which everyone knew was bull-shit, but since Tony was a celebrity, the authorities had to look like they were doing *something.*

Lola, ever mindful of her public image, had reluctantly broken off their engagement and hurriedly married Matt, who could not believe his luck and had willingly signed an ironclad prenuptial agreement.

Now she was stuck with him. But not for long. Lola had plans, and those plans included Linc Blackwood.

Cat Harrison was not happy to be at the Cannes Film Festival. Celebrity events were so boring, full of stars with enormous egos. Not that she'd been to that many, but ever since she'd written and directed her first movie, *Wild Child,* a film loosely based on her own somewhat unconventional life, she'd been forced to work the circuit. And ever since her low-budget (try nonexistent-budget) movie had become a cult hit, Cat was flavor of the month.

Big freaking deal. She *hated* being the center of attention. She *loathed* having to get dressed up and play nice to the money-men and movie big shots who were hot to finance her next project.

"Ya gotta do it, luv," advised her Australian musician husband, Jump Jagger—no relation to Mick, although he wished.

"Why?" she'd argued.

" 'Cause it'll be good karma for us both. An' I could do with a bit of karma."

Trust Jump to put himself in the mix. He had an annoying habit of always putting himself first. It didn't matter, though, because she was crazy about him.

The child of divorce, Cat had grown up dividing her time between an eccentric English mother and a totally insane American father, which meant that she'd spent most of her childhood drifting between the two countries, until at seventeen she'd decided she needed her own space and her own career (Daddy was a hugely successful sculptor and Mummy an award-winning photographer). So she'd moved to New York, where she eventually met Jump—who'd saved her from a downward spiral of drugs and craziness. She was heading along a bad road, and he'd managed to pull her back just in time. Then they did the conventional thing, got married, and settled into a SoHo loft.

While Jump worked on his music, Cat took various gigs as a nanny, dog walker, and personal assistant to a sullen but extremely creative theater director. One weekend, full of ideas and enthusiasm, she'd started writing a screenplay. Six weeks later she began shooting her film on an old Sony Handycam she'd taken from her father's basement. She'd used their weird and wonderful assortment of friends as actors, while Jump had worked on putting together an edgy and interesting sound track with his group. *Voilà!* Instant movie.

A friend's uncle had introduced her to a small distributor, who'd picked up her film, and from the first screening—like *The Blair Witch Project* before it—the buzz began. First there was a website, then there were two, then three. Within weeks there were twenty-one websites devoted to discussing *Wild Child.*

Cat was beyond excited, until reluctantly she was thrust into the spotlight. The media loved her. It helped that she was now nineteen, tall and agile, with short, spiky, natural blond hair, olive green eyes, and a challenging face with high cheekbones. She could've easily been a model or an actress. Neither profession interested her; she got her kicks out of being on the other side of the camera, the side where she was able to maintain a certain degree of control.

Merrill Zandack, head of Zandack Films, had taken over distribution of *Wild Child,* and now he was planning to finance her next project, *Caught,* a quirky film she'd written about a womanizing con man and a duplicitous female undercover cop. Hence her visit to the Cannes Film Festival.

"Be nice to everyone, kitten," Merrill had told her when she'd arrived. "You're on the fast track."

"I'll be nice if *you* stop calling me 'kitten,'" she'd responded, a tad irritably. It pissed her off that men thought it was quite okay to call women cutesy names. How would *he* like it if she called *him* "puppy"?

Merrill, a plump, balding man, who spent most of his time sweating profusely while sucking on a large Cuban cigar, found Cat to be a refreshing presence. He admired the way she didn't kowtow to anyone. He enjoyed her nonconformist attitude. Merrill had a gut instinct for talent, and if Cat kept her head and didn't annoy too many people with her ballsy approach, she was destined to soar.

Shelby did the dance and she did it well. Linc did it better. Linc was an expert at making everyone feel they were his best friend. He had charm and then some. Shelby watched him as he flirted with a very svelte looking Sharon Stone. She got a kick out of watching him when he didn't know she was looking. He was *so* damn sexy.

"You're a beauty, hon," Merrill Zandack said, puffing on his cigar as he lumbered up behind her. "Can't wait to see your movie."

"Thanks, Merrill," she said, turning toward the powerful studio head as he planted a sweaty kiss on her cheek, leaving an irritating wet spot that she was dying to wipe off.

"You an' me gotta work together," Merrill continued, blowing a stream of expensive cigar smoke directly into her face. "I hear tell you're dynamite in tonight's flick."

"You do?" she said, surreptitiously attempting to wipe her cheek dry with the back of her hand.

"I was supposed to give it a private screenin'," he wheezed. "Never had time."

"Sorry to hear that."

"Naw, this way's better," he said, blowing more cigar smoke in her face as he managed a not-so-discreet peek down her cleavage.

She took a step back and smiled politely at Merrill's date, a statuesque Anjelica Huston clone. Since his wife had died several years ago, Merrill had rarely been seen with the same woman twice. He appeared to favor a long line of interchangeable brunettes, women he never saw fit to introduce.

"Well . . . I do hope you enjoy it, Merrill," Shelby said, once more glancing over at Linc, who was now in an intense conversation with Woody Allen. No rescue there.

"You look beautiful, hon," Merrill repeated.

"Thanks," she murmured, and to her relief, Merrill spotted Lola Sanchez making a much admired entrance, and immediately headed in her direction, his brunette date trailing regally behind him.

Shelby's appointed P.R. person, a young Frenchwoman with her hair worn in a tight bun, and a sulky, turned-down mouth, hovered nearby. "Do you wish to meet with the reporter from *Paris Match* now?" the woman asked.

Shelby shook her head. The last thing she wanted to do was speak with a journalist. "Tomorrow, at the press conference," she said.

The woman's thin lips tightened. "He has to leave for Paris early in the morning. He will not be able to attend the press conference."

A couple of years ago Shelby would've said yes to anything. Two years of therapy and she'd learned to say no.

"If he's so anxious to speak with me," she suggested, "then perhaps he should stay over."

Before the P.R. woman could reply, Linc reappeared and took her arm. "C'mon, sweetheart," he said warmly, winking at the P.R. woman. "Let's go take our seats."

Shelby nodded, her stomach fluttering. This was her big night and she was determined to relax and enjoy it.

CHAPTER
2

Cat was staying on Merrill Zandack's yacht, a luxurious ninety-footer with six guest bedrooms and a staff of twenty. It was some setup. She wished Jump could see it as she prowled around her cabin getting herself together, finally taking a long look in the bathroom mirror, squinting at her full-length reflection. She'd made a supreme effort. Low-slung Juicy Couture jeans, showing off her finely toned abs and a recent diamond piercing in her navel; a black Rolling Stones cutoff tee, Loree

Rodkin chains and crosses hanging around her neck; and large gold hoop earrings.

Her outfit probably wasn't everyone's idea of how to impress at a big film festival, but screw it, at least she was comfortable. She hadn't worn a dress in years and she wasn't about to start now. Besides, Jump was on tour with his band in his native Australia, and without him by her side she felt ever so slightly vulnerable.

Whenever she went anywhere by herself, guys came on to her. She did not get off on the attention. Cat was a one-man girl, and in spite of her fiery independence she kind of missed having Jump beside her. They did everything together. Or at least they used to, before her career took off at such a startling pace and Jump decided to hit the road. Not that she minded him getting out there; it was something they'd both been working toward, and the success of his sound track had thankfully helped him score a few good gigs. Opening for mega rock legend Kris Phoenix in Sydney was a *real* break. Jump and his band were *totally* psyched. She was happy for him, although she still couldn't help wishing he was with her tonight.

A knock, and Jonas Brown, Merrill Zandack's diligent assistant, put his head around the door.

"The tender is ready to take us to shore," Jonas announced.

"Where's Merrill?" she asked, staring at Jonas, who was the complete opposite of his loudmouthed, somewhat uncouth boss. For a start, Jonas was young—probably still in his late twenties. And quite good looking in a low-key, not at all her type, way.

"Mr. Zandack has already left," Jonas said. "He asked me to tell you that he'll meet you at the premiere."

"You mean I've got to go there on my own?" she complained, hating the thought of walking in by herself.

"*I* will accompany you," Jonas said.

"I don't know why he wants me there," she grumbled, reaching for her fringed purse.

"Mr. Zandack feels it is important for you to be seen," Jonas said, his narrow gray eyes inspecting her outfit. "Is that what you're wearing?" he asked, unable to conceal the note of disapproval in his tone.

"No," she snapped, annoyed that he

seemed to be judging her sense of style. "I'm planning on changing into a black Prada uniform so I can look exactly like you."

"I wasn't criticizing," he said quickly.

"Yes, you were," she retorted, adding an airy "That's okay, I'm totally secure in the way I dress. Who needs affirmation?"

"Then we should go," Jonas said unblinkingly. "Mr. Zandack does not appreciate being kept waiting."

"Glad you shared that with me," she drawled with a sarcastic edge. "Wouldn't want to be the one who kept the big man waiting."

Lola spotted the back of Linc walking into the theater. Damn! She'd wanted to impress him. And who wouldn't be impressed with the way the cameras were flashing just for her, while every journalist in the place clamored for her attention?

Linc Blackwood might be married to a movie star, but she, Lola Sanchez, was *the* movie star of the moment. Nobody was hotter or more desirable.

A big difference from her last encounter

with Mr. Blackwood. Oh yes, things were very different then.

Flash Back Six Years

Lucia Conchita Sanchez. A pretty girl of eighteen. A would-be actress-singer-dancer getting nowhere fast. Waitressing by day and playing records by night—helping out Carlos, her disc jockey boyfriend, who worked three nights a week at a Hollywood club. Lucia had long, chestnut brown hair that reached below her waist, and a curvaceous body. She lived at home, in Silverlake, with Claudine, her half-black, half–Native American mother, and her philandering Mexican father, Louis Sanchez, a small-time boxer who considered himself a regular stud. She had two older, married sisters, Isabelle and Selma, and a lazy, out-of-work brother, Louis Junior, who aspired to be exactly like his dad. Lucia couldn't wait to leave home.

At school she had excelled at singing, dancing, and drama class. Acting was her passion, so as soon as she graduated high school she had set out to pursue an acting career. She was very ambitious and quite determined to break into show business. Problem was, nobody wanted to hire her. She couldn't even get an agent to take her on. "You're too ethnic looking" seemed to be the general opinion.

Ethnic looking? As far as she was concerned she was gorgeous, with her sultry looks, smooth olive skin, and voluptuous body. Okay, so she wasn't cookie-cutter pretty, but she had her own particular style.

After numerous rejections and no callbacks on the auditions she did manage to get into, she tried approaching a modeling agency. "Too fat," announced a skinny bitch with legs like a couple of twigs and no ass.

Too fat. Ridiculous! Just because she did not conform to Hollywood's obsession with thinness. She went on a diet anyway—eschewing Claudine's delicious fried chicken and her dad's favorite enchiladas.

Her parents thought she was crazy. Her papa sat her down one night and told her that she had absolutely no chance of making it, and since she'd been quite good at math in school, she should get herself a proper job, working in a bank like Selma, where she had a chance of eventual promo-

tion. *"Waitressin' ain't gonna take you nowhere,"* Louis informed her.

Like boxing was such a big deal. Louis Sanchez had two cauliflower ears, scars all over his face, and a permanent limp. It certainly didn't seem to stop women from throwing themselves at him.

Her mother was a real beauty, with exotic features, waist-length hair, and a sexy, rounded figure—maintained in spite of having given birth to four children.

Lucia liked to think she'd inherited the best of both her parents in the looks department. She had her mama's long legs, big bosom, and thick chestnut hair. And her papa's slightly flat nose, seductive brown eyes, and full lips. "Lover's lips," Louis was fond of saying. "They run in the family."

Yeah, *Lucia thought.* Those lips of yours have run all over the neighborhood.

Sex was not an open subject in the Sanchez household. Although everyone knew about Louis's indiscretions, they were never mentioned. When Lucia was old enough to hear the stories about her unfaithful dad, she was shocked. It always amazed her that Claudine allowed him to get away with it, and never said anything.

As soon as Lucia hit puberty, boys were all over her. They coveted her big breasts, fine ass, and the flirtatious attitude she'd inherited from her dad.

"Do not give it up," Mama had warned her, wagging a skinny finger in Lucia's face. "Let 'em look, watch the poor fools drool, then let 'em beg for more. You give it up, girl, an' you'll be good an' sorry. The last thing you want is a baby growin' in your belly."

Those ominous words were enough to frighten her off sex, until at sixteen she fell for a bad-boy rapper who lived down the street, and after several delirious months with him she did get pregnant. Claudine was so mad that she refused to speak to her daughter for weeks. Louis was more understanding. He took her for an abortion at the local clinic. Selma came too. It was one of the worst days of her life.

After that experience she swore off sex, taking it no further than an occasional blow job—and that took place only if she really liked the boy.

Oral sex was a two-way street with Carlos, and although, when he had her skirt around her waist and her bra off in the back of his car, he pleaded with her to let him take it further, she held fast. No more abortions for Lucia Conchita Sanchez. She'd learned her lesson.

One night Carlos informed her that he'd scored a gig disc-jockeying at a fancy party in Bel Air, and he wanted her to assist him. For a moment she was too excited to speak. Bel Air. Stomping ground of the rich and famous. Maybe she'd finally be discovered, or at the very least meet an agent who was prepared to represent her.

She did not let on to Carlos how psyched she was. Carlos was kind of laid-back, with long greasy hair and gaunt rock star looks. Music was his thing; he was a master at putting together the sounds that everyone wanted to hear. According to all their friends, Carlos had a future.

The party, thrown by megaproducer Freddy Krane, was taking place in Freddy's magnificent old mansion at the top of Bel Air. It was reached by driving up a long, winding, palm-lined driveway.

Lucia sat next to Carlos in his 1968 souped-up silver Mustang, savoring every moment. When they arrived, she helped him set up his equipment out by the enormous black-bottomed swimming pool. There were servants and caterers, bartenders and waiters swarming everywhere, preparing for the evening's festivities.

Lucia took it all in—the hundreds of votive candles in exquisite crystal holders surrounding the pool, the lavish flower centerpieces on every table, the white-and-silver tablecloths and black silk napkins. She willed herself to remember every detail so that she could tell Mama, Isabelle, and Selma.

Although quite impressed, she forced herself to maintain a cool exterior as she sorted through Carlos's extensive CD and record collection, setting everything out in neat piles. Carlos was very particular; he liked things just right.

There were times she daydreamed that if she didn't get a break in show business soon, perhaps she should consider marrying Carlos. He was hot to screw her, so she knew it would be no problem nudging him into a proposal, if that's what she decided she wanted.

Would marrying Carlos be such a bad thing?

Maybe not.

Once the party got going it was a blast, full of faces Lucia recognized from the popular entertainment magazines she devoured each week. It could be her imagination, but after a while she began to think that Freddy Krane kept glancing her way. Freddy, a big, sloppy-looking man, with an unruly reddish beard and small piggy eyes, was old, at least fifty, and that was ten years older than her dad.

Lucia had dressed for the occasion in a short brown fake-leather skirt (unfortunately the real thing was far too expensive) and a midriff-baring white tee shirt that showed off her large breasts, encased in a flimsy bra, her nipples at attention through the thin material. Her long chestnut hair hung below her ass—she hadn't cut it since she was eight.

She knew she looked hot. A couple of the waiters sniffed around trying to get her phone number. She politely declined, although she was secretly pleased they'd asked.

Carlos played and she swayed, moving her body in an undulating, provocative way. The sounds were primo, everything from N.W.A. to Santana to Mötley Crüe, with

*plenty of Marvin Gaye and Smokey Robin-
son thrown in for the nostalgia junkies.*

*Yes, Freddy Krane was definitely taking
notice, even though he was surrounded by
a bevy of blond beauties. Earlier in the
evening one of the waiters (a would-be actor) had given her a list of the host's credits.
According to the waiter, Freddy Krane spe-
cialized in high-budget action movies and
had worked with all the macho stars from
Eastwood to Schwarzenegger. "He's the
real deal," the waiter confided. "Word one
from him, an' you're in his movie. You
should go for it."*

*"No thanks," Lucia retorted. She craved
stardom, but not at any price.*

*Just before midnight she spotted Linc
Blackwood walking in. Linc Blackwood! Her
favorite movie star! She'd seen all his
movies at least three times. She could
hardly believe it!*

*She nudged Carlos, who could have
cared less. Carlos wasn't into movie stars,
he was into his record collection, his precious Mustang, smoking a little weed, and
getting a lot of head.*

*"Look who it is," she said in a low, excited
voice.*

"*Stay cool,*" Carlos responded, throwing her an irritable look.

"I can't stay cool!" *she wanted to scream.* "It's Linc Blackwood—recently voted the Sexiest Man Alive by *People* magazine. How can I possibly stay cool?"

She was breathless, in awe, her stomach churning. There were other famous faces at the party, but as far as she was concerned they meant nothing. Linc Blackwood was it.

She kept her eyes on him, checking out his every move. Women began swarming all over him, silicone-breasted blondes with overteased hair and all-American smiles. He didn't seem to take much notice. He sat at a poolside table drinking and holding court. After a while he was joined by Freddy Krane and several more gorgeous girls. Freddy kept patting him on the back and howling with laughter.

Lucia moved her body to the sounds, giving a raw and sexy performance, the music sweeping away her inhibitions. She saw Freddy nudge Linc and gesture in her direction. Then, to her delight, the two men began watching her. She glanced at Carlos, who didn't appear to have noticed. Her heart started beating fast—she was about to be discovered! After a few minutes Linc Blackwood was on his feet, holding a drink, pointing her out to one of the many girls who surrounded him.

The chosen girl nodded, then circumvented the pool and hurried over. "Hi," the girl said.

"Hi," Lucia replied. She wasn't stupid; she knew the girl had been sent on a mission.

"I'm Zara Light," the girl said in a distinctly English accent. "And you are . . . ?"

"Lucia."

"Okay, Lucia," Zara said briskly. "It's your lucky night. Linc and Freddy have requested that you join them for a drink."

"They did?" she responded breathlessly.

"That's why I'm here," said Zara, a pretty girl with dark curly hair.

"When?" Lucia asked blankly.

"Now," Zara said, rolling her eyes.

Lucia glanced at Carlos. He was spinning away—caught up in an extended track of Ja Rule. Did she have to ask his permission?

No. It wasn't as if they were married or anything. She was free to do whatever she wanted. And she wanted to go meet Linc Blackwood—her living, breathing fantasy.

She grabbed Carlos's arm, causing a nasty glitch on the record.

"Fuck!" he exclaimed.

"I'll be back," she said quickly, and without any further explanation she was on her way to meet her favorite movie star.

Twenty-five minutes later, Lucia Conchita Sanchez and Linc Blackwood were rolling around on top of the king-size water bed in Freddy Krane's master bedroom, clothes half off.

"I . . . I can hardly believe this is happening," she murmured, completely starstruck.

"Believe it, kiddo," Linc responded, pulling off her tee shirt. "You got great tits," he added, expertly unclipping her bra and flinging it across the room. "They're real, aren't they?" She nodded speechlessly. "You got any idea how hard it is to come across real tits in this town?" he complained, caressing her nipples with his fingertips.

She didn't know and she didn't care. She only knew that from the moment she'd met him, her destiny was about to be fulfilled, and nothing else mattered.

When Linc wanted to, he could handle a woman in bed exactly the way he knew they all craved. He gave Lucia his full attention, enjoying her full, ripe breasts, the silky mound of black pubic hair between her long legs, the smooth curve of her generous ass.

He didn't go for the gold immediately; many women along the way had taught him that plenty of foreplay led to real pleasure. So he got her hot first, spending time on her breasts, sucking on her large, erect nipples until she began moaning aloud.

Then he spread her legs, going down on her as if he really enjoyed it—which he didn't. But what the hell, this one tasted sweeter than most.

Lucia was dazed and confused. How had this happened? She was not the kind of girl to jump into bed with someone on a first date. And this was not even a date. And she had a boyfriend, so obviously this was total insanity.

Or was it? Linc Blackwood was her hero, and how many times would she get an opportunity to be with the man of her dreams? An opportunity to be with a man who had the tongue of an angel or a devil . . . or . . . She gasped, struggling for breath, grabbing a pillow to cover her face as he went down on her. She was half embarrassed, half thrilled, half ashamed, half ecstatic.

What was she doing?

What was he doing?

Whatever it was, she was not stopping him.

They stayed in Freddy Krane's bed all night, indulging in everything Lucia had ever dreamed of doing with Linc Blackwood. He made love to her every way imaginable, and he did not use a condom.

"You're clean, aren't you?" he asked at one point. "A virgin, right?"

If that's what he wanted to think, it was okay with her. And she didn't even care if he made her pregnant, because this time things were different, this time he would marry her and they'd live happily ever after in a big Hollywood mansion—the one she'd seen photographs of in People. *And she'd become a movie star too. All her dreams would be realized.*

Eventually she fell asleep in his arms, sticky and naked and satisfied.

The next morning she was awakened by someone shaking her shoulder. She opened her eyes. The events of the night before came flooding back. "Linc," she murmured, rolling over to greet him.

Only it wasn't Linc, it was Freddy Krane, standing beside the bed, bleary-eyed in a striped toweling bathrobe that flapped open, revealing that he had nothing on underneath.

"Ohmigod!" she muttered, grabbing a sheet to cover herself. "Why are you here?"

"Hate ta tell ya, doll," Freddy said, pulling his robe closed. "Ya happen t' be sleepin' in my bed."

"Where's Linc?" she asked, alarmed.

"He hadda go, some kinda early meeting. Asked me t' tell ya he had fun last night."

She sat up abruptly, her mind racing in a hundred different directions. "Is that all he said?"

"Ya gotta realize Linc's a busy man," Freddy said, eyeing her as if she were prey and he were a hungry tiger.

"So . . . so you mean he's gone?"

"That's what I said."

Suddenly realization dawned, the ramifications of what she'd done becoming horribly clear. She'd made love to a man she hardly knew. She'd spent the night with him. She'd done everything with him, opening up sexually in a way she never had before. And now he was gone. God! He might be a movie star, but what kind of man left her in a strange bed without a word?

"Hate ta rush you, only ya gotta move it," Freddy said. "You can use the shower in the guest room, then hustle your cute ass outta here."

"Where's my . . . boyfriend?" she asked hesitantly.

"You got a boyfriend?" he said disbelievingly.

"The disc jockey, Carlos. Where is he?"

"Oh yeah, that's the dude who was askin' 'bout you," Freddy said, yawning. "Told him you were with Linc."

"What did he say?"

"Guess he was pissed."

"Oh God!" she moaned, shaking her head.

"Don't sweat it, he got paid cash for last night's gig," Freddy said, clearing his throat. "Ya gotta get goin', puss. I'm a busy man."

She was too embarrassed to look at him. "Can you turn your back?" she muttered.

"Sure, doll, only you don't got nothin' I ain't seen before." He turned around, whistling tunelessly.

She quickly grabbed the sheet, twisting it around her body. Then she gathered her clothes, which were scattered across the floor.

"What's Linc's phone number?" she asked, pausing at the door, convinced there must be some mistake.

"Ya ain't gonna get through, honey," Freddy said sympathetically. "Linc's got assistants an' minders up the kazoo."

"Then I'll give you my number, and you can ask him to call me," she said, knowing she probably sounded like some desperate fan, only she couldn't help herself, she'd honestly thought Linc cared.

"Look, sweetie," Freddy said in a kindly tone. "Ya had a great time. Why doncha leave it at that?"

"Excuse me?" she said, her cheeks blazing with embarrassment. "I'm sure Linc wants to see me again."

"Yeah, yeah, doll, I'm sure too," Freddy said quickly. "But in the meantime, why don't I take ya ta dinner tonight? Who knows—you an' I might hit it off."

"Linc wouldn't like that," she said, fighting back tears, still living with the hope that

this was all some big misunderstanding and that Linc would come walking into the room.

"S'matter of fact, he suggested it," Freddy said casually. "Y'know, seein' as he's so busy an' all."

"I can't believe he'd do that," she said miserably.

"Hey—what's wrong with me?" Freddy said indignantly.

"Nothing," she muttered.

"Then let's get together for dinner. You an' I can have our own party." He winked knowingly. "If ya know what I mean."

She knew what he meant only too well. "No thank you," she said stiffly.

"Suit yourself," he said, shrugging. "Guest room's first on the left. Give me a holler when you're finished an' I'll get the maid t' call you a cab."

She marched from the room with as much dignity as she could muster.

So this was Linc's deal—he'd used and discarded her like a disposable doll, then passed her on to his friend as if she was nothing. What a bastard! How could he treat her in such a way?

Her parents were furious that she'd stayed out all night. She'd had to make up some lame excuse about getting sick and sleeping over at a friend's house. As for Carlos, he wanted nothing more to do with her, and quite frankly she couldn't blame him.

A few weeks later, to her horror, she discovered she was pregnant. How could this happen to her again? Well, she knew how, only it simply wasn't fair.

For several days she contemplated trying to reach Linc Blackwood to tell him. Finally she decided she had too much pride to do that. Her once-favorite movie star had treated her like a one-night whore, and she was not about to beg for his assistance.

Petrified that her parents would find out, she managed to pull a double shift at her waitress job. The extra money allowed her to move from her family's home into a small apartment with her best girlfriend, Cindi Hernandez, who was also trying to break into show business.

Her parents were not pleased. They didn't like Cindi; they considered her a bad influence. Lucia pointed out to them that she was eighteen and they couldn't stop her.

As soon as she could, she scraped together enough money for a cheap abortion.

*It turned out to be a horrifying experience.
No clean clinic. No one to help her. Just
some old gnarly Mexican man in a back
room who forced her to lie on a table,
spread her legs, and treated her as if he was
doing her a big favor.*

*She'd bled for days afterward, until Cindi
forced her to go see a legitimate doctor. The
doctor cleaned up the botched job, and before she left his office, the doctor callously
informed her that she could never get pregnant again.*

His words still haunted her.

In her heart, Lola had always known that
one day she would get her revenge on Linc
Blackwood.

Now, as she watched him enter the theater, she realized that day was enticingly
near.

CHAPTER
3

"We're late," Jonas said, hurrying Cat up the red carpet, steering her by the elbow.

"Not my fault," she responded.

"I wasn't blaming you," he said, still fuming because they'd had to wait for the tender to bring them to shore, even though he'd informed the purser exactly what time they needed it. Once Mr. Zandack left the yacht, the crew seemed to have no regard for anyone else.

"Perhaps you should've picked me up

earlier," Cat suggested, trying to shake free from Jonas's firm grip.

"Mr. Zandack will not be pleased," Jonas said, almost talking to himself.

"What's he gonna do—eat you?" Cat said mockingly, thinking that Jonas was obviously some sort of drama queen who threw a shit fit if everything didn't go his way.

Jonas gave her a blank stare. This girl had a mouth on her and he wasn't sure he liked it. He had long ago decided she was annoying. She had an *I-don't-give-a-shit* attitude and a definite lack of respect toward Merrill Zandack. Mr. Zandack was a powerful force in the film industry, and Jonas felt lucky to be working for him. He was getting an education that would help him tremendously when he struck out on his own, which he planned on doing as soon as he felt he'd learned enough.

A couple of lingering photographers recognized Cat and began calling her name. She didn't know how to react; the whole posing thing was such a downer, she found it plain embarrassing.

"Stop and smile," Jonas commanded, letting go of her elbow and taking a couple of steps back so he was not included in the picture.

Cat offered the photographers a fake smile and an awkward wave before hurrying up the steps of the Palais des Festivals. Jonas had to sprint to keep up with her.

"I hope the movie hasn't started," he said, worrying.

"Bet it has," Cat said, irritating him even further.

"Maybe not."

"Shit!" she exclaimed, stopping short.

"What now?"

"My diamond stud popped out of my navel."

"Jesus!"

"We have to go back and look."

"Look where?" he asked, exasperated.

"On that dumb red carpet. I must've lost it there."

"No," he said firmly, attempting to move her forward.

"It's my first diamond," she complained.

"You're late," he said abruptly. "I'll show you to your seat, then *I'll* go back and look."

"And what if you don't find it?" she demanded, challenging him with her green eyes.

"Mr. Zandack will buy you another one," he said, hurrying her along.

"He will?"

"I'll make sure."

"Didn't know you had that much influence."

"You'd be surprised."

Hmm, she thought, *Jonas isn't as bland as I imagined.*

She wondered if he was gay. Could be. It was difficult to tell—although he was rather well groomed for a straight man, with his perfect haircut, Prada outfit, and well-manicured nails.

Gay?

Definitely.

The movie had started, which put Jonas in a foul mood. He indulged in a quick verbal argument with an uptight French usher who tried to prevent Cat from entering the theater. Jonas spoke excellent French and won the battle.

"This man will show you to your seat," he said to her, giving her a quick shove toward the usher. "I'll see you after the movie. Oh yes, and try not to speak while the film is running. Mr. Zandack doesn't appreciate noise."

"Fine," she said irritably. "And don't come back without my diamond."

"I'll find it," he said, adding a snarly "That's if you had one in the first place."

"Well," she answered slowly, "I guess *you* weren't staring at my belly button like every other guy in the place. But don't *you* worry—I *totally* understand why."

"Oh *please*," Jonas retorted, getting her drift and not liking it one bit.

The uptight usher led her to her seat with the help of a flashlight.

"Where were you?" Merrill growled.

"Shhh," said a large woman sitting in the row of seats behind him.

Cat settled back to watch the movie. She didn't have to explain anything to anyone; that was Jonas's job.

Flash Back Six Years

When Cat Harrison was thirteen, she found herself alone in a villa in the south of France with one of her father's acquaintances, a seventy-three-year-old, extremely famous artist. Her father had left her there while he went to Paris for a few days. They were sup-

posed to be on vacation together—only it never happened.

"What age are you?" the old man asked, peering at her with rheumy eyes.

"What age do you want me to be?" she replied challengingly, tall and tanned and blond and lovely.

"The younger the better," the old man said, leering lasciviously.

She knew what was coming next. Men had been on her case since she was a lot younger than thirteen.

The old man reached for her. She backed away. Even though she was young, she knew how to handle horny old leches—kick him in the balls and run. Only this one was no threat, so she didn't bother. Instead she agreed to his request to pose nude for him, but only if he paid her an exorbitant fee for the privilege of doing so.

The painting he did of her was an enormous success and ended up hanging in the National Gallery. It was called Girl on the Brink. Her father, the renowned sculptor Gable Harrison, was quite amused. Her mother, Bethany Harrison, the photographer critically acclaimed worldwide and legendary beauty, was not.

"If you're going to pose naked, at least get your pubic hair groomed," was her mother's only comment.

Negative! Negative! Negative! When it came to her daughter from her first marriage, Bethany never had anything positive to say. Five times married, Bethany Harrison was jealous of her daughter's burgeoning beauty. She loved Cat, but only on her own terms.

Cat understood. She was an old soul, wise beyond her years. She'd had to grow up fast because both her parents were too busy with their extremely successful, all-consuming careers to pay her much notice.

As an only child, Cat was left very much to her own devices. Discipline from either parent was nonexistent. They both spoiled her with money and material goods, when all she really craved was their love and attention.

She attended school in London, where more often than not she played truant. She'd stuff her book bag with jeans and a tee shirt, make her way to the nearest underground station, change out of her uniform, and hit the movie theaters in the West End. Movies were her passion. She de-

voured everything, from out-of-control teen gross-out movies to films by Tarantino and Scorsese.

Since she looked at least four or five years older than her actual age, she had no trouble attracting men, and picking them up was a habit she soon got used to. Getting them hot was an adventure. The game was to get them out of control, then reveal her true age. Ha! The horrified looks on their faces as they backed off were classic!

She was not interested in boys her own age, finding them to be crass and inexperienced. Not that she went all the way with her conquests. Oh no. Men were not to be trusted. Her father was an example of that. Gable Harrison, an imposing-looking man with his long, snow white hair, frivolous beard, and flirtatious eyes. Cat resembled her mother; she had that tall, blond, perfect thing going. Sometimes she wished she was short and dark and Italian looking, but she had to go with what she had.

By the age of thirteen she'd absolutely perfected the art of sexually doing everything but. She was totally adept at driving grown men crazy—a teenage nymphet with a hot body, a ton of curiosity, and no desire to get knocked up. She felt wise way beyond her years, and was much traveled—vacations in the south of France, Sardinia, and Capri with her father's famous and exotic friends; safaris in Africa and trips through India with her much-married traveling mother and whatever husband Bethany was married to at the time.

Ah . . . Bethany's husbands. They were a trip indeed, each one younger than the last. At least three of them came on to her. Fortunately she knew how to handle horny men—especially horny men married to her mother.

By the age of fourteen she was bored with almost everything. "Been there, done that" was her motto. Then one day, while staying with her father in New York, she met Brad Kravitz, a twenty-something Internet whiz kid who'd made millions of dollars in a very short period of time. She was about to celebrate her fifteenth birthday. Brad was twenty-two. With her father's blessing and her mother's encouragement she moved in with Brad, and it wasn't long before he introduced her to the wonderful world of real sex and recreational drugs.

Good-bye, boredom.
Hello, ecstasy and speed.

Cat wished she had a bag of popcorn to munch on. Jonas would've probably thrown a fit if she'd asked him to find some.

Too bad. The movie was riveting—and good movies and popcorn absolutely went together.

Shelby was nervous. Following her image on the screen was quite an ordeal; all she could see was her faults. Half the time she wanted to cover her eyes, because viewing herself larger than life was never something she enjoyed.

Staring at the screen, she had to admit that *Rapture* was an extraordinarily power-ful movie, and that the performance her di-rector, Russell Savage, had gotten out of her was excellent—quite possibly her best work yet, and certainly her biggest oppor-tunity.

She shot a sideways glance at Linc. His eyes were closed.

How insulting! Her own husband was napping his way through *her* movie. Sometimes he could be the most selfish man in the world.

She nudged him. *"What?"* he muttered, startled.

"You were sleeping," she whispered accusingly.

"I wasn't," he responded, covering a yawn with his hand.

She shook her head in exasperation before refocusing her attention on the screen. Soon it would be over, and people would either love her performance or hate it.

She shivered in anticipation.

Matt's hand descended on his wife's thigh. Lola promptly removed it. She was doing her best to concentrate, studying Shelby Cheney on the big screen, wondering what Linc had seen in her that had made him place a ring on *her* finger. Shelby wasn't *that* hot, kind of ordinary looking. There were hundreds of girls who looked exactly like her in Hollywood. *I'm sexier and younger,* Lola thought. *Why did he choose her and not me? She's too white-bread. No spice. Not exciting like me.*

In spite of all her success, Lola could not get Linc Blackwood off her mind. And the surprising thing was that she had never run into him. Quite remarkable, considering the number of award ceremonies, parties, and premieres she'd attended. A few times she'd spotted him from a distance, and that was it. No face-to-face confrontation.

One night, lying in bed, she'd come up with a plan. She'd recently read an interview in *Premiere* magazine about how Linc was looking to do something different. "I'm getting too old for action movies," he'd said to the female interviewer, self-deprecating grin firmly in place. "So I was thinking of changing directions. Maybe try a romantic comedy." Elliott Finerman's new movie—*New York State of Mind*—was a big-budget romantic comedy with an excellent role for her male costar, who had not yet been cast. It occurred to her that Linc might accept the role if it was offered to him. The only thing she *didn't* know was how he'd react the fateful moment when they *did* come face-to-face. Surely he must know that she was now this famous creature, a fantasy goddess to millions of men? She was actually quite surprised that he'd never attempted to contact her; perhaps he was too embarrassed.

Tonight should be interesting. Linc was at the screening, so no doubt he'd be at the party after, and they were bound to be introduced. She couldn't *wait* to savor the look of surprise on his face, or perhaps the look of lust when he saw her.

Ha! He could lust away, because he was *never* getting anywhere near her again. And when he accepted the role in her movie, she would torture him with her quite considerable charms.

She would not be satisfied until she brought Linc Blackwood to his fucking knees.

Matt's hand was investigating her thigh again. This time she gave him a sharp slap on the wrist.

"Wassamatter?" he mumbled.

"Don't," she hissed.

"Why not?"

"Because I don't want you to."

Faye, sitting on the other side of her, leaned forward. "Something wrong?" Faye whispered.

"No, everything's fine," Lola said, returning her gaze to the screen. "In fact, everything's perfect."

*   *   *

Cat had to admit that *Rapture* was good. Russell Savage was a stylish and talented director, and the writing was sharp, if slightly overwrought at times. She wasn't sure that she would've cast someone as pretty as Shelby Cheney in the lead role, but the actress was doing an excellent job.

Cat was psyched about making the leap into the big time. It was one thing shooting *Wild Child* on the streets of New York, but now Merrill Zandack had promised her a fat budget for her second film, *Caught,* which was exciting, because this time she'd be able to hire a proper crew, a decent cinematographer, *and* pick and choose who would star. She kind of entertained the idea of going with unknown actors again. Stars always came with all kinds of baggage. Although Angelina Jolie would be sensational as the undercover cop. And she wouldn't say no to Colin Farrell as the womanizing con man. He was certainly sexy enough, with plenty of macho heat.

"You'd better be nice to Merrill," Jump had warned her before he'd left for Australia. "Zandack's the money guy. Don't piss him off."

"How *nice* do you want me to be?" she'd asked, teasing him.

"Not *that* nice," Jump had replied with a dirty laugh. "The geezer's old enough to be your fuckin' granddad."

So what? In Hollywood age didn't seem to matter. Men of sixty often married girls of twenty. The age difference appeared to bother people only in reverse. Older women were reviled for being with younger men, although it was certainly getting easier. She'd read a long piece about it in the *New York Times.* Women like Demi Moore and Madonna were setting a new trend.

Women who don't give a crap, Cat thought, smiling to herself. *My favorite people.*

She returned her attention to the screen. The more she watched, the more she learned.

When *Rapture* reached its conclusion, the audience rose to its feet, indulging in a hearty round of applause.

Shelby experienced a flurry of butterflies in her stomach. She had never been in such a quality film before; it was an exhilarating feeling.

Linc put his arm around her, squeezing her waist. "Not bad, sweetie," he whispered.

Not bad, sweetie. Well, what did she expect from Linc?

Merrill Zandack, sitting in the row behind, tapped her on the shoulder. "You an' I gotta talk," he wheezed, recognizing a great performance when he saw one. "You'll meet my new discovery, Cat. I'll have my people messenger her latest script to your people. It's dynamite. Could be right for you."

Overhearing this conversation, Cat was shocked. She did not see Shelby Cheney in her movie at all. Especially as she'd been thinking along the lines of an Angelina Jolie. The role called for somebody younger and tougher than Shelby Cheney. Not that Shelby wasn't a terrific actress; she'd just proven so in *Rapture.* However, no way did that make her the perfect choice for a sexy, savvy, *American* undercover cop.

How dare Merrill Zandack start offering actresses a role in *her* movie?

One thing Cat intended to keep, and that was control.

CHAPTER
4

At the after party, Shelby found herself swept up in a sea of congratulations. The French P.R. woman hovered by her side. Linc immediately drifted off on his own.

For a moment Shelby felt lost, then she took a deep, life-affirming breath and decided she'd better start embracing the compliments that were coming her way. What actress wouldn't appreciate hearing how great she was?

Russell Savage hurried over to kiss and

hug her. So did Beck Carson. The photographers jostled for position.

For once Shelby relaxed, posing with her director and costar, allowing herself the pleasure of basking in the adulation. She'd worked hard for a reception like this. It was every actress's dream to appear in such a fine movie.

She smiled her dazzling smile, while continuing to enjoy every satisfying minute.

Lola was creating her own circle of excitement. The French loved her. They loved her lips, they loved her legs, and they especially loved her fine ass. She was a huge star in France.

"I wish I talked French," she grumbled to Matt.

"Bonjour, mademoiselle," he said with a stupid smirk on his bland face.

"Oh great," she said disparagingly. "Is that all the French you know?"

"Learned it at school," he boasted, like it was some huge achievement.

She had to do something about Matt. He wasn't up to her standards. Divorce was *definitely* in their future. Thank God her lawyer had gotten him to sign that prenup, because as soon as they got back to America she planned on dumping him fast. The thrill was definitely gone.

Elliott Finerman was standing nearby. "Elliott," she said imperiously, beckoning him over. "Isn't that Linc Blackwood? Don't you think I should meet him?"

"You've never met him?"

"I don't think so."

"Then how come you're so hot to have him in our movie?"

"I'm not *hot* to have him in my movie," she said, tossing back her hair. "He's a huge star who's looking to do something different, and this might be the perfect opportunity. Besides, I think the two of us have chemistry."

"How would you know *that?*" Elliott asked.

"So many actors today are just boys. Brad Pitt and Leonardo DiCaprio are sexy, but they're not men. *I* like men. And *that's* what I like about Linc Blackwood. Believe me, Elliott, we'll have *plenty* of chemistry."

You're not looking for a costar, Elliott thought. *You're looking for a convenient fuck.*

"I'll see what I can do," he said.

"He's right there," Lola said, pointing. "Bring him over."

What kind of balls did this broad have? Who did she think she was dealing with? A lackey? An errand boy? He was one of the biggest producers in Hollywood and this bitch was trying to tell him what to do.

He attempted to remain calm because the smart move was to keep her happy. No happy star, no movie.

He walked over to Linc, who was busy knocking back a hefty glass of scotch while flirting with an attractive Frenchwoman. Naturally.

"Hello, Linc," Elliott said, falsely jovial.

Linc didn't take a beat. "Had a hunch you and I weren't talking," he said offhandedly.

"That was then, this is now," Elliott said. "Time passes, so I . . . uh . . . figured it was time to forgive and forget."

"Can't say I blame you," Linc replied with an easy grin. "After all, you *were* married to her, so maybe there *should* be an apology."

"I agree," Elliott said, relieved that Linc was ready to move on. "I think there should."

"Okay, Elliott," Linc said magnanimously. "Then I accept your apology."

Elliott was outraged. Once a jerk, always a jerk. The asshole was supposed to be apologizing to *him.*

He cleared his throat and glanced over at Lola, who was waiting impatiently for him to bring her the arrogant prick.

"Uh, listen, Linc—there's someone who wants to meet you," he said in a strangled voice.

"Yeah?" Linc said. He didn't like Elliott Finerman, never had. "And who might that be?"

"Lola Sanchez."

"Yeah?" Linc said, his interest perking. Everyone knew who Lola Sanchez was. The hot Latino actress with the body to die for.

"She's over by the bar."

Linc's eyes swiveled, checking her out. "See you later, sweetheart," he said to the woman he'd been talking to, and accompanied Elliott to the bar.

"Lola, Linc Blackwood," Elliott said, making the requested introduction.

"This is a real pleasure," Linc said, taking her hand and bringing it to his lips.

"Uh . . . me too," she murmured, waiting for him to recognize her.

"I'm a big fan," he continued, eyes roaming all over her spectacular body.

"You are?"

"Yup," he said, his eyes coming to rest on her partially exposed breasts. "I've been following your career."

"You've been following *my* career?" she said, utterly dumbfounded. Was it possible that Linc didn't remember her? That he was actually under the impression they were meeting for the first time? Unless, of course, he was playing it cool because her husband was standing right next to her.

"Sure have," Linc said, easy grin in place.

No, she decided, he wasn't being cool— the bastard simply did not remember her. Unbelievable! Not to mention insulting. She was the same girl, wasn't she? Certainly more polished, but the same girl. Her hair was shorter, her nose a touch thinner— thanks to an excellent plastic surgeon who'd also given her more pronounced cheekbones. Her figure was still luscious, although she was fifteen pounds lighter. How *could* he forget her? How could he *not* remember the girl he'd taken to bed, made love to all night long, then dumped in the morning?

Matt decided it was time to jump in. "Hi," he said, proffering his hand. "I'm Matt Seel, Lola's husband."

"Lucky man," Linc said, not taking his eyes off her.

This was the final insult. The sonofabitch obviously had no memory of their one long, steamy night of passion.

She decided to put him to the test. "I've a feeling we *have* met before," she said, toying with the stem of her martini glass.

"Do you honestly imagine I'd forget someone who looks like *you?*" Linc replied, turning up the charm. "You're more beautiful in the flesh than on the screen."

She swallowed hard, licking her suddenly dry lips. This man was responsible for her being barren. *And he did not remember her!* How she hated him.

Sensing that the famous movie star was coming on too strong, Matt once again joined in. "How long are you in Cannes for?" he asked, inserting himself between them.

"Not long," Linc replied, completely uninterested in anything Matt might have to say.

"We're leaving soon," Matt announced, placing a possessory arm around Lola, who did not appreciate his show of affection.

"We can't wait to get back to our house in Bel Air."

"That makes us almost neighbors," Linc remarked.

"Where do you live?"

"Beverly Hills."

"You should come over sometime with your wife," Matt said. "Play some tennis. We'll make up a foursome."

Linc continued staring straight at Lola. "Do you play?"

She returned his gaze, edging away from Matt, who was continuing to irritate her. "I certainly do," she purred. "And I'm *very* good."

Linc smiled. "I *bet* you are."

Merrill Zandack did not stay long at parties. Once he'd circled the room and spoken to everyone he deemed worthy of his attention, he was out of there.

Jonas was waiting outside.

"Did you find my diamond?" Cat asked, pouncing on him.

"Yes I did."

"Where is it?"

"Why? Are you planning on sticking it back in your navel *now?*"

"What are you two talking about?" Merrill asked, lighting up his usual strong-smelling Cuban cigar.

"Nothing important," Jonas said. "How was the movie?"

"Shelby Cheney's got a great rack," Merrill remarked, exhaling smoke. "Told her she'd be right for *Caught.* Messenger her people a script."

"I'd like to speak to you about that, Mr. Zandack," Cat said quickly.

"How many times I gotta tell you? Call me Merrill. 'Mr. Zandack' makes me sound like I'm a hundred years old."

"Okay, *Merrill,*" she said, fuming. "We have to discuss it."

"Sure, kitten. We're on our way to the Carlton Terrace for a drink, we'll talk about it there."

"I asked you not to call me kitten," she muttered.

He didn't hear her; he was already heading for the waiting car.

Cat turned to his dark-haired date, who was lingering. She felt sorry for the woman tagging along behind the fat man. "Do you have a name?" she asked.

"She doesn't speak English," Jonas said.

"What nationality is she? Perhaps I can talk to her in her own language."

"Russian," Jonas said, giving Cat a superior look. "Do you *speak* Russian?"

"No," Cat retorted, returning his look with one of her own. "Does your boss?"

"They communicate in other ways," Jonas said, ushering them both into the car.

"Let's go," Merrill said, filling the backseat with cigar fumes. "It's champagne time."

The crowd was thinning out. Shelby looked around for her husband. He was easy to spot, muscular, tanned, and rugged. Linc was an extremely masculine looking man and every woman picked up on his macho scent. Fact of life. If he wasn't a movie star, they'd still be all over him.

She hoped he was sober. She needed him tonight. She had an urge to cuddle up in bed and have *him* look after *her.* Compliments from her husband would make such a welcome change.

On the other hand, she knew how painful intimacy was for Linc. He'd had such a tough childhood, full of beatings and rejection. Giving unconditional love was extremely difficult for him.

"No more interviews tonight," she said to the P.R. woman. "I'd like to go back to the hotel now."

"Very well," the woman said. "I'll make sure your car is waiting."

"Please tell my husband I'm ready to leave."

"Certainly."

She watched as the woman crossed the room toward Linc. What kind of life was it for someone like that? Looking after celebrities, putting up with their outrageous demands, dealing with the press. It must be so unfulfilling.

I want a baby. The thought popped into her head out of nowhere. *I want Linc's baby.*

Maybe tonight was the night. The south of France. Her movie triumph. A luxurious hotel suite overlooking the Mediterranean. She'd waited long enough. Why not?

Here came *why not.* Linc. Her husband. Smirking like an idiot. Unsteady on his feet.

Damn! He was loaded.

"Hi, baby," he drawled, pawing her arm. "You havin' a good time?"

"Actually I'm quite tired," she said quickly. "Can we go back to the hotel?"

"No way!" he said in a loud voice. "The evening's just beginning. There's parties all over town. We gotta celebrate, sweetheart. We gotta celebrate *you* takin' it all off."

"Linc, it's late," she said, trying not to lose it. "You've had a lot to drink. I think—"

"C'mon, sweetie, relax," he cajoled. "We're on vacation."

"This is *not* a vacation," she reminded him. "It's work."

"Some work, sitting on your ass watching a movie," he said, his lip curling. "Although," he added, "I gotta admit—it's a cute ass."

"Not *a* movie, *my* movie," she corrected. "And I've done a ton of interviews today, with more tomorrow. Plus I'm jet-lagged, and don't forget that we're still on L.A. time."

"You're on L.A. time," he said pointedly. *"I'm* ready to party."

She had a choice. She could go back to the hotel and get some well-needed rest, or she could accompany her husband on his prowl around town.

There was no choice—she couldn't leave

Linc to his own devices. He was drunk and on his way to being out of control. She had to stay by his side to protect him.

It was too bad. He'd faithfully promised her that he wasn't going to drink on this trip, and now look at him. Linc was fast turning into the king of empty promises.

"Okay," she sighed. "One party, and then bed. Is that a deal?"

"Deal," he said, grabbing her and twirling her around. "I got me the best little wife in the world."

CHAPTER

5

The group sitting around a table on the terrace of the Carlton Hotel included Merrill Zandack with his mystery date; Lola Sanchez and her husband, Matt; Jonas; Elliott Finerman; and Cat. There were stars, producers, investors, and directors congregating at all the surrounding tables. The Carlton Terrace was a popular meeting place, especially at the end of the evening, when everyone was ready to wind down and catch up on all the day's gossip.

Cat had already checked out the action, had a drink, been ignored by Lola Sanchez—who obviously didn't consider her important enough—and now she was anxious to get back to the yacht.

Unfortunately, Merrill was in no hurry. He was fawning all over Lola, who was basking in the attention. She'd once made a movie for him, and they were apparently old friends.

Cat had an urge to call Jump, find out how his tour was going. They'd spoken only once, and she missed him, especially since they'd hardly been apart since their marriage, two years ago.

She daydreamed about what they'd do if Jump was with her. Knowing her husband, he'd be into adventure. They'd hire a speedboat, go waterskiing, hit the beaches and mountains, and generally explore. On their honeymoon he'd taken her to the Great Barrier Reef, off the coast of Australia, where they'd had *the* most amazing time.

The simple life. When she wasn't working, that's what she was into, not all this fancy party crap.

"Do you think I'll get through to Australia on my cell?" she asked Jonas.

"Checking up on hubby?"

Who the hell used the word "hubby"? *Of course* Jonas was gay. Why had she ever doubted it?

"I don't check up on people," she answered crisply.

"I've been meaning to ask . . . ," Jonas ventured.

"Yes?"

"Aren't you kind of *young* to be married?"

"Aren't you kind of *nosy* to be questioning me about stuff that's none of your business?" she retorted.

"Give me the number, I'll try it for you."

She scribbled the number on a drink napkin and handed it over with her phone.

Jonas got up and walked away from the table, cell phone in hand.

Cat wasn't sure whether she should follow him or not. Then she decided that she should—anything to get away from the cigar smoke permeating their table, polluting the balmy night air.

Just as she was about to run after Jonas, Matt Seel grabbed her arm. "Merrill's raving about *Caught,*" he said, preventing her from taking off. "How long did it take you to write?"

She knew exactly where this question

was leading. Since the huge success of *Wild Child,* everyone thought they were capable of writing a successful script. After all, if a nineteen-year-old girl could create a hit movie, why couldn't they? Now Matt obviously thought *he* could write a screenplay, and he was expecting *her* to tell *him* how easy it was.

"Uh . . . it's difficult to say," she answered, being purposely vague.

"A month? Two? Three?" he persisted.

"It's not really a question of time."

"What, then?"

"Talent," she wanted to say. But she didn't. It couldn't be a laugh a minute being married to Lola Sanchez—the woman came across as a total diva. "Tenacity," she said. "And stamina."

"I'm writing a script," he announced.

Surprise! Surprise!

"That's great," she murmured.

"It's loosely based on my life."

"No kidding?"

"Yeah. My dad's a cop and I was a championship tennis player before I married Lola."

"Sounds interesting."

"It is," he said enthusiastically. "Can I tell you more?"

"Later," she said, extracting herself from his grip. "Right now I gotta go talk to my old man."

She hurried over to Jonas, who informed her he was unable to get a signal.

"Crap!" she exclaimed. "Can we go back to the boat now?"

"When Mr. Zandack is ready."

"When will *that* be?"

"Do I look like a mind reader?"

Jonas was so fucking uptight. He'd been drinking Perrier all night; maybe a shot of vodka would get the stick out of his ass.

"Can't the tender take me back on my own?" she persisted.

"Mr. Zandack doesn't like people leaving before he's ready."

"Like I care?"

"Word of advice," Jonas said, poker-faced. "Don't piss him off."

"Hey," she said, sick of his attitude. "He's bought my movie—not my soul. I'm a free spirit, and I intend to remain one. Tell him I'm going to the boat."

Jonas was not giving an inch. "How do you plan on getting there?"

"I'm taking the tender," she answered, equally stubborn. "Please call and have it come fetch me."

"This seems like a good time to remind you that I work for Mr. Zandack, not you."

"Then I'll have to ask Mr. Zandack to speak to you, won't I?"

"About what?"

"About getting me the fucking tender," she said, finally losing patience.

"Go ahead."

"I will," she said, snatching her cell phone and marching back to the table, where she found Merrill sucking limes and downing tequila shots along with Lola Sanchez—both of them enjoying themselves immensely. Merrill's Russian girlfriend and Lola's husband looked on with glum expressions. Elliott Finerman was long gone.

What was she supposed to do? Sit and watch?

No way. That wasn't her style. She could only kiss ass for so long, and Merrill's time was now up.

"Uh, Mr. Z. . . . Merrill, I'd like to go back to the yacht," she ventured. "Can you tell Jonas to call the tender for me?"

Ignoring her request, Merrill downed another tequila shot and sucked on a lime.

"Merrill," she repeated. "I want to leave."

"Ten minutes," he said, beaming. "An' we'll all go back together. Okay, kitten?"

The smile on Shelby's face was becoming more fixed by the moment. She was desperate not to let it slip, for the paparazzi were everywhere, ready to pounce. There were big bucks to be made from a picture of her and Linc involved in any kind of altercation.

Linc was loud and boisterous, coming on to every woman in sight, grabbing and pawing. If only she could get him back to the hotel before he did something he'd regret in the morning.

Unfortunately she knew the routine only too well. Basically Linc was an alcoholic who refused to admit he had a problem. Oh yes, a couple of times he'd conceded that maybe he needed help, and had actually spent time in rehab. But as soon as he got out, he'd laughed at the idea that he was addicted and done nothing about it. His glass was full, something he refused to acknowledge.

There were times he didn't drink for months on end. There were other times one glass of wine would be all he could tolerate. Then there were the times like tonight, and these were the times she dreaded most. Linc on a binge. It wasn't a pretty sight.

"Linc is damaged goods," Brenda, her therapist, had explained to her. "He's experienced an extremely traumatic childhood, and that colors everything he does."

"How can I help him?"

"Tell him to come and see me, I'll do what I can."

After much persuasion, Linc had finally agreed to sit down with Brenda. A couple of lengthy sessions later, he'd pronounced the whole therapy deal total crap.

Brenda didn't think so. "The man needs help," she'd informed Shelby. "He's suffering from an overload of guilt. He feels he could not protect his mother, and in some way failed his father. He drinks to take away the painful memories."

Determined to lure him away from the party without incident, Shelby quietly whispered in his ear. "Sweetheart, you promised one party only. I'm very tired. Can we go now?"

"Wassamatter?" he slurred, his eyes becoming glittery and mean. "Doncha *want* me havin' fun?"

"We'll have fun at the hotel," she promised, knowing exactly what would happen when she got him there. He'd collapse on the bed and she'd have to undress him, shoes and all. In the morning he'd awake with a vicious hangover, beg her forgiveness, and faithfully promise it would never happen again.

Linc belonged in AA. Much to Shelby's dismay, his tolerance level for alcohol was steadily declining. When they'd first gotten together she had not considered it too much of a problem.

But now . . .

Flash Back Four Years

"Who's the girl with Pete?" Linc asked his closest pal and longtime agent, Marty Zimmerman. They were standing by the pool table at Marty's house, while a few dozen people mingled at the party taking place. Ever since his latest divorce, Marty was famous for his casual Sunday night drop-ins;

the usual ratio was three girls to every man. Marty was a major player.

Grabbing a drink, Marty cocked a somewhat bushy eyebrow. He was a short, wiry-looking man in his late forties, with a shock of thick brown hair and a prominent nose. "Off-limits," he said. "Pete found her first and he's in deep lust."

"He is?" Linc said, staring at the girl in question.

"Yup," Marty said, nodding vigorously. "He's taken her out four times and according to him—barely gotten a good-night peck."

"Pete?" Linc said, laughing incredulously.

"Yeah, Pete the Peterman. Can you believe it?"

"No," Linc said, picking up a pool cue. "Pete scores more pussy than I do."

"Not with this one," Marty responded, selecting his own personal cue, embossed with his initials in gold. "She's holding out pretty good."

"Maybe I should move in," Linc mused. "Put him out of his misery."

"Naw, you don't wanna do that. This is the real thing. Pete's talkin' marriage."

"You gotta be shittin' me?" Linc said, chalking his cue.

"Nope," Marty said matter-of-factly.
" 'Fraid our Pete's a goner."

"How come I never heard about this?"

"Could be because you've been on location in Asia for the last three months," Marty said, racking up the balls.

"That'd do it."

"You break," Marty said with a magnanimous wave of his hand.

"Mr. Generous," Linc replied, starting off the game. "Hold tight 'cause I'm about to cream your ass."

"You wish!"

"I know."

"Lucky shot!" Marty exclaimed as several balls zoomed into various pockets.

"Thought you were gonna come visit me on location," Linc remarked, preparing for his next shot.

"Everyone knows I hate flying."

"You're my agent, Marty," Linc chided, leaning over the table. "You're supposed to service the client."

"Talkin' of getting serviced," Marty said. "How was the pussy over there?"

"Same as here," Linc said, taking another successful shot. "The difference is—three hours later, you're hot for more."

Both men laughed.

"'S good to have you back," Marty said warmly. "This town's not the same without you."

"Thanks," Linc said, taking another long look at the girl with Pete. "Believe me," he added. "It's great to be back."

He blew his next shot, and Marty took his turn.

"How come I've never seen her before?" Linc asked.

"Because you do not go to other people's movies," Marty said, squinting at his options. "And she doesn't frequent your favorite hangouts."

"Does she have a name?"

"Shelby Cheney. She's an English actress, starred in a couple of independents. Word is she's up for the lead in the new Tom Cruise."

"Fuck Tom Cruise," Linc said forcefully. "How about my next movie?"

"Jesus!" Marty groaned, stepping back from the table and leaning on his cue. "Aren't you listening to me. She's taken. T-A-K-E-N."

"You said Pete's not fucking her."

"Linc," Marty said gravely. "Do me a personal favor. Leave this one alone."

"Sure."

But of course he didn't, even though Pete, one of the top stuntmen in town, was a close friend.

The next morning he had his manager find out all about Shelby Cheney. She was a fairly successful English actress who'd moved to Hollywood eight months earlier. Her career was definitely on the rise, and she was definitely not a girl about town.

Linc liked the sound of her—he already knew he liked the look—so a couple of days later he arranged to have her come in for a meeting with his director, casting people, and himself.

The moment Shelby entered the office he knew she was different. Coolly beautiful, with a mane of raven hair, intelligent hazel eyes, and a body she could not conceal beneath a simple cashmere sweater and knee-length beige skirt.

She sat on a chair in front of them, crossed her spectacular legs, and did not lose her composure. Most actresses with an opportunity to star in a Linc Blackwood movie would be selling themselves like crazy. Shelby didn't do that. She was thoughtful, serious, and quite charming.

Linc leaned back and let the others do the talking.

"You're English, is that right?" asked the casting woman.

"Guilty," Shelby replied with a soft smile. "However, if you're at all worried about my accent, I can assure you that I do a perfect American."

"Lucky guy!" Linc joked.

"Excuse me?" Shelby said, throwing him a cool look.

"Just a dumb joke," he said, wondering what she would look like naked in his bed.

"Would you mind reading a scene?" asked the director, already smitten.

"Not at all," she answered politely in her melodious voice. "Although I think I should warn you that I'm not sure I'm right for this role." She smiled another dazzling smile. "I'm not exactly the athletic type. And I find the topless scene somewhat gratuitous. I would not be prepared to shoot that scene as written."

The room was silent. An actress talking herself out of a leading role. Unheard of.

"Uh . . . Millie will read with you," said the

director, indicating the casting woman's assistant.

"That's not necessary," Linc said, standing up. "If it's okay with Ms. Cheney, I'll read the scene with her."

He gave her the look. The irresistible, rugged, macho movie star look that worked with every woman he ever encountered. They all wanted a piece of Linc Blackwood. He had it going and then some.

"Whatever you like," Shelby said, as if it was no big deal.

Hmm . . . she wasn't falling all over him. Unusual but intriguing. Surely she couldn't be in love with Pete? Pete was a major womanizer who'd get her into bed and then dump her.

It did not occur to Linc that when it came to women he followed exactly the same pattern.

Shelby scored the role in his movie. Three weeks later the cast and crew left for a two-month location shoot in New Zealand. Pete was furious that she was heading out on location with Linc, but there was nothing he could do about it since he was working on a movie in town and was unable to leave. He called Linc and threatened that if he so *much as touched her, there would be some reckoning. "I love this girl," Pete informed him. "So lay off." Linc laughed and assured Pete that she wasn't his type.*

But of course she was, and a month after their movie wrapped, Linc Blackwood and Shelby Cheney were married on a Hawaiian beach in a romantic ceremony attended by Shelby's family, whom Linc flew over from London, and a few close friends. Pete was not among them.

Linc was ecstatic. For the first time he finally understood what caring for a woman was all about. He loved Shelby, she was it. And as far as he was concerned, his drinking, drugging, and womanizing days were over.

The honeymoon period lasted a year, and then it was back to his bad old ways. Linc simply couldn't help himself; there were too many temptations out there, and he had no willpower.

Playing around did not mean that he wasn't still crazy about his wife. Shelby was the best. An angel. And one of these days he really would settle down. Maybe he'd even give her the baby she wanted so badly.

Maybe.
One of these days.

"Love you," Linc said, pulling Shelby down on the bed beside him. "Love you *so* much, babe. You're the best."

He was drunk, but at least he wasn't in one of his mean and nasty moods, and she'd gotten him back to the hotel without any embarrassing incidents. Thank God for that.

"C'mere, baby," he mumbled, pawing at her gown. "Take it off an' come t' bed."

She could smell the booze coming off him in waves; it made her quite nauseous. She loved him deeply, yet there were times like this when she couldn't stand to be near him.

"Wanna make love t' you," he mumbled. " 'Cause you're my wife. My wunnerful, boo-ful li'l wife . . . My . . ." His hands dropped off her and his eyes closed. He was out. Gone. And he wouldn't surface again until noon the next day.

Unfortunately, she knew the routine only too well; she'd experienced it many times.

Feeling let down and abandoned on a night when she should've been feeling nothing but triumphant, she wearily pulled off his shoes and loosened his belt. She had neither the inclination nor the energy to undress him further. Let him sleep in his clothes. She didn't care how uncomfortable he was when he awoke, because by that time she'd be long gone. She had a morning of interviews and photographs, lunch with a journalist from *USA Today,* and another mass press conference in the afternoon with her costar and the director of *Rapture.* Sleep was imperative, otherwise she would look a wreck.

Damn Linc! He was impossible. Why couldn't he think of *her* for once? After all, she thought of him all the time.

CHAPTER
6

Cat had never been a patient girl, and waiting around for Merrill Zandack to decide when he was ready to return to the yacht was pissing her off.

Finally, after Lola Sanchez and her husband left, she jumped to her feet, exclaiming, "Man, I'm exhausted!"

"The night is only just beginning, kitten," Merrill said, puffing on his cigar. "Next we go to Regine's."

"Not me," Cat said firmly. *I'm* heading back to the boat. So if you're *not* coming, please tell Jonas to arrange for me to get there."

"Headstrong," Merrill muttered.

"What?" she said sharply. He wasn't her fucking father, for crissakes, and he was speaking to her as if he was. Not that her father was any kind of disciplinarian; quite the contrary, in fact.

"Okay, okay," Merrill said, snapping his fingers at Jonas, who jumped to attention. "Call for the tender. *Now!"*

Cat shot Jonas a triumphant look.

He went out of his way to pretend not to notice.

"Did you sleep with Merrill Zandack?" Matt demanded the moment he and Lola reached their luxurious suite.

"You're not *serious?"* she replied, removing her borrowed diamond Chopard earrings, which she was hoping they'd allow her to keep as a gift. "Me and that fat old man. Is that what you think of me?"

"I heard Merrill Zandack has a reputation around the actresses he works with," Matt said, pressing on. "There's a rumor that he makes them give him head."

"Like I would do something like that with *him*," she said in disgust.

"The two of you seemed pretty cozy tonight," Matt said accusingly, not realizing that if he was smart he would drop the subject.

"Cozy, huh?" Lola said, her expressive brown eyes flashing major danger signals.

"Doing tequila shots. Sucking limes," Matt continued sulkily. "While *I* sat there like an idiot."

"You said it."

"Huh?"

"That you're an idiot."

Matt's face flushed a dull red. They'd been married only five months, so why was she treating him like he was nothing more than an accessory to have on her arm? "I wish you wouldn't talk to me like that," he responded.

"*You* said it," she repeated, stepping out of her dress, standing before him in all her glory—naked except for a thin diamond chain around her waist, a rhinestone encrusted thong, and Jimmy Choo stilettos.

He couldn't take his eyes off her. Lola Sanchez was magnificent, and *he* was her husband.

His eyes lingered on her nipples, so big and brown and tempting.

He started getting hard.

His nagging went out the window as he reached for her.

She backed off. "I have to make a call," she said evasively, and walked into the bathroom.

Matt attempted to follow her. Anticipating his move, she slammed the door in his face with a succinct "I don't appreciate being accused of things."

Safely locked in the bathroom, she stared at her reflection in the mirror above the marble sink. She knew she looked good; no false modesty there. And so she should; she broke her back to look her best. Not to mention spending a fortune on her own personal trainer, with whom she spent two hours a day six days a week whether she was working or not. Plus she had a waxer who came to her house every two weeks; a manicurist every five days; a hairdresser, stylist, and makeup artist on permanent call.

Even though she was only twenty-four it took hard work, time, and money to look as good as she did. It wasn't easy maintaining the image. However, she wasn't complaining. Oh no, not after all the things she'd gone through to get where she was today.

Matt might be dense, but he'd certainly called the shot when it came to Merrill. She *had* given the powerful mogul a blow job. It had happened early on in her career when she was desperate to score the lead in one of his movies, and the only thing standing in her way was Mr. Zandack's sexual pleasure. So she'd done it. Once.

The good news was that it had gotten her the part, and that role had signaled the start of her ascent. She'd played a sexy young dancer who protects a small child and an adorable puppy from the wrath of an abusive husband. Excellent strong-heroine stuff. The public ate it up, and suddenly she was a name, and scripts started coming her way, and the two years of struggling in a series of humiliating bit parts playing maids and hookers was over.

One blow job for her shot at stardom. Not such a big deal.

Later she'd found out that Merrill Zandack expected the same from all the actresses he worked with. She'd felt a lot better when she'd heard that it was a rite of passage. A simple blow job to establish his power, and then they could be friends. He treated her with nothing but respect now.

She wondered if the skinny young blonde in the weird outfit with the odd name had done it yet. His protégée. Cat.

Probably. They all had to. It was part of the deal.

The phone rang in Tony Alvarez's Hollywood Hills home. He almost fell off the bed reaching for it.

"Tony, baby," Lola purred into his ear. "I miss you."

"Who the fuck's this?" he mumbled.

"You *know* who it is," she replied in a husky voice.

"Lola?"

"Who else?" she said, as if he didn't know.

"Jesus holy *Christ!*" A beat. "What's the freakin' time?"

"Let me see," she said coolly. "It's midnight here."

"An' where the fuck is *here?*"

"I'm at the Cannes Film Festival."

"Jeez, Lola," he groaned. "Y'know I'm not into early mornin's."

"Tony," she said patiently. "It's nine hours ahead in France, so therefore it's three o'clock in the afternoon in L.A. I'd hardly call that early morning, would you?"

"Shee . . . it."

"Aren't you happy to hear from me?"

"Oh sure," he said, groping for a half-finished joint on the bedside table. "I'm real psyched gettin' an early-mornin' wake-up from my *married ex*-fiancée."

"That's what I called to tell you."

"So tell me."

"Things aren't working out between me and Matt."

"No shit?"

"In fact," she said, pausing dramatically, "I'm divorcing him."

"You mentioned this to *him* yet?" Tony said, lighting up.

"I will."

"Why you callin' me?" he said, taking a drag off the half-smoked joint.

"I told you," she murmured softly. "I miss your hot body."

"You do, huh?"

"Yes, Tony, I do."

"You ran, baby," he said, his voice hardening. "You ran like a fuckin' thief in the night. Couldn't get away from me fast enough."

"I had to. It was all getting too much."

"You had to?" he said disbelievingly.

"That doesn't mean *we're* over," she said quickly. "I mean, you and I—we could *never* be over."

"Lola, Lola," he said, scratching his head. *"You* are somethin' else."

"I miss us being together." A long beat. "In bed. All warm and wet and hard and—"

"Too bad," he interrupted.

"Look, I understand you're mad at me, and that's why I want to make everything right."

"An' how d'you plan on doin' *that?*"

"First I have to ask you a very important question."

"Keep talkin'."

She hesitated for a moment, unwilling to set him off. Tony had a dramatic temper, for that matter so did she. "It's not easy," she began.

"Spill, Lola."

"Are you still . . . using?"

"What're you—a fuckin' narcotics cop?" he exploded, furious she would ask such a question.

"Here's the thing," she said, speaking fast. "I want us to get back together, but I can't do it if your habit is likely to drag us both down."

"Who the fuck *needs* this shit?" he said, abruptly cutting her off.

Unfazed, she immediately redialed. She knew Tony was not an easy get. She also knew that she'd hurt him badly by dumping him and marrying Matt, so now she had to make amends.

"Whaddya want from me, Lola?" he sighed, answering on the first ring.

"I told you."

"One thing about you, babe—you got yourself a set of big brass balls, that's for sure."

"Thought you liked that in a woman," she teased.

"Listen, I hate t' break the news, but this is one dude who's moved on."

"I don't believe you."

"Same old Lola," he said with a dry laugh. "Think you're the only woman in the world."

"The only one for you," she countered.

"Get it into your brain, baby," he said harshly. *"You* made the goddamn break, now *you* gotta live with it."

"Wrong."

"Right. 'Cause there's no way I'm gonna have any woman policin' me."

"I'll be back in L.A. in a few days," she said, confident that he didn't mean a word of it. "I'll call you then."

"Don't bother."

"Trust me, Tony—we'll work things out." He was silent. "You *know* you want to," she added in her most seductive voice, clicking off her phone just as Matt began hammering on the bathroom door.

"What're you doing in there?" Matt yelled.

"Can't a girl have any privacy?" she yelled back.

"You've been in there for half an hour."

"So what?"

She stepped out of her high heels, removed her makeup, brushed her teeth, and sauntered back into the bedroom, where Matt waited impatiently.

"What's wrong with you?" he said in a whining voice. "You've turned really cold on me lately."

"I'm too tired to talk now," she said, climbing into bed and pulling up the covers.

"When *can* we talk?"

"Soon," she murmured, and ignoring her irate husband, she drifted off to sleep.

The Mediterranean was eerily dark and quite rough as the tender made its way back to the yacht, careening over the waves. Apparently Merrill Zandack did not like his yacht to come into dock; he preferred to distance himself from the action.

Sometimes Cat had nightmares about the sea. Although she was an excellent swimmer, sitting in a crowded tender in the dead of night was hardly her favorite thing to do. She concentrated on thinking about Jump. Australia seemed so far away, and yet it would take her only a day to fly there. Maybe she'd hop a plane and surprise him, which wasn't such a bad idea.

The only problem was that she was supposed to stay in Cannes for several more days, trapped on Merrill Zandack's yacht. "You gotta meet people, kitten," Merrill had informed her. "Distributors, foreign sales, press. People who'll help make your next movie bigger than your first."

When they reached the yacht it was a performance getting Merrill safely aboard.

The tender was rocking and bumping against the side of the yacht, and the big man was slightly unsteady on his feet after God knew how many shots of tequila.

How awful if he falls in the sea, Cat thought.

How funny! As long as he doesn't drown.

Two of the crew gamely hoisted him up the unsteady rope ladder, one pulling him from the front, the other shoving him from behind. His Russian girlfriend didn't say a word. Well, she couldn't, could she, considering she didn't speak any English.

Once they got Merrill safely aboard, Cat was next. She climbed the ladder with Jonas right behind her. *Hmm . . . he's probably checking out my ass,* she thought. *I do have an ass like a boy—just his style.*

The captain was waiting to greet them, looking snappy in his pristine white uniform. "Do you wish to sit outside on the deck, Mr. Zandack, or in the living room?" the captain asked.

Merrill chose to sit outside.

The chief steward approached. "And what can I get everyone to drink?" he inquired, falsely jovial, because it was past midnight and he was ready to get some sleep.

"Nothing for me," Cat said, stretching and yawning. "I'm off to bed."

"No!" Merrill said forcefully. "Have a drink with me. I did what *you* wanted, now you do what *I* want."

Crap! How much rope did she have to skip to get her movie made?

"Okay, I'll have a glass of water," she said, reluctantly sitting down.

Ignoring her request for water, Merrill told the steward to bring a bottle of Cristal and a dish of caviar.

"I don't like champagne," Cat remarked. "It gives me a hangover."

"You've been drinking the cheap stuff," Merrill snapped. "No hangover with Cristal."

Since it was quite obvious his Russian girlfriend was being ignored, the woman got to her feet and marched inside. Merrill did not appear to notice.

"Anything else I can do for you tonight, Mr. Zandack?" Jonas inquired, hovering by the table.

"No, no, you can take off," Merrill said, waving his cigar in the air.

"Then I'll say good night to everybody," Jonas said, shooting Cat a quick look as if to say, *I'm out of here. Sorry, but you've got to stick around.*

Oh man! Cat thought. *Now it's just Merrill and me. Wonderful!*

When the caviar and champagne arrived, Merrill clicked his fingers at the steward and instructed him to pour Cat a glass.

"I asked for water," she said, wishing she was anywhere but here.

"You're having champagne," Merrill argued.

The steward filled a champagne glass and placed it in front of her.

She had no intention of drinking it.

"How you liking Cannes?" Merrill asked, giving her his full attention. "It must be quite somethin' for a girl like you."

What was *that* supposed to mean? She wasn't some kid straight out of nowheresville.

"I've been here many times before," she said quickly. "My father has plenty of friends who own villas here." For a moment she flashed onto the famous old artist and the nude painting he'd done of her. Age thirteen seemed like light-years away.

"Thought this was your first trip," Merrill said, obviously miffed that he was not the first to introduce her to the south of France.

"No," she said patiently. "My family's very cosmopolitan. I have an American father and an English mom, so I grew up traveling between the two countries." *If you'd concentrated on my movie,* she thought, *you would've realized it was based on my life.*

"I've been around talent all my life," Merrill announced. "And you're going places, kitten. With my help and backing, nothing's impossible."

"Cool," she murmured, watching him as he proceeded to knock back a full glass of champagne.

"Now," he said, getting up and holding out his hand. "Come with me, I got somethin' t' show you."

"What?"

"You'll see."

Oh great! Now he was slurring his words.

"Here's the thing, Mr. Zandack . . . Merrill," she said, coming up with a fast excuse. "I promised I'd call my husband. He's in Australia, and the time difference is wacko, so I'd better get to it."

Merrill couldn't care less *where* her husband was. "You'll talk to him later," he said, pulling her up.

Reluctantly she followed him inside as he swayed unsteadily down the long corridor to his master suite. He flung open the door.

She ventured inside, checking out the luxurious space, tastefully decorated with expensive antiques, a large bed, and a wide-screen TV. She was actually looking for his Russian girlfriend, who appeared to be nowhere in sight. Rumor was that he kept her stashed in another cabin and brought her out only when he required her sexual services—whatever they might be.

"So," she said, lingering near the door, "what is it you want to show me?"

"This," Merrill said. And quick as a flash he unzipped his pants, slipping out his somewhat shaky member.

If it wasn't so funny it would be incredibly sad. As she stood there staring at his flabby prick, she recalled a joke her mother used to tell about a man exposing himself to a woman on the street and saying, "Whaddaya think *this* is?" And the woman replying, "It looks like a cock, only smaller."

She stifled an insane urge to burst out laughing. This was *such* a cliché situation. The mogul and the almost hard-on. If she wrote about it nobody would believe her.

"Suck it!" Merrill commanded, red in the face.

"You've *got* to be kidding," she said in amazement.

"Suck it!" he repeated.

She managed to stay cool. There had to be a civilized way to handle this. "Uh . . . I think you might've had too much to drink," she said at last.

"If you want me to make your movie, then get down on your knees an' suck it now," Merrill roared. "That's an order."

"You know what?" she said, backing toward the door. "You can take my movie and shove it up your sorry ass. Because, Mr. *Zandack*—I am out of here."

"Don't you *dare* leave me," he bellowed.

"Screw you!"

And with those words she marched out of his cabin, hurried straight to her room, and started packing.

Men! Young or old. They were all the same when it came to sex.

She might be only nineteen, but she'd certainly covered the waterfront.

Flash Back Two Years

There was one thing Cat had always possessed, and that was strength of character. Where it came from, she didn't know. Maybe she'd inherited it from one of her eccentric parents; they had to be good for something.

Growing up, she'd soon realized that her parents couldn't stand each other, although they'd obviously once enjoyed an extremely passionate and complex relationship. She knew this was so, because they always had nothing but bad things to say about each other. Gable couldn't wait to put down all her mother's husbands, while Bethany openly laughed at her father's series of much younger girlfriends—none of whom he married.

Cat didn't care. As long as she didn't have to go to school and nobody was on her case, she was content. Especially once she got caught up in the drug scene.

At fourteen—thanks to her live-in boyfriend, Brad—she was into ecstasy and speed. At fifteen she was dabbling in crack. By the time she was sixteen she and Brad were experimenting with heroin.

When her father found out about her experimentation, he'd merely laughed. "It's a phase," he'd said. "Went through it myself. I know what I'm talking about."

Bethany never said a word, although Cat was sure that Gable must have told her. Cat had a feeling that Bethany was simply happy that she was out on her own. Bethany did not appreciate having a young, attractive daughter; it made her feel old.

One memorable night—a few days after Brad lost all his money in a sudden Internet crash—Cat came home late from a party. Brad had not gone with her, claiming he didn't feel like it.

She entered their apartment, quite bombed and happy with her never-ending round of parties and drugs. Brad was sprawled on the floor in the living room. A mournful Lou Reed crooned depressing songs on the stereo, while Howard Stern inspected women's breasts on TV.

Brad had a tourniquet around his arm, a needle clutched in a death grip, and no pulse. His eyes were wide and blank. He was quite dead.

Time to move on, Cat thought, too stoned to realize the severity of what had happened.

Later that week she left Brad's apartment and moved in with two gay friends, who loved her and tried to protect her.

A few months later, she was hanging with the usual crowd of misfits she spent all her time with, when she ran into Jump. She and her friends had covered the club scene, and later they'd crashed a party. She'd sneaked into the bedroom and was about to shoot up—which was her new favorite thing to do—when Jump walked in on her.

"What're you doing?" he asked.

"Playing tennis," she responded rudely, staring at the tall skinny dude with the long ratty hair and heavily tattooed arms. "What do you think?"

"Your funeral, mate," he said, staring back at her.

"What's that stupid accent?" she asked.

"Australian," he answered. "Why? You wanna rag on it?"

"No," she said, shaking her head, thinking

*he was just another guy on the make. "So,"
she offered generously, "wanna share?"*

*"What kind of moron shares needles?" he
said in disgust, glaring at her like she was
the stupid one.*

*"You gonna stand there an' watch?" she
inquired belligerently.*

*He backed out of the room without
another word.*

*When she rejoined the party and discov-
ered it was his apartment, she was embarrassed. Then he started jamming on the gui-
tar with some musicians, and she began
getting into the music. Later she told him so,
and he gave her what she perceived as a
pitying look.*

*Cat was used to men coming on strong.
Jump was different. He had girls all over
him; it seemed he hardly noticed her. Except
he did, because when she was on her way
out, he caught her at the door, surprising
her. "Get straight, an' I'll take you out sometime," he offered.*

*And that was the start of her first real
love. She was seventeen. Jump was twenty.*

*He told her he thought they should get
married five weeks after they were together.
"Only you gotta give up hard drugs," he*

warned her. "You can do weed. Anything else an' I'm outta here. Got it?"

Yes, she got it. And that's where her strength of character came in. She could give it up if she wanted to. Now that she had Jump, she didn't need drugs.

When she informed her parents she was getting married they did not put up any objections. Why should they? They didn't care. All they'd ever done was hand her money and drag her along on their exotic trips, competing with each other to get her to like them best. The result was that she didn't like either of them very much.

Neither of them attended her wedding, which took place in Bali. It was her and Jump on a private beach, very romantic. Then Jump took her to visit his widowed mother in Sydney, and they spent a couple of weeks exploring the outback and the Great Barrier Reef. It was a whole new experience, and she loved it.

Jump was the kind of man who made her want to get up in the morning. He energized her, forcing her to realize there were more important things than partying and getting high—although he was not averse to smoking weed morning, noon, and night.

Jump was very into his music; he had a passion. Cat decided she'd better get a passion of her own, and one day she came up with the idea of writing and directing a movie. The story of a poor little rich girl, a girl who had everything except love, then found it with the right guy.

Jump encouraged her to write the script. She found it easy, considering her real education had been spending three quarters of her life in movie theaters.

She knew she could do it. She had the fire and the will to achieve.

When Jump read her script he said, "You're a bloody good storyteller. You gotta go for it."

So she did, and Wild Child *was that movie—full of eccentric characters and crazy people, full of the stories she'd encountered along the path of her somewhat unconventional life.*

When her movie became a runaway success, her father saw it and laughed. "You certainly nailed Bethany for the bitch she is!" he cackled, obviously not recognizing himself. "I'm glad. The cunt deserves it."

Bethany saw it a few weeks later. "What a charming work of fiction," she said curtly, refusing to acknowledge that it was the truth. However, she did recognize Gable, whom she called an egocentric asshole.

Wasn't it comforting that her parents thought so well of each other?

Cat was not a girl to mess with. Movie or no movie, she had no intention of putting up with Merrill Zandack's insane sexual antics. Old men with hard-ons. Part of her past. Sometimes she thought *that* was the story of her life.

Well, Merrill Zandack was not getting away with his bad behavior. First thing in the morning she was out of there.

CHAPTER

7

The muscles in Shelby's cheeks ached due to the fact that she'd been smiling all morning. Interview after interview. Photo after photo. Now it was lunch with a journalist from *USA Today,* and after that, more interviews.

She dreamed of getting up one morning and having nothing to do except nothing. What utter bliss!

Then once more she dreamed of having a baby, Linc's baby, even though he had expressed no desire to start a family.

Surely she could persuade him?

Why not? She was convinced he'd be happy if it was a fait accompli situation and she got pregnant.

No more birth control pills, she thought. *A baby might solve all our problems.* Because even though Linc would never admit it, their problems were escalating every day.

The journalist from *USA Today* was a sandy-haired, middle-aged man dressed in a leisure suit. He wore steel-rimmed glasses and had an obvious crush. "Very much enjoyed your performance in *Rapture,*" he enthused as soon as they sat down.

"I'm glad you liked it," she answered politely, ordering a bottle of Evian and a salad Niçoise from an attentive waiter.

"You're quite marvelous in it," he added, fiddling with his glasses. "And extremely brave."

"Thanks," she said modestly, hoping the interview would not take too long.

"I'm trying not to sound like a gushing fan," the journalist continued. "Only I'm forced to speak the truth."

"Well," she said, bestowing one of her dazzling smiles on him, "if *you're* going to speak the truth, then I'll attempt to do the same."

"I'm sure you're aware that your smile lights up the screen," he said admiringly. "You must've been told that dozens of times."

This was more like a fan fest than an interview. Shelby reminded herself that even though the man was all over her, she should not let her guard down. Sometimes journalists tried to lull their interview subjects into a false sense of security. They softened them up with compliments, then wrote an all-out bitchy piece.

"Your husband has to be very proud of you," the journalist continued, tapping his stubby fingers on the table.

"He is," she replied, thinking of Linc passed out on their bed, still reeking of liquor. Was he proud? Probably. In his own way.

"Linc Blackwood is a much more accomplished actor than everyone thinks. It's a shame the public don't get to see how good he is."

"I agree," she said, happy to talk about Linc. "My husband is definitely underrated."

"Surely it upsets him, not getting the recognition he deserves?"

"Not really," she answered carefully, aware how her words could be twisted and turned.

"I read that he's considering tackling a romantic comedy."

"Yes," she said, wondering where this interview was headed. "Linc would be wonderful in that kind of role. It's not exactly general knowledge, but he has an excellent sense of humor."

"I bet he didn't find your nude scene too funny."

There it was. The zinger. Up went her guard. "Excuse me?" she said, a touch frostily.

"Well, you know," the journalist said, leaning closer. "A man watching his wife with everything on show up there on the big screen. It can't have been easy for either of you."

She glanced around for her publicist, who appeared to have vanished. Damn! This man was not to be trusted; she sensed it.

"We're both actors," she said, endeavoring to remain calm. "Linc understands that it's my job."

"And his of course." A beat, then: "How do you feel about *him* doing steamy love scenes with beautiful younger women?"

"Perfectly fine," she replied, trying not to grit her teeth. And what was that crack about younger women? She was only thirty-two, for God's sake. "As I said before," she added graciously, "we're both professionals."

"You certainly are."

How she loathed the process of giving interviews. Unfortunately it was a necessary part of her job.

Smile firmly in place, she continued to be as charming as humanly possible. The power of the pen was a dangerous and slippery weapon.

The first thing Cat did when she awoke was to try and reach Jump on the phone. It seemed there was never any answer from his hotel room. She dressed, finished packing, and immediately went to see the captain, thinking that the sooner she was off this boat, the better.

"I'll be leaving today," she said briskly.

"Please arrange to have the tender take me to shore as soon as possible."

"Mr. Zandack didn't say anything about this," the captain said, frowning.

"Mr. Zandack has no say about when I come and go," she replied, sounding a lot calmer than she felt.

The captain nodded unsurely, while Cat made her way onto the deck, where breakfast was laid out.

It was a glorious day, the sea was calm and smooth like Venetian glass, and the sky a perfect blue. She poured herself a glass of freshly squeezed orange juice and sat down at the table.

A few minutes later Jonas appeared, his hair kind of rumpled as if he'd recently fallen out of bed. She decided that he looked much better when he wasn't so groomed.

"The captain tells me you want to leave," Jonas said, coming right to the point.

"Correct," she replied.

"Why?" he demanded, staring at her.

"Because I want to," she said, sipping her juice and returning his gaze, daring him to argue. "Is that okay with you?"

"Does Mr. Zandack know?"

"What *is* this obsession with Mr. Zandack?" she said irritably. "I keep on telling you—I'm a free person. Don't you *get* it?"

"You can't leave without his knowledge," Jonas said, circling her.

"I can do what I want."

"I'll have to wake him, and believe me— he does not appreciate being disturbed this early in the morning."

"Tough, huh?" she said sarcastically.

"Maybe you can tell me exactly what happened?" he said, ignoring her sarcasm as he sat down next to her.

"What makes you think *anything* happened?" she said defensively. *Ha! Like he doesn't know what his boss is all about.*

"*Something* must've happened to make you want to leave so abruptly."

Absently she picked up a piece of watermelon with her fingers and popped it in her mouth. "Come on, Jonas. You know *exactly* what his trip is."

"No. I don't. How about filling me in?"

A long, meaningful pause. "Your boss is a major pervert," she finally blurted. "Is that what you're waiting to hear?"

There was a short silence during which Jonas remained stony-faced. "I'll have to wake him before I can authorize your departure," he said at last.

She was fed up with his attitude, not to mention disgusted with Merrill. Screw her movie; she wanted out. The old man *was* a pervert, and she was not about to put up with his crap.

"If you *don't* let me get the hell off this fucking boat," she said, green eyes blazing, "I'm sure you realize that keeping me here against my will could be construed as kidnapping. And you'd be an accessory."

"Then I guess you'd better consider yourself kidnapped," Jonas said. And he got up and walked inside.

Linc Blackwood awoke with a major hangover. "Jesus!" he groaned, rolling off the bed. "I gotta stop doin' this to myself."

He staggered into the bathroom, where he peered at his reflection in the mirror and did not like what he saw. Bags under his eyes, blotchy skin, and thick eyebrows screaming out for the talented attention of Anastasia—the best little plucker and waxer in Beverly Hills. "Crap," he muttered, stripping off his crumpled clothes. Then he yelled out his wife's name. "Shelby? Shelby, where are you, sweetie?"

He didn't expect her to answer. He knew that she had a shitload of interviews to get through, so it was highly likely that she'd left early.

He glanced at his watch, noting that it was half past twelve. His mouth felt like a birdcage that hadn't been cleaned in a week, and his head throbbed as if a jack-hammer was busy doing double duty. Reaching for a bottle of mouthwash he tried recalling the events of the previous evening. He could just about remember seeing Shelby's movie, hitting the after party, and that was it, although he *did* recall that watching his wife on the screen had been a most uncomfortable experience. He'd seen a rough cut of *Rapture* earlier, and it hadn't bothered him that much when she'd taken off her clothes for the extremely graphic sex scene. But sitting in an audience filled with his peers, he was incredibly pissed. It wasn't a pleasant feeling sharing his naked wife with the world.

Oh yeah, he knew he was probably being unreasonable, Shelby was an actress and it was part of her job. But he still couldn't help feeling disturbed.

Shit! Maybe it was time he gave her the baby she was always carrying on about. Knock her up. Keep her off the screen. Show the world she was his and only his.

A baby. That was a big responsibility. Children always got in the way. However, if it's what she *really* wanted, then he should do it for her.

He loved his wife; she had so many amazing qualities apart from being talented and beautiful. The quality he appreciated most of all was the way she watched his back at all times, refusing to let him get out of control. Before they'd married, he'd spent endless nights out with the guys, nights where he'd get piss-faced and end up with a stripper or a semihooker in a hotel room, thoroughly regretting it the next morning. He'd always been petrified of commitment; women were there for the taking. He was a movie star for crissakes. He could have his pick, so why make it more than a one- or two-night stand?

Then along came Shelby, and her inner strength and kindness completely changed his world. With Shelby by his side he felt safe and protected. She wouldn't allow him to get into trouble, she loved him too much. And he loved her, although sometimes he needed to let loose, and booze always helped.

Today she'd be mad at him, he knew it. He'd ruined her special evening, and he couldn't blame her for being angry. Had to do something about *that.*

He wandered back into the bedroom, picked up the phone, and spoke to the concierge. "Call Chopard and arrange to have some pieces sent up to my suite. Diamond bracelets, earrings, something expensive."

"Certainly, Mr. Blackwood," said the concierge obligingly. "I will speak to the manager at Chopard, and they will send you a magnificent selection."

"Make it soon."

"Yes, Mr. Blackwood."

"Morning," Matt said, stroking Lola's smooth-as-satin back, hoping she was in a responsive mood.

Lola opened her eyes slowly. For a moment she lay there imagining she was in bed with Tony Alvarez, until she realized that if it *was* Tony, she would be awakened with far more than just a stroke. Tony was an extremely virile Latino man, a very powerful and skilled lover. Matt was just the opposite. He was a white-bread puppet with no raging passion, a one-minute man with a distinct lack of technique, although she had to admit that he *did* have a big cock. It was his one major asset.

Unfortunately there were times size simply wasn't enough. Lately she was beginning to realize exactly how much she missed Tony, *especially* his presence in her bed.

Matt began making another move. She hurriedly rolled away from his eager hands.

"What's the matter?" he asked, sounding hurt.

She was tempted to say, "You." Only this was not the time or the place to tell him it was over. Besides, she planned on having her lawyer do the dirty deed. She'd been thinking about it a lot, and divorcing Matt was definitely the right move. He was a big boy, he'd soon get over her. And to sweeten his departure she was prepared to pay him a healthy sum of money to walk away quietly, as long as he agreed not to sell his story to the tabloids.

God! How she hated the tabloids. They were always making up scummy stories about her—calling her a demanding diva and all kinds of other things. She often threatened to sue. Her lawyers always talked her out of it, assuring her that getting involved in a lawsuit was more trouble than it was worth.

"My hair and makeup people will be here any minute," she said, stretching languidly. "I'm lunching with Merrill at the Hotel du Cap."

"We are?" Matt said, perking up.

"No. *I* am," she corrected.

"What about me?"

"You'll find something to do," she said, sitting up and stretching again. "Do me a favor, Matt, call room service and order orange juice, croissants, and coffee for six. Faye will be here soon, so you'd better get dressed."

Matt was not giving up easily. He had a major hard-on and a gorgeous wife. What was wrong with a quickie? He started with the stroking again.

"Matt!" she scolded sharply. "Aren't you *listening* to me? There's no time."

"Yes, there is," he said sulkily, thinking how much she'd changed from the warm and loving woman he'd married only months ago.

"No, Matt, there's not," she replied.

Lola Sanchez was a busy woman. Even though she did not have a movie showing at the festival, she was very much in demand. There was nothing like being a hot commodity, with everyone wanting a piece of her. She loved all the attention; it suited her just fine.

How different from her first visit to the famous Cannes Film Festival. How very different.

Flash Back Five Years

"You gotta change your name, kiddo," Lou Steiner said, slurping down a cappuccino.

"Why?" Lucia Sanchez demanded, her big brown eyes scanning the crowded Croisette, secretly thrilled that she'd been transported to such a magical place.

"Too ethnic."

Oh man! If she only had a dollar for every time she'd heard those words.

"*I'm not changing anything,*" *she said stubbornly.*

"*Who's the boss here?*" *Lou said rudely.* "*I say change—you change.*"

Who did he think he was? She wasn't his girlfriend; her roommate, Cindi Hernandez, was. Cindi, now known as Cindi Heart—thanks to Lou's name-change fetish—had been sleeping with Lou for several months.

They'd both met Lou at the same time. He used to come into the diner where they worked as waitresses. Every day he arrived promptly at eight ready for his breakfast, a skinny man with pale yellow hair carefully arranged across his scalp in a crossover style designed to hide the fact that he was rapidly going bald. Lou favored tight suits, striped shirts, and featured a large diamond ring on his pinky. He soon informed them he was a personal manager and dropped many famous names, including Pamela Anderson's and Carmen Electra's, both of whom he claimed he'd discovered.

Lucia didn't believe him; she thought he was a boastful creep. Cindi was convinced he had career-advancement potential, es-

pecially when she found out he drove a Rolls-Royce—even though it was twelve years old.

Now the three of them were at the Cannes Film Festival, thanks to Lou and a deal he'd made with a cheapo hotel and American Airlines.

Before leaving the States he'd taken them to Frederick's of Hollywood and bought them a series of sexy and revealing outfits. Then he'd asked them both to sign ten-year contracts giving him exclusive management rights and twenty-five percent of any future earnings. Lucia flatly refused. Cindi went for it. He took Lucia to Europe with them anyway, because two girls were better than one, and Lou wanted to put himself back on the map. His plan was to parade Cindi and Lucia along the beach where all the photographers gathered. When he gave them the signal, the girls would begin posing, attracting plenty of attention.

"How will that help our careers?" Lucia had asked.

"It'll get you noticed," Lou shot back. "From there you'll leave it to me. It'll be an all-win situation."

Lucia was uncomfortable with the whole

deal, but since she'd never been to Europe, Lou's invitation was too tempting to turn down.

"At least you don't have to sleep with him," Cindi had grumbled. "I'm doing it for both of us."

"How can you?" Lucia had replied. "He must be at least—I dunno—fifty?"

"Yes, but he certainly knows how to treat a girl," Cindi had confided. "And he discovered Pamela Anderson."

"So he says."

Lucia was very fond of her best friend, only she didn't think Cindi had the potential to be another Pamela Anderson—not even a Carmen Electra—because even though Lou had paid for Cindi's makeover, including a nose job and large silicone breasts, Cindi did not have that special something that Lucia knew she possessed.

Lucia was quite disillusioned with her progress as far as breaking into show business was concerned. She'd been going out on audition after audition, and the only jobs she'd managed to score were a couple of walk-ons, playing maids. She'd been offered the role of a stripper in a Steven Seagal film, a part she'd turned down because *it called for total nudity and she couldn't bring herself to do that; her family would disown her.*

Coming to Cannes with Lou and Cindi was an exciting diversion, especially as she'd never been out of America and it was an all-expenses-paid trip. Who knew what could happen? She certainly had nothing to lose.

Lou had his scenario down. He'd found out about a photo session that was to take place on the beach for an Italian starlet, and when the girl finished and left the scene, he planned for Cindi and Lucia to sashay past the photographers wearing the very briefest of thong bikinis.

"If you really wanna grab their attention," Lou suggested with a sly smile, "you'll take your tops off."

"No way," Lucia said firmly.

"Understand this," Lou answered with a stern shake of a bony finger. "To be a star, that's what you gotta do."

Cindi was up for it; she wasn't sleeping with Lou Steiner for the pure joy of sharing his bed. Like Lucia, being discovered was her constant dream.

The scene went exactly as Lou had prom-

ised it would. The moment the Italian starlet made her exit, Cindi and Lucia undulated into the picture. The photographers—spotting two pretty, scantily clad girls—began snapping away.

Lucia immediately experienced an addictive sensation of power. She'd never had this much attention and it was quite a kick.

Lou, standing on the sidelines, began waving his hands in the air, indicating to them that they should drop their tops. The photographers got into it, too. "C'mon, girls," yelled a couple of the English ones standing at the front. "Show us your titties."

Cindi unhooked her bra. Out tumbled her enormous new silicone breasts with huge, erect nipples.

Now the flashbulbs really started popping.

Lucia hung back, suddenly feeling quite shy.

"You, too," yelled one of the photographers. "C'mon, darlin'. Show us your boobs."

She wasn't ashamed of her body, but the thought of her dad and the rest of her family seeing the photographs stopped her. "Sorry, this is all you're getting, guys," she said, still trying to pose provocatively like she'd seen in the magazines.

But their focus was no longer directed at her. Cindi was the one getting all the attention.

By the time the photographers lost interest and drifted off, Cindi had posed for hundreds of photographs.

Lou came running over as Cindi put her top back on. "You did it!" he said excitedly. "These photos will hit the front pages everywhere."

"The front pages of what?" Lucia asked, a tad jealous.

"Magazines, newspapers," Lou crowed. "You lost out, honey. Shoulda listened to me."

Unfortunately—much to Lou's chagrin—the photographs did nothing for Cindi's career. Topless photos were no big deal anymore, so she and Lucia returned to America disappointed and undiscovered.

Lucia kept slogging away at her waitress job, going to auditions whenever she could, not dating much and having dinner at her family's house every Sunday night, where her dad lectured her on the importance of giving up her dreams and getting a proper *job in a bank like her sister Selma. He kept nagging her about making sure she had a secure future.*

Secure future indeed. No thank you. One way or the other she was going to become a star.

The only good thing that came out of her brief encounter with Lou Steiner was his name-change idea. A few weekends later she was watching TV with Selma when on came a Barry Manilow special. "Can we switch channels?" she asked, preferring a more soulful kind of music.

"No way!" Selma protested. "This Manilow guy is so cute! You gotta sit still an' watch him."

So she did. And when Mr. Manilow—resplendent in a white suit and gold brocade vest—began singing his famous hit "Copacabana," she suddenly sat up very straight. "Her name was Lola," he sang; "she was a showgirl . . ."

Yes! That was it! Lola. Lola Sanchez. It had a certain ring to it.

The moment she changed her name from Lucia to Lola, good things began to happen. She landed a legitimate agent who thought she had potential, then a small role on a cable soap show, and finally a minor but pivotal role in a real movie. After that, her big break starring in Merrill Zandack's film.

Stardom, when it came her way, was fast and furious.

Now, five years later, she was back in the south of France. Only this time she wasn't staying in a cheap hotel desperately trying to get noticed. This time she was a star.

Lola Sanchez.

Superstar.

It had been some trip.

"Take your pick," Linc said, indicating a treasure trove of exquisite diamond jewelry laid out in open black leather boxes lined with rich crushed velvet. "Or maybe you'd like to choose everything." He grinned—the little boy grin she found so damned appealing. "Catch me while I'm in a generous mood, sweetheart. You know it doesn't happen every day."

Shelby sighed, happy to see him sober, yet still disturbed about the previous night. "You don't have to do this," she said.

"I know I don't *have* to," he said, still grinning. "I *want* to. There's a big difference."

She sighed again. Why did he feel he always had to overcompensate? A simple apology would've been enough. Or a promise that he would never do it again.

"What's it gonna be?" he said, putting his arm around her.

She stared at the glittering jewelry, unable to decide on any of it.

"Personally I favor the pink diamond," he said. "Got a feeling it matches my eyes."

She couldn't help laughing as he picked up the magnificent seven-carat ring and slipped it on her finger. "Perfect fit. Now I'm gonna hafta marry you all over again."

The ring was certainly beautiful, but she didn't want him buying her expensive presents simply because he felt guilty.

"I hate it when you drink," she said softly.

"I know," he replied. "You don't have to remind me—I turn into jerk of the year."

"Then why do you do it?"

"Ah . . . ," he said ruefully. "Wouldn't it be nice if I could come up with a simple reply?"

They both knew it wasn't simple. Nothing about Linc was simple.

At least he realized he'd behaved like a jerk; that was something.

"How about making up your mind to

quit?" she suggested. "That's what would *really* make me happy."

"It's not that big a problem, sweetheart," he said, anxious to move on.

"Yes, Linc," she persisted. "It is."

"No, baby," he said, his voice hardening. "It isn't."

They'd had this conversation many times and nothing ever changed.

One of these days she had a nagging feeling that she'd have to leave him.

The sad thing was that he'd force her into it.

CHAPTER

8

"Mr. Zandack would like to see you in his stateroom," Jonas said, catching Cat outside her cabin.

"Forget about it," she answered brusquely. "I told you—I'm outta here."

Jonas was on a mission, there was no way he was allowing her to escape. "You could show him the courtesy of explaining why."

"Trust me," she said, narrowing her green eyes. "He *knows* why."

"Can't you give him two minutes?" Jonas

urged, well aware that Merrill had a nasty way of punishing the wrong people, and he was directly in the line of fire.

"Why?" she asked.

"For me," he said. "I'll be right outside the door. And if you don't work it out with him, I promise I'll personally put you on the tender. How's that?"

"Y'know, this isn't fair," she said, running a hand through her short blond hair. "This scene doesn't interest me. I want to split."

"I know you do," he said, peering past her into her cabin. Shit! She was packed and ready to go. "If you could just do it for me, I'll be forever in your debt," he said calmly. It hurt him to beg, but what else could he do?

Hmm . . . forever in her debt, huh? Not such a bad thing. "Well . . . okay," she sighed, agreeing, although she'd already made the decision that she didn't care *how* difficult it was finding somebody else to finance her movie, she was through with Merrill Zandack.

"Thank you," Jonas said, sounding properly grateful. "I owe you one."

She followed him upstairs and down the long corridor that led to Merrill's stateroom.

Jonas knocked tentatively, then opened the door. She walked into the room while Jonas remained outside.

Merrill was sitting up in bed wearing chocolate brown silk pajamas. His Russian girlfriend—fully made up—was in bed beside him, clad in a lacy negligee. A tray of breakfast goodies sat on his lap. It was a cozy scene of domestic bliss that hardly rang true.

"Uh . . . y'know I wasn't exactly planning on saying good-bye," Cat said, hovering by the door. "But apparently it's the rule around here." She took a bold step forward. "Would you *please* instruct your captain to let me off this boat before I'm forced to jump."

"Ah, Cat, Cat," Merrill said, shaking his head. "You are a very impulsive girl."

She was impulsive! What about him? Was it possible that he actually *didn't* recall demanding that she suck his pathetic erection last night? "Excuse me?" she said, glaring at him.

"If I did anything that offended you, I deeply apologize. Perhaps I had too many tequilas. I remember nothing."

Oh, so now he was coming up with the tried and true *I-remember-nothing* excuse.

Didn't that go out of style with the old Rock Hudson and Doris Day movies that she saw so often on late night TV?

"Of course, you may leave if that's what you're certain you want," Merrill continued. "As long as you don't forget that tonight I am throwing a party for you, and there will be many people attending that you should meet for the sake of your career."

Oh man, now he was laying a guilt trip on her; she'd totally forgotten about the party.

"If you like, Jonas will accompany you into town," Merrill added. "You can spend the day shopping. Buy anything you want. Jonas has my credit card."

"No, thanks," she said, shaking her head. "Shopping's not my thing."

"You could walk around the town," he suggested. "You're not a prisoner on my boat."

"Well, yeah," she said indignantly. "That's exactly how I feel."

His Russian girlfriend was staring at her with a totally blank face. Cat wondered if she actually spoke perfect English and couldn't be bothered to get involved. Highly likely, and quite wise.

"Take the tender to shore," Merrill said

magnanimously. "Jonas is yours for the day. He'll buy you lunch, and tonight you'll attend my party." A crafty pause. "Or should I say *our* party."

Now what was she supposed to do? Fortunately she hadn't reached Jump, because if she'd told him about the incident he'd insist she get the hell out of there. On the other hand, if she was smart, she'd stay and hopefully cement the financing and support for her movie.

"Okay," she said at last, mad at herself for weakening. But it wasn't as if Merrill was a *threat*—he was simply a fat old producer who obviously got off on trying to control women sexually.

"Excellent decision," Merrill said. "You're a clever girl."

Was she? She didn't *feel* clever.

"Jonas," Merrill yelled. "Get in here."

Jonas entered the room. "Take Cat to lunch," Merrill ordered. "And whatever else she wants to do. Be back here by five."

Jonas shot her a quick glance. She wondered if he thought she'd caved too easily. So what? She didn't care *what* he thought.

"Tonight's the party," Jonas said, obviously not thrilled at the prospect of spending the day with her. "I should be here."

"Not necessary," Merrill said, dismissing him. "You haven't had a day off since we arrived."

"It would hardly be a day off," Jonas pointed out.

"Go," Merrill said, waving them both out of his room.

"Hmm . . . ," Cat said once they were outside. "Looks like you're stuck with me."

"Yes, it does," he said dourly.

"Don't worry," she said. "Soon as we hit the shore you can take off and I'll do my own thing."

"I have my orders," he said rigidly. "And that's to take you to lunch."

"Do you always do everything he says?"

"Mr. Zandack is my boss. I'm getting the best education possible. There's nothing wrong with that."

"If you say so."

"Yes," he said, uptight as usual, "I do."

Lola wasn't sure what she wanted to do after *New York State of Mind.* She'd just finished shooting a thriller in Atlanta, and there were several scripts she was considering for the future. Last night Merrill Zandack had mentioned Cat's next project was going to be big. She'd seen *Wild Child,* and even though it was quite rough, it had a frantic energy and moved fast. Cat was not an experienced filmmaker, however; according to Merrill she had heat and a built-in young audience. Lola liked the thought of that. "What's the role?" she'd asked.

"A sexy, captivating woman like you," Merrill had replied.

Lola admired Merrill. He was responsible for her first big break, and even though she'd had to service him orally, she didn't mind, because it wasn't as if she was involved with anyone at the time, and a simple blow job wasn't *that* big a deal. In fact, ex-President Clinton didn't even consider it sex.

Yes, Merrill was a powerful man who could make things happen.

By the time her makeup artist and hairdresser had finished with her, and her stylist had helped her into a dazzling white sundress, she was ready for anything.

Faye Margolis was on the phone in the living room. Lola always felt secure when Faye was around; she considered her hard-working publicist better than a dozen body-guards. People were scared of Faye. She was a genius at what she did, and everyone knew it.

"Morning," Faye said briskly, putting down the phone. "Did we all sleep well?"

"Sure did," Lola replied, applying a touch more lip gloss with her finger. "What's my agenda today?"

"While *you* lunch with Mr. Zandack, I'll be setting up a room with TV crews from Sweden, Denmark, and Norway," Faye said. "Those interviews will take you half an hour after your lunch, then at three-thirty you're having a drink with the journalist from *Vanity Fair.*"

"Why aren't *I* coming to lunch?" Matt asked in a whiny voice.

"It's all business," Faye explained.

"Besides," Lola added, unable to resist a tiny dig, "Merrill didn't invite you."

"That's not very polite," Matt said sulkily.

"Nobody *forced* you to come here," Lola pointed out. "You could've stayed in L.A."

"I thought you *wanted* me to come," he said, pulling on his goatee.

"You heard Faye," Lola said impatiently. "It's an important business lunch. Surely you can see that it wouldn't look right having my husband trailing behind me?"

"I don't understand why I can't come," he complained, following her around the room.

"You'll be escorting her to the party tonight on Merrill's yacht," Faye said, interceding. "I'm sure that'll be more interesting for you, Matt."

"Then what'm I supposed to do today?" he said, scowling like a truculent child.

"Sorry," Lola said, picking up her Dolce & Gabbana sunglasses. "I'm not responsible for planning your leisure time."

Faye quickly hustled her out the door before the two of them became embroiled in a fight. No man enjoyed being relegated to the background. Famous women and non-famous men—it was an ongoing problem.

A group of eager photographers were gathered outside the hotel. They jumped to attention as soon as Lola appeared. She flashed them a smile and a few poses while wondering if any of them were the same photographers who'd captured her and Cindi on their first trip to the Cannes Festival. Little did they know what a bonanza they'd have if they discovered her early pictures.

Her mind flashed on Cindi for a moment. She hadn't spoken to her in years. The last she'd heard, Cindi had married Lou Steiner and was dabbling in soft-core porno movies. How sad if it was true.

She climbed into the waiting car, Faye right behind her.

The moment the car set off, Faye was on her case. "Do you have something you want to tell me?" Faye inquired in her raspy voice.

"What might that be?" Lola asked, casually removing her purple-tinted shades.

"I think you know what," Faye said, her tone brooking no argument. "And since *I'm* the one who'll have to deal with it, shouldn't you be giving me a heads-up?"

Lola sighed. She knew exactly what Faye was getting at. "It's not *my* fault," she answered defensively. "Matt is simply not right for me."

"He's trying," Faye said, uncharacteristically sympathetic.

"Not hard enough," Lola replied.

"I hope your plans do not include getting back together with Mr. Alvarez."

"What's wrong with Tony?" Lola asked, springing to her ex-fiancé's defense. "He's not doing drugs anymore."

"How do *you* know?" Faye said, squinting at her in a knowing way.

"Tony's had a bad rap, that's all."

"And because of his *bad rap*," Faye said pointedly, *"you* endured a ton of *bad* publicity."

"It wasn't *that* bad."

"You have a short memory, dear. The first time Tony was arrested for possession, *you* were with him. They took you to the station and kept you there for three hours. Your lawyer had to call in a lot of favors to make it go away. And so did I."

"Relax," Lola said. "I'm not planning on getting back together with Tony."

"Good," Faye said sternly.

Sometimes Faye's know-it-all attitude drove Lola crazy. Why couldn't the woman understand exactly how difficult it was for her?

"It's just that Matt is like a great big lummox who hangs around me with nothing to do," she said, unable to let it go. "He depends on *me* to entertain him. Isn't it about time he realized that I'm not an entertainment director? He's *boring,* Faye, and I can't *stand* boring."

"Then why did you marry him?" Faye asked, sensible as usual.

"You *know* why I married him," Lola said irritably. "Because my manager and my agent and my lawyer *and* you advised me to do so. 'Get as far away from Tony as possible,' you all insisted. 'He's ruining your career.' So I did."

"I'd call that excellent advice," Faye said. "It distanced you from a man who was bringing you nothing but damaging publicity. It saved you from being dragged down with him."

"You don't understand," Lola insisted, her eyes gleaming. "I have to be *passionate* with a man. There's no way I can settle for mediocre."

"And apparently you're not going to," Faye murmured dryly.

As soon as they arrived at the Hotel du Cap, Lola forgot about Matt and Tony and launched into career mode, sweeping through the spacious lobby as if she owned the place. Faye accompanied her to the outdoor patio overlooking the blue Mediterranean, where a solicitous maître d' ushered her over to Merrill Zandack's table.

Merrill was sitting by himself reading *Va-*

riety while puffing on his usual fat cigar. He did not get up as Lola approached. She tapped him on the shoulder. "Lola, dear," he greeted. "You look delicious as usual."

"I don't know how, considering the way you plied me with tequila last night," she said, flirting outrageously. "You're such a bad boy, Merrill," she added, wagging a playful finger in his face as she slid into the chair opposite him. "I have a monster hangover. I must look like a hag."

"Impossible, my dear. You're one of the sexiest and most talented actresses around."

"I *love* that you think that," Lola said, wondering what other actresses he had in mind. "You were the first one to give me a break. I'll always be grateful for that."

"Me too," he said with a dirty-old-man leer.

Oh, God! Was he remembering his shriveled old cock in her mouth? How humiliating!

"I have that script we talked about for you to read," he said. "Cat's written a very complex character. Personally, I think you're right for it."

"Did your people messenger copies to

my people?" she asked. Translation: *I can't be bothered to read it, so send it to my manager.*

"Who needs agents and managers?" Merrill said. "I want *you* to read it. You'll do that for me, Lola, won't you?"

"Of course I will, Merrill," she answered graciously. "I trust your judgment all the way."

Sitting with her director, Russell Savage, and her costar, Beck Carson, on a raised platform with a microphone in front of her, facing an army of international journalists, Shelby wished she hadn't accepted the damn pink diamond ring. Linc probably thought all was forgiven, which meant that he'd do it again. Maybe not this week or even this month, but he had a pattern he always followed. No Alcoholics Anonymous for Linc Blackwood—the man who claimed he didn't have a problem. Shelby was becoming more convinced every day that if he didn't do something about it, his drinking would eventually destroy their relationship.

Russell Savage, a short, wiry, staccato-voiced man, with stand-up black hair and thick, bushy eyebrows, nudged her. "Your answer, sweetie," he urged.

Her answer. To what? She was thinking about Linc and hadn't heard the question.

"Excuse me," she said into her microphone. "Could you please repeat the question?"

"Would you be prepared to do more on-screen nudity?" asked a pie-faced woman with a thick Swedish accent.

"Uh . . . it would very much depend on the script and, naturally, the director. Mr. Savage made me feel extremely at ease. And so did Beck," she added, indicating the actor sitting on her right. "Both of these wonderful men were always respectful. Plus there were only essential people on the set when we shot the love scene everyone seems to be talking about."

"Love scene?" said the female journalist sneeringly. "Is that what you call it?"

"Yes," Russell Savage said, taking over. "It's a raw, very sexual *love* scene, and only an actress of Shelby Cheney's caliber and talent could've pulled it off."

"Some people have compared it to the graphic sex scene between Billy Bob Thornton and Halle Berry in *Monster's Ball*," said a male journalist. "How do you feel about that comparison?"

"Flattered," Shelby replied. "Halle Berry is an amazing actress."

"She certainly is," agreed Russell, rapidly joining in again. "But let's face it, guys—comparisons are lazy journalism. *Rapture* is a completely different movie."

And so it went, most questions involving the nudity and sexual content of the film.

Shelby couldn't wait for the torture to be over. She was an actress, not a talking puppet.

After Shelby left, Linc decided that since he'd never made it to all *his* morning interviews, he'd better catch up. He was well aware that there were many journalists waiting to speak to him, and pissing off the press was never a good idea. So reluctantly he wandered downstairs, unshaven, hiding his bloodshot eyes behind dark glasses.

Women's heads still swiveled. Linc exuded a rugged sex appeal that they obviously found irresistible.

Norm Johnson, his publicist, was pacing the lobby, tearing out his hair—metaphorically speaking, because Norm featured a flat red rug that perched on his bald scalp like an Indian's trophy. It would take an army to dislodge it.

"Hey, Norm," Linc said, patting the short man on the back like he hadn't missed a dozen interviews.

Norm glowered on the inside. Linc was not an easy actor to deal with at the best of times, especially when he'd been drinking. And last night he'd obviously experienced quite a bender.

"You're late!" Norm wanted to yell at him. "You're late! And rude! And a pain in the ass!"

He didn't say any of those words—instead he manufactured the perfect publicist's noncommittal expression and got down to business. Dealing with stars was never easy, especially big macho studs who thought they owned the world.

"So what's happenin', Norm?" Linc asked, grinning lazily.

"There's a woman from *Premiere* magazine who's been waiting since ten A.M. She's in the bar."

"Wise choice," Linc said, thinking that maybe one Bloody Mary was exactly what he needed to get him through the day. One Bloody Mary and that was it. "Let's go," he said. "I'm ready to charm."

"Glad to hear it," Norm said through clenched teeth as they headed for the bar.

CHAPTER
9

"We should have the tender drop us in Juan-les-Pins, where we can walk around," Cat suggested.

"Walk around and do *what*?" Jonas said, not very pleased at the prospect of spending the day with Cat when he'd sooner be checking over every detail of the upcoming party.

"Like hang out and do nothing," she replied vaguely, inspecting his outfit of linen slacks and crisp white shirt. "You'd better go put on something more comfortable before we take off."

Reluctantly he acquiesced, changing into shorts and a tee shirt before jumping into the tender.

"Nice legs!" she teased. "Shame about the face!"

A few hours later they both realized what a welcome change it was getting away from the razzle-dazzle of the festival. They'd perused the many small boutique shops, strolled along the seashore, and finally they'd settled at an outside café in the middle of the main square.

"So, Jonas," Cat said, sipping a Pernod on the rocks and lowering her shades, all the better to give him one of her penetrating green-eyed looks. "You've got to admit this is more fun than all those uptight events we've had to suffer through."

"Suffer through?" he said, raising an eyebrow. "People would pay fortunes to attend these events."

"You know what I mean."

"You have no idea how lucky you are, do you?" he said, shaking his head.

"Lucky?" she said casually. "How come?"

"You've got Merrill Zandack behind you. What more can you ask for? He'll make *sure Caught* gets made. Admit it—you're *unbelievably* lucky."

"Or maybe I'm simply talented," she said quickly.

"That too," he conceded. "Only there are thousands of talented people who struggle for years and never get a break."

"That's *their* karma. Mine is pretty good."

"How old are you, Cat?"

"You *know* how old I am," she said, not appreciating his superior tone. "And what's *that* got to do with anything?"

"You're lucky, that's all," he said, thinking how easy she'd had it.

She stared at him for a moment. She'd always felt Jonas did not like her, now he'd proven it by making out she was a spoiled little rich girl who simply happened to get lucky. "Hey," she responded sharply. "I had an idea and I pursued it. Most people talk a good game, then never do anything about it. *I* got off my ass and called in every favor I could to make my first movie. Nobody handed me anything. The fact that it worked doesn't make me *lucky.* That's insulting."

"I didn't mean it to be," he said, backing down.

"How about *you?*" she said challengingly. "Do *you* have a dream that hasn't happened 'cause you're too busy kissing Mr. Z.'s ass?"

"Some people have to work for a living," he said, keeping his temper in check. He was annoyed with himself because it was true, he *did* kiss Merrill's ass, but that was because it was his only option if he ever planned on making it as a producer. He always remembered the Joel Silver story—Joel Silver, producer of many megahit movies including the *Die Hard* series, started out his career as another big producer's gofer and driver. If it could happen for Joel Silver, why couldn't it happen for him?

"I've worked bloody hard to get where I am," Cat said earnestly. "I'm *entitled* to everything I've achieved."

"Even though you're only nineteen?"

"What's *with* you?" she said, amazed that he was carrying on about her age. "Young is where it's at today. Don't you get it—*young,* Jonas. How old are *you?*"

"Twenty-six."

"You look older," she said rudely.

"Why would you say that?"

" 'Cause you've got an old attitude."

"Thanks."

"You're always dressed up in your Prada, running after Mr. Zandack, and y'know, I think you get on people's nerves."

"I do not," he said indignantly. "Perhaps I get on *your* nerves. Other than you, I'm well liked."

"Ha! Well liked? Nobody even notices you."

"That's not very nice."

"You're not very nice to me," she responded, knowing she sounded like an argumentative kid, but unable to help herself. "Ever since I arrived here you've been on my case."

"Do you think it's because I didn't have international parents like you who could afford to let me roam around the world?"

"Careful," she said caustically. "Your resentment is beginning to show."

"I don't resent you."

"Then stop being such an uptight asshole toward me."

"Didn't know I was."

"Apology accepted," she said sarcastically. "What is it you want to do, anyway?"

"One of these days I hope to be producing films that have something meaningful to say."

"That's very Oprah Winfrey of you."

"I'm using this opportunity as Mr. Zandack's personal assistant to learn."

"Hmm . . . then be very careful exactly what you learn from dear old Merrill."

"Mr. Zandack is a major force in the film industry."

"Tell me the truth, Jonas, are you pissed he's prepared to finance my movie?"

"I can assure you, this isn't personal."

"Oh, *really?*"

"Maybe we should drop the subject."

"I'm cool with that," she said, checking her watch. "What time is it in Australia? I want to phone my husband."

"You got married way too young."

"Oh, here we go with the age thing again," she sighed. "What *is* your hang-up with age?"

"It's a well-known statistic that most women wait until they're in their mid-twenties to get married."

"Why wait?"

"Sensible people do."

"Who said I'm sensible? I'm a nutter. Surely you've guessed by now?"

"Was Jump your first boyfriend?"

"Ha!" she said, taking another sip of Pernod. *"That's* hilarious. Where do you think I got all that info for my first movie? It's *my* story, you know." A beat, then, "How about you?"

"Why is it that you always manage to turn the question around?"

"I've got an inquisitive mind."

"You sure do."

"So, do *you* have a . . . partner?"

"What do you mean by 'partner'?"

"You know," she said, pressing on. "Someone you live with."

"Are you intimating that I'm gay?"

"Didn't say that."

"What do *you* think 'partner' means?"

"Okay, so yeah, you *are* gay, right?"

"Christ!" he said, thinking that this girl was too much. "Sorry to disappoint you, but I am most definitely *not."*

"Oops!" she said, realizing that she'd made a mistake. "It's just that, y'know, we're here in this cool place and there's all these hot girls parading by in shorts and bikinis, and you're not even eyeballing any of them."

"I don't look at other women when I'm with one."

"It's not exactly like we're together, Jonas."

He frowned. "What made you think I was gay?"

She shrugged, feeling somewhat awkward. "I dunno. You never . . . well, I guess I've only seen you at work."

"I can assure you," he repeated. "I am *not* gay."

"Okay, okay, I believe you."

"Good."

"Can we order food now? I'm starving."

"There's one thing I feel I should mention before I read your script," Lola said, toying with the stem of her wineglass in a sexually suggestive fashion.

"What?" Merrill responded, lighting up a fresh cigar.

"You're not planning on letting that girl direct, are you?"

"It's her project, Lola."

"So *what? You're* the boss."

"She's talented. You saw *Wild Child.*"

"She's also inexperienced. There's no way I could work with someone so new. I'll read it, and if I like it, we'll talk. I'm sure you know that I now get costar and director approval."

"Not a problem," Merrill said, sweating profusely. "If you wanna make the movie, you'll get whatever you want."

"Here comes my publicist," Lola said, waving at Faye, who was fast approaching their table. "Interviews and more interviews—you know how it goes."

"You work hard for your movies," Merrill said. "Some of my actresses get paid a fortune an' refuse to do shit. You're a professional, Lola. I admire that."

"It was a lovely lunch, Merrill," she said graciously, reaching for her sunglasses. "It's always a pleasure seeing you."

"You'll be at my party tonight?"

"Wouldn't miss it."

"You bringing that husband of yours?"

"Of course."

"No more Tony Alvarez in your life, huh?"

"No," she said, putting on her sunglasses.

"Tony's trouble. You're a smart girl getting rid of him."

She nodded, pretending to agree, although she was seething inside. How come everyone thought they were free to criticize her love life? She would sleep with whomever she wanted. If they didn't approve, too bad.

Faye reached their table. Lola got up. Merrill didn't.

He's such a rude sonofabitch, she thought. *Rude, but powerful. And powerful always wins out.*

"Bye, darling," she said, bending down to give him the Hollywood peck on both cheeks.

"See you tonight," he said, blowing acrid smoke in her face. "We'll talk more."

He watched her as she walked away, big ass tightly encased in clinging white jersey. Director and costar approval indeed. Actresses! They were all the same. Jesus! How quickly it went to their heads. He could remember her down on her knees sucking his cock like her life depended on it. And perhaps it did, because he'd had the power to make her a star.

Power. That's what it was all about. And how better to feel the power than to have some eager little cocksucker down on her knees servicing him.

As they moved away from the table Lola turned to Faye. "Merrill will do anything for me," she murmured. "Men are so easy. Especially unattractive ones."

Faye wasn't interested in hearing about her client's conquests. "There are three TV crews waiting," she said. "I've checked the lighting and it's good."

"What points should I hit?"

"Talk about anything except your love life," Faye warned.

"My love life?" Lola said, raising an eyebrow. "Surely you're forgetting I'm a married woman. Nothing to talk about."

"And don't *you* forget it," Faye said firmly. "If they *should* mention Tony Alvarez, you wish him the best, you'll always be there for him as a friend, but you haven't seen him since you got married."

"Thank you, Faye," Lola drawled sarcastically. "What *would* I do without you?"

She'd already decided that the first person she'd call the moment she got back to America was Tony. They belonged together, and it was about time she followed her instincts instead of listening to everybody else's advice.

"You handled yourself well," Russell said admiringly as they left the press conference. "Didn't need my help at all."

"Yes I did," Shelby answered ruefully. "Your comments were perfect."

"I kinda know how to handle 'em," Russell said. "Done it a time or two."

She sighed. "Are we *constantly* going to be compared to *Monster's Ball?*"

"You know what the press are like, they always need a hook."

"It's upsetting that people think I'm hanging on to Halle Berry's coattails because she did an outrageous sex scene and now *I* have."

"We were shooting our movie before she even won her Oscar," Russell pointed out. "Forget about it."

"I can't stand these press junkets."

He laughed dryly. "This is nothing. Wait until we get back to the States and our movie hits the screens there. You'd better prepare yourself."

"As long as you're beside me, Russell.

You've got a way of always making me feel secure."

It was true. Filming *Rapture* with Russell Savage had been an extremely rewarding experience. Not only was he a fine director, he was also a caring human being, and that made all the difference. She was quite convinced she would never have been able to get through the graphic love scenes with another director in charge. Her role was too personal, plus Russell brought out a side of her that she had not known she possessed.

"Terrific answers, honey," said Beck Carson, winking at her on his way past. "You're quite a pro."

Beck had been another source of strength to her. He was one of those low-key actors who never stopped working. He had world-weary eyes and a phenomenal screen presence. Twice nominated, it was quite possible he could be nominated again for his role in *Rapture.*

"When are you leaving?" she asked.

"Flying to New York later this afternoon," he said. "How about you?"

"Linc and I are off in a couple of days. We're stopping by to see my parents in London."

"What a city!" Beck said, rolling his eyes. "Spent quite a bit of time there last summer. English people are the best."

"I'll take that as a compliment," she said, smiling. "Even though I now live in Hollywood."

"You'll *always* be English," Beck said. "You've got that English thing going. I hope Linc realizes what a lucky sonofabitch he is."

"I hope so too," she said, turning back to Russell. "Will you be at Merrill Zandack's party tonight?"

"Yup," Russell said, nodding. "When Merrill throws his annual party, *everyone* shows up. It's a Cannes staple. At least the caviar is the best."

"That's very Hollywood of you, Russ. *Where* did you say you were born?"

"Brooklyn, honey, and I don't *ever* forget it."

"Really?"

"That's the trick of surviving in this business—never forget where you came from."

Shelby nodded. Perhaps that was Linc's problem. He could never forget his abusive father and the shocking violence he'd endured as a child. It was one of the reasons she always forgave him for his out-of-control drinking and vile moods.

That's why she loved him so much—because deep down he wasn't the big macho movie star, he was a little boy lost and he needed her. He also needed therapy, and one of these days she was convinced that he'd give in and she'd get him to spend more time with Brenda. If only he would, it might solve all their problems.

CHAPTER
10

Lunch was a feast. Giant pink shrimp followed by succulent, grilled chicken and tomato-and-mozzarella pizzas. For dessert there was rich chocolate cake and coconut gelato.

"I haven't eaten this good since I got here," Cat announced, licking her fingers with great glee.

"You're a fast-food girl, then, huh?" Jonas said, leaning forward to remove a speck of chocolate from her lips.

"This isn't fast food, this is amazing."

"You're easy to please," he said, thinking that sometimes she actually acted her age; it was most endearing.

"Jump says I'm not."

"He's wrong."

She grinned. "You know what I'd like to do now?"

"Go back to the boat?" he said hopefully. "Because there's a lot more party details I should be taking care of."

"Oh, no," she said, vigorously shaking her head. "Merrill promised I had you for the day, so now *I* want to go waterskiing."

"You're not serious?"

"Perfectly serious. Why?" she said, wrinkling her nose. "Don't you ski?"

"I tried telling you earlier—didn't have your privileged upbringing."

"Privileged upbringing my ass! Warring parents who were always on the run. Jump taught me in Australia. We spent ten days exploring the Great Barrier Reef. It was way cool!"

"He sounds like quite a guy."

"You'd like him," she said, adding a mischievous, "and now that I know you're not gay, you two could be friends."

"Does that mean he's homophobic?"

"No way."

"Then why couldn't we be friends if I *was* gay?"

"Which you're not."

"Not."

"Jump gets along with everyone."

"Is he bisexual?"

"Come *on,*" she protested. "Stop teasing me."

"Do I have to?" he said, mock-serious.

"Yes, Jonas, you have to."

"Y'know," he said, stretching, "I've got to admit that this has been kind of relaxing, getting away from the big man for a day."

"You need to do it more often," she said, leaping up and reaching for his hand. " 'Cause now I'm about to teach you how to water-ski."

He started to protest, but she was having none of it. "What's under your shorts?" she demanded.

"Excuse me?"

"Have you got on underwear?"

"Of course," he said, alarmed. "And I'm *not* skiing in them."

She stifled a grin at the thought of Jonas in his underwear. Boxers or briefs? Aware of his label fetish, she decided they had to be Calvin Klein and tight.

"Come on," she said, pulling him up. "I'm buying you swim shorts to protect your modesty, then you can learn."

"Don't *want* to learn," he objected, shaking his head.

"Yes you *do,*" she said insistently. " 'Cause when you're a big producer making huge, meaningful movies, you'll come here and knock the pants off everyone with your cool athletic abilities. How about *that?*"

He liked the fact that she had confidence in him. Maybe she wasn't such a pain in the butt after all. "So you actually believe I'll make it?" he said.

"Anyone who has a passion is gonna make it. Hey—I'm a classic example. Dropped out of school at fifteen, was a major druggie—only don't mention that to Merrill."

"I quit school at fifteen too."

"You did?"

He nodded.

"How come?"

"My old man needed extra drinking money."

"Sounds like a story I should hear."

"Another time."

"Promise?"

"Sure," he said, uncomfortable because he didn't like revealing stuff about himself. After all, she couldn't possibly be interested, she was merely killing time until she hooked up with her rock 'n' roll husband.

Two hours later, half drowned and surprisingly content, they lay side by side on sun beds on a half-empty beach. Cat was oblivious to the attention coming her way, for stripped down to her bikini she was a total looker—tall, with an athletic body, spiky blond hair, and classic features. Even her various small tattoos and piercings failed to detract from her beauty.

Jonas had trained himself not to have feelings for any of the actresses he came in contact with—and working with Merrill, there were many. But Cat was not an actress, she was a writer/director, and he suddenly found himself extremely attracted to her, which he realized was not a wise thing. This kind of attraction had not happened to him in a while. He'd given up on girlfriends because they were too time consuming—not to mention demanding. He preferred to concentrate all his energy on Mr. Zandack, a most demanding boss.

Watching Cat, it suddenly occurred to him what he was missing.

"Man, you were so hysterical on the skis," she said, breaking into a fit of giggles. "I *warned* you not to bend your arms. The moment you bent 'em, it was all over. You took such a dive."

"Glad you're amused."

"I wish you could've seen the expression on your face!"

"I had a better time sitting in the boat watching you."

"I'm a fine skier, huh?" she said boastfully. "A champion!"

"Not bad."

"Ha! Admit it—I *am* a champion!"

"Yes, Cat, you're pretty damn great."

Christ! He'd better put a hold on his feelings before he made an idiot of himself. She was being friendly and he was falling in love.

"We should be getting back to the yacht," he said, checking his watch.

"How'll we get back?"

"I thought maybe we'd swim."

"*And* he has a sense of humor too," she said, laughing.

"You were under the impression I didn't?"

"Well . . . I *am* getting to know you better. You're not as uptight as I thought."

"Uptight?"

"Don't sound surprised. You're *so* into your work, it's frightening."

"And that's a bad thing?"

"All work and no play," she said flirtatiously.

"Let's go," he said abruptly. He didn't want *anyone* getting to know him better, not even Cat.

"Five more minutes," she pleaded, rolling onto her stomach and, to his extreme discomfort, unclipping her bikini top. "I'm having *such* an amazing time."

"You can sunbathe on the yacht," he pointed out, trying not to stare.

"No, I can't. The crew are everywhere, and I don't fancy the idea of Zandack leering at me with a hidden camera. I bet he has them stashed all over the place."

"No, he doesn't."

"Face it, Jonas. He's a dirty old man. And old perverts get off on hidden cameras.

By the way," she added casually, "does he proposition all his actresses too?"

"How would I know?"

" 'Cause you know everything he does."

"Not everything," he said, marveling that this girl possessed such an extraordinary talent for moviemaking. Where did it come from? Today she was just a kid having fun.

"C'mon," she said persuasively. "We're friends now. You can tell me."

"Nothing to tell," he said. "And if there was—I'd be loyal to my boss."

"Loyal, my ass," she snorted. "You think he'd be loyal to you?"

"Yes."

"You could've warned me about him," she said accusingly.

"Why would I do that? You might have liked it."

"Yeah, sure," she said sarcastically. "There's *nothing* I like better than sucking—"

"That's enough," he interrupted, hurriedly holding up his hand.

She giggled. "You're a prude."

"No, I'm not. Can we please go now?"

"If you insist," she said, sitting up and fastening her top.

He attempted to avert his eyes, an impossible feat.

"Tell me about tonight," she said, reaching for her shirt. "Who'll be there I should play nice to?"

"You don't have to be nice to anybody," he assured her. "Your talent speaks for itself."

"Jonas," she said, wriggling her long legs into her shorts, "that's the coolest thing you've ever said to me."

Granting an interview for *Vanity Fair* was a treacherous path indeed. Faye had already negotiated the cover, so Lola felt confident that the photographs would be fantastic since *Vanity Fair* employed only the best. She was hoping the photographer would be Annie Leibovitz or Greg Gorman, both of whom she'd worked with before. However, she was nervous about the interview, especially as for once Faye had been unable to secure copy approval.

Starting off in the south of France was not bad, and thankfully the interviewer was male. She always enjoyed a better rapport with men. Sometimes women were jealous of her, even though she did nothing to promote their feelings of inadequacy. In fact, she went out of her way to be extra nice to them.

She walked into the interview, attitude in place. Gorgeous yet humble. Sexy yet approachable. A girl who'd made it from nothing, and now appreciated every minute of her phenomenal success.

The interviewer, an older man of stature, put her at ease immediately, and then they were off.

As usual, Faye had warned her that she was not to talk about Tony. "What if *he* brings him up?" she'd said. "I have to say *something.*"

"You'll say what I told you before," Faye had answered sternly. "And remember, you are now a married woman, so it would not be appropriate for you to discuss another man."

"I know," Lola had argued, "but by the time the magazine hits the stands I might not *be* a married woman."

"Nobody knows that, do they, dear?"

"Surely the magazine will be pissed if I talk lovingly about Matt, then dump him? They won't have time to change their copy."

"Go ahead and *pretend* that you're happily married," Faye had insisted, refusing to change course. "We'll deal with the divorce when it comes."

So that's exactly what she did. She talked about her past movies, her future career plans, Matt, and the things they enjoyed doing together. "We like sending out for pizza and watching videos," she found herself saying. "The simple things are best. Family, close friends. Our favorite evenings are spent staying at home."

Thankfully, after an hour and a half it was over, to be continued in L.A.

"God!" she complained in the car, driving back to the hotel. "It's so tough. I have to keep a smile on my face, listen to everything he says, ask him about *his* family, and appear to be interested. The truth is if I saw him on the street tomorrow, I wouldn't even remember his name."

"Why do you feel you have to put on this persona for journalists?" Faye asked. "Why not be yourself?"

"*You* try it, Faye," she said irritably. "It isn't easy. They come in with a preconceived idea of who I am and what they intend to write. Because I'm sexy and successful, they immediately think I'm going to be a diva or a bitch. It takes mucho energy and concentration to change their minds."

"You do a good job, Lola."

"Thanks."

"Try and get some rest before the party tonight."

"I plan to."

"And since I won't be there, make sure that you and Matt do not fight in public. There will be photographers everywhere."

"Yes, Faye. I promise, Faye," Lola chanted, fed up with hearing the same old thing.

She ran into a couple of producers and an important director on her way up to her suite. It was always good to be seen in the right places.

She entered the suite on a high, from which she rapidly came down when she was greeted by the sight of Matt lying on a massage table in the middle of the living room wearing nothing but a towel. The masseuse, clad in an electric-blue halter top and crotch-hugging shorts, looked more like a hooker than a professional.

"Oh," Lola said sarcastically. "I do hope I'm not disturbing you."

"Naw, that's okay," Matt said, not getting it as usual. "Nadine's easing the tension in my back."

Lola checked out his towel, noticing that he had an impressive hard-on.

"I'll be in the bedroom, I need my privacy," she said, seriously pissed that he had some strange masseuse in their suite. For all he knew the woman could be a spy for the tabloids, and *he* was lying there with a hard-on. It simply wasn't cool. Plus her stylist and her makeup and hair people would be arriving soon for touch-ups, and she wanted to be free to wander around in her robe. Matt was an albatross hanging around her neck. She would be so much happier when he wasn't around.

Deciding to take a shower, she marched into the bathroom and slammed the door.

Standing under the stream of warm water washing away her cares, she began to relax.

Naturally, after a few moments she started thinking about Tony and whether she should call him one more time. She couldn't blame him for being mad; his macho pride was hurt. If the situation were reversed she would be livid, and probably never speak to him again. Perhaps he needed more persuading that they should get back together.

Tony Alvarez. She thought about his long black curly hair, dark sexy eyes, low-down dirty laugh, and the way he touched her in all the right places.

Yes. Tony Alvarez. He was the man.

And she wanted him back.

The moment Shelby entered their suite, Linc was all over her, barely giving her a chance to catch her breath. "You look beautiful. I missed you *so* much. C'mere, sweetheart, I love you," he said, pulling her toward him. "Lemme see your ring. It sparkles like your eyes."

He smelled of mouthwash, a bad sign. And he was extremely loving—even more so than usual. She wanted to ask him if he'd been drinking, but she knew he'd get furious and deny it, so what was the point?

He almost carried her into the bedroom. The bed was strewn with rose petals; a bottle of champagne stood in an ice bucket close by.

"It's not our anniversary," she said, quite startled. "What is all this?"

"It's for *you,* baby. I'm showing you how much I love you."

"Then let's not open the champagne."

"Don't you trust me?" he asked, sounding hurt. "I told you, I'm not drinking anymore. Hey—one lousy glass of champagne never hurt anyone. Right, sweetie?"

"You never stop at one glass, Linc."

"Don't nag, Shell, I promise I'll behave," he said, starting to kiss her.

She couldn't resist him. Ever since the first time they'd met he'd always had a certain effect on her. Physically he was the most exciting man she'd ever been with. Not that there were many—only two before Linc that she'd actually slept with.

He pushed her down on the bed. "When did you get time to do all this?" she gasped, overwhelmed by the sweet smell of the rose petals and Linc's relentless touch.

"I have my ways," he said mysteriously, his practiced hands moving up and down her body.

"I like your ways," she said, shivering.

"You do?" he said, releasing the clip on her bra.

"Yes," she murmured.

"And you like this?" he continued, fondling her bare breasts.

"Oh, yes, yes."

"Y'know, sweetie, I've been thinking," he said, stopping for a moment and propping himself up on one elbow.

"About what?" she asked breathlessly.

"I think it's about time you quit taking the pill."

She didn't dare tell him that she'd stopped taking the pill three months ago. He was so paranoid about her getting pregnant that he usually pulled out before he reached orgasm.

"Are you telling me something that you know I want to hear?" she asked softly.

"I'm telling you you're the most beautiful, sweetest woman I've ever met," he said, caressing her nipples with his fingertips.

Did this mean he was actually ready to make a baby?

Yes, she was sure it did.

A feeling of euphoria swept over her. This was the Linc she loved, the man she'd married. And now he was telling her that she could have his baby.

She put all thoughts and doubts out of her mind, lay back, and totally surrendered to the moment.

CHAPTER

11

"It's about *time* you got your lazy, good-for-shit, fuckin' dumb ass back here," Merrill screamed at Jonas as soon as they returned to the yacht.

Cat was shocked. She'd never seen Merrill like this—red in the face, eyes bulging, sweaty double chins quivering like jelly. Since she was used to standing up to bullies—her father was a classic example—she was not at all intimidated. "Quit with the screaming," she said, staring defiantly at the angry mogul. *"You* were the one who made him spend the day with *me.* And we've had a very nice time, thank you—in case you're interested."

"He's got work to do," Merrill yelled. "Fuckin' *work.* We're throwing a goddamn party, in case you've forgotten."

"Whatever you need, Mr. Zandack," said Jonas, quick to fall back into loyal assistant mode.

"I *need* you to get your useless ass in gear," shouted Merrill.

Cat headed downstairs to her cabin. She didn't care to watch Jonas being humiliated in front of everyone. Today she'd discovered that he was a nice guy; he didn't deserve to be treated like shit.

Once in her cabin she picked up the phone and finally got through to Jump in Australia. "I've been *desperate* to speak to you," she said, totally psyched to hear his voice. "What's going on? You're never in your room."

"I'm here now," he mumbled. "An' it's the middle of the freakin' night."

"Oh, *sorry.* How's it going?"

"Rock 'n' roll, babe," he said, giving a loud, audible yawn. "What can I tell you?"

"Merrill's behaving like a pig. I can't wait

to fill you in on all the horror stories when I see you. The best news is that I'm definitely getting my movie financed."

" 'S good."

"So tell me everything about the tour. What's Kris Phoenix like?"

"He's a cool dude, big star." Another loud yawn.

"You sound out of it."

"You'd be freakin' out of it if *you* were woken up in the middle of the night," he grumbled.

"You could've called *me."*

"Gettin' through to a boat is a hassle."

"What're you *talking* about?" she said, frowning. "It's a *boat,* not the freaking moon."

"You tryin' to pick a fight with me?" he said belligerently. "Is that why you called?"

"No, Jump," she answered patiently. "I *called* to tell you that I miss you. Don't you miss me?"

"Yeah, yeah."

He was in one of his obnoxious moods, probably zoned out on weed. He was a big stoner—joints for breakfast, lunch, and dinner. "I think you should call me when you're conscious," she said, determined not to lose her cool.

"Whatever," he mumbled.

She slammed down the phone. What kind of a bug did he have up *his* ass?

Grabbing her iPod, she lay down on the bed, put on her Bose headphones, and began listening to Eminem at full volume. Playing loud music always made her feel better.

Donatella Versace had designed Lola a drop-dead, in-your-face, cut-down-to-the-crack-in-her-butt, and plunging-in-the-front gown. There was not much material involved, but what there was, in slinky white silk cut on the bias, showed up every inch of her spectacular body. Her olive skin gleamed; her chestnut hair was wild and curly, swirling around her shoulders; diamond starburst earrings adorned her ears; and an emerald bullet hung around her neck, nestling between her breasts. She knew she looked hot.

When she left the hotel on Matt's arm, the photographers confirmed it by causing a small riot, all of them struggling and pushing to get the best shot. Matt was happy to

pose beside her, the proud husband, determined to score a career of his own.

Merrill Zandack's people had organized a
flotilla of small boats to take the guests out
to his yacht, which was majestically moored
in the bay like a solitary shimmering summer jewel.

"How will I get on a boat in these heels?"
Lola worried, pointing at her Manolas.

"Take 'em off," Matt suggested, adding a
gallant "I'll carry you."

"You'd do that for me?"

"I'd do anything for you, you're my wife,"
he said, thinking of the photo opportunities.

She hated it when he was nice; it gave
her an attack of the guilts. And Matt *had*
been nice when she'd first met him. Nice
and sexy and well endowed. Now he was
just plain boring.

Fortunately the sea was smooth as glass,
making the ride to the yacht fast and easy.
Several crewmen began tripping over one
another to help her aboard. She realized as
she climbed onto the yacht that she was
giving everyone a fine view of her ass. Let
'em have a cheap thrill, she didn't care.

The yacht was festooned with fairy
lights and exotic flowers; a Brazilian group

played seductive background music; uniformed crew members were everywhere, plus good-looking, hot young waiters in tight white jeans and tee shirts with *The Zandack* emblazoned on the front in red lettering.

Lola plucked a glass of champagne from a tray and basked in the attention coming her way.

Merrill greeted her with a sloppy wet kiss on both cheeks. She wished people wouldn't do that, it ruined her makeup.

Sharon Stone wafted by; the woman seemed to be everywhere. And then Lola spotted Linc Blackwood and Shelby Cheney, who, according to the buzz, was *the* actress of the moment.

Lola felt a shiver of resentment. Why couldn't *she* score a role like Shelby had in *Rapture?* Why couldn't *she* work with an Oscar-winning director like Russell Savage?

She glanced around, seeing if she could spot Elliott Finerman. He'd better have made an offer to Linc, because if he hadn't done so, she would be seriously angry. Elliott needed her to get his movie made. Surely *he* realized that without her he *had* no movie.

"There's Linc Blackwood," she said to Matt. "Let's go say hello."

"Sure," Matt responded obligingly, and they headed in Linc's direction.

Shelby was surrounded by well-wishers all telling her how great her performance was in *Rapture.* She listened appreciatively, while all she really wanted to do was hold on to her husband. When he wanted to be, Linc was so attentive and full of love, and now that he'd promised they could try for a baby, she felt blissful. It was such a relief to hear him say those words.

She wondered if she was pregnant already. He'd made love to her in such a beautiful fashion. The moment they made a baby she wanted it to be the result of a special night of love exactly like tonight.

Soon they were separated. She didn't mind because Linc had faithfully promised he wouldn't drink.

Merrill Zandack greeted her effusively, hanging on to her arm. "Magnificent!" he enthused. "An Oscar-worthy performance, my dear." Then he started talking about the script written by his young protégée. "I want you to read it," he said. "It's a perfect role for you."

"I'll read it, Merrill," she said agreeably.

"Good, good. We *should* work together. Can't imagine why we haven't."

"I'd like that."

"Come," he said, throwing his arm around her shoulders. "I'll show you around."

"I'm sure Linc would want to join us."

"He'll see it later. Come with me," Merrill insisted, leading her past a burly security man who guarded the long corridor leading to his stateroom.

"Your yacht is spectacular," she said, admiring the oak-paneled walls lined with framed posters of his many films. "How long have you owned it?"

"Too long," he said. "Wait until you see the new one I'm building. It's twice the size."

Grabbing a glass of wine from a passing waiter, Linc quickly swigged it down before Shelby noticed. Not that she was anywhere in sight, so he considered himself safe. He couldn't figure out *why* she objected to his drinking. It wasn't as if he got falling-down drunk or anything, although he had to admit that there *had* been times he'd blanked out and couldn't remember *what* he'd done. Hey—the bottom line was he could control his drinking. It was no big deal.

He smelled musky perfume, turned around, and Lola Sanchez was upon him. Good-looking broad—voluptuous and sexy and married. Not that it mattered. He wasn't interested; Shelby was enough for him. He loved his wife, and from now on he was determined to stay faithful.

"How nice to see you again, Linc," Lola purred, behaving in an extremely friendly fashion.

He responded by checking out her outfit. It was impossible for the delectable Ms. Sanchez to expose one more inch of skin without being arrested. The tits were almost out, the ass was a sight to behold, and the face—well, she had lips a man could kill for, and seductive brown eyes that promised a myriad of sexual delights.

"Hey, Lola," he said. "And, uh . . . Matt. How's it hangin'?"

"Pretty good," Matt said, proffering a manly handshake.

Lola licked her glossy lips before taking a

sip of her martini. It infuriated her that Linc still made her edgy after all this time. He was a prick. Superprick. And she couldn't wait to bring him down for what he'd done to her.

"Linc," she said, toying with the emerald nestling in her quite considerable cleavage, "has Elliott Finerman talked to you?"

"Elliott, Elliott," he said vaguely. "Oh yeah, I ran into him last night."

"Did he say anything?"

"About what?"

"He, uh . . . mentioned that you'd be on top of his wish list for our upcoming movie."

"Then he'd better speak to my agent," Linc responded, his eyes lingering on her breasts.

"It's a romantic comedy," she continued. *"New York State of Mind."*

"Yeah?"

"I'm starring in it."

"Too bad," Linc said lightly. " 'Cause I *always* get top billing."

"And so you should," she said, making a mental note to tell Elliott that if she had to, she'd accept second place.

This was important. Linc deserved to be

punished, and she was prepared to do any-thing to make it happen.

Emerging from her cabin, Cat scanned the hordes of guests, her green eyes searching for Jonas. They'd had fun that afternoon; she'd felt comfortable with him. She did *not* feel comfortable with the overdressed bunch of party guests busy talking, net-working, ass kissing, and generally bullshit-ting. Hollywood by the sea. This crowd did not appeal to her.

She thought about Jump and their unsat-isfactory phone call. Some conversation. She'd been anxious to hear all about Kris Phoenix and the tour, and she'd also wanted to tell him all *her* stories about the festival and what a bullying despot Merrill Zandack was. So it was three o'clock in the morning in Australia. Big freaking deal. Since when did Jump go to bed early? He was a night person; they both were. He could be such an asshole! She wouldn't be phoning *him* again in a hurry; it was his turn to pick up the phone and call *her.*

She spotted Jonas in a corner and hur-ried over. He was safely back in his black

Prada suit, hair slicked back, the perfect executive assistant.

"Has Merrill stopped screaming at you?" she asked.

"He gets concerned," Jonas said, making excuses for his uncouth boss.

"That doesn't mean he should talk to you like you're nothing. Especially in front of people."

"It's part of my job to take anything Mr. Zandack hands out," Jonas said, refusing to make eye contact.

"No it's not."

"Yes, Cat, it is." He hesitated for a moment. "Y'know, I've got to work. And you should be circulating, meeting people. Go find Mr. Zandack and stick by his side."

"Do I have to?" she groaned.

"That's why you're here," he reminded her.

"Okay, I'll go circulate, but only if you promise we can get together later and trash the party."

"If that's what you want," he said guardedly.

"Take notes," she joked. "It'll be a blast dissing this group. Did you *see* Lola Sanchez's dress? It's pure stripper city."

"*You* should try wearing a dress sometime."

"And look like that?" she said, making a face. "Are you *insane?*"

"There's Merrill," he said, pointing out his boss. "You'd better go over."

"I'm on it. Later, okay?"

He nodded, although he had no intention of meeting up with her later. He had his job, she had hers. They were miles apart. There was nothing to be gained by palling up with her.

By the time Shelby caught up with Linc, he was drunk. Disappointment flooded over her. Did he have *no* control? His promises meant nothing.

He was busy amusing a group with stories about the time he'd met Fidel Castro on a visit to Cuba. Self-deprecating and charming, he kept his audience enthralled. He had not reached the bad stage yet, the stage where he slurred his words, became belligerent and mean, and began grabbing women in a most inappropriate way.

Fortunately she was just in time to rescue him. She gave him a hug and a peck on the cheek, at the same time deftly extracting the glass of booze from his hand.

"Here's the wife," Linc announced, grinning broadly at his attentive audience. "Miss Control Freak. Thinks I drink too much. *Me?* Ain't *that* a kick in the head." And he proceeded to launch into a cheerful rendition of some old Dean Martin song. Then he reached out for a woman in the group and began swinging her around in an exaggerated dance routine.

Shelby smiled and pretended it was all good fun and that she didn't care about her husband making a fool of himself.

But of course, she did. She hated watching Linc fall to pieces.

CHAPTER
12

A few days after Merrill's successful party, the Cannes Festival began to wind down, and most of the major players boarded their private planes and left. Merrill gave several people a lift on his jet to London, where he was staying for a week. The group included Cat, Lola, Matt, and Jonas. Merrill's Russian girlfriend had been left in the south of France, and now he had another statuesque brunette accompanying him. This one spoke English, which did not seem to please Merrill, because every time she opened her mouth he told her to shut up.

"Where *does* he find them?" Cat whispered to Jonas as they boarded the plane.

"They find *him,"* Jonas replied. "He's always got a new one."

"How convenient."

Cat had decided that from London, she was hopping a Quantas flight to Australia for a fast visit. Surprising Jump was a good thing. He'd never been on tour without her, and she had a feeling he was in a resentful mood because she wasn't with him.

According to Merrill, the financing for *Caught* was a done deal. Several foreign distributors had come in, so it was now a go situation. She was excited, although she tried not to show it. Cool was better.

Halfway to London she was shocked to discover that not only had Merrill offered the lead in *Caught* to Shelby Cheney, but he was also trying to persuade Lola Sanchez to say yes. And the *only* reason she discovered this was because perched on Lola's knee was her script.

Outraged, she shot out of her seat, cornering Jonas at the back of the plane. "Exactly *why* is Lola Sanchez reading my script?" she demanded.

"Because Merrill asked her to," he explained.

"She's totally *wrong* for it," Cat fumed.

"Who's right? You don't like Shelby Cheney either, so who *do* you have in mind?"

"Angelina Jolie, that's the actress I want."

"Then you'd better tell Merrill."

"Don't worry, I will."

Merrill was sitting at a round table, magazines spread out before him, puffing on a cigar, filling the cabin with acrid smoke.

Cat slid into the seat opposite him. She was steaming. How come he'd conveniently forgotten to mention that he'd given her script to Lola Sanchez? Who else did he have in mind that he wasn't going to tell her about? Gwyneth Paltrow? Nicole Kidman? Madonna!

Yes, she could understand that he wanted a star, but if that particular star was wrong for the role, then they shouldn't even be considered. And Lola Sanchez was *definitely* wrong.

"Merrill," she said. "Can we talk casting?"

"Premature," he said, dismissing her with a wave of his cigar.

"No, it's not," she said stubbornly, determined to be heard. "About Lola Sanchez—"

"Not now," he interrupted, blowing smoke in her face. "We'll talk about it another time."

He was the most annoying man in the world. But right now he was her ticket to ride, and this probably wasn't the right time to make waves.

Lola flicked through the script, her eyes barely registering the words. She wasn't at all interested in appearing in a movie written by a girl like Cat Harrison. Who cared? Cat was a flash success story. One amateur movie and everyone was doing handstands, including Merrill—who should know better. This kind of project did not intrigue Lola at all. She was more interested in finding a script like *Rapture,* and a director of Russell Savage's caliber.

It wasn't fair. She never got to work with top directors, and yet she knew she had it in her to do so. Nobody had thought Salma Hayek could pull it off until she'd starred in *Frida,* and Jennifer Aniston was certainly not taken seriously until she appeared in a small film called *The Good Girl.* Lola decided that she had to work on Merrill to come up with a project worthy of her talent.

She was well aware that after *New York State of Mind* she'd better do something careerwise that made an impact. Shelby Cheney's reviews were spectacular, and it galled her. *She* could have played that role; *she* would have been just as good—if not better.

She glanced across at Matt, who had obviously decided he would be Merrill Zandack's new best friend, and was regaling him with tales about the tennis circuit.

Merrill obviously wasn't listening. The only reason he was bothering to give Matt the time of day was that the schmuck was married to her.

Lola knew this. Matt, of course, did not. He thought people liked him because he was a friendly guy. He had no clue that as soon as she announced they were divorcing, he would return to being a nobody. Sure, the tabloids would follow him for a short while, just so they could write about whom he was dating next, then his name would fade from the headlines.

She tapped her long, manicured red fingernails on the open script balanced on her lap, hoping Elliott Finerman had finally gotten his act together and offered Linc *New York State of Mind.* Linc's latest reviews in the trades were abysmal; he should leap at the chance of making something different.

Faye, sitting in the seat behind her, passed over a copy of *USA Today.* "Read the interview with Shelby Cheney," Faye ordered. "Read it and learn how careful you have to be with the press."

Oh yes, that's exactly what she wanted to do, read another story about Shelby Cheney. She was sick of reading about the woman.

She took the paper anyway. There was a large photograph of Shelby on the front page, and a heading that read: SHELBY CHENEY—MARRIAGE TO LINC BLACKWOOD IS NOT EASY.

Hmm, Lola thought. *This looks interesting.*

And she started reading.

Shelby and Linc sat side by side on an Air France flight to London. Linc was not in a good mood. Shelby was forever carrying on about his drinking, and her constant nagging was beginning to get him down. Why couldn't she shut the fuck up? It was okay for her—she had a hit movie and glowing reviews, whereas his movie had not been received well, and he'd had to endure the usual shitty reviews in the trades, such as, "Another Linc Blackwood action adventure with not enough action and certainly no adventure in Linc's performance."

Did Shelby *really* expect him to stay sober after reviews like that? He was on a binge and he knew it. Only he couldn't stop, didn't *want* to stop. Fuck! Why should he?

So they were barely talking, and then he picked up *USA Today* at the airport, and once they were airborne he began reading Shelby's interview aloud.

"Shelby Cheney settled into her seat while every red-blooded man in the restaurant turned to stare at her. What a beauty! 'I've been told my smile lights up the screen,' Shelby murmured, smiling seductively." He took a beat. "Christ!" he said, throwing her a disgusted look. "You didn't actually say this shit?"

"You *know* I'd never say anything like

that," she assured him, highly embarrassed. "The journalist said it to *me.*"

Linc shot her another look and continued reading aloud.

"'Everyone thinks Linc can't act. It's a shame that he's so underrated. It really upsets him, especially in view of *my* big success.'"

"That's not true," she wailed. "I told you—he's putting *his* words into *my* mouth."

"Quote: 'And Linc hated *Rapture,*'" Linc said, really getting into it. "'He hated watching me make love to another man, and quite frankly, I'm jealous watching him with all the beautiful young actresses *he* works with. Our marriage isn't easy. Although we're both professionals, we try to do the best we can.'"

He threw the paper down in a fury. "Try to do the best we can, huh, Shelby? Is that what we do?"

"He's twisted what *he* said to *me* and made it look as if *I* picked those words," Shelby repeated miserably, her face flushed.

"Well, honey, you'd better learn to be a lot smarter than that if you wanna stay in this business," Linc said in a hard voice, clicking his fingers for the flight attendant. "I'm having a drink and I don't want to hear any more of your bitching and nagging. Okay?"

Then he picked up the script Elliott Finerman had sent over and started reading.

It was cold and raining in London, a damp drizzle that refused to quit.

"My God, it's *freezing,*" Lola complained, wrapping her lynx coat around her and shivering as she alighted from the aircraft. "I wish I could stay on Merrill's plane all the way home."

"You can't," Matt said, touching his annoying little goatee. "Not unless you're prepared to spend a few days in London. Hey—if we do that, I'm sure Merrill would give us a ride to L.A."

"No way!" she said, frowning. "It's too cold and miserable here. I need the sun. Besides, British Airways is comfortable enough. They have those seats that turn into beds."

"I hope you told the concierge to book us the middle seats so we can sit together."

"Faye tried—they were already booked," she lied, having no desire to spend the next ten hours side by side with Matt. She wanted her privacy so that she could day-dream about Tony Alvarez and how great their reunion would be. She also wanted to plan the punishment she would dole out to Linc. After the dismal reviews he'd received for his movie, she was certain he'd be into taking on a different role. Why *wouldn't* he want to work with her? She'd been all over him in Cannes; he hadn't been able to take his eyes off her cleavage.

Yes, in spite of his precious wife he was hot for her already. Lola knew these things.

Simone, an attractive woman from British Airways, met them at the plane, whisked them into a private car, and sped them over to the British Airways terminal, where she checked them in, then accompanied them upstairs to the first-class lounge.

Several people came over to ask Lola for her autograph. She obliged, a big movie star smile on her face.

Lola knew how to put it on better than anyone. Besides, she genuinely loved the attention. The little girl from Silverlake had made it all the way to the top, and the feel-ing was exhilarating.

* * *

Cat was psyched to be getting away from all the bullshit and on her way to see Jump. A week apart seemed like a year, and even if she was able to spend only a few days with him, it was worth it. The big Kris Phoenix concert was coming up in Sydney, and that was the most important night for Jump and his band. After a few more unsatisfactory phone conversations, she wanted to be there for him—front row and center—supporting him in every way, just as he'd supported her when he'd gotten her off drugs.

When Merrill's plane landed, she had to hurry to make her connection, barely finding time to say good-bye to everyone. She saved Jonas for last; he'd been the one bright spot of her trip. Once she got him out of his Prada he'd turned out to be a cool guy—and not even gay! When she got to L.A. she'd have to hook him up with one of her girlfriends.

Even though she considered herself a New Yorker, she'd rented an apartment in L.A. for the next six months, because that's where *Caught* was set, and that's where Zandack Films was based. Australia would be a nice break between the south of

France and getting back to work. She could have stayed in London for a couple of days and visited her mother; that's if her mother had been there. Mommy Dearest was currently on a photographic safari in Africa with a man twenty years her junior—who, if he played his cards wrong, was about to become husband number six.

Oh well, that's my mother, Cat thought wryly. *Nothing's going to change her.*

"I'll see you in L.A.," she said to Jonas.

He nodded, busy on his laptop.

"Anything you want from Australia?" she asked, thinking that he'd been kind of elusive for the last few days—ever since their fun time at the beach.

"No thanks," he said, closing his laptop and standing up.

"You okay?"

"Sure," he said noncommittally. "Why wouldn't I be?"

"I just wondered."

"Did you tell your husband you're coming?"

"Nope," she said, grinning. "Surprises are the bomb!"

"Not always," he cautioned.

"What do you mean by *that?*"

"Nothing. Jump is a lucky guy."

"And I'm a lucky girl."

"Didn't I already tell you that?"

They exchanged a look.

"Well . . . I guess I'm outta here," she said.

"Have a safe trip."

"I will." Impulsively she kissed him on the cheek before hurrying from the plane. "See you in L.A."

CHAPTER
13

The first thing Lola did upon arriving home was rush upstairs, shut herself in the bedroom, and call her lawyer, Otto Landstrom. "You've got to help me, Otto," she pleaded. "This is urgent."

"What's the problem, Lola?"

"I want a divorce."

"That's impossible. You only recently got married."

"It simply isn't working out. Europe was especially bad, and the truth is . . . marriage is not for me."

"What does Matt have to say about your change of heart?"

"He doesn't know. I want *you* to tell him."

"You want *me* to tell him?"

"Yes," she said persuasively. "After all, you *are* my lawyer. You're supposed to take care of this kind of thing."

"I'm a lawyer, not a marriage counselor," Otto said, sounding pissed. "I can't call him up and say, 'Your wife is divorcing you.'"

"Why not?" she said petulantly.

"Does he have any hint you're thinking of divorce?"

"No. We just got back, and all he's interested in is sitting in front of the TiVO checking out what sports programs he missed."

Otto sighed. "Exactly *why* did you marry him, Lola?"

" 'Cause I *thought* I could make it work. And anyway," she added truculently, *"you* advised me to, along with everyone else."

"Then why are you divorcing him?"

"He's *boring,* Otto. And since when did I need a *reason* to get divorced?"

"You *always* need a reason."

Why did everyone have to make it so difficult? "You're my lawyer, Otto," she said sharply. "This is an instruction. Do it."

Otto did not appreciate her tone. The time was coming in the not too distant future when he would give up representing movie stars. They were too much damn trouble.

"When do you expect me to take care of this?" he asked.

"Like yesterday. I'll go to a spa with my sister; you can tell him then. That way he can be gone by the time I get back."

"When are you leaving?"

"Maybe tomorrow," she said vaguely. "I'll let you know."

"I'll do it, Lola. But you have to talk to him first. At least give him some indication that all is not well."

"I'm not *good* at confrontations," she wailed, mad at Otto for refusing to make it easy for her. *"You* handle everything, that's what I pay you for." She clicked off her phone. God! How come Otto was making it such a major deal? She shelled out big bucks for him to take care of business—*including* personal.

The intercom buzzed, and Jenny, her assistant, informed her that her mother was on the phone.

Damn! She'd have to tell her family before they read about it in the tabloids. They'd all been at the wedding, her many cousins and other assorted relatives, mingling with the stars, their mouths half open in awe as they recognized many famous faces.

She'd tell Mama first. Claudine Sanchez was fond of Matt, and why shouldn't she be? In *her* mind her daughter had married a white-bread sports hero.

Yeah, sure. A loafer. A sponger. A man who expects me to pay all the bills.

On the other hand her dad wasn't so crazy about Matt. "He don't have that macho thing goin'," Louis Sanchez had complained the first time she'd brought him home. "You'd be smarter to find yourself a Latino man." A caveman grin. "Sexy, like me."

Yeah, well, Louis Sanchez should know all about *that.* Mr. Stud. The bull of the neighborhood.

Lola often wondered how Claudine had put up with his philandering over the years. She would *never* take that kind of crap from a man; it was disrespectful and insulting.

Hmm . . . she'd better arrange a visit to a spa with one of her sisters. Both of them enjoyed all the perks that came with her stardom. They loved it when she went to an award event and scored a huge basket filled with thousands of dollars' worth of stuff, which she always handed over to them. She was very generous to her family; Mama called it sharing the luck. Recently she'd bought her parents a house in Hancock Park. The house had cost a fortune, but it was worth every dollar to see the look on Claudine's face. Her dad wasn't so thrilled; he didn't like leaving the old neighborhood and his many cronies; so she'd bought him a new red Corvette to make up for his loss. That soon shut him up; now he could visit his lady friends in style.

"You must do something for your sisters next," Mama had informed her before she'd left for the south of France. "They need your help."

Why? They both had husbands. Still . . . to appease Claudine she'd agreed to create a trust to pay for her nieces' and nephews' future education. It wasn't such a hardship because she could certainly afford it, and she adored the kids, especially as she knew she could never have any of her own. That was *her* secret, a secret she kept close to her heart. A secret that haunted her and drove her crazy.

She clicked on her phone. "Hi, Mama."

"Welcome home, Miss Movie Star," joked Claudine. "I'm happy you're safely back."

"Thanks."

"Did you have a wonderful time?"

"Of course."

"Who did you see? What did you wear?" Claudine was totally into hearing all the details.

They chatted for a few minutes, then Lola promised to phone her in the morning.

Next she called Tony. His voice mail picked up.

"Hey," she purred into the receiver. "Guess who's back in town?"

When she finally made her way downstairs, Matt was still in the library, switching sports programs on the TiVO.

"What're you searching for?" she asked impatiently.

"I've got plenty of catching up to do," he said, busy clicking his remote. Obviously it did not take much to turn Matt on.

"Can't you do it later?" she said, yawning. "I'm going to bed and you'll disturb me when you come up."

"Go to bed later," he advised. "That way you won't get jet lag."

"What're you, an expert?"

"Why are you so bad tempered lately?" he asked, taking his eyes off the TV for a moment.

She shrugged. This seemed like a good opportunity to give him a hint. "We don't seem to be getting along so good, do we, Matt?"

"I think we get along fine."

"It's just that now we're married, you don't *do* anything. And if you want the truth—it bugs me."

"I told you," he said firmly. "I gave up tennis because I'm writing a screenplay and planning on being an actor. Give me time and I'll surprise you. You'll see."

"It's not that simple."

"Yes, it is," he said stubbornly.

"No, it's not," she countered.

"You made it from nothing," he said pointedly. "Why can't *I?"*

"Because you've got to be realistic, Matt. You're married to *me."*

"So?"

"So there's no way you can go out on auditions for bit parts; it wouldn't be dignified for either of us."

"Then put me in one of *your* movies," he said. "You have plenty of control. Elliott Finerman likes me. I could even play the lead in *New York State of Mind.*"

Was he *insane?* "You're *not* an actor," she reminded him sharply. "You're a tennis player."

"And what were *you* before you started acting?" he retaliated. "I seem to remember that you were a waitress."

"The difference is that *I* wanted to be an actress ever since I was a little girl," she said heatedly. "It was my lifelong ambition. I worked hard to get where I am today."

"Yeah," he sneered. "And what did you have to *do* along the way, Lola?"

"*Excuse* me?" she said, outraged.

"Is it true what they say about Merrill Zandack?"

"Who's *they?* And what do *they* say?"

"That he has to get serviced by all the actresses he works with."

"Oh, for God's sake," she hissed, prancing out of the room.

Now she didn't feel so bad. Matt had a stupid, dumb-ass attitude. Let Otto go ahead and do her dirty work. She didn't care anymore.

Martha and George Cheney lived in a large house in St. John's Wood, an upmarket area of London. George, a retired stockbroker, worshiped his daughter. Shelby reminded him of her mother; she was kind and giving, with a genuinely sweet nature. It often surprised him that she'd chosen to become an actress. Such a strange and difficult profession.

Martha Cheney had invited them to stay at their house, but Shelby knew it would not be a good idea, for Linc was extremely demanding. He expected room service, cable TV, and all the amenities of a luxury hotel. Instead, she'd opted for a suite at the Dorchester, where Linc would have everything he required—including a gym where he could perform his daily workout.

Ever since he'd read the unfortunate *USA Today* interview, Linc had been in a foul mood. He absolutely refused to believe her protestations of innocence.

"Goddamn it, Shelby. You should be smart enough to know that journalists twist

your words," he said, once they were settled at the hotel.

"Hasn't it ever happened to you?" she
asked, tired of his relentless complaining.

"Yeah," he retorted. "When I was young
and stupid. You've been a working actress
for long enough. You should know better."

"In future I'll have a publicist and a tape
recorder present so I can prove it to you."

"You *must* have said some of those
things."

"No, Linc, I didn't," she answered wearily.
"He told me he thought you were an underrated actor and I agreed with him."

"Christ!" he muttered, heading for the
minibar.

"The truth is, you *are* underrated," she
said, following him. "You *should* be doing
different things."

"I am," he said, swigging from a bottle of
scotch, daring her with his eyes to stop him.
"I'm instructing my agent to accept Elliott
Finerman's movie."

"What movie is that?"

"I read the script on the plane. It's a romantic comedy with Lola Sanchez."

"Lola *Sanchez,*" she exclaimed. "Do you
honestly think the two of you have chem-

istry? I mean, she takes over the screen, and the last thing you should do is play second fiddle."

As soon as the words left her mouth, she knew she'd made a mistake.

"You think I'd be second to Lola Sanchez, huh?" he said, glaring at her. "How come you didn't put *that* in your fucking interview?"

"I'm sorry," she said haltingly. "I didn't mean—"

"I'll be in the gym," he said, and stomped out of their suite.

Shelby realized that lately she couldn't say anything right. Linc's lackluster reviews had set him off, and the *USA Today* piece hadn't helped his black mood. The interview wasn't *that* bad, but unfortunately it had given him something to vent his anger and frustration on.

Her immediate problem was that they were expected at her parents' for dinner that night, and how was she going to ask him not to drink? Whatever troubles they were experiencing, she did not want her parents to know.

Meanwhile, according to her agent, everyone was anxious to work with her.

Word of her performance in *Rapture* had reached the States. The trades had given her glowing reviews, while Linc's reviews were dismal. "Your price is skyrocketing," her agent told her over the phone. "Word is that when the time comes, you've got a good chance of being nominated. Congratulations, Shelby. You've done a great job."

She was excited, and yet she couldn't let Linc see her excitement, because she knew it would only upset him further.

What a dilemma! If only she could enjoy her amazing success and not have to worry about Linc all the time. Sometimes she felt as if she were treading on eggshells.

Later, when he returned from the gym, Linc flopped down on the bed and calmly announced that he wasn't going to her parents' for dinner.

"You can't do this to me," she said, struggling to remain calm. "They're expecting you. If you don't come with me it will look bad."

"I'll give you a choice," he said, activating the TV remote. "You can go by yourself. Or if I come, I'm drinking, and I don't want you nagging me in front of them."

Great, what kind of a choice was *that?*

"Okay," she said tightly. "But you *will* behave, won't you?"

He threw her a filthy look. "Y'know, Shelby, sometimes you talk to me like I'm a fucking kid, and I'm bored with it, okay? You've got a habit of boring the shit outta me."

Obviously he'd had another drink or two at the bar.

She nodded miserably. Dealing with Linc was becoming more and more of an ordeal.

Cat managed to view several DVDs on her flight to Australia. She also had time to listen to some new CDs she'd picked up at the airport.

During the long flight she got to talking to a friendly flight attendant who informed her she was the biggest Kris Phoenix fan in the world.

"I'll get you tickets," Cat promised.

"Oh my God! That would be incredible!"

"*And* a backstage pass," Cat added. "How about that?"

"Fantastic! And I'll give *you* a bag full of miniature bottles of booze."

"Deal," Cat said, grinning. "I'm sure Jump won't object." Although she had no doubt that there was no shortage of booze on the tour.

Not that Jump was a big drinker; he wasn't. He was into his weed and that was about it. In view of her insane drug past she was happy that he didn't indulge in anything else.

Jump had saved her from a total wild-child life, although if she hadn't been such a wild child, she would never have had the material to write her movie, so it had all worked out in the end.

A stern-faced customs officer took one glance at her standing in line, clad in her tightest, frayed jeans, with her cropped top and studded earlobes, and decided she looked suspicious, so he pulled her out of place and began searching through her luggage piece by piece—checking everything.

Man, she was pissed! Now that she'd finally arrived in Australia, she couldn't wait to see Jump.

By the time she got out of customs, hailed a cab, and reached his hotel, it was past midnight. She marched up to the front desk, announced that she was Mrs. Jagger, and requested his room key.

The clerk gave it to her without any argument, which pissed her off, considering she could have been some crazed groupie trying to get to him. But at least she had access, and if he wasn't there she'd slide into bed and surprise him when he got back. It was no good searching around the city looking for him; he could be anywhere.

Riding up in the elevator, her mind was racing. If he *was* in his room he wouldn't have the security chain on. Jump wasn't into security locks and things like that; his claim was that if somebody was out to get you, they'd do it anyway, citing John Lennon as a prime example.

There was a DO NOT DISTURB sign on the door of his room, which meant nothing, because he always left it on. He had a phobia about maids and housekeepers coming in and rifling through his stuff.

She slipped the key into the lock. Ha! Just as she'd thought, no security chain in place.

His room looked like a bomb had hit it: clothes thrown all over the floor, half-empty beer bottles on every surface, lights blazing, TV blaring—another of his charming habits; he never slept without the TV at full blast.

All this and no Jump.

She was disappointed, yet at the same time kind of pleased. She had a mental vision of him opening the door, finding no TV making noise, no bright lights. "What the bloody hell's goin' on?" he'd roar. "The bloody maid's been in here." Then he'd discover her. Man, would he be shocked!

Grabbing a bottle of water from the minibar, she drank it down, then hurried into the bathroom and turned on the shower.

Soon they'd be enjoying a great reunion. It was certain to be an amazing night.

CHAPTER
14

Isabelle Sanchez was a Lola Sanchez wannabe. Older than her sister by five years, and thirty pounds heavier, with a mass of frizzed red hair, thick eyebrows, and too much makeup, she still considered herself pretty hot stuff, even though she was married with two kids. *"I should've been the actress in the family,"* she was fond of saying to whoever would listen. *"I would've kicked butt."*

Like I don't? Lola thought. Only she never

said anything, because family was family and it was best to keep the peace.

Selma was her favorite sister, but Selma was busy with her job at the bank and couldn't get away, so Lola had to settle for Isabelle, who couldn't wait to dump her two small boys at a cousin's and accompany her famous movie star sister to a spa.

"We're gonna have ourselves a time!" Isabelle singsonged in the limo on their way to a luxury women-only spa in Palm Springs. "Will we get to see any famous people?"

Lola shrugged. "How would *I* know?"

"You could find *out,*" Isabelle insisted, wagging a finger in her sister's face. *"You're* someone. They'll tell you."

"No they won't."

"Yes, they *will.* You have to learn to work it, Sis. You're supposed to be a star."

Lola soon realized that she'd made a mistake. They'd been in the car for only ten minutes, and already Isabelle was driving her crazy. Plus her sister had doused herself with so much cheap perfume that Lola thought she was about to be asphyxiated.

"I *love* this!" Isabelle exclaimed, playing with the automatic tinted windows. "Luxury living is so fine. I suppose *you* get to do it all the time."

"Not *all* the time," Lola replied, willing Isabelle to shut up.

"Yeah," Isabelle continued, stroking the leather seats. "An' I bet you get everything for free."

"Sometimes."

"Well," Isabelle said knowingly, "it's not as if you have to *work* for a living. It's all handed to you on a silver plate."

"Platter."

"What?"

"Nothing."

And so the journey progressed, with Isabelle in full nag about how tough it was raising two kids, holding down a job—which she was currently out of—*and* taking care of her husband, Armando, who was on sick leave from *his* job because of a minor injury to his foot.

"I'll tell you frankly," Isabelle said, just before they pulled up to the spa. "We're stone cold broke. We're gonna need help to get us outta trouble."

Lola couldn't believe that they hadn't even arrived yet, and already she was getting hit up for money. The year before she'd given her sister at least fifty thousand dollars because of an emergency with her house and delinquent car payments. Now she was after more.

It wasn't that Lola didn't have the money—she did. But she'd sooner give it as a gift than be asked. It galled her that they all expected something for nothing.

She'd left the house with Matt still firmly ensconced in front of the TV. He'd waved her off, completely unaware that he wouldn't be there when she returned. Otto had promised to take care of things, and he'd better deliver, otherwise she'd be looking for a new lawyer.

Tony had not returned her call. She wasn't worried; Tony wasn't going anywhere. When she was ready, he'd be back in her arms, exactly where he belonged. The sex was too hot for him to resist.

"More potatoes?" Martha Cheney asked her handsome son-in-law.

"No, thanks," Linc said, shaking his head. "But I gotta tell you, your cooking is delicious."

Martha smiled modestly. She was fond of Linc, even though he was an American.

She and her husband had been quite disappointed when Shelby had first moved to America to pursue her career. They'd accepted it, because they knew that her acting was important to her, and she certainly had talent. But they still hadn't liked it. Then Shelby had met and married the very famous American movie star Linc Blackwood, and they knew they'd never get her back.

To Shelby's surprise, Linc seemed to be on his best behavior. He'd had a sherry before they sat down for dinner, and during the course of the meal he'd drunk only one glass of wine. Maybe he wasn't going to embarrass her.

When her mother got up from the table to clear the dishes, Linc got up too, grabbing Martha around the waist. "Martha, you're some wonderful woman," he said enthusiastically. "You and your daughter, you're both the greatest."

"Why, thank you, Linc," Martha said, quite flustered as she attempted to escape from his powerful clutch.

"So," Linc said, finally releasing Martha and turning to George, "have you seen your little girl's new movie?"

"Not yet," George said, lighting his pipe.

"However, I hear she gives an excellent performance."

"Oh yeah," Linc said, shooting Shelby a spiteful look. "She gives a performance all right. You're in for quite an eyeful."

"Linc," Shelby said sharply. She'd already warned him that she was not allowing her parents to see *Rapture;* it was not their kind of film. Besides, she refused to upset them, and viewing their daughter with her clothes off in an explicit sex scene would definitely upset them.

Linc was set on making trouble; there was no stopping him now. "You told them about your movie, sweetheart?" he asked, all loving and innocent.

Now it was her turn to shoot *him* a look. Sometimes he could be a mean sonofabitch. And this was obviously one of those times.

Cat slept fitfully, all the while waiting for Jump to return to his hotel room. Finally she was awoken by a key in the door and a mumbled *"Fuck!"* as he tripped over a shoe.

She held her breath. He'd say more than "Fuck" when he discovered her in his bed.

She could hear him fumbling for the light

switch, then suddenly the room was flooded with light.

"Surprise!" she exclaimed, sitting up in bed.

"Holy *shit!*" Jump yelled. "Where the *fuck* did *you* come from?"

The spa was buzzing. There were three famous women there, all in the process of getting a divorce. Isabelle had all the news when she rushed into Lola's room a couple of hours after they arrived. "I got the skinny from one of the girls in the beauty salon," she said excitedly. "Guess what? Petra Flynn's here. Seems like her old man beat the crap out of her. She's got a black eye, *and* a leakin' boob. It's a horror story. She's come here to recover before she hits the lowlife with a lawsuit."

Petra Flynn was a sexy TV star with the biggest implants this side of Texas.

"Really?" Lola said, not at all interested.

"And *that's* not all," Isabelle continued, "there's that girl, the one who sued that billionaire guy for like, y'know, a zillion dollars a week for child care. She's here, too."

"How do you know all this?" Lola asked.

"Mm . . . it's easy," Isabelle said, shrugging. "All I had to do was ask the questions. And," she added, "this is the best one of all. Serena Lake's here."

Serena Lake was a perky girl-next-door movie star, married to a successful heart surgeon. Several months ago she'd run off with her costar, a macho English actor who had a wicked reputation with women. Her marriage had broken up, and then the English actor promptly and quite publicly dumped her and returned to his girlfriend in London. According to the tabloids, Serena was now desperately trying to win her husband back.

"Do you *know* any of these people?" Isabelle asked, her eyes wide with gossip. "We should all get together, have kind of like a hen party, where they'd tell us everything. What d'you think?"

"I think we're keeping to ourselves while we're here," Lola said, completely uninterested in hearing about other people's problems. "And I also think *you* should stop asking questions."

"It's good *you're* happily married," Isabelle said, inspecting her sister's clothes hanging in the closet. "Otherwise this place could be called the Divorce Club. How about *that?*"

"Yes," Lola said flatly. "How about that?"

They were in a cab on their way back to the Dorchester when Shelby finally spoke. "You're a bastard, you know that?" she said, her eyes filling with tears.

"How come it took you so long to find out?" Linc answered, egging her on.

"I wish I'd never married you."

"A little louder, sweetheart. I don't think the driver heard."

"My parents are nice, sweet people; there's no need for them to hear you talking trash about me."

"What trash?" he said casually. "All I told 'em is that you flash your tits. You're hardly doing a Sharon Stone in *Basic Instinct.* Although if the part was right, I guess you'd do that too."

"Shut up," she said, biting her bottom lip. "I don't want to speak to you."

"Oh, I see," he said sarcastically. "It's okay for you to talk trash about me in an interview, but God forbid I mention your movie to your parents. Then it's the end of the fucking world. *So* sorry, Miss Fucking Perfect."

She stared out of the cab window, ignoring him. He'd embarrassed both her parents. Her father because he couldn't stand the thought of his daughter on-screen without her clothes, and her mother because she felt let down and humiliated that Shelby would do such a thing. They didn't understand that it was a brilliant movie, and that the nude scene was an integral part of the action. It was hardly exploitive, merely necessary.

Damn Linc! Why couldn't he keep his big mouth shut?

They rode the rest of the way to the hotel in silence. When they arrived, Linc refused to leave the cab. "I'm going gambling," he said. "Wanna come?"

"No," she replied, getting out of the cab. She was tired of being his nursemaid. Let him go lose money, let him get photographed falling down drunk, let him pick up women. The way she felt about him right now, she simply didn't care.

There was a group of fans gathered outside the Dorchester. The last thing she felt like doing was signing autographs, but it was cold and the doorman informed her that some of them had been waiting all night. A few were holding glossy photos from her early days on British TV.

She placed a smile on her face and signed their pictures, then, shivering, she entered the hotel.

Safely upstairs, she called her mother. "Don't take any notice of Linc," she said, attempting to smooth things over. "He received bad reviews for his film, so he isn't in a good frame of mind."

"Your father's upset," Martha said, sounding quite frosty. "You always promised us when you became an actress that you would be respectful of yourself, and never lose your integrity."

"I *am.*"

"Being respectful of yourself means no nudity," Martha said sharply.

"It's an acting role, it's not real," she protested. "And nudity was necessary for the role. I didn't mention it to you before because I *knew* you'd be upset."

"You're old enough to do what you want," Martha snapped. "However, I must say that I'm *very* surprised you would do this to your father."

"I'm not doing anything to Dad," Shelby objected, feeling like a little girl again. "I'm thirty-two years old. I'm an actress playing a role. People are saying all kinds of great things about my performance, so please try not to be small-minded about this."

She knew it was useless trying to explain. Her parents were old-fashioned people with old-fashioned values; they would never understand.

She wished there was someone she could talk to; she hadn't kept in touch with her friends in London, because along with her career, Linc was a full-time job.

It suddenly occurred to her that somehow or other, Linc had managed to isolate her from all her old friends. It was sad, yet she'd allowed it to happen.

No more. Things were about to change. This time it was different. If he didn't do something about his drinking, she was seriously thinking of leaving him.

"*You* are the craziest bird in the world," Jump yelled, hugging her. "How'd you manage to sneak in here without me knowing it?"

"Booked me a ticket, got on a plane," Cat said, with a huge grin.

"Gotta say I'm chuffed t' see you, darlin'."

"I should hope so. I came a long way for you. *And* . . . guess what?"

"What?"

"I wore my best dress." Giggling, she leaped out of bed totally nude.

"Hello, Sydney." Jump whistled.

"Hello, *you,"* she said, locking her arms behind his neck while twisting her long legs around his waist.

He responded appropriately, and before long they were cavorting around on the messed-up bed.

Exactly as Cat had imagined, it was a great reunion.

As soon as Isabelle left to track even more gossip, Lola picked up the phone and called Tony.

This time he answered on the first ring. "Yo, Tony," she said. "Did you get my message?"

"Yeah, I got it."

"So . . . ," she purred. "Are you excited?"

" 'Bout what?"

"About *me,* of course."

"Where are you now?"

"In Palm Springs, at a spa with my sister."

He sighed. "What d'you want, Lola?"

"What do *I* want," she said slowly. "Hmm . . . let me see . . . I want double helpings of chocolate ice cream, an Oscar, a new Porsche, and, oh yes, I want *us* back together."

"In that order?"

"Maybe I'll give up on the ice cream and put you in first place."

"Lola—"

"Remember the fun we used to have, Tony?" she interrupted. "The games we used to play."

"Yeah," he said flatly. "Mind games."

"No, I mean the games *you* got off on," she said seductively. "Like—oh—I don't know . . . the schoolgirl and the teacher, or the housewife and the repairman, or how about the starlet and the big producer? That was always one of your favorites."

"Tempting, baby. Only I gotta tell you—there's no way we're gettin' involved again."

"And why is that?"

" 'Cause I ain't interested in your old man chasing me down with a shotgun."

"The only shotgun Matt's got is between his legs. And trust me, Tony, he does *not* know how to shoot."

"When you comin' back from this spa place?"

"In a day or so. Right now my lawyer's getting rid of Matt."

"What's he doin'—burying him in the desert?"

"That's not funny, Tony."

"Wouldn't put it past you, babe."

"As a matter of fact," she said, "he's offering him mucho bucks along with his prenup settlement."

"No shit?"

"We both know he'll take the deal, then you and I are free to be together. And *this* time, Tony, there'll be no hiding out. I want the world to know how much I love you."

"You do, huh?" he said, warming up.

"Bet on it."

"Uh . . . Lola."

"Yes?"

"There's somethin' I gotta tell you."

"Go ahead."

"I'm . . . uh . . . kinda gettin' engaged."

She laughed disbelievingly. "Tony, Tony,

Tony, you always *were* the master at making up stories. It must be the director in you."

"This is no story, babe," he said quickly. "It's real."

"You're crazy."

"No," he retaliated, getting angry. *"You're* the crazy one, thinkin' you can walk back in on me like nothin' happened."

"Whoever it is, dump the *puta,"* she said, unperturbed, because there was no way Tony would choose another woman over her. They were soul mates, tried and true.

"Just like that, dump her, huh?" he said.

"Yes, baby, you can do it."

"Jesus, Lola—"

"I'll call you tomorrow and tell you when I'll be back." She put down the phone as Isabelle entered the room. "I wish you'd knock," she said irritably.

"Who were you talking to—your lover?" Isabelle joked, picking up her sister's Chopard diamond-studded watch and admiring it.

"What have you found out now?" Lola asked, not really interested.

"It's all good," Isabelle said, fastening the exquisite watch on her wrist. "We have to go downstairs to the dining room for dinner."

"And exactly *why* do we have to do that?"

"To see everyone," Isabelle answered vaguely.

"No. I'm ordering room service."

"You've *got* to come down," Isabelle pleaded. "If I go sit by myself, nobody will know who I am."

"I'm sure you'll tell them," Lola said dryly.

"Don't be a bitch," Isabelle said, still admiring the watch. "I'm your *sister;* it's a treat for me to see famous people. *You* see them all the time, so it's not fair to shut me out. *Please* let's go down."

"Fine," Lola said reluctantly. "Just this once, 'cause the rest of my time here I'm only leaving the room for treatments."

"Okay," Isabelle said, heading for the closet. "Can I borrow one of your silk shirts? My clothes are crap. How about the purple one? It's not a good color on you."

"Go ahead," Lola sighed. "And give me back my watch."

"Can I wear it to dinner?"

"I suppose so."

It wasn't as if she had a choice. The annoying thing was that Isabelle always managed to get her own way. She always had.

"Mr. Blackwood, it's a pleasure to welcome you back, sir," said the doorman at the Ritz Club.

"Nice to be back," Linc said, slipping the man a hefty tip.

He'd joined the club when he'd first come to London with Shelby several years ago. Gambling was a passion he'd picked up in Vegas. Gambling in London was more civilized, especially when the croupiers were mostly pretty girls in low-cut dresses, although none of them were any competition for his wife, or Lola Sanchez for that matter.

He'd been thinking about Lola, and the movie he was about to say yes to. There was something about Ms. Sanchez. She had an animal sexuality that was quite intriguing. And if Shelby was so intent on giving him a hard time, there was nothing wrong if he cared to take it further.

He was fucking married, not dead.

Cat was asleep when she heard the key in the door. She'd always been a light sleeper. Jump, on the other hand, slept through anything; it would take a major earthquake to wake *him.*

She wondered if it was a burglar breaking in, and lay very still, waiting to see what would happen next.

The door opened, and somebody entered the room. She heard the rustle of clothes, and the next thing the weight of a body flopped down on Jump's side of the bed.

"Sorry about earlier, hon," said a female voice with a strong Australian accent. "You were right as usual. *I* was wrong. We shouldn't let a stupid fight get in the way of another fab fuck. An' *this* time I've got something special for you. Wakey, wakey."

Cat hit the light switch.

Straddling Jump's sleeping body was a bubblehead brunette, quite pretty in a zaftig kind of way, and totally naked apart from a wicked-looking piercing in her left nipple.

"Who the hell are *you?*" the girl shrieked, glaring at Cat in shock and horror.

"I'm his wife," Cat said. "Which means *I* belong here. So, here's the *real* question of the night—who the *fuck* are you?"

CHAPTER
15

Against her better judgment, Lola accompanied Isabelle to the dining room—a high-ceilinged, airy space overlooking a huge Olympic-size pool and exquisite gardens filled with jacaranda trees and lush walls of bougainvillea.

She had to admit that the surroundings were more than tranquil, or at least they would be if Isabelle would only shut up.

"You don't understand what a break this is for me," Isabelle said. *"You* try taking care of two boys under six. My kids drive me loco. I get no sleep, then I have to work. Now Armando is home, hangin' around the house all day—gettin' in my way. It's a zoo."

"You have help," Lola pointed out, remembering that Mama had asked her to pay for a woman who cooked and cleaned several days a week.

"Not as much as I need," Isabelle said resentfully. "You don't realize how lucky you are, Lucia. You have a big mansion with people runnin' to do everything you want, while you lie back eatin' chocolates an' watchin' TV."

"The *reason* I have a big house," Lola explained, "is because I worked extremely hard to afford it."

"Acting's not *work,*" Isabelle snorted derisively. "Acting is play. A bunch of people kissin' your fat ass. I'd give *anything* for that." She laughed. "'Course, *my* ass is fatter than *yours,* but if *I* had nothin' to do, like you, *I'd* be in better shape. Mind you," she added with a self-satisfied smirk, "Armando has no complaints."

Lola attempted to tune out. She wondered if Otto had ousted Matt by now. She hoped so, because two days of listening to Isabelle was bound to drive her totally nuts.

It occurred to her that she should have asked Claudine to accompany her. However, Mama would've asked too many questions, and before long she would've gotten her daughter to reveal that a reunion with Tony Alvarez was in her future. Then Mama would've started contributing her opinion— "You can't do it," she'd say. "Why would you want to be with a drug addict like that?"

The trouble with family was that they felt they could say anything—and usually did.

Across the room Lola spied Serena Lake, a petite brunette with big blue eyes and a tentative girl-next-door smile. They vaguely knew each other, but Lola was hardly in the mood to socialize. However, once Isabelle saw her, it was all over. Isabelle nudged her sister. "Do you know her?" she asked in a reverent whisper. Lola shook her head. "You go to all the same premieres an' parties," Isabelle insisted. "You *must* know her."

"I kind of do," Lola admitted. "We're not friends, though."

"I should go over and tell her you're here," Isabelle said. "She looks awfully lonely sitting by herself."

"No!" Lola said.

"Why not?" Isabelle argued. "I'd give

anything to meet her, then I can get an autograph for my boys."

"Your boys are too young to know who she is."

"Yes," Isabelle said—never at a loss for words. "But when they grow up they'll know."

"Do me a favor," Lola said, sipping mango juice. "Leave her alone. She's come here to relax, like me."

"She's so pretty," Isabelle said, craning her neck to get a better look.

"Do you think so?" Lola said. *"I* don't."

"Well, she's not *sexy* like us," Isabelle said, placing herself in the same league as her sister. "She's got that all-American kinda sweet thing. Some men go for that."

"I'm sure they do."

"Gotta go to the little girls' room," Isabelle announced, jumping up.

Lola picked at her salad and thought about Tony. Almost engaged indeed! What utter crap. The man was scared, frightened of the passion they'd once shared. He was wary of getting burned again, and she couldn't blame him.

On her way back from the ladies' room, Isabelle stopped at Serena Lake's table.

Lola saw this from across the room and inwardly groaned. What was her pushy sister up to now?

Within minutes Isabelle came running back to the table, beaming. "Serena has promised to sign pictures for the boys," she said proudly. "An' I told her you'd be happy to get together while you're here."

"You did *what?*" Lola said, frowning.

"She's by herself."

"I *told* you I didn't want to socialize. Serena's not a friend, she's an acquaintance."

"Please, Lucia," Isabelle begged. "Do it for me."

"No, I won't."

"You've changed," Isabelle said accusingly. "You've forgotten how you used to come over to my house, an' I'd cook you your favorite spicy chicken, an' we'd talk about clothes an' boys an' stuff. Now you're Miss Big Fancy Star, an' everythin' I do is wrong."

"That's not true."

"When you were workin' as a waitress, my God—*nothin'* was too much trouble. I remember the time you saw Linc Blackwood at a party when you were datin' that disc jockey guy. You were *so* excited. Bet you wish you'd got *his* autograph."

"I do not."

"I'm your *older* sister, Lucia, an' don't you forget it."

"How can I forget it when you're always reminding me?"

Isabelle was determined. "Serena Lake needs us," she said dramatically. "And *I* need to meet her."

"I am *not* getting into Serena Lake's business, and neither are you," Lola responded. "What did you say to her, anyway?"

"Told her we were willing to help her in any way we could."

"I don't fucking *believe* you!"

"Nice language, Lucia. It's a good thing Mama's not here."

"Stop calling me Lucia. I've been Lola for the last five years."

"Lola's a stupid name," Isabelle said, tossing back her frizzy red hair. "You'll always be Lucia to me."

"Hello."

They both glanced up in tandem; they'd been so intent on arguing that neither of them had noticed Serena Lake approaching their table.

"Oh . . . hi," Lola said, taken by surprise. "How *are* you?"

"Okay, I guess," Serena answered wanly. "Do you mind if I join you?"

"Um, no," Lola managed.

"Oh yes, please do sit down," Isabelle said, turning into an awestruck fan with manners. "My sister and I are here for you. You must have suffered terribly. Those supermarket rags are nasty. How do you put up with all the horrible things they say about you? As an ordinary person, my sympathies are with you."

"Thanks," Serena said, sitting down.

There goes my peace and solitude, Lola thought. *Better get on the phone to Otto. I'm never going to make it here for two days.*

Shelby began experiencing pangs of regret around 3 A.M., when she couldn't sleep and Linc had not yet returned to the hotel. Where was he? What was he doing? Was he making a fool of himself?

She should've stayed around to protect him. The London press were notorious, and that's all she needed, lurid stories about Linc getting drunk and out of control in the morning papers. Her parents would appreciate *that*.

She sat up in bed, switched on the light, and called down to the concierge, requesting to be put through to the Ritz Club.

"Certainly, ma'am," said the concierge.

She waited impatiently until someone at the club answered. "This is Mrs. Blackwood," she said. "I believe my husband might be there."

"Mr. Blackwood left a couple of hours ago," said the receptionist.

"You're sure?"

"Quite sure, madam."

Damn! Where could he be? The bar in the hotel was probably closed by this time, so it was no good looking for him there.

She had no idea what to do. Trust Linc to mess with her mind as usual.

"It's not what it looks like," Jump yelled—after he'd shoved the bubble brunette out of the room, clothes and all.

Man, he must think I'm pretty naive to believe that old chestnut, Cat thought, glaring at him. *Not what it looks like, indeed. Some naked bird crawling all over him.*

"Then what is it?" she asked, pulling on her jeans.

"Some skank groupie who thought she was about t' get lucky."

"Yeah?" Cat said, throwing on her tee shirt. "And since she had the key to your room, she must've been pretty secure in that knowledge."

"Hey, babe—"

"Hey, babe, *what?*" she said furiously. "We've been married two years and you're screwing around on me. This ain't gonna fly, not with me."

"I told you—it's not what it looks like," he said sulkily.

She shook her head in wonderment. "I believed in you, Jump. Thought you were different. Guess I was wrong. There's an old expression my dad taught me—'A standing prick has no conscience.' Hey—why don't you write a song about *that?*"

"Aw jeez, Cat, so what if I did screw her? It doesn't mean shit."

"Are you telling me that you *did?*"

"I got birds throwing themselves at me all the time. I might've been out of it one night. It coulda happened. Who remembers?"

"Who fucking *remembers?*" she said, outraged.

"I got no clue why she came waltzing in here."

"You know what?" Cat said, grabbing her bag. "I'm out of here."

"Don't do that," he groaned.

"I can do what the fuck I want."

"It was a one-off; she's a slag."

"How do I know she wasn't lying next to you the other night when I called?"

"She wasn't."

"Oh, really? I'm glad *you're* so sure."

"Look," he said. "I'll be straight with you. She happens t' be an old girlfriend I was with way before I met you. We hooked up earlier tonight an' it kinda happened. I told her I was married an' slagged her off. *That's* why she came here."

"Conveniently with a key."

"She must've pinched it."

"You know what, Jump?"

"What?"

"I can't stay with somebody I don't trust, and *I don't trust you.*"

"Didn't we just fuck? Wasn't it mind-blowing?"

"Yeah," she retorted, green eyes blazing

with fury. "It totally blows my mind imagining where your dick was before you stuck it into me."

"You can't leave, not over this."

"Watch me. It's over. Sayonara. Goodbye. S'long."

"Some skank groupie breaks into my room an' you're telling me it's over?"

"That's *exactly* what I'm telling you. If you can't keep your dick in your pants, then unfortunately, you can't keep me."

And with those words she said good-bye to her marriage.

Serena Lake was not shy about revealing the sordid details of her extramarital affair to Lola and Isabelle. She told them all about her long-suffering husband, Ward, and the English bad-boy movie star she'd had the best sex ever with. How devastated she was when Richard had left her, and how she now wanted to get back together with Ward for the sake of their two small children.

Isabelle was in heaven. She was actually sitting in a luxurious spa with her sister, who didn't really matter, and the big movie star Serena Lake, listening to Serena Lake reveal her innermost thoughts. It was simply too incredible.

"I'm so adrift," Serena said, flapping her hands in a helpless fashion. "And the tabloids are no help; every week they print another vile story about me."

"Oh, I know, I know," Isabelle agreed. "It must be awful."

"Why don't you sue?" Lola asked, knowing full well what a tricky and expensive road *that* was.

"My lawyer advised me not to."

"The tabloids stink," Isabelle said vehemently. "My sister's right there alongside you. A different story every week."

"Yes," Serena said, turning to Lola. "I've read about you and Tony Alvarez. He's an amazing director. I'd give anything to work with him one day."

You should only know how amazing he is, Lola thought. *The man is a human sex machine.*

"What will you do next about gettin' back with your husband?" Isabelle asked, loath to get off the perils of Serena.

"Who knows?" Serena said, shrugging. "Ward has promised we can meet, talk things through. He has custody of the children right now, which is so unfair."

"I understand about the kids," Isabelle interjected. "I have two boys, and if I couldn't be with them I'd be lost. Fortunately, my Armando *never* looks at other women, and *I* never look at other men, although I've had plenty of opportunities. Oh yes, *plenty.*"

"You see, *I'm* the one who left the family home," Serena explained. "That makes a big difference in the eyes of the law."

"Surely your lawyer can do something about *that?*" Lola asked.

"Not with the way the tabloids are carrying on," Serena said. "Every week they give my husband all kinds of new ammunition against me."

"You mean it's *true* what they say in the tabloids?" Isabelle said, completely enthralled.

"There's always a *germ* of truth," Serena admitted. "They sniff out a story, then they elaborate."

"Last week they printed that I travel around with fifteen assistants and six bodyguards," Lola sniffed. "Do *you* see anybody here? I'm with my sister and one bodyguard, who doubles as my driver. I'm a perfectly normal person when I'm not in front of a camera."

"You're not normal," Isabelle argued. "Sometimes you have *two* bodyguards when you go out. Surely you remember the day we went shopping on Rodeo Drive and you got mobbed, and we had to call the police?"

"There's nothing wrong with using bodyguards occasionally," Lola said defensively. "It's for my protection. There's too many obsessive fans out there. I know you don't understand, Isabelle, but people *do* get obsessed with me. I receive thousands of fan letters a week."

"*I* was stalked once," Serena mused, joining in. "The man was under the impression that we were married. He wrote me hundreds of threatening letters, sent disgusting e-mails, then he killed himself."

"That's terrible!" Isabelle exclaimed.

"Yes, especially as he did it outside my house," Serena added.

"How did he do it?" Isabelle asked, bug-eyed with curiosity.

"He set himself on fire."

"Oh my Lord!" Isabelle shrieked.

"I know it's early," Lola said, yawning, "but I've got to get some sleep."

"You go on up," Isabelle said, still enthralled with all the stories. "I'll stay here and keep Serena company."

"That's okay," Serena said. "I should be getting to bed myself. It's been nice talking to you two. Isabelle, you're so kind. And Lola, I'm glad we've had this chance to get together. Whenever we see each other it's always kiss-kiss and 'What a great dress.' There's never time for anything meaningful."

Lola nodded. She hadn't expected to like Serena, and she did. It was a pleasant surprise.

Later, back in her sister's room, Isabelle couldn't stop talking. She was filled with excitement. "Wait till the girls hear about *this,*" she announced.

"What girls?" Lola asked, diligently removing her makeup.

"My girlfriends."

"You shouldn't repeat anything you've heard here today," Lola warned in a stern voice. "Serena was telling us things in confidence."

"I won't repeat *everything.*"

"You shouldn't repeat *anything.*"

"If I wanted to," Isabelle said slyly, "I could call up the tabloids and make myself five hundred dollars. They pay cash, you know."

Interesting that Isabelle knew the going price. Lola couldn't help wondering if that's where some of the stories about *her* had come from.

Would her sister really do such a thing? Hmm . . . she wouldn't put it past her.

"Okay, now I've absolutely got to get some sleep," she said, climbing into bed. "Why don't you go to your room and watch TV?"

"I think I'll take a walk around," Isabelle said, bursting with adrenaline. "See who else I can find to talk to."

"No, go to bed," Lola ordered. "You're here for a rest. You told me that you never get any sleep, what with the boys waking you every day at six. Take advantage of your time here."

Reluctantly Isabelle left. As soon as she was sure her sister had gone, Lola reached for the phone and called Tony again. He was on her mind big time; she couldn't wait to hear his voice.

"Hi," she murmured.

"You again," he said.

"Who is she, Tony?"

He gave a low chuckle. "I wondered how long it would take you."

"Tell me who she is, then you can tell me when you're getting rid of her."

"She's a beautiful eighteen-year-old Puerto Rican singer, an' I love her."

"Get real, Tony. We both know who you love," Lola said scornfully. "I'll be back soon. Prepare yourself."

She put down the phone. He didn't fool her. Tony Alvarez. Lola Sanchez. They belonged together.

Linc rolled in around seven in the morning, bleary-eyed and disheveled. By this time Shelby had gotten over her feelings of regret that she hadn't stayed with him. She was now angry.

"Where were you?" she demanded, tight-lipped.

"I'm gonna get the third degree, am I?" he said, collapsing on the bed. "I wanna sleep. Wake me when it's time to go to the airport."

"I asked where you were, Linc."

He closed his eyes, managing a fake snore.

She could smell the booze a mile away. It was wafting from his pores.

Damn! She hoped that when he awoke he had the mother of all hangovers.

She went into the bathroom and slammed the door. Linc Blackwood was *not* going to ruin her triumph. She had a hit movie, amazing personal reviews, and now it was her time to shine.

Sydney Airport was deserted. Cat hurried straight to the Quantas desk and booked a ticket on the next plane to L.A. Unfortunately it didn't depart for another five hours. Upset, angry, and disillusioned, she checked into a nearby hotel.

The whole deal was such a fucking cliché. Surprise husband. Discover he's been playing on the side. Walk out.

Only it hadn't happened that way. He'd slept with her *before* she'd discovered his infidelity. What an *asshole!*

She needed a shower. He could've caught something from that girl, and he hadn't even bothered taking a shower before sleeping with *her.* Yuck!

She felt let down, used, and dirty. Bastard! Did he honestly think she would forgive him?

No fucking way.

It was all surreal. Two years of total togetherness, and now this.

Her mother had always warned her that men were not to be trusted. Could it be that her much-married mother was right?

She felt like such a fool. Why had she thought Jump was different? Why had she trusted him?

He must be pretty stupid, too, because he'd actually admitted it, confirmed he'd screwed someone else, and that was it for her. Jackass!

Fortunately she didn't have to go back to their New York loft and all the memories. She had an apartment waiting for her in L.A. and Jump was not part of it. She'd settle into her new place, and when she felt like it, she'd fly to New York, pack up all her things, and that would be *it.*

One divorce coming up.

CHAPTER

16

First thing the next morning, Lola phoned Otto to check on his progress regarding the Matt situation.

"He's out, gone. Packed up and left," Otto assured her.

Lola clutched the phone to her ear. "Are you *sure*?"

"I personally escorted him off the premises."

"What happened? Tell me everything."

"I informed him that we had to have an

urgent meeting, then I went over to the house and laid it out."

"You told him about the extra money he was getting on top of the prenup if he signs a paper agreeing not to sell his story?"

"Yes, Lola."

"Was he upset?"

"I would say so. He doesn't seem to think there's anything wrong between the two of you."

"Did he ask why I had *you* do it?"

"It's done. He's out of the house. I'm having the locks changed now."

"Why? Do you think he'll come back?"

"No, I think he'll go away, but eventually he wants to see you to find out what went wrong."

"No way," she said vehemently. "I'll be cordial if I bump into him, but I don't care to see him."

"Fine."

"Thank you, Otto, I appreciate it."

"I'm glad, Lola, because it wasn't easy."

"Well," she said succinctly, "I guess the only *easy* part is the enormous bills you send me every month."

Before Otto could reply, she hung up the phone, feeling deliciously free. Now she could go home with no worries. And yet she wouldn't mind staying at the spa for a couple of extra days. It was relaxing and she was quite enjoying being pampered and waited on by all the various beauticians in residence, people who were totally dedicated to caring for their perfection-hungry clients.

Besides, it was a treat for Isabelle, and much as her sister got on her nerves, Lola *did* love her, and it was fun to see her so caught up in it all. Isabelle was in heaven, for not only had she befriended Serena Lake, but she'd also managed to strike up a conversation with the TV star Petra Flynn.

Lola stayed well away from that one. It was okay to be friendly with a fellow movie star, but Petra was TV, and Lola considered that beneath her.

She went downstairs for her scheduled seaweed wrap, meeting up with Isabelle in the treatment room. They lay naked on beds side by side as their bodies were brushed with a thick gooey liquid, then wrapped in filmy, leaflike sheets.

"I feel like a seaweed tamale," Isabelle giggled. "This is so *bad!*"

"Enjoy it," Lola said, wriggling her toes.

"Oh, I am!" Isabelle exclaimed. "By the way, what happened to your pubes? You've hardly got any left; it looks loco."

"I had a Brazilian wax," Lola answered casually. "You should try it; your bush is almost as big as the hair on your head."

"That's so rude!" Isabelle said, blushing.

"But true," Lola insisted.

"Armando likes it that way."

"He does?"

"Oh yes," Isabelle boasted. "Armando is a *real* man, he enjoys a *real* woman."

Hmm, Lola thought, *nothing like sneaking in a quick jab against me.*

"I'm sure he does," she said cheerfully. "That doesn't mean you shouldn't try it. Surprise him. It's a definite turn-on."

"You think?" Isabelle said, quite tempted to do something bold and daring.

"I'm sure they do it here. Say yes and I'll treat you."

"Well . . . ," Isabelle said hesitantly.

"Do it!" Lola insisted. "Live dangerously for once."

"Okay," Isabelle said, secretly pleased.

Why not? She, too, could look like a movie star.

* * *

Shelby attempted to wake Linc half an hour before they were due to depart from the hotel. Even though she was shaking him hard, he was difficult to rouse.

"Get up," she said, continuing to shake his shoulder. "We have to leave for the airport."

Fortunately there was nothing in the morning papers about her erstwhile husband. She was dying to question him, find out where he'd been. On the other hand, she wasn't sure she wanted to know.

"Aw, Jesus!" he groaned, surfacing slowly. "My head's *killing* me. I can't get on a fucking plane like this. I'm sick, sweetie, really sick."

She had no sympathy for him. "I packed your stuff," she said coldly. "I left out the sweat suit you always travel in."

"Gee, thanks, honey," he said, reaching out for her.

She moved away. Obviously he'd put the *USA Today* piece to rest and was in a better frame of mind toward her. It didn't make any difference, she was still mad.

He got up, making his way noisily into the bathroom. Soon she heard the shower running.

Did he honestly think she was going to excuse his behavior as usual? Was that the way this was supposed to go?

No. She was too angry. This time he had to learn a lesson and check himself into re-hab.

He emerged from the bathroom, a towel knotted casually around his waist. "I still feel like shit," he complained, in case she hadn't gotten it the first time.

"Take a couple of aspirin," she suggested.

"That's very sympathetic."

She gave him a long, cool look. "Since when did you imagine I was sympathetic to a hangover?"

"Oh Christ," he said, yawning. "Here we go."

She decided ignoring him was better than getting in another fight, so she finished packing, then called down to the concierge to send up a bellboy to collect their luggage.

Outside the hotel there were quite a few photographers waiting, plus a gathering of fans.

Linc put his arm around her, smiling his movie star smile for the cameras, his bloodshot eyes safely hidden behind extra dark glasses.

The crowd was delighted. Shelby Cheney and Linc Blackwood. A movie star couple sent to thrill.

The fans waved and cheered enthusiastically as the driver and doorman loaded their suitcases into the car.

They rode to the airport in silence. Halfway there Linc fell asleep, snoring the rest of the way.

When they arrived there were more photographers waiting, and several airport personnel ready to whisk them to the VIP lounge.

Once there, Linc settled in a comfortable chair.

"I'll be right back," Shelby said.

"Where you going, sweetie?" he asked, like a small kid about to be abandoned by his mother.

"I want to buy magazines and a book to read on the plane."

"You're going to read?" he said in his best little-boy-lost voice. "You're not planning on cuddling up with your husband?"

Here came the turnaround. *I need you, I want you, I love you, you're everything to me.* Linc Blackwood could go from being mean and nasty to the most needy man in the world. Only this time she wasn't falling for it. This time she was too disappointed with him to care.

"Can I get *you* anything?" she asked politely.

"C'mon, sweetheart," he said, almost pleading. "Quit with the cold treatment. You know I can't help the way I am."

"That's just it, Linc, you *can.*"

"No, sweetie," he protested, reaching for her hand. "I'm weak that way. You *know* why."

Damn. He was playing the vulnerable card. Sober and sorry, Linc was extremely difficult to resist.

Matt Seel had never suffered from a shortage of girls. Ever since he was a teenage jock they'd always been available to him. And not dogs, pretty ones, because he was tall and blond and athletic. A professional tennis player with a big cock and a ready smile. Women were never a problem; in fact, he usually couldn't get rid of them.

Then he met Lola Sanchez and everything changed. She was so different. A sexy and exotic temptress who had the ability to transport him to another world. In bed she was an angel *and* a devil. She had tricks he'd never known existed. She was perfectly capable of taking him to heaven and back again. Before long he fell deeply in lust.

So when her lawyer turned up at the house and informed him he had to get out, he simply couldn't believe it. "Lola's doing this to me?" he said, completely shocked.

"Miss Sanchez is being very generous," Otto Landstrom informed him. "Not only is she living up to the prenuptial you signed, but she also wants to give you a bonus check, contingent on you not selling your story."

"She's dumping *me?"* Matt exclaimed. He'd never been dumped by a girl in his life. Tall, blond, and athletic meant always doing the dumping himself. "I gave up everything for Lola," he said. "I gave up my tennis career. No prenup will cover that."

"Let's not forget that you signed in all good faith," Otto said smoothly. "The prenuptial will hold up in any court you care to take it to. If you're difficult, you can forget about the extra bonus. However, if you cooperate, you'll get the money *and* Lola's friendship. I'm sure that's worth something."

"When is she coming back?"

"It doesn't matter when, she wants you out today."

This was a further shock.

"Be out in two hours," Otto said, waving a check in front of Matt's face, "and this is yours, but only if you sign right here." He proffered a letter of intent.

Matt realized that the only smart thing to do was to go along with the program, even though he knew he should run it by a lawyer. Only he didn't have one at the present time, and anyway, what was he *supposed* to do? Turn down a very generous settlement? Plus Lola had a fiery temper; it wouldn't be wise to piss her off.

"Why is she doing this to me?" he asked.

Otto shrugged. "Lola's a movie star, she does what she wants."

That made sense. Lola always did what she wanted. She'd never treated him as an equal, or worried about his opinion. Unlike her mother and sisters, who were always sweet to him.

He went upstairs and packed his belongings. He used her best suitcases, the new set of Louis Vuitton she'd gotten for free.

Screw her! She wanted him out. What a cold piece of work she'd turned out to be.

He returned downstairs, accepted the check, signed the letter, and took off in Lola's new Bentley.

One of these days Lola would get hers, and he wouldn't be sorry.

The apartment Cat had rented in L.A. was light and spacious, located in a high-rise building overlooking the city. Sparsely furnished, it was all she needed for a six-month stay in L.A. The moment she arrived she missed the New York loft she shared with Jump, and she especially missed all her stuff. She felt secure having her possessions around her—books, manuscripts, CDs, DVDs, and favorite paintings she'd picked up at street markets. A bare apartment with nothing personal was not going to work for her.

She was putting on a brave face, although on the inside she was breaking up. Life without Jump would be a challenge. He'd saved her from herself, gotten her off drugs, and straightened her out. Since that time they'd done everything together, and now she was alone. There was no way she cared to drift back into her bad old ways simply because she was by herself. Going through her L.A. phone book she was dismayed to realize that most of her friends who resided in the City of Angels were pals from her drug days. Reconnecting with them could turn out to be fatal. Not that she was contemplating returning to her old ways; she was wise enough to realize that temptation was always dangerous.

Nobody to call. Nothing to do. Hire a freaking lawyer, that's what she *should* do.

She called the Zandack office and asked for Merrill. He was still in London. Then she requested Jonas. He was in London with the boss. Naturally.

It was all too depressing, alone in L.A. with nothing to do and no one to call. She sent out for pizza, switched on the small TV, and fell asleep watching a mindless reality show about ten pathetic women vying for the love of some stupid, preening jerk.

Getting dragged into the drama of Petra Flynn's upcoming divorce was inevitable.

Once Isabelle was on the case there was no stopping her. After befriending Serena, she went after Petra big time. Now here they were—a cozy quartet. Soon Petra, Serena, Isabelle, and Lola were taking every meal together, setting out on long hikes, and monopolizing the Jazzercize class.

Lola wasn't sure how it had happened, although she had to admit that she was quite enjoying herself. Since she'd become a star, girlfriends were a thing of the past. She was too busy, and the women she came in contact with lived in another reality. Now, here were these two famous women she could relate to. And they were fun to be around—even though Serena was moping about her lost lover and Petra was livid about her abusive soon-to-be-ex.

On their last night at the spa, after a couple of bottles of red wine—smuggled in by one of Petra's handlers—Lola finally let loose and revealed all.

"Guess what?" she announced. "While I'm here, I had my lawyer tell my husband to get out."

"Get out of what?" Isabelle asked, still an innocent in the ways of movie stars—even after three days of concentrated boot camp.

"You did?" Petra said, getting it immediately. She was an impossibly doll-like twenty-five-year-old, with amazing implants, scads of white-blond curls, and a pouty face. She ruled late night TV with her sexy hit series, where she played a billionaire who fights crime—usually undercover in the skimpiest of outfits.

"Yup," Lola said. "Just like that. It was easy. My lawyer took care of it."

"Who's your lawyer?" Serena inquired.

"Is he cute?" Petra asked. "I only like dealing with cute lawyers since I seem to spend half my time with them."

Lola would hardly describe Otto as cute, although his bald, polished head *was* quite intriguing.

"Take care of *what?*" Isabelle asked, still not getting it.

"She's divorcing him, silly," said Petra, pouring herself another glass of wine.

"Yes," Serena said. "And apparently she's doing it the easy way."

"You're divorcing Matt?" Isabelle said, totally shocked. *"Why?"*

"It was inevitable," Lola said. "He's *boring!"* And then she dissolved in a fit of wine-induced giggles.

"Boring's not good," Serena said, wrinkling her cute girl-next-door freckled nose.

"Boring sucks!" Petra agreed, her huge implants almost bursting out of her skimpy white tank top. "I can take anything but boring."

"Richard wasn't boring," Serena sighed, naming her English bad-boy lover who'd dumped her.

"Nor was Andy," Petra said, naming her violent, soon-to-be- ex, football star husband.

"And neither was Tony," Lola said, naming her cocaine-addicted ex-lover. "So I've made a decision—*I'm* getting him back."

"Lucia!" Isabelle exclaimed. "Are you *crazy?*"

"No, dear Sis, I'm finally sane, and I want my Tony back."

"Tony Alvarez is a hottie," Serena remarked.

"Tony *Alvarez?*" Petra said. "The director guy?"

"That's him," Lola said proudly.

"Baby, go for it!" Petra encouraged her. "That man is *gorgeous.* Why'd you ever leave *him?*"

"Don't you read the tabloids?" Isabelle snapped.

"Only about myself," Petra retorted.

"Tony Alvarez is a drug addict," Isabelle said flatly.

"Who isn't?" Petra responded. "I can't get through the day without a couple of Vicodin and a shot of vodka."

"God! Lucia!" Isabelle cried, rapidly sobering up. "What will Mama say?"

"It's *my* deal," Lola answered boldly, full of smooth red wine. "Nobody's business but mine."

"I bet Tony's a wild man in the sack," Petra said, eyes gleaming.

"Richard was a wild man," Serena said wistfully. "I've never experienced anyone like him."

"Big dick?" Petra asked matter-of-factly.

Serena blushed. "I can't tell you that."

"Why not, honey?" Petra said, admiring her gold fake nails. "They talk about *us.*"

"He went back to his girlfriend in England," Serena said miserably. "I hate him! He *used* me."

"You can get him back if you *really* want him," Lola offered. "Men are easy."

"For you," Serena said.

"For any woman with half a brain and great boobs," Petra said, fluffing out her white-blond curls.

"I don't *have* great boobs," Serena wailed.

"Then *buy* 'em," Petra said. "*I* did. And in case anyone's interested, my Andy is a solid eight and a half inches, and I'm walking away from *that* 'cause he's a no-good, battering bastard, and I've *had* it."

Both Lola and Serena applauded. Isabelle didn't. She was too shell-shocked by her sister's announcement and the direction this conversation was taking. Isabelle considered herself a worldly woman; however, discussing the size of a man's member was plain dirty—although she couldn't help making a quick mental note to bring a ruler to bed. Armando would definitely be a winner!

Much to Shelby's surprise, Linc agreed to go into rehab. "I don't need to," he said resignedly, "and the rags'll make a meal of it, but if that's what'll make you happy . . ."

Shelby was relieved. Since getting back to L.A., her cold and unforgiving attitude toward him had obviously had the required effect.

She called Brenda, who said, "Yes, get him in there immediately."

The next day she drove him to a discreet Malibu retreat where many of the big stars went when they needed help.

"You *do* know this is a big joke," he said as he got out of the car. "I'm perfectly sober. Haven't had a drink in days. You *know* I don't need this."

For a moment she weakened. He was right; no drinking had taken place since they'd arrived back from Europe. Unfortunately that didn't mean it was over. Linc needed professional help.

Unbeknownst to her, Linc had switched from booze to cocaine. He'd discovered that a quick snort got him through the day and was less detectable than a swig of scotch. Shelby would never suspect drugs; she was too naive, which was one of the things he loved about her. Even though she was an actress, living and working in the thick of Hollywood, she'd managed to maintain her innocence when it came to the wilder things in life. The truth was he didn't want to lose her, and sometimes he knew he came perilously close. London had not been good. He'd blown a shitload of money at the casino, and later he'd ended up in some bimbo's apartment getting a mediocre blow job.

Christ! Not smart. Thank God Shelby hadn't found out.

Upon entering the facility, a polite man at the front desk asked to go through his bag, then searched the clothes he had on.

Linc didn't care. It wasn't as if he was addicted or shit like that. Cocaine. Booze. He could leave them both alone if he wanted to.

The problem was that he didn't want to.

Cat embarked on a major shopping spree—not for clothes; she was more interested in getting her apartment in shape. She took a trip to Melrose and discovered an interesting rug shop where she purchased several colorful rugs. Next she ordered two Shabby Chic couches and an ornate Mexican mirror. Then she found a stately stone Buddha, and an old oil painting of jazz great Billie Holiday. After that came the big splurge—she moved on to Robertson and purchased a highly expensive oversized bed, and tons of enormous soft cushions. Then, finally, two flat-screen TVs, a DVD player, an Apple computer, and an extremely extravagant Bose stereo system.

At last she felt at home. Now she could get back to work.

CHAPTER 17

Claudine Sanchez called a family conference. Lola was surprised it had taken so long, since she'd been home from the spa for almost a week. She phoned Mama back, told her she was busy and couldn't make it.

"You *will* make it, Miss Movie Star," Claudine retorted with gusto. "And you *will* make it tonight."

There was no arguing with Claudine Sanchez. Once her mind was set, everyone in the family had to jump—including Lola, although she still couldn't figure out why she had to comply. She was rich. She was famous. But the bottom line was that she was still Claudine's daughter.

On the business front things were good. She was pleased because Elliott had gotten Linc Blackwood to sign on for *New York State of Mind.* She'd already started costume fittings and getting her head in the right place. Every movie was different, and this one was bound to be more than interesting. It was payback time, and now she had the perfect opportunity.

Big Jay, her bodyguard/driver, delivered her to her parents' house, where the entire family was gathered. Louis Sanchez, Isabelle (with a smug, I-had-to-tell-them look on her face), her other sister, Selma, and Louis Junior—like it was any of *his* business.

Lola marched into the living room. *"What?"* she demanded impatiently, throwing down her new Gucci bag. "Why did I have to come here tonight? I'm about to start a movie. This is not good timing for me."

"In this family," Claudine said sternly, "divorce is not good timing either."

"What are you *talking* about?" she said irritably.

"I'm talking about the things your sister told me."

"And what exactly did she tell you?" Lola said, shooting Isabelle a killer look.

Claudine gave a long-suffering sigh. "It's no good trying to deny it, Lucia. Isabelle says you're planning on divorcing Matt."

"What if I am?" Lola said, exasperated. "Is it anybody's business except mine?"

"I don't understand what's become of you," Claudine said, shaking her head. "I taught you to be a *good* daughter. Now it seems that all this fame and stardom has gone to your head."

"How's the house, Mama?" Lola said, standing her ground. "Comfortable? Because all my *fame* and *stardom* is what bought it for you."

"Don't sass me, girl," Claudine said, her tone sharpening.

"I warned her not to marry Matt," Louis said, joining in. "The poor bastard's got no *cojones.* He's not a man. It was never a match."

"Be quiet," Claudine said, silencing her unfaithful husband with a steely glare.

"It's true, Mama," Louis Junior said, slouching across the room.

"You stay out of this," Lola snapped, turning on her brother. "It's none of your business. Do you get it?"

"No, *I* don't get anything," Louis Junior whined. "Mama and Papa get a house, my sisters get all kinda shit—an' *I* get nothin'."

"What is it you expect from me?" Lola demanded.

"You're my sister," he said sulkily. "You should give me a job."

"Why *me?* I'm not responsible for you. If you shifted your lazy ass you might manage to get a job on your own."

"Who're you callin' lazy?" Louis Junior retaliated. "If *you*—"

"Stop fighting," Claudine ordered. "Lucia—what do you have to say for yourself?"

"I'm twenty-four years old, Mama," Lola said, furious that she had to deal with this crap. "I can do anything I like. And if I decide to divorce Matt, it's between him and me."

"What happened with you an' Matt?" Louis Senior asked, scratching his chin. "The bastard beat you? 'Cause if he did—"

"Ha!" Lola scoffed. "I'd like to see a man

beat *me.* I'd kick him in the balls exactly like you taught me, Papa."

Louis grinned, proud of his famous daughter, who quite obviously possessed the *cojones* her husband lacked.

Selma spoke up. "It's really none of our business," she said. "If Lucia feels this is the right thing for her to do, then she must go ahead and do it."

"Thank you," Lola said gratefully. "And as for you," she added, shooting another venomous glare at Isabelle, who sat on the couch, hands clasped in front of her as if she wasn't Miss Gossip of the World, "I gave you three fabulous days at a luxury spa, and *this* is how you repay me? You couldn't *wait* to run to Mama and tell her about me and Matt. I'm surprised you didn't sell your story to one of those supermarket rags."

"Your mama's right," Louis Senior said, deciding to take on the role of man of the house. "You better have a special reason for divorce."

"Yeah," agreed Louis Junior. "A very special reason."

"Oh, for God's sake!" Lola exploded, fed up with being spoken to as if she were a child. "Will you all butt out. It's *my* fucking divorce."

"Excuse me, Miss Movie Star?" Claudine said, her face thunderous. *"What* did you say?"

"It's *my* fucking divorce," Lola repeated.

"Leave now," Claudine said, standing up, full of rage. "I will not put up with street language in my house. Come back when you can behave yourself like a lady."

"Why should I answer to any of you?" Lola said, getting more angry and frustrated by the minute. "You can *all* go screw yourselves."

She turned around and walked out.

Damn! They were ignorant. How dare they think they could still boss her around? She was a star. A rich movie star. She was important and famous.

Big Jay jumped to attention, hurriedly opening the car door for her. She got in, muttering to herself.

"You say somethin', Miss Lola?" Big Jay asked. He was a huge tree trunk of a black man with Rastafarian dreadlocks and a soft, Michael Jackson voice.

"Yes," she said, still simmering. "Unless

there's a gun to my head, *never* bring me here again. And *that's* an order."

"Casting is a strange and wonderful thing," Merrill lectured, sitting behind his enormous desk in his vast office overlooking the city of Los Angeles.

"I know," Cat replied carefully. "But if the casting's not right, then nothing works."

"You're still a neophyte in this business," Merrill said, puffing on his usual fat Cuban cigar. "If I can persuade Lola Sanchez or Shelby Cheney to play the lead in *Caught,* you should kiss my ass. And I think I got Nick Logan hooked for the con man. A star makes all the difference at the box office."

"I don't care," she said, her mouth set in a stubborn line.

"You're not dealing with a small, piece-of-shit movie now, Cat. You've moved into the big leagues. So grow up and start realizing how lucky you are to have *me* behind you." More thick smoke wafted in her direction.

She glanced over at Jonas. He was sitting at the side of Merrill's desk, taking notes. No help there.

"But Mr. Zandack—" she argued.

"How many times I gotta tell ya—call me Merrill."

"What if you sign an actress who's completely wrong for the role?"

"You tellin' me my business?"

"I'm just—"

"Shut up an' listen," he said, interrupting her. "If I say we hire a big star, that's what we do. An' if that big star doesn't want you to direct—you gotta go along with that too."

"If I don't direct," she said, sitting up very straight, "there'll be no movie."

"No kiddin'?" Merrill said. "Guess you're forgetting about the contracts you signed."

Alarm bells started going off in her head. *What* contracts?"

"Let me jog your memory, kitten. When my company took over distribution of *Wild Child,* you signed contracts givin' me all rights on your next project. Which means you'll direct if the star wants you to—and if she doesn't, too bad."

"I don't believe this," she said, standing up.

"Believe it. You wanted a big-budget movie, you got it."

Dazed and confused, she left his office. She needed time to digest what he'd said and study the contracts that she must have signed. It wasn't enough that she'd had such a shattering experience with Jump. Now this.

Downstairs in the parking lot she climbed into her rented car—a red convertible Mustang. Her mind was racing. She knew what she had to do: hire a sharp lawyer and stop behaving like a foolish little girl. It was quite apparent that Merrill Zandack was a man used to doing things his way, and she was naive for not getting professional advice in the first place. And that was Jump's fault; he'd always had an aversion to lawyers. "Why pay when you can figure it out for yourself?" he'd said. So when Merrill's business affairs people had given her contracts to sign, she hadn't bothered consulting a lawyer; she'd simply gone ahead and signed, thinking she could trust Merrill not to screw her.

Wrong! She was an idiot. A fool. According to Merrill she'd signed away all rights.

As she was driving from the parking lot, Jonas came running up to her car. "Glad I caught you," he said.

"Oh, it's you," she said flatly.

"We should go for coffee, talk about things."

"What's to talk about?"

"Plenty."

She frowned. "Can you explain what just happened?"

"I can try," he said, genuinely eager to help her out.

"Then get in the car and let's go," she said, deciding she had nothing to lose.

He shook his head. "Can't do it now, I'm working. How about later?"

"Come by my apartment."

"I'll be there soon as I finish."

"What time?"

"Depends on his mood."

"Great," she said irritably. "You can't even tell me what time you get off work."

"Don't start with me, Cat. I'm trying to help you."

"In that case, do me a big one and bring me copies of the contracts I signed."

"Hasn't your lawyer got them?"

"Uh . . . I don't have a lawyer," she admitted, knowing how dumb she must sound.

"That isn't smart."

"Like tell me something I *don't* know."

"Look," he said sympathetically. "Every-thing'll work out."

"Sure," she replied, unconvinced. "My heroine will either have a Latino accent or an English one. *And* a big, sexy ass. Perfect for the role of an edgy undercover cop."

Jonas made a valiant attempt to change the subject. "You didn't mention Australia. Was it fun?"

"Oh yeah," she answered sarcastically. "An absolute blast."

"That's not a happy voice."

"I don't want to get into it now," she said, realizing that for some inexplicable reason she felt like crying, and wouldn't *that* look weak in front of Jonas. "Later," she said, revving her engine.

And with that she drove off.

The woman sitting at the bar was mys-terious, in her tinted glasses, big hat, long straight black hair, with heavy bangs con-cealing most of her face, and formfitting black tailored suit. Her legs were encased in the sheerest of black stockings, and on her feet were the highest of heels.

"Hey," the man said, sliding onto the bar stool next to her.

"Hey, yourself," the woman responded.

"You come here a lot?" the man asked. He was Latino and handsome, not particularly tall, with longish jet-black hair, full lips, and brooding eyes.

"Occasionally," the woman replied, sipping a martini.

"What do you do?"

"I'm a housewife. And you?"

"A salesman."

She placed her glass on the bar. "Is there something you'd care to sell me?"

"Come up to my room and we'll see if I got anything that interests you."

"I'm sure there's a possibility," she murmured.

The man slid a key into her hand. "Room three-oh-six, five minutes." He left the bar.

Slowly the woman finished her martini, paid the bar tab, got up, and sashayed from the room. Several eyes swiveled to watch the mysterious creature.

Traveling up in the elevator she took several deep breaths before walking down the corridor to room 306. The anticipation was a killer.

The woman slipped the key into the lock and entered.

The man was lying on the bed in black bikini underwear. Naturally he was hard. The woman would not have expected anything less.

"Is that what you have to show me?" she said boldly.

"Lock the door," he said in a low voice. "Strip, baby. Gimme a show."

The woman turned around and locked the door. Then she removed her sunglasses and hat. Her long straight hair still mostly concealed her face. Anyone with a practiced eye could tell it was a wig.

The man stared at her, his dark, brooding eyes alive with lust.

Slowly, standing at the foot of the bed, the woman began taking off her clothes. First she unbuttoned her tight jacket, button by button, taking her time. Underneath she had on a skimpy black bra—the kind usually favored by Las Vegas showgirls. Her breasts swelled from the confines of the lacy garment.

"Nice," the man said.

Next the woman unzipped her skirt and stepped out of it. Almost naked except for a Frederick's of Hollywood garter belt with the black stockings and high heels, she was a magnificent specimen.

The man's erection was straining at his underwear, but the woman still took her time as she knelt provocatively on the bed, crawling toward him like a predatory panther.

"You got a name?" the man asked, his voice thick with desire.

"Names don't matter," the woman replied.

The man reached forward, pulling her down on top of him. The woman raised her body, her warm skin grazing his. Then she put her hands into his underwear and slowly peeled them down.

The man was harder than she'd imagined. So hard that when he entered her she experienced a sharp combination of pleasure and pain.

The woman gasped, throwing her arms above her head and moaning with an overwhelming passion.

The man placed his hand over her mouth. "Quiet," he ordered. "You'll wake the neighbors."

"I'm not home," the woman reminded him, pushing his hand away.

"Oh yeah, baby," the man said, flipping her so that he was on top. "This is home. This is *definitely* home, an' it's *so* fuckin' good to be back."

Yes, Lola thought, happy in the arms of her much-missed lover. *It certainly is.*

Five days was all Linc could take at the Malibu retreat, then he walked out and took a cab home.

"What happened?" Shelby asked, taken by surprise.

"Absolutely nothing, sweetheart," he said, pulling her into his arms and kissing her. "I did everything they asked me to. Went to all the meetings, made my own bed, and all that crap. Then today I talked to one of the counselors, and he told me to get the hell out, that I didn't need to be there."

"He sent you home?" she said, not sure whether to believe him or not.

"Yeah, the guy said I didn't have a problem. Check it out."

"I'm not checking up on you, Linc."

"So don't. It's your choice," he said, kissing her again. "Didja miss me?"

"Yes," she admitted. "I missed you a lot."

"You too, baby. You too."

"Are you sure you're—"

"Hey," he said, interrupting her. "This is what we're gonna do. We're taking all the booze out of the bar, locking it in a closet, and throwing away the key. How's that?"

"Yes, Linc," she said obediently.

"You wanna know why?"

"Yes."

" 'Cause I ain't drinkin'."

"Is that a promise?"

"For you, my lovely wife, it's a promise," he said, embracing her again.

Relief overwhelmed her. This was a new Linc. Obviously the five days away had done him some good.

"I *do* love you," she murmured, feeling safe and secure in his arms.

"I know you do, sweetheart, and I love you too," he said, tipping her face back so he could gaze into her eyes. "Here's the deal. I love you more than anything in the world, so if it's a question of you or booze, guess what I'm choosing?"

"Me, I hope," she said, smiling softly.

"You got it."

Five minutes later he was on the phone in his study talking to his agent, discussing his upcoming movie, the clothes, the schedule, and everything else connected with it.

Shelby wanted to tell him what was going on with *her* career, so as soon as he was finished, she perched on the edge of his desk and started talking. "I've been offered several new projects," she told him. "Two I'm taking seriously. One begins shooting almost immediately, and the other wouldn't begin for another six months."

"What are they?"

"The one that starts immediately involves nudity."

Christ! Did she honestly think he was allowing her to be naked in a movie again? How would *she* like it if *he* was on-screen bare-assed naked?

"You've done it once, that's enough," he said, remaining calm like it was no big deal. "Trust me on this, Shelby."

"I agree," she said. "Although it's an excellent script and a lot of money."

"*I* make a lot of money," he said forcefully, surprised she was pushing it. "Which means *you* don't have to. What else?"

"There's kind of a James Bond–type film. The only problem is that it takes place on various locations, and I wouldn't want to be away from you."

"I start shooting in a week, so I'll be finished by that time. I could come with you—be your location groupie," he grinned. "How about *that?*"

"I've always wanted my own personal groupie."

"Sweetheart," he said, reaching for her again, "here I am."

Later, when Shelby was busy in the kitchen cooking dinner—something she still enjoyed doing in spite of their large staff—he made his way upstairs, locked himself in his dressing room, located his stash, laid out a couple of lines, and took a few quick, satisfying snorts of cocaine.

The magic powder made him feel powerful and full of strength. Who needed booze? Not him. Jesus! He could do anything he wanted.

Things were going to work out just fine, and Shelby would never know the difference.

CHAPTER
18

Lola felt that finally everything was going her way, in spite of her continuing troubles with her family. Elliott Finerman was obviously a first-rate producer; he'd hired an experienced director with an impressive track record, an award-winning cinematographer who she knew would make her look fabulous, and best of all, he'd signed Linc Blackwood.

She had a strong suspicion that *New York State of Mind* was about to be a breakthrough movie for her. She'd always had a desire to play comedy—smart comedy, not slapstick. *New York State of Mind* could be it.

Most exciting, Tony Alvarez was back on the scene. Well, not exactly back; they'd had a few secret assignations where they role-played—one of their favorite things to do. She'd not actually gone public with the news that they were together again. She sensed it wasn't wise until Matt was total history, plus she had no desire to put up with the flak she was bound to get from all the people around her, especially Faye, for she knew that her long-suffering publicist would complain bitterly.

Tony went along with the secrecy; he got off on intrigue. She'd pick up the phone, tell him where to meet her, and he'd be there. It was an exciting game, one where she got to play dress-up with an array of wigs and many different outfits. Whatever her disguise, she always managed to make herself unrecognizable to the general public. It added to the spice. And Tony was still as spicy as ever. Hot and horny and sexy and dark. Everything about him turned her on.

She'd spent the morning haranguing Otto Landstrom over the phone. "Listen, Otto,

I'm leaving for New York tomorrow to start my movie. And I want my Bentley back. How many times do I have to tell you— when Matt left the house he took my Bentley. Surely you saw him do it? Why didn't you stop him?"

"I wasn't standing on the doorstep watching his every move," Otto said dryly.

"It's *my* car," she said petulantly, "and I want it back."

"Did you buy it while you were married?"

"Yes, Otto, with *my* money."

"Then it *could* be construed as community property, in which case he's entitled to use it."

"He *signed* the fucking agreement, Otto," she retaliated, fast losing patience. "Get my car back."

"I'll do my best."

"And another thing, he took my luggage."

"Let's not get petty here."

"It's my new set of Vuitton luggage and I want that back too."

"Lola—"

"You know he only did it to piss me off."

"You can hardly blame him, can you?"

"Whose side are you on, Otto?"

"I'll take care of it. Good luck with the movie, dear."

She hated it when Otto called her "dear," it sounded so patronizing. *Note to self— think about hiring new lawyer.*

She was happy to be leaving. Selma had come by, pleading with her to make the peace with Mama.

"No," she'd said, refusing to weaken. "I've *had* it with the way the family thinks they can walk all over me. I buy them a house, give them money. Nothing seems to mean anything. And as for Isabelle, she's a tattling bitch."

"Please, Lucia," Selma had pleaded. "Talk with Mama before you go. We live in a dangerous world; it's not right to keep bad blood between you."

"I'll call her from New York," she'd finally agreed, impatient for Selma to leave.

She had one last assignation with Tony before she left, and half of the fun was the preparation.

The struggling starlet and the powerful film director. One of their favorites. Tony liked it because he got to play himself. She liked it because it was total fantasy.

She went to her closet and chose a Marilyn Monroe blond wig, pedal pushers, and a Second Skin tee shirt. Then she added huge Jackie O. sunglasses, borrowed her maid's old car, and drove to Tony's office.

Tony's receptionist was a cow, Eurasian and exotic looking. Lola was sure he'd screwed her, but he would never confess to it. Unrecognizable, she told the cow she had a reading with Mr. Alvarez, and the cow made her wait five minutes before buzzing him and sending her through.

Tony was sitting behind his desk, legs propped up, smoking an herbal cigarette. He glanced up when she entered.

"Did you get the sides?" he snapped.

"Yes, Mr. Alvarez," she answered, suitably subservient.

"Can you act?"

"Do I have to?"

"It might help."

"I can do . . . other things."

"What other things?"

"If it'll get me the part . . ."

"Can you suck cock?"

"Excuse me?"

"You heard. Can you suck my cock?" He stood up and unzipped his pants. "Down on your knees," he ordered. "Let's see how much talent you got."

She didn't need asking twice.

True friends were hard to come by, so when Jonas came to her aid, Cat genuinely appreciated his help, even though he was going against his boss by advising her. He'd recommended two lawyers and she'd gone to see them both, finally choosing Leo Napoli, a thirty-five-year-old bald gay man, ambitious and razor sharp.

After looking over her contracts, Leo shook his head in amazement. "Who advised you to sign these?" he asked.

"My husband."

"You're married?"

"Yeah," she said, running her hand through her short blond hair. "I know, I'm young. But that's another story."

Leo shook his head like he couldn't quite believe it. "You were dealing with Merrill Zandack and you didn't get professional advice," he said. "That's crazy."

After studying the contracts he explained that she'd signed away all rights to *Caught*. "There's not even a clause giving you final script approval," he informed her. "If Merrill

Zandack decides he wants to use only your name and title and bring in other writers, he's free to do so. *And* he has an option for your next script."

"What can we do?" she asked.

"Nothing. You lost out on this one. But one thing I promise you—we'll win on the next."

"What do you mean I've lost out on this one?" she said, dismayed. "Merrill *promised* I could direct."

"And maybe he'll keep his promise. Who knows? We'll arrange a meeting with Mr. Zandack, let him know you're represented now."

The next day she and Leo sat down with Merrill in his office. Puffing on his usual cigar, Merrill laid it out. He announced that he'd hired a line producer and put *Caught* on a fast track. He also informed them that he was on the point of signing a famous actress, and if the actress agreed to Cat directing, then she had the gig.

"It's all about the bottom line," he said to Leo. "You know it's to Cat's advantage if this film is big."

"You had her sign away all her rights," Leo pointed out. "That's not fair."

This sent Merrill off into a choking fit of sarcastic laughter. "Fair? Are you *in* this business?"

"We're screwed," Leo told her when they got back to his office. "Let's hope that whoever this actress is he's talking with agrees to you directing."

"Speaking of getting screwed," Cat ventured, prowling restlessly around his office. "Do you deal with divorces?"

"Divorce is one of my specialties."

"Really?" she said, flopping into a chair. "I thought L.A. lawyers spread it around the firm so they can charge double fees."

"No," Leo said, with a quick smile. "I specialize in contracts, negotiations, *and* divorce."

"Great! You're my kind of lawyer."

"Who is this guy you're married to? Is he in the business?"

"Kind of. He's Australian."

"Not Russell Crowe, I hope."

She couldn't help laughing. "I can assure you he's no Russell Crowe. And since I haven't mentioned this to anyone yet, including Jonas, I'd prefer you didn't say anything."

"Naturally."

"Thanks."

Leo took out a yellow legal pad and picked up his pen. "Let's get some details. I need his name and profession."

"Jump Jagger, he's a rock 'n' roller."

"Any relation to—"

"No," she interrupted. "Everyone asks that. I wish."

"Did you sign a prenuptial?"

"Of course not. I was seventeen when I got married."

"Does he have money?"

"I don't want anything from him."

"How about the reverse?"

"Jump would *never* ask me for a dime."

"Divorce puts a new slant on things. People change."

"Not Jump."

"Why are you seeking a divorce?"

"It's a major cliché."

"You still have to tell me."

So she did, the whole sad story.

Leo listened intently, and when she was finished he assured her that he would be able to take care of everything.

She left his office feeling more positive about things.

That night she and Jonas went to dinner

at Orso's on Third Street. They sat outside in the garden.

"What's going on?" Jonas asked as soon as they'd ordered. "You haven't been your usual obnoxious self since you got back."

"Did Leo say anything to you?" she asked, sipping a glass of red wine.

"No, was he supposed to?"

"Okay," she sighed. "Here's the deal. Only please—do *not* laugh at me."

"You didn't laugh at me when I fell off my skis," he reminded her.

"Actually I did," she admitted.

"As long as you didn't take my photo."

"Does that mean you won't laugh at me?"

"No, I'll respect whatever you have to tell me."

"Well, it's um . . . it's like, y'know . . ."

"C'mon, Cat, give it up. Did you catch him with another girl?"

"How did you know that?"

"I warned you not to surprise him."

"It's worse than that," she said miserably. "I got to his hotel room and he wasn't there, so I slid into bed all ready to do the whole jumping-out-of-bed-naked thing. Finally he came in, was thrilled to see me, and we had this, uh . . . well, I don't have to tell you what happened next."

"Please don't."

"All I can say is it was great, then we went to sleep, and the next thing I know there's some skanky unclothed bitch climbing all over him. He admitted he'd been with her earlier, told me he was drunk and she was an old girlfriend."

"Jesus, Cat, I'm sorry."

"Wonderful story, isn't it?" she said ruefully. "The kind of stuff you read about."

"Or write about," he interjected.

"Y'know," she mused, "my father always told me all men are dogs; so did my mother." She gave a regretful laugh. "That's about the only thing my parents taught me."

"Have you heard from him since?"

"He keeps on calling. I don't answer his calls."

"Maybe you *should* talk to him, see what he has to say."

"What's *wrong* with you?" she exploded. "Aren't you listening to me? The asshole *cheated* on me."

"Sorry."

"Sex is *the* most intimate act between two people," she said, narrowing her green eyes at the thought of Jump with another woman. "And the jerk blew it."

"I guess he did."

"I'm nineteen, Jonas," she said earnestly. "Not some forty-year-old housewife with six kids who depends on the old man to bring home the bacon. Believe me, Jump is history, I'm divorcing him."

"You're sure about this?"

"Yes, I'm sure," she said, taking another sip of wine. "Y'know, I was looking forward to coming to L.A. I wanted you to meet Jump. *And* I was planning on setting you up with one of my girlfriends."

"So you think I need fixing up?" he said, looking perplexed.

"I never see you with anybody." A beat. *"Is* there someone special?"

"I'm too busy."

"You must have *some* kind of sex life," she persisted, determined to find out.

"So now that you've revealed everything to me, *I'm* supposed to reveal everything to you—is that the way this goes?"

"No, be your usual silent self. Dunno why, but I like you that way."

"You like me, huh?" he said, pleased.

"You're my friend," she answered warmly.

"We'll always be friends, only let's not act too friendly in front of Merrill, otherwise he's likely to can my ass."

"Never. The old pervert couldn't possibly manage without you."

"You think?"

"I *know*. He totally depends on you."

"Really?"

"Yes, really."

"Let's order," he said, picking up a menu. "Are you hungry?"

"Always."

"At least you never lose your appetite."

"For food."

He decided to let that one go.

Shelby drove Linc to the airport with the thought that she would soon be joining him on the New York location. She was unable to go with him because of the L.A. press junket for *Rapture* and an upcoming charity lunch in L.A. where she was being honored for her work raising money for various cancer charities.

"I'm sorry you won't be here for it," she said wistfully, driving down La Cienega because she refused to drive on freeways.

"So am I," he agreed. "My wife being

honored is quite something. Did you ever think that would happen when you came over here as a struggling English actress?"

"I never struggled, Linc," she said, smiling. "I came here to make a movie, liked it, and stayed."

"Then *I* saw you at Marty's party, and that was *it*—you and I were destined to be together."

"Destined?" she said, still smiling. "That's very dramatic, coming from you."

"And true."

"Pete wasn't too happy," she remarked, remembering her last conversation with her onetime boyfriend, whom she'd left for Linc.

"Who gives a fuck about Pete?" Linc said sharply. "I can never figure out what you were doing with him in the first place."

"Pete's a nice guy. He was one of the first people I met in L.A."

"Nice guy, my ass!"

"Linc—"

"You're lucky you never fucked him, 'cause if you had, I wouldn't have gone near you."

"Charming," she said, pulling up at a red light. "You and the double standard go hand in hand."

"I'm tellin' you the way it is."

"*You* slept with dozens of hot little starlets," she said accusingly, "and *I* went near *you.*"

"That's 'cause you couldn't resist me," he said with a knowing grin. "Played it smart, didn't I? Knew it wouldn't take long before you fell in love with me."

"No," she corrected, "*you* fell in love with *me.*"

"Yeah, I fell in love with your beautiful tits."

"Don't be so crude."

"Jesus, Shelby, sometimes you sound like your mother."

"And sometimes you *don't* remind me of my father," she chided. "My father is a gentleman, and you're not."

"Hey, this is the new me, remember? No drinking."

"Let's not get carried away, Linc. It's only been a few days."

"You gotta have faith, sweetheart."

"I do. Now—important question—are you *sure* you'll be all right in New York without me?"

"It won't be easy," he teased.

"I'll be joining you in a week."

"And I'll miss you every minute of every day," he promised, leaning toward her and nuzzling her neck. "What do you think of that?"

"I think I love you," she murmured, attempting to concentrate on her driving.

"Guess you must," he said, basking in her love. "You cook me dinner, drive me to the airport. Meanwhile we've got a ton of people working for us, so how come you feel you gotta do everything?"

"It's the English in me."

"That's what I like," he said, moving even closer and sliding his arm around her shoulders. "The English in you. That's what I *really* like—getting inside you."

"Linc!" she gasped, almost rear-ending a Cadillac. "I'm trying to drive."

She dropped him off at the private section of the airport.

"You're not coming in?" he asked.

"You know I hate good-byes."

"Love you," he said, kissing her on the lips. "I'll call you when I get there."

"You do that, Mr. Blackwood. Fly safely."

At home there was an urgent message waiting from her agent. She phoned him back. "Yes, Ed, what's so important?"

"Did you make a verbal agreement with Merrill Zandack?"

"What kind of verbal agreement?"

"He says you agreed to star in *Caught.*"

"I certainly didn't."

"I presume you've read the script?"

"Yes, he gave it to me in Cannes. I liked it a lot, but I wasn't sure I was right for it."

"Are you interested?"

"I hadn't thought about it."

"Word is it's a hot property. The girl who wrote it directed *Wild Child.* They've got it on a fast track, and Zandack is offering a ton of money."

"Linc says I don't need money."

"And that would be because . . . ?"

"He's got plenty."

"Yeah, well, Linc's got *his* career to look after, and you should look after yours. If the deal is right, it's a six-week shoot in L.A., starting in ten days."

"I'm only here for a week, then I'm supposed to be joining Linc in New York."

"This might be something you should do, Shelby. Zandack has the touch. Last year he had three movies nominated, and if this script is as good as he says it is . . . ."

"Let me read it again."

"We'll both read it and talk tomorrow. Zandack needs an immediate answer."

"Fine," she said, clicking off the phone. "I'll get right on it."

CHAPTER
19

Movie crews loved Lola. She'd learned early on that playing the diva did not go down well, so she always made sure to make herself known to all the key people on the set and act in an approachable fashion.

On the first day of location shooting in New York, she arrived in a car loaded down with boxes of chocolate cookies, *New York State of Mind* tee shirts, and baseball caps for the crew. Usually the producers gave out presents at the end of a shoot, but Lola had found it was to her advantage if she arrived with gifts on the first day.

Elliott Finerman was there to greet her. Since he'd given in and hired Linc Blackwood, she was overly nice to him, before moving on to the film's cinematographer— Dudley Wayne, a seasoned veteran. Dudley was the most important man to her; *he* was the one who would make her look out of this world.

"Darling," she said, enveloping him in a big hug. "All I ask is that you cover up my bags."

"I don't see any bags," Dudley said, peering at her with a professional eye.

"You will after I've been in New York a few days." She laughed, bringing him in on the joke.

"You have perfect skin, Lola," he said, quite sincerely. "I'm sure the camera loves you."

"And *you'll* make sure it loves me even more, won't you, Dudley?" she said in her sexiest voice.

"I'll do my best," Dudley replied, mesmerized.

Watching her, Elliott marveled at her seductive skills. This girl would fuck a snake if it could do something for her in return. Actresses! They were all the same. Phony as a game of three-card monte.

The director, Fitch Conn, was a big, gangly blond man in his thirties. He'd directed several successful movies and was all over Lola immediately. They'd had a couple of meetings in L.A. and he was already enamored. He was on her side, exactly the way she wanted it.

The first day's shooting took place outside, on a street downtown in the Village. Linc was not around. Lola was pleased because it gave her time to bond with the crew. Trailed by Big Jay and her assistant, Jenny, she handed out the cookies, tee shirts, and baseball caps, talking and joking with whoever crossed her path. By the end of the day she'd won everyone over.

The following morning, when Linc turned up, she was ready. They were shooting more location street scenes, and the excited crowds had to be cordoned off by several burly New York cops, who kept on sidling over and asking for her autograph.

Lola greeted Linc with a friendly hug. "I'm thrilled you're making this movie with me," she purred, establishing that it was *her* project. "We'll have so much fun."

"Sounds good," he said, thinking how sexy Lola Sanchez was in her formfitting red dress, emphasizing every delectable curve.

"Is your lovely wife with you?" Lola asked, glancing around as if she expected to see Shelby.

"She's flying in next week," Linc replied, accepting a mug of coffee from an assistant.

"Then we must all have dinner," Lola insisted. "I'll arrange everything."

"Great," Linc said. "With, uh . . . it's Matt, right?"

"Matt isn't here," she said, managing to look a tad forlorn.

"When does he arrive?"

"Can I tell you a secret?" she said, lowering her voice and leaning close.

"Sure," he replied, inhaling a strong whiff of her heady scent.

"This is not public knowledge yet. But unfortunately we're getting a divorce."

"You and Matt?" Linc said, surprised. "The guy I met in the south of France?"

She nodded.

"That was only a few weeks ago; the two of you seemed real tight."

"As you well know, Linc," she said in a sad voice, "illusion is everything."

"Jeez! I'm sorry to hear that you've split."

"*Are* you?" she said, giving him a long, meaningful look, which he chose to ignore.

At the lunch break Lola ate outside with her hairdresser, her makeup artist, Jenny, and Faye. They all sat at one of the long trestle tables set up in a parking lot, along with the rest of the crew. Lola knew it was important to show everyone she was a girl of the people, not a stuck-up princess like so many stars.

Her group surrounded her, making sure that no intruders got anywhere near her. They were a close-knit posse who'd all worked together on her last two films.

Linc chose to eat in his trailer, which pissed her off. Later that day she questioned him. "Are you a snob?" she asked in a teasing fashion. "*I* eat with the crew. Where were you?"

"Here's the deal," he answered with an easy grin. "I prefer staying in my trailer, where I can relax, study my lines, make phone calls. When you've been in the business as long as I have, you'll do the same."

Translation: *Lunch break is getting-high time. In private.* He'd already set up his supplier, a real estate guy who dealt on the side and was available to come by the set anytime he called. The coke was flowing freely and he felt no desire to drink. The perfect solution.

"Shame," Lola said, licking her glossy lips. "I always think it can be so helpful if costars get to know each other."

"Right," Linc replied, fully aware that she was coming on to him. Nothing new about *that;* most women did. But he wasn't into responding. He recognized that Lola Sanchez was dangerous territory, and now that he'd given up drinking, and she was getting a divorce, he knew enough to stay away—although he had to admit that she was some hot number. Exactly what he *didn't* need. He had Shelby, and he would do nothing to put their relationship in jeopardy.

"How would you feel about me accepting a movie in L.A.?" Shelby asked over the phone.

"Huh?" Linc said, safely back at the hotel.

"If you don't want me to do it, I won't. It all happened very suddenly."

"It's not the movie we talked about—the one where you take your clothes off again? 'Cause if it is—"

"No, Linc," she interrupted. "I promised you I wouldn't do that."

"What is it?"

"The script Merrill Zandack gave me to read in the south of France. Ed recommends I do it. It's a completely different role from the woman I played in *Rapture.*"

"Yeah?"

"I'd be playing an undercover cop."

"*You?*"

"Yes, me. I'm an actress, remember?"

"Hey—sweetie, I'm not gonna stop you. There's nothing for you to do here except hang around the set while I'm working, and we both know how boring that can be."

"True. Although we'd be together at night."

"Not really," he said, stifling a yawn. "We have a shitload of night shoots coming up."

"My movie would shoot six weeks in L.A. By the time I'm finished you'll be home."

"Go ahead and say yes. Sounds like you're into it."

"I'll miss you, though."

"I'll miss you too, but I've got a nice hotel setup, my agent's flying in this week, my publicist's already here. So I'm surrounded by people."

"Are you *sure* you'll be okay?"

"Hey—if you're worried about me drinking, I'm *not.*"

"Promise?" she said, anxious to believe him.

"Yeah, I promise. You don't have to be here to protect me, Shelby."

"Then you think I *should* say yes?"

"Who's directing?"

"Cat Harrison."

"You mean the kid?"

"She's not such a kid, she's almost twenty."

"Sweetheart, *that's* a kid."

"Merrill told me if I have doubts I can choose any director I want. But you know what? I had Ed run *Wild Child* for me again, and I like her work. She's got an offbeat, quirky style."

"Who else is in it?"

"Nick Logan."

"He's not bad."

"I wanted to make sure you were okay with me not coming there. Although I'll fly in for the *Rapture* press junket. Merrill promised I can use his plane."

"Listen to my little movie star wife," Linc said, amused. " 'Merrill says I can use his plane.' Jeez!"

"People do that for you all the time," she chided. "Don't make *me* feel spoiled."

"I'm teasing you. Can't you take a joke?"

Shelby hung up feeling pleased. She'd already said yes to the James Bond–type movie that did not start for six months, and *Caught* would be an interesting interim film.

Linc was right, there was nothing more depressing than hanging around a set, especially when he was into concentrating on his work and did not appreciate diversions. Basically she'd be sitting in New York doing nothing.

She called Ed and accepted the movie.

He was one happy agent.

Talk about an accelerated preproduction schedule. Things were totally crazy. So crazy that Cat did not have time to dwell on her personal problems. According to Leo

Napoli, he'd arranged for divorce papers to be sent to Jump in Australia. She was relieved; the sooner her two-year marriage was over the better.

Merrill had gone ahead and signed Shelby Cheney and Nick Logan to star in *Caught.* Cat still felt Shelby Cheney was wrong for the role; however, Nick Logan was perfect for the smart-mouthed con man. In his early thirties, Nick had a bad-boy edginess about him, plus he was also a dynamic actor. Currently finishing off a modern-day cowboy movie in Arizona, he was flying in as soon as his film wrapped.

Cat wished she'd had more to say about the casting of her two stars, but she couldn't complain; at least she was about to direct her own movie, since apparently neither Shelby nor Nick had voiced any objections.

Her excitement level was in overdrive. She was getting ready to direct her own movie with two star actors and an actual budget! How cool was *that!*

Merrill had surrounded her with a first-rate team of people—all of whom had worked for him before. She was well aware that he was making sure she wouldn't screw up. It was aggravating and assuring all at the same time.

The line producer, Gary, seemed like a great guy. He was energetic, smart, and noncritical. He steered her through production meetings, casting sessions, and location scouts, making her feel secure, even though she knew he probably regarded her as a total amateur.

Jonas was also there for her, arriving at her apartment every night after work, breaking down the script with her as she bounced ideas off him and discussed the shooting schedule, laying each scene out on index cards.

In her mind she had a master plan for *Caught.* She wanted to capture a degree of realism. She wanted her movie to have a gritty edge, with a documentary feel to it.

"Everyone loves the script," Jonas assured her. "Usually Merrill brings in one or two other writers. This time he hasn't mentioned doing that, so it's quite a compliment."

After one particularly creative session with Jonas, Cat requested a private meeting with Merrill, and informed the big man that she would like him to appoint Jonas as an associate producer on *Caught.*

At first Merrill laughed at her, then after a lot of persuasion he realized it wasn't such a bad idea. After all, he'd taught Jonas everything he knew, so why *not* put him out there? Merrill was also canny enough to realize that it could be useful having Jonas permanently on set to report back.

"Please don't mention *I* asked you to do this," Cat insisted.

Merrill agreed, although it didn't stop him grumbling about losing the best assistant he'd ever had.

When Jonas got the news he was delighted. He immediately asked Cat if she'd had anything to do with it. "Who me?" she said innocently, not fooling him one bit.

"I know it's you," he said. "Do I thank you now, or later?"

She was sitting on the floor of her apartment, surrounded by storyboards, notes, and her laptop.

"Just be there for me," she said. "That's thank-you enough."

"All the way," Jonas replied.

"I'm worried about Shelby Cheney," Cat said, swigging from a can of 7 UP.

"Why?"

" 'Cause she's English and too beautiful to play my cop."

"She's also an excellent actress," Jonas pointed out.

"I know, but—"

"Maybe you should take another look at *Rapture,*" he suggested. "Her American accent is right on. I'll arrange a screening."

"I'm glad *you're* so confident. She'll probably hate me anyway."

"What makes you think that?"

"I dunno," she said miserably.

"Come on," Jonas said, cheering her up. "Where's the cocky, *I-can-do-anything* Cat we all know?"

"She's on hiatus."

"Bring her back."

"Maybe she's not available. Maybe she's scared."

"Not Cat."

He didn't tell her about Merrill's backup plans; it would only make her more nervous.

A few nights later, when they were once again sitting around in her apartment working on the storyboards while eating pizza and drinking wine, Cat started talking about her drug-addicted past. She had no idea why she suddenly decided to confide in him. She simply felt like unburdening herself, and Jonas was an excellent listener. "I don't *ever* want to go back to doing that," she said with an exaggerated shudder. "But I have this recurring dream that being a druggie is like being an alcoholic, and since an alcoholic is *always* an alcoholic, I guess I'll always be a druggie."

"Not the same thing," Jonas said, watching her carefully. "They *call* people alcoholics because the temptation is always there. If they have one drink they know it's over."

"You think *drugs* are different?" she said, thinking that he was obviously naive. "I bet you've never even smoked a joint."

"We're talking about *you,* Cat, not me."

"Oh yeah, me," she said ruefully. "The girl who was dabbling in heroin, doing crack." She sighed. "What a moron!"

"Do you miss it?"

"Come *on!* I look back in horror."

"Then there's no way you'll do it again. You're too smart."

"Jump saved me, y'know," she mused. "Without his help . . ."

"You've got to stop thinking that way," Jonas said, irritated that she still considered her cheating husband some kind of savior. "You were an easily influenced kid. Now you're a big-time writer and director, which gives you every reason to stay straight."

"Thanks," she said softly. "I must say, Jonas, that you've got this knack of calming me down. You're like the big brother I never had."

"Glad to oblige," he said, realizing that he was becoming far too attached to this crazy, talented girl, and since she regarded him as nothing more than big-brother fodder, it was time to distance himself. Although distancing himself was almost impossible now that he was officially working on the movie. He was grateful for the opportunity to show what he could do—it was something he'd been working toward—and if everything worked out it could only lead to bigger and better.

A celebration was in order, so shortly before principal photography was due to begin, he informed Cat he was taking her out for dinner.

"No, no, no," she said, panicking. "I have to work all night. I'm kind of freaked. I won't be talkable to for the next six weeks, then after that I'll be locked in the editing room."

"*That's* why you're coming out," Jonas said firmly. "I'm getting you while I can."

"Aren't you *listening?*" she wailed. "It's impossible for me to go anywhere."

"Too bad."

She shot him a look. "Since when did *you* get so forceful?"

"Since *you* became a prima donna," he responded.

He took her to L'Orangerie, a fashionable French restaurant on La Cienega, and although the restaurant was very elegant, they both felt out of place amongst all the well-dressed, affluent people and the fancy French food.

"Man!" Cat groaned, as the maître d' seated them. "The waiters are staring at me as if I'm from Mars."

"You could've worn a dress," Jonas suggested, although he was getting quite used to her uniform of low-rider jeans, combat boots, and skimpy tanks. It didn't matter what she wore; she was so striking looking that she could've gotten away with an old sack and bare feet, and still be the most beautiful woman in the room.

"Ugh! Dresses are not for me, thank you," she said with a mock shudder.

"Why? I'd go shopping with you."

"No way," she said, frowning. "I *hate* shopping. It's a total waste of time. Besides, you do enough for me."

Before he could reply, a waiter appeared at their table and offered them menus.

"Can we split?" Cat asked after the first course, eggs mixed with caviar. "I'd sooner grab a Fatburger, wouldn't you?"

"Only if you're buying," he said, signaling for the check.

"Hmm . . . ," she said. "Think I can manage that. I'll add it to the budget. Merrill will never notice."

"You know, Cat," he said, smiling, "when I start producing my own films, I'm hiring you to write and direct every one."

"You'd better hurry," she said with a big, wide grin. " 'Cause soon you won't be able to afford me."

"I got your Bentley back," Otto informed Lola, speaking from his car phone in L.A.

"You did?" Lola said, pleased. "How about my luggage?"

"Do not expect miracles," Otto said, turning onto the Pacific Coast Highway. "It wasn't easy. I gave him your SUV in exchange. I imagine that's all right with you."

"I suppose so," she grumbled.

"How's the movie going?"

"We've been on location, shooting street scenes. It's freezing."

"The weather is beautiful here. I'm on my way to Malibu to meet with a client."

"Stop it, Otto," she groaned. "You know I miss L.A."

"Well, you'll have a nice new Bentley to drive when you get back. I had it detailed for you."

"Thanks," she said, certain that he'd add another grand to her exorbitant monthly bill. It wasn't easy being a single woman and watching over her money. What she needed was a man to check up on him.

She'd been shooting in New York for almost a week, and she'd hardly seen Linc at all. The majority of their scenes together were interiors, although very soon they'd start shooting on a soundstage in Tribeca, and then she could start working on him.

The New York papers were busy stalking her. Everywhere she went there were paparazzi lurking, waiting to see who she was with and what she was up to. The gossip columns carried daily items about the absence of Matt. Faye answered all their questions with a terse statement announcing that all was well with Lola Sanchez's marriage; her husband, Matt, had business in California and would be joining her soon.

Then Tony called. "I'm flying in," he announced. "Gotta check out the club scene for my next movie."

"But Tony—," she began, not quite sure that she was ready to go public with their relationship.

"You with me or not?" he said tersely. "Remember—no more hiding, babe. We're out in the open, or nothin'. Right?"

"Right, Tony."

"You gotta forget about playin' games, Lola. This time I want it real."

Tony was an *I-want* kind of guy. It was one of the things she found so sexy about him.

"When will you be here?" she asked breathlessly.

"Friday night. We'll turn that town *out.*"

"Wouldn't miss it!" she said, already planning her outfit. It had to be something sensational; Tony was into high style and flash. A lethal combination.

"I'll call you."

"Yes, Tony."

Ah . . . the two of them together again; she could only imagine the furor it would cause. Paparazzi heaven!

She decided against telling Faye. Why look for trouble? Faye could read it on the front pages along with everyone else.

Lola Sanchez and Tony Alvarez. The hottest couple in America.

Mama Sanchez would throw a fit.

Too bad. Like the TV show said—one life to live. And Lola was about to live it all the way.

CHAPTER
20

"Pete? What a surprise!"

"Shelby. How are you?"

They bumped into each other outside the soundstage in Culver City where Shelby was soon to start shooting Cat's movie. She was on her way to her car, having recently completed her second round of costume fittings.

"It's *so* nice to see you," she exclaimed, smiling warmly at her onetime boyfriend—the man she'd left to marry Linc. "What are you doing here?"

"Stunt coordinator on *Caught*," Pete said, shifting uncomfortably.

"You mean we're working on the same film?"

"Looks like it."

She couldn't help noticing how cool he seemed toward her. It was no surprise; they hadn't spoken since she'd married Linc. She'd called him a day or so before the ceremony and told him she was about to take the step. He'd been livid. "How can you do this?" he'd said. "We were a couple. You *know* I wanted to marry you."

"It just . . . happened," she'd explained, knowing how lame she sounded.

"Linc's a no-good sonofabitch," he'd said. "I warned him to stay away from you. But oh no—he couldn't keep it in his pants, could he? Not our Linc."

That conversation had taken place four years ago. She hadn't seen or spoken to Pete since. Now here he was, standing in front of her, a rugged-looking man in well-worn blue jeans, cowboy boots, and a denim shirt, with piercing blue eyes and a strong jaw.

"It's lovely to see you, Pete," she said, genuinely meaning it.

His voice was rough. "Where's Linc?"

"On location in New York."

"So I guess the two of you are living happily ever after?"

"I hope so."

"I hope so," he repeated. "That doesn't sound very promising."

"Look," she said awkwardly, "I *do* feel I owe you an explanation."

"Time passes," he said, shrugging as if he didn't give a damn. "I've forgotten about it. We had a thing going and you moved on, that's all."

"Can we have lunch?" she asked impulsively. "For old times' sake."

"Would Linc allow you to have lunch with me?"

"I don't need his permission," she said, brushing back her long hair.

"That's nice to know," he said, softening slightly.

"Since we'll be working together, I think it's an excellent idea, don't you?"

"If you say so," he said, flashing a rueful smile. "You always *were* able to talk me into anything."

She smiled. "I'm talking you into it, am I?"

"How about Jerry's Deli in the Valley?" he

suggested. "Or is that too out of the way for you now that you live in Beverly Hills?"

"One o'clock tomorrow?" she said, ignoring his veiled crack.

"I'll be there."

Driving over to Merrill's office, she decided it was best not to mention to Linc that she was lunching with her old boyfriend. He wouldn't understand, and yet she felt she owed Pete more of an explanation. Besides, Linc was so busy on *New York State of Mind* that they'd barely had time to talk.

Over the last few days she'd had a couple of meetings with Cat Harrison. She liked her a lot. The girl was young, but she was also smart and seemed to know exactly the way she wanted things done. They'd gone over the role of the undercover cop at length, both coming up with ideas about the character. Fortunately their ideas seemed to jell.

Merrill greeted her effusively. As soon as she'd signed on for the movie he'd sent her three dozen purple roses, a case of Cristal, and a pound of caviar. He was obviously pleased to welcome her aboard.

"Cat and I can *definitely* work together. I

like her a lot," Shelby said, settling on his couch.

"That's my kinda news," Merrill said, staring at the English actress. She was such a classy beauty, with her flawless skin, wide-set hazel eyes, and thick raven hair. It was a great tribute to her acting skills that he was sure she could bring Cat's edgy cop to life on the screen.

He contemplated unzipping and giving her a thrill. Then he thought, why risk another turndown?

Besides, without popping a couple of Viagra, he couldn't get it up anymore.

Merrill Zandack was finally realizing that it didn't have to be a necessary rite of passage for the actresses he worked with to service him. There'd be exceptions, of course, but Shelby Cheney was not one of them.

"You're cute," Nick Logan remarked.

"Excuse me?" Cat responded.

"I wasn't expecting cute," Nick said, squinting at her.

"And *I* wasn't expecting asshole compliments in my face."

Nick Logan laughed. He was a skinny thirty-one-year-old with unruly dark hair, a scruffy beard, sleepy eyes, and eyelashes longer than any girl's. "Didn't mean to insult you," he said, digging at his teeth with a raggedy toothpick.

"Didn't take it as an insult," she responded. "Merely stupid."

"I've never worked with a girl director before," he ventured.

"You must mean *woman,*" she responded.

"You're a girl," he said, grinning insolently. "I know a girl when I see one."

"Like how long do I have to listen to this crap?" she snapped.

"And she's got a mouth too. I get off on that."

"You know what, Nick," she said, deciding to cut it short. "Let's get something straight. This is *my* movie. *I* wrote it, *I'm* directing it, *you're* starring in it. Now I know you've been successful for a few years and I haven't, but since this is my project, can we keep a little respect going here?"

"Cute with a mouth—even better."

Nick Logan was obviously a major smart-ass, which fortunately would work very well for the role of the con man in her movie.

Jonas loathed him on sight. "He's one of those playboy actors," he said. "The kind that hangs out with his posse at bars every night, picking up girls and getting drunk."

"As long as he doesn't do playboy acting in front of the camera," Cat retorted, "then I'm down with it."

"He's planning on flirting with you," Jonas said irritably. "That's the way he'll try to railroad you into doing things his way."

"Men always flirt with me," Cat answered flippantly. "Got a hunch it's the diamond in my navel; turns 'em on big time."

"Very funny," Jonas said, quite unamused, and scared of his growing feelings for this girl.

"Like I have *time* to flirt," she retorted. "Besides, aren't you forgetting I'm in the middle of a divorce? Who needs flirting?"

"Yeah, right," Jonas said, unconvinced. She'd caught her husband with another girl. It was only human nature that she'd want to get back at him. And what better way than screwing some smart-mouthed, cocky movie star?

"So make *sure* I don't flirt, will you

please?" she added, although she had to admit that she did find Nick Logan quite attractive in a bad-boy kind of way.

"What am I, your keeper now?" Jonas snapped.

"Isn't that why Merrill put you on the movie, to watch over me?" she said, wondering what kind of bug he had up *his* ass.

"No," Jonas said. "We both know the reason Merrill put me on the movie is because *you* asked him to."

"That's what *you* think."

"That's what I *know.*"

As their start date drew nearer, Cat was feeling less tense. Hitting it off with Shelby Cheney had helped considerably. The actress was totally down-to-earth and nice. Even better, she seemed to know instinctively what Cat expected of her. Plus, as Jonas had pointed out, her American accent was impeccable.

"I keep on annoying American actresses," Shelby had confided. "They all think they should be playing *my* parts, but when you get someone like Renee Zellweger as Bridget Jones—a classic English heroine—it's only fair that I play American roles, don't you think?"

Cat had nodded her agreement. Now she was wondering how Shelby and Nick would match up. They were both so different, yet her gut instinct told her they would have great chemistry together.

They'd better, because soon it would be movie time, and she was finally ready.

Tony Alvarez hit New York like a wild tornado. He was handsome, flashy, full of zest—a purveyor of sexy excitement everywhere he went. He took over the biggest penthouse suite at the Four Seasons in New York and called Lola immediately.

"Tonight, ten o'clock," he said, lolling in his suite, enjoying a manicure and a pedicure. "I'll come get you."

"Can't wait," she replied, shivering with anticipation. She'd already chosen the dress she would wear—a Versace number that left little to the imagination. Over it she planned on throwing a white mink coat she'd rushed out and purchased at Bergdorf.

Faye had flown back to L.A. for the weekend. Was *she* going to get a shock when she saw the Monday morning papers!

It so happened Tony arrived in New York

on the day Lola was due to shoot her first bedroom scene with Linc. Fitch was wandering around the set, most concerned that everything went well. Lola assured him that he wouldn't be disappointed. "I'm a love scene veteran," she informed the panicky director. "Leave everything to me."

Later that day, Linc walked onto the set wearing a white toweling bathrobe. He was surrounded by his entourage.

Lola, lounging in her chair, was also in a bathrobe. Underneath she wore a brief thong with flesh-colored pasties covering her nipples. She was not shy about getting almost naked on-screen—the key word was "almost"; never let them see everything. Why take away the mystery?

"What you got on under there, Linc?" she asked teasingly.

"A hard-on and a smile," he joked, not at all intimidated by the sexy actress. He was in good shape due to five hundred push-ups a day, an hour on the treadmill, plus lifting weights. For a man his age he looked pretty damn good. Not that he was old, but you had to be twenty-two in Hollywood these days.

"What's under *your* robe?" he asked.

You bastard! she thought. *If you had any kind of memory you'd know exactly what was under my robe.* "Wouldn't *you* like to know," she said, faking a sexy smile.

Maybe. If I wasn't married, he thought.

When it came time for a rehearsal, Fitch suggested that they both keep their bathrobes on.

"Why?" Lola demanded. "If we want to get this right, let's do it properly." She stood up, shedding her bathrobe and handing it to the wardrobe woman, who gave her a fluffy white towel in exchange. Very slowly and sensuously she wrapped the towel around her almost naked body.

An audible gasp went around the crew. "Holy cow!" the focus puller muttered. "What a woman!"

The scene took place in a bedroom, with Lola emerging from the bathroom clad only in the towel.

Fitch was settled behind the camera, issuing instructions. "Linc, enter the shot, grab Lola, and as you both fall on the bed, take her towel away, making sure you block her body."

"Think I can do that," Linc said.

"Keep your bathrobe on until you get her to the bed, then she'll take it off you."

"No, no!" Lola said heatedly. "She *rips* it off him. This woman is impatient."

"That's not how it's written in the script," Fitch said.

"Words," Lola scoffed. "I *know* this character. This woman is passionate—like me. And since this is their first time together, she can't *wait* to feel the heat of his skin against hers."

"We'll try it your way, Lola," Fitch agreed, not about to argue with the fiery actress, who seemed to know exactly what she was doing. "That okay with you, Linc?"

"Sure," Linc said.

The moment the scene started, Lola was all over him. As he started to pull the towel away from her, she grabbed him and they began kissing.

Linc immediately felt himself beginning to get erect. This woman was some kisser, plus she had her almost naked body pressed against him real close, and he hadn't seen his wife in over a week.

After a few moments he knew he'd better slow things down. "Somebody call cut," he yelled.

"This is a rehearsal," Fitch said. "What's your problem?"

"The colonel is saluting—if you get what I mean."

The entire crew broke up laughing.

Lola smiled a slow, seductive smile. "I'm sorry, Linc," she said demurely. "Is it something I did?"

"I'll get over it," he said, unable to keep his eyes off her spectacular body.

"Don't feel embarrassed, it happens with most of my costars," Lola murmured innocently. *Hmm . . . Mr. Blackwood. You're going to be easy . . .*

"I'm sure it does," he said. Christ! If Shelby knew about this she'd be most unhappy. He took Fitch to one side. "This could be an ongoing problem," he muttered.

"Your problem is my problem," Fitch agreed. "We should take a short break."

"You mean—"

"Yeah," Fitch said, man to man. "I mean, go take care of it and let's get this shot in the can."

Lola had the best afternoon. Not only was Linc hot for her, but so were the rest of the crew, staring and panting and probably all fantasizing about her. It put her in an excellent mood to meet Tony that night; she was primed and ready.

When Tony arrived at the hotel he had a minion call her suite to inform her that he was waiting in his limo downstairs. Lola was excited; hanging with Tony Alvarez was a kick. He surrounded himself with bodyguards and a mixed entourage of friends and hangers-on, creating a stir wherever he went. Tonight would be no different.

She took one last critical look in the mirror. Not much else she could do, because without false modesty she knew she looked amazing. Her chestnut hair was swept up in a sexy tumble of curls, her Versace dress was fabulous, her Jimmy Choo stilettos emphasized her long legs, while her white mink coat and the sparkling diamond bracelet and earrings that Cartier had sent over that afternoon added major glamour. It was all good.

This was the first time since they'd gotten back together that she was seeing Tony as herself and not as one of their favorite play-acting characters.

Filled with sexual anticipation, she rode the elevator downstairs with Big Jay in close attendance. Once there, Big Jay escorted her through the lobby and outside to the sidewalk, where a sleek white limousine waited. Tony had a thing for white limos, the bigger the better.

A bevy of photographers sprang forward. There was a rumor in the air that Tony Alvarez might be in the car.

"Who're you with, Lola?" called one of the photographers. "Who's in the limo? Is it Tony?"

She smiled at the cameras and posed for a few fleeting seconds. "Wouldn't you like to know," she said, teasing them.

Then Big Jay guided her into the limo and slammed the door shut, leaving everyone wondering.

Tony was leaning back against the leather seat, smoking. He had on a pale beige Armani suit, a black silk shirt, plenty of Bling Bling, including an enormous diamond stud embedded in his earlobe. His teeth were whiter than white, his black hair curled over his collar. Lola was turned on just looking.

"I finally get to see the beautiful Lola Sanchez," he drawled, flashing a sexy smile. "The *real* Lola Sanchez."

"I hear tell you've been meeting with several friends of mine," she replied, also smiling.

"Ain't nothin' like the real thing," he sang.

"Here I am," she purred.

"Gotta say I missed you, babe," he said, reaching out to pull her close. He smelled of a rich, musky aftershave.

"Careful," she said, eluding him. "I wouldn't want to get lipstick on you."

He removed a white silk monogrammed handkerchief from his pocket and handed it to her. "Wipe it off. You know what I want."

"This is not exactly private," she said, indicating the driver and Tony's martial arts bodyguard, both sitting up front.

Tony pressed a button, and the black dividing glass slid into place, separating them from everyone. "C'mere, baby, an' do it just for me," he coaxed, leaning even farther back and unzipping his pants.

She obliged. What better way to start a memorable evening?

CHAPTER
21

Shelby drove herself over the Canyon to meet Pete for lunch. She was not into bodyguards and minders; that wasn't her reality. And since she'd never had to deal with any serious threats from deranged fans, she still felt comfortable driving around on her own.

It was no big deal, even though Linc didn't like it when she took off to the dry cleaners or the market. "We've got people to do that for us," he'd said.

"No, Linc, you don't understand," she'd

explained. "It's important for me to feel normal."

"Sweetheart," he'd insisted, "you're *not* normal, you're a movie star, and movie stars have people who do everything for them. Okay?"

She begged to differ. She did not want to be one of these actresses who were surrounded by assistants and minders, publicists and stylists, with everyone laughing at their jokes and telling them how wonderful they were. Besides, she certainly did not regard herself as a movie star until seeing *Rapture.* And even now, the term "movie star" was far too Hollywood. She would much rather be regarded as an accomplished actress.

The night before, she'd spoken to Linc on the phone, omitting to mention that she'd run into Pete or their upcoming lunch. Linc wouldn't approve; he had a wild jealous streak, which he didn't exhibit often, but when he did, it was not pretty.

Actually, she saw nothing wrong in meeting up with Pete. He'd been a good friend to her when she'd first arrived in Hollywood, and she didn't see why they couldn't continue to be friends.

She was happy that Linc was obviously enjoying his movie in New York and seemed to be staying sober. It was good for him to be involved in a different kind of project; perhaps it would force the critics to realize how talented he was.

"What's Lola Sanchez like?" she'd asked.

"A spitfire," he'd replied. "All the guys on the set are hot for her."

"And you?" she'd asked teasingly.

"Me, honey? I'm a married man."

She'd laughed softly. "I'll be there next weekend. Can't wait to see you."

"Don't overwork yourself," he'd said.

"I'm not a delicate little flower, Linc," she'd reminded him. "I'm a big, strapping English girl."

"Not so much with the strapping," he'd said with a quick laugh. "I'll be waiting for you."

"Linc?" she'd said hesitantly. "Are you *sure* everything's okay?"

"Stop with the questions. If I *wasn't* okay, you'd hear it in my voice, right?"

"I suppose so."

"You *know* so."

"What are you doing every night?"

"Sitting around in my hotel playing cards and ordering room service. Exciting, huh?"

"I miss you," she'd said wistfully.

"You too, sweetheart."

She'd hung up the phone reassured that he was doing well. Yes, she realized it was naive of her to think that a few days in a Malibu rehab center had cured him of drinking forever, but maybe this movie was what he needed. Something different, something to show the public that he was capable of more than over-the-top action films.

She parked her car in the lot next to Jerry's Deli, and entered the crowded delicatessen. Dressed in casual slacks and a silk shirt, large blackout sunglasses covering her eyes, and her long hair tied back in a ponytail, she could often get away with not being recognized.

Pete was already there. As soon as he saw her, he jumped up from his table and waved. She strolled over.

"You made it," he said, obviously pleased.

"Yes," she answered, dazzling him with her smile. "All the way to the Valley. Aren't *I* a clever girl?"

"It's great to see you, Shelby," he said, a touch awkward. "I'm glad we're doing this."

"So am I," she said, settling into her seat as a waitress came over with menus.

"What do you feel like having?" he asked. "They make a helluva sandwich here."

"*Giant* sandwiches," she replied, perusing the menu. "You Americans eat enough for three people."

"That's 'cause we need our energy."

"So you can fight the rest of the world?"

"Low blow."

"Sorry," she murmured, deciding on a tuna melt.

Pete went for a hamburger with everything on it and a side of french fries.

"I'm sure you're aware that you have a few stunts in our movie," he said, after the waitress left their table. "I'll be coordinating your stunt double, which means we'll be working together quite a bit. I was thinking you should build up your strength."

"Why would I want to do that?"

"In case you decide to try some of the stunts yourself."

"Me?"

"Is there a reason you can't?"

"I've never done anything like that before," she said hesitantly.

"Now's the time," he said, full of enthusiasm. " 'Cause I got a hunch you'll love it."

"I will?"

"I could start you on a training program," he said. "Nothing too strenuous."

"I don't know . . ."

"C'mon," he said encouragingly. "I'll take you to my gym in Santa Monica, work out a program for you to follow."

"You have a gym now?"

"A chain of 'em."

"That's terrific," she said, picking up her glass and taking a sip of water. "You know, I *am* kind of interested in learning about self-defense. Would you be able to teach me?"

"How about shooting a gun?"

"Let's not get carried away," she said, laughing softly. "I'm hardly planning on appearing in a cowboy movie."

"The way the world's going, learning to shoot is not such a bad idea."

"Guns scare me," she said, remembering Linc's graphic stories about the night his father shot himself in the head.

"Not when you know how to use 'em."

Their order arrived, and Pete began attacking his burger as if he were a starving man.

Shelby leaned forward, stealing a french fry from his plate. "So tell me, Pete," she said, attempting to sound casual. "Are you married?"

"No," he answered, giving her a long, penetrating look. "Truth is, Shelby, I gave up trusting women after you."

She lowered her eyes. "I'm sorry."

"I'll be honest," he said, speaking slowly. "After you ran off an' married Linc, I have to admit I was kinda bitter for a while. 'Cause, well . . . you're not exactly easy to get over."

"I wish I could make you understand how overwhelming it was for me when I met Linc. We fell in love and I was . . . helpless." She paused for a moment, wondering what her life would've been like if she'd stayed with Pete. Different, that was for sure. "Y'know, Pete," she continued, her eyes meeting his, "it was never my intention to let you down."

He nodded. "I know that."

"I would be so happy if you and Linc could be friends again. I hate thinking it was me who came between you."

"Me and Linc—friends," Pete said scornfully. "That's *never* gonna happen. I'll be *your* friend, not his. There's no way after what he did to me."

"Pete," she said, impulsively reaching across the table and squeezing his hand, "we *both* did it. Why can't we be grown-ups and forget about the past?"

"Oh, Shelby, Shelby," he sighed. "You make it sound so damn simple."

"It *is* simple."

"For you, maybe."

"For you, too," she urged. "All you've got to do is let go."

"Easy for you to say."

"It would mean so much to me."

He gave her a long, lingering look. "Here's the big question—does he make you happy?"

"Of course he does," she replied, once more meeting his gaze. "Linc's a *great* guy. I mean, he has his problems, but we've managed to work through them."

"That's more than most women were able to do."

"I promise you, he's a changed man."

"Because if he *doesn't* make you happy . . ."

"What, Pete?"

"Then he'll have to deal with me."

Somehow it was comforting to know that she had a man who was totally on her side.

Cocooned in a haze of champagne, grass, and decadence, Lola surfaced slowly. She was naked in Tony Alvarez's bed in his hotel suite, with Tony asleep beside her. Flung casually across the bed was a mink-lined satin throw, while on the bed were Tony's black silk sheets—he never traveled without several sets. Tony was an extravagant hedonist.

Thank God it's Saturday and I'm not on call, she thought, gently touching his back. She could feel the heat still there, vibrating through his dark olive skin. God, Tony Alvarez was an addiction she'd *never* gotten over.

Naked, she stepped out of bed and padded into the bathroom. What a night! Tony had insisted on exploring all the new Latino supper clubs. They'd covered three or four, with the paparazzi dogging their every step, growing in number as they exited each place. It was exhilarating, running out through back entrances, sneaking into their limo, seeing if they could outrun the paparazzi. Tony, with his sly smile, flashy entourage, and way of doing things with such style.

After she'd gone down on him in the car, he'd presented her with a single ten-carat yellow diamond on a thin diamond chain to wear around her neck. "It's your slave chain, baby," he'd said with a cunning smile. "Every time you wear it, you'll think of me."

He certainly knew how to please her. But then again, she certainly knew how to please *him.*

"Where's your so-called fiancée?" she'd asked, knowing for sure that the girl was history.

"On ice," he'd replied, pouring more champagne.

End of *that* story.

They'd started off the evening with Cristal in the limo. It was not until later that he'd begun snorting coke. She was not happy about his habit. "Tony," she'd pleaded, "you *know* that's why I had to leave you last time."

"You wanna be with me—you take me how I am," he'd said, full of confidence.

"Nobody's gettin' busted, baby. I got body-guards on top of bodyguards."

"But Tony—"

"Fuck, Lola," he'd interrupted, his voice hardening. "I'm on probation. You think I wanna go through any legal shit?"

Somehow it added to the danger. Tony, the drugs, the excitement.

Not that she indulged. She'd decided early on that she was never getting into drugs; she knew how they affected people's looks. She'd watched one actress on a TV series whose face had gotten more bloated and disgusting every time an episode ran. Plus cocaine wasn't for her, champagne was more her style.

"I don't understand why drinking doesn't do it for you," she'd complained. "What's the fascination you have with cocaine and the other stuff you're into?"

"Hey—just know I'm ecstatic *you* ain't into it," he'd said. "Nobody wants to mess with a coke whore. 'Specially not *this* dude."

They'd danced the night away with crowds of people watching and surrounding them, clapping them on. They were both fine salsa dancers who took pleasure in excelling. It wasn't simply because they were famous that they cut such a swath; some couples were meant to be.

Lola knew she should call Otto and warn him that they were back together, and she should certainly inform the formidable Faye. Then she decided the hell with them, it was *her* decision, she could do whatever she liked.

Wrapping herself in one of Tony's luxurious cashmere robes, she leaned forward, carefully examining her face in the mirror. Fortunately, she was blessed with perfect olive skin, and this morning she was positively glowing. Who needed diamonds when she had Tony?

Thankfully she'd inherited her mother's beauty and her father's zest for living. Poor Isabelle and Selma had not; they were both quite ordinary looking. *She* was the star of the family, although it helped that she was surrounded by experts who helped her look the best she could.

Piling her hair on top of her head, she stuck a pin in it, then returned to the bedroom.

"Tony," she murmured, leaning over him,

her full breasts grazing his chest. "Time to get up, it's way past noon."

"Oh, baby, baby," he muttered, throwing out his arms. His chest was covered in a smattering of fine black hair. She would've hated it if he shaved his chest like so many Hollywood actors; she loved the way a thin line of hair headed straight down his stomach, making a steady line toward his crotch, where it curled around the stem of his magnificent cock.

"Tony," she murmured again, fluttering her fingers lightly across his stomach. "Lola desires your company, so please quit snoring in my face."

He opened one eye and squinted at her. "Who snores, baby? Not me." He opened his other eye. "How ya doin'?"

"Sensational, thank you," she replied, teasing his lips with her tongue.

He undid the tie on her robe. It fell open. He reached in and began squeezing her nipples with his fingertips. "Gotta say I missed this," he said, continuing to caress her.

She began stroking his cock, which immediately sprang to attention. "And I missed this," she said in a low, throaty voice.

"Nice," he said, thrusting himself toward her. "We both got somethin' we missed."

She shrugged off her robe.

"Where's your diamond, babe?" he asked.

"I left it on the bedside table."

"Put it on," he ordered.

"Now?"

"Yeah now."

She picked up the exquisite diamond, fastening the thin chain around her neck. The diamond hung between her breasts like a talisman.

"Wanna fuck you, babe," Tony said, pulling her down next to him. "You and your great big diamond."

She spread her legs, welcoming him into the place he truly belonged.

Tony Alvarez was *her* addiction, and she'd never stopped loving him.

It was a crisp, sunny New York morning. Freddy Krane was in town, so Linc decided to take him on a jog around Central Park. Freddy bitched and moaned, but went along with the program when Linc insisted it was good for him. " 'S long as we make it to the deli an' have a good brunch," Freddy said, huffing and puffing as he lagged along behind Linc. "Don't forget I'm on L.A. time. My stomach's screamin'."

"All you think about is your goddamn stomach," Linc remarked, jogging at a steady pace. "It wouldn't hurt for you to lose a few pounds. You got a gut like a pregnant cow."

It was impossible to insult Freddy, he was impervious. "Listen to Mr. Fit," Freddy chortled. "You *gotta* stay in shape, I don't."

"Dead right if I'm doing your next movie," Linc agreed.

"Bet your ass," Freddy said, swatting a fly from his face. "The studio was screamin' for Vin Diesel. I told 'em to go fuck 'emselves. This script is yours."

Freddy had flown in the night before to meet with Linc and talk about the film he wanted him to sign on for. Although it was another big action adventure, Linc figured that after the romantic comedy it would be a wise move to return to the action genre.

He hadn't had a chance to mention Freddy's movie to Shelby, although he was sure they could work it so that they'd be able to spend time on each other's location. After all, work was work, and she'd chosen to do another movie rather than stay with him in New York. He conveniently forgot that he'd persuaded her to do so.

Freddy insisted that they go to the Carnegie Deli for brunch.

"Can't go there," Linc objected. "I'll get hassled for autographs an' shit."

"You got security," Freddy pointed out. "This is New York, nobody gives a crap about you."

"Thanks. Did you happen to see the paparazzi hanging out the fuckin' trees?"

"What they gonna say about you?" Freddy said. "That you're a fag 'cause you're out joggin' with me?"

Linc laughed. *"That'd* make a change."

"Have your guys meet us at the deli," Freddy suggested, leaning against a tree, totally out of shape.

Linc signaled one of his security team. "I'll see you at the Carnegie Deli, I'm going in Mr. Krane's car."

Freddy's car and driver were waiting at the entrance to the park. The two men got in the car and the driver took off.

"How was Cannes?" Freddy inquired, lighting a cigarette. "Same old rat fuck?"

"I got my usual shitty reviews."

"Throw 'em in the crapper. I *never* had a decent review, an' I'm the richest goddamn producer in Hollywood."

"Yeah, you and Arnold Kopelson."

"Arnie's the greatest. But *I* make the best action films," Freddy boasted.

The Carnegie Deli was crowded. Freddy pushed to the head of the line. When the hostess saw Linc, she immediately made room, seating them at a corner table. Freddy summoned a waitress and ordered eggs, smoked salmon, lean corned beef, bagels, and cream cheese for the two of them.

"No surprise you got a gut," Linc remarked. "Whatever happened to fruit and yogurt?"

"Screw the healthy crap," Freddy scoffed. "My cholesterol's rising—but who gives a shit?"

"You should look after yourself," Linc lectured. "You're no kid."

"Yeah, yeah," Freddy said, not listening. "We'll have dinner tonight, you'll meet my new girl."

"Christ, Freddy," Linc groaned. "Not *another* would-be actress."

"You did okay, an' *you* married an actress," Freddy pointed out, attacking a large onion bagel.

"Shelby's different."

"You always were one lucky sonofabitch," Freddy said, slathering on the cream cheese.

"You can say that again."

An energetic, tanned man approached their table. Freddy jumped up and they exchanged high fives.

"Kenny—m'boy!" Freddy greeted. "How're they hangin'?"

"No complaints," Kenny replied with a big smile.

Freddy turned to Linc. "This guy knows everyone in New York," he enthused. *"And* he manages t' keep a sharp eye on my portfolio. Made me a bundle last year. Kenny Rickle, meet Linc Blackwood."

"A pleasure," Kenny said, slipping his card in Linc's direction. "Anything you want while you're in town—call. I'm a *big* fan."

"I'll do that," Linc said, pocketing Kenny's card.

Kenny drifted off, joining a table crowded with several New York models.

"The dude's a player," Freddy said, sitting down and piling even more cream cheese on his bagel. "Jeez!" he added, waxing nostalgic. "Remember *our* single days?"

"You rarely *had* a single day," Linc reminded. "You skipped from one wife to the next."

"Fuckin' alimony whores," Freddy grumbled. "Those bitches are worse than the IRS."

"Who's this one tonight?" Linc asked.

"One of those supermodel types—she's lookin' to break into movies."

"Ambitious. The worst kind."

"You'll like her, she's a far-out broad. An' talkin' of broads—how ya doin' with La Sanchez? She as hot as everyone says?"

"She's a number all right."

"I *bet* she is," Freddy said, busily stirring three lumps of sugar into his creamy coffee. "Saw her on Letterman the other night. Y'know, there's somethin' about her that's kinda familiar."

"Sure there is," Linc said, drinking his coffee black. "She's been in—what—five movies in the last four years?"

"I'm wonderin' if she was an extra on one of *my* movies," Freddy said, slurping his coffee. "It's like I know her from before."

"Before what?"

"Before she was a star, schmuck."

"Yeah, yeah," Linc said sarcastically. *"You* discovered her. According to you, everyone from Meg Ryan to Julia Roberts was your discovery."

"It probably *was* me, I got the eye," Freddy said, watching two tall blondes who were standing by the counter.

"You've got an eye all right," Linc said, swiveling his head to check out the blondes. "New York women, stylish, right?"

Freddy rubbed his hands together. "Forget about style," he said with a raucous chuckle. "Gimme a hot L.A. body any day. Fake tits an' a cocksuckin' mouth. That's *my* style!"

CHAPTER
22

Working with Nick Logan turned out to be a pleasant surprise. He was on time, knew all his lines, looked almost handsome once the makeup and hairdressing department had shaved off his beard and cleaned him up, and best of all he was a terrific actor.

Cat had dealt with a raggle-taggle band of amateurs on her previous movie; now, working with professionals was a major kick. Her cinematographer was a thoughtful and extremely helpful collaborator who advised her, but not in a superior way, which made her feel that she was getting the best out of him and *still* implementing her own ideas.

There was so much to think about, so much to do. As the director, everyone came to her for decisions. It was a huge responsibility, but one she felt she was capable of taking on. She even had her own assistant, Kodi, a cute Chinese girl who was probably older than her and did everything she asked, which was kind of cool.

Fortunately Jonas was there for her, watching her back, making sure it all went smoothly. Even Merrill visited the set on the first day of shooting to wish everyone luck. He was his usual powerful presence, puffing on a huge cigar, trailed by a temporary assistant—a skinny man with bright red hair, handpicked by Jonas.

On the second day of principal photography Cat's lawyer called her on the set. "I know you're in the middle of a thousand things," Leo said. "Only I thought you should know that I've had a response from your husband. He doesn't want a divorce, refuses to hire a lawyer, insists that he talk to you, and says this can all be worked out when he gets back."

"That's crap, Leo," she said angrily, cradling her cell phone. "He doesn't get it. There's *no way* I'm putting up with him screwing around on me."

"I hear you," Leo said. "Don't worry. I'll deal with it."

"Please do," she said, clicking off her phone.

Like she didn't have enough to deal with, and Jump was *not* a priority.

"What's up?" Nick Logan asked, sidling over, a cigarette dangling from his lower lip. "Boyfriend problems?"

"Were you listening to my conversation?" she demanded.

"Half the set heard it," he said, squinting at her with sleepy amber eyes. "You were fuckin' yelling."

"I was *not,*" she responded indignantly.

"If you say so."

"And I don't *have* a boyfriend," she added. "If you *must* know, I have a husband."

"Nasty."

"What?"

"Husbands who dick around," Nick said,

flicking ash on the ground. " 'Specially on a knockout babe who looks like you."

"Don't hit on me, Nick," she said, fixing him with a steely glare. "I'm not into it."

"Then you'd better let me know when you are, an' maybe we'll do somethin' 'bout it."

Before she could reply he drifted off, conferring with the script supervisor, who definitely had a crush on him.

God, he was annoying! Although his cocky attitude didn't seem to stop every woman on the set from developing a crush on him.

Cat couldn't care less, as long as he did good work; that was all that mattered. She had no eyes for getting involved, and certainly not with an actor.

Shelby continued to see Pete, reasoning to herself that she wasn't doing anything wrong. And even though she was well aware that her husband would hardly approve of her spending time with an old boyfriend, what Linc didn't know wouldn't irritate him.

On the other hand, Pete was a good friend, and it wasn't as if she'd ever slept with him. During the time they were together they'd indulged in a few steamy necking sessions, never taking it all the way, which was kind of juvenile, considering the amount of women Linc had slept with in his past.

The truth was that she enjoyed Pete's company. He didn't drink or smoke, he simply got on with things in a down-home kind of way. He reminded her of normal life—the way it was before she'd moved to Hollywood and married a famous movie star with a drinking problem.

She drove to Pete's gym in Santa Monica, found a parking meter, and left her car on the street.

The gym was massive, with huge windows overlooking the ocean, and all the latest equipment. It was full of toned, hard bodies working nonstop to make them even fitter. "I feel so out of shape," she said ruefully, looking around.

"You're not," Pete responded, once again obviously delighted to see her. "You're very toned and, uh . . . very beautiful."

"Thanks," she murmured, wishing he wouldn't go there. She wasn't seeking compliments, merely friendship.

"I'll give you the tour," he said.

"I'd like that," she said, following him around as he showed her the steam room, lap pool, and massage rooms.

"Gotta say I'm looking forward to seeing you in *Rapture,*" he remarked. "I hear your performance is quite something."

"Oh," she said, suddenly shy. "You must've heard about the nude scene."

"The word's around."

"Do you have any idea how embarrassing it was to shoot? I *begged* the director for a closed set, yet people managed to sneak in anyway."

"That's the way it goes."

"At one point there were men actually hanging off the rafters. It was most disconcerting."

"And I bet you handled it like you handle everything—with your usual style."

"I try," she said modestly.

After the tour they sat down in his cluttered office, where he offered her a bottle of Evian, picked up the script, and began going over the stunts he thought she might be up to attempting. "The car stunt's a breeze," he assured her. "You can handle it, no problem."

"I can?" she asked unsurely.

"You bet," he said, nodding vigorously. "I already spoke to Cat about it."

"You did?"

"Yeah, it's important, Shelby, 'cause sometimes the audience spots it when a stunt double takes over."

"Not in your movies they don't."

"I appreciate that."

"Have you ever doubled for Linc?"

"Sure did. There was no way you could tell us apart on the screen."

"You're not as tall as him."

"We fake it with shoes, hairpieces, whatever."

"Show me the movie and I'll guess who's who."

"I have a DVD of it," he said. "Hey—wanna come by my place later an' take a look?"

"No, Pete," she said quickly. "I don't think that's a good idea."

"Why?" he said, challenging her. "We're friends, aren't we?"

"I wouldn't feel comfortable."

He gave her a long look. "Is there a reason for that?"

"Well . . . ," she began, wishing he hadn't asked. "I . . . uh . . . haven't mentioned to Linc that we bumped into each other."

"You haven't, huh? How come?"

"I'm sure you remember that Linc can be quite jealous."

"Oh yeah, I remember." A long silent beat. "Y'know, Shelby, I thought by this time he would've gotten you pregnant. I always imagined you with a couple of kids. You'd be a sensational mother."

"We, uh . . . we've discussed having children," she said. Then she stopped abruptly. "You know what, Pete?" she said, brushing back her long hair. "Talking about this is too personal."

"Sorry," he said quickly. "I shouldn't've gone there. It's none of my business, right?"

She nodded, suddenly feeling disloyal to her husband. "I've got to go," she said, getting up. "Thanks for the tour."

"Anytime," he said, throwing her a quizzical look. "Don't forget, I'm always here for you."

Lola did not return to her hotel until Sunday evening, having spent *the* most glorious weekend with Tony. In her heart she could not imagine why she had ever left him. Tony Alvarez understood her better than any man ever had. They were soul mates, destined to be together.

Big Jay escorted her up to her suite, where there were a ton of messages waiting for her. She had not bothered to turn her cell phone on all weekend, therefore she'd been unreachable.

Naturally she'd seen the papers. TONY AND LOLA—TOGETHER AGAIN! With huge front-page pictures in the *Post* and the *Daily News.*

She was thrilled to see how fantastic they looked together. The story inside was not such a thrill: "Lola and Tony Alvarez a couple again? Where does that leave Lola's husband, Matt Seel? Sitting in California by himself? Or maybe Lola and Tony are just friends. . . ."

Damn! There was no doubt that Matt would see this and be hurt. She hadn't wanted to hurt him; it was just that he was so damn *boring,* she'd *had* to get away or go crazy. Besides, she'd known Tony much longer than she'd known Matt, so her soon-to-be-ex shouldn't feel dissed that she'd decided to go back to her original love.

She sat on the edge of the bed and clicked on the TV while listening to her voice mail.

Faye was first, naturally. "What the *hell* do you think you're up to?" her bossy publicist rasped. "And why didn't you tell *me* first, so that I could maintain *some* degree of control? I'll be back on Monday; we'll have to deal with it then."

Oh good, she couldn't wait.

The second call was from her highly expensive attorney, Otto Landstrom. "Not a smart move, Lola," Otto said in his disapproving-father voice. "We should talk as soon as possible. You're putting ammunition into the hands of the enemy."

What did *that* mean?

The third message was from Selma. "Mama's about to have a heart attack," her sister wailed. "You'd better call me back immediately."

And so on and so on, with many other messages from friends and relatives, all putting in their ten cents' worth.

Why couldn't they leave her alone? Didn't anyone understand? No bad publicity was about to frighten *her* off. Tony Alvarez was her man, and this time she was staying with him, come what may.

She *loved* Tony. She loved him passionately. And no bad publicity would ever split them up again.

Freddy Krane's idea of a good time was staying up all night. Since Freddy was also into doing coke, Linc decided it wasn't such a bad idea.

Freddy's latest supermodel girlfriend, Allegra, joined in the fun too. She was a six-foot-tall beauty who hailed from Australia, with a strong accent that could cut glass. She talked a lot, assuring them that when she finally broke into movies, she would make Nicole Kidman look like a Girl Scout.

"Been a supermodel for five years," she announced. "Been on the cover of *Sports Illustrated* twice. I'm like *huge* in the modeling world."

Linc and Freddy didn't care what she was as long as she joined them in their habit.

Linc had a feeling that he shouldn't be indulging in front of some strange model with a loud mouth, but then he thought, *What the hell?* He was in New York, far away from

Shelby, and what she didn't know wouldn't hurt her.

The three of them started off having dinner at Coco Pazzo, where Linc bumped into several acquaintances. After dinner they stopped by a few clubs, all of which Allegra was extremely familiar with. She sailed past the door people with a disdainful flip of her hand, and headed straight to the VIP room where she downed apple martinis as if they were lemonade.

"I'm out every night," she boasted. "Staying up late never affects me. I'm what they call a natural beauty."

Yes, and modest too, Linc thought.

"I'm gonna put her in my next movie," Freddy announced, winking at Linc behind her back. "Is it *my* fault if she ends up on the cuttin' room floor?"

At around 3 A.M. Linc decided he was tired and ready to go home. Freddy cornered him, informing him that Allegra would not be averse to a threesome.

"Sorry," Linc said, remembering that he had an early call. "Not my scene."

Freddy jeered that he was getting old.

Maybe he was. He was forty-something, not exactly a kid anymore. Besides, he was looking forward to seeing Shelby on the weekend.

There was nothing wrong with missing one's wife.

After a restless night's sleep, Lola reported for work accompanied by Big Jay and Jenny. They were shooting a scene on location at the Central Park Zoo and the paparazzi were in full evidence. She hid in her trailer until she was called, then with Big Jay by her side, protecting her, she headed for the set.

Linc Blackwood was already there. She'd been so caught up with Tony all weekend that she'd forgotten about Linc and her plan. The moment she saw him it all came rushing back. Staring at him from a distance, she realized that she could never have babies with Tony, the love of her life. She could never have a little girl that looked like her, or a little boy that looked like Tony, and it was all because of Linc Blackwood. He'd treated her like she was less than nothing, used her, got her pregnant, and dumped her all in one night. What a piece of shit he was.

Now, staring at him, she was more determined than ever to smash his dreams the way he'd smashed hers.

So . . . what was she waiting for? Let the games begin.

Clad in a beige cashmere Valentino coat and a wide-brimmed hat, she casually waved at him.

"Hey," he said, strolling toward her. "You're all over the front pages."

"I know," she answered demurely. "I've been a very bad girl, haven't I?"

"Bad girl suits you," he said with a half smile.

"You think?"

"You're glowing."

"I am?"

"Oh yes."

They exchanged a long look before Lola quickly changed the subject. "Is your wife here yet?" she asked, as if she cared.

"Flying in this weekend."

"I bet you're looking forward to seeing her."

"Sure am."

A wistful sigh. "It must be nice to be happily married."

"It certainly is."

"Matt and I, we had so many plans . . ."

"What happened?"

She lowered her eyes. "I can't talk about it, Linc. It's too upsetting."

"Sorry."

"Tony's an old friend," she explained. "He's helping me get through it."

Yeah, Linc thought. *I can see that.*

"Y'know," Lola said, "I was hoping we could run some lines later."

"Is there a particular scene you have in mind?"

"The dialogue in the party scene doesn't work for me."

"It doesn't?"

"No. I was thinking we could go over it, make some changes."

"When do you want to do this?"

"Well," she said coyly, "I realize we can't be seen out to dinner together; it would drive the paparazzi insane."

"Wouldn't think you were free for dinner anyway, what with Tony consoling you and all."

"As a matter of fact, I *am* free. Tony had to fly to New Orleans on a location scout. He won't be back until the weekend, which means I'm all alone in the big city."

"That makes two of us."

"*Would* it be a mistake for us to be seen out together?" she said, wide-eyed. "After all, it's not as if there's anything going on between us."

"The gossip rags would go nuts," Linc said. "And I'm sure Shelby wouldn't appreciate it."

"Scared of wifey?" she asked, lightly mocking him.

"Me?" he said, raising a cynical eyebrow.

"Yes, you," she said, flirting.

"Just trying to be smart, Lola. Let's not forget we're making a movie, not having an affair." Now it was his turn to mock her. "Wouldn't want anyone thinking otherwise, would we?"

"*I* don't have *time* for an affair, do you?" she said, licking her lips in a suggestive way.

"It *would* be kinda difficult to fit it into our busy schedules," he said, grinning at her obvious come-on.

Man, Lola Sanchez was *definitely* a piece of work. Flirting with her was a kick, but there was no way he had any intention of taking it further.

*　*　*

Rapture was opening across America the following week and Shelby was on edge about it. Suddenly she was about to be exposed to the world, and it was a scary prospect.

The next day was the L.A. press junket, which meant major maintenance. She spent the afternoon at the hair salon having her hair done, getting a manicure and pedicure. The studio had already sent designers to her house with a selection of clothes she could choose from, so later she selected a simple white Galanos dress and gold jewelry from Van Cleef & Arpels.

Early the next morning, Kara, the studio publicist for *Rapture,* arrived to pick her up and escort her to the Beverly Hills Hotel, where the junket was taking place. "It'll be a long day," Kara warned. She was a Southern girl with crinkly red hair down to her waist and funky tinted glasses. Rumor had it that she was sleeping with Beck Carson.

"I can take it," Shelby said, getting into the limo parked in her driveway. "The only problem is forgetting what I've said to one journalist, and wondering if I've already said it to another."

Kara gave a high-pitched laugh. "I'll try to

prompt you. They've each got four minutes, unless it's *E.T., Extra!* or *Access.* They get six minutes—more if they send Mary Hart. You'll break for lunch at twelve for an hour, then after makeup and hair touch-ups, we're back in the room. The morning's all print. The afternoon's all TV."

"Wonderful," Shelby sighed, not relishing the thought of a day locked up with probing journalists. "Where are the others?"

"Russell's in the next room. Beck's on his way."

"Do I get to see them?"

"I'll put in a request that everyone break for lunch at the same time."

"Thanks."

"You'll be great," Kara said, adjusting her glasses, which kept on falling off the bridge of her nose. "You've done it a thousand times before."

"Not exactly a thousand," Shelby said modestly. "However, I'll do my best."

And she did, answering numerous questions, dodging difficult ones, avoiding the comparisons to *Monster's Ball,* flattering other actresses, talking about her director and costar, being very careful not to say one negative word about Linc.

At the lunch break she got together with Russell and Beck. The three of them sat around swapping war stories about the various members of the press.

"Watch out for the guy from Chicago," Russell warned. "He's out for a kill. You'll recognize the rug, the twitch, and the bad breath."

"And don't forget the sexy little number from Vegas," Beck said, joining in. "She managed to slip me her phone number two times."

"Can't wait!" Shelby murmured. "Do you think *I'll* get lucky too?"

"Only if you cut your hair and lower your voice," Beck joked.

She loved hanging out with them. Making *Rapture* had been an intense experience, one she'd never forget. Both men were true professionals and a pleasure to work with. If only every movie could be as enjoyable.

By the end of the day she was all talked out. She phoned Linc at his hotel and got his voice mail. She left a message that she was going to bed and would call him in the morning, then she took a long hot bath before settling down for the night.

Just as she was drifting off to sleep, her

private line rang. Thinking it was Linc, she reached for the phone and murmured, "I know. You don't want me falling asleep until you've told me how much you love me."

"How did you know?"

It was Pete's voice.

"Oh," she said, embarrassed. "I thought it was Linc."

"Sorry if I'm a big disappointment."

"No . . . uh . . . it's just that . . . when did I give you this number?"

"You wrote it down for me. Remember?"

Yes. She remembered writing down her phone number. And by mistake she'd obviously given him her private line.

"I didn't wake you, did I?" he asked. "It's only eight, I thought you might want to grab a burger after your press thing today."

"Actually I'm in bed."

"Did you eat?"

The truth was that she hadn't eaten anything since lunch. Her housekeeper had left a fully stocked fridge, but she hadn't felt like eating alone. Now Pete was on the phone, and what was she supposed to do?

Linc was in New York, Pete was her friend, and she *was* hungry.

"What d'you think?" Pete asked, pushing for an answer. "Burger or no burger?"

A big, fat, juicy hamburger with a side order of greasy french fries. Yes!

And tomorrow she'd tell Linc.

CHAPTER

23

Nick Logan was an outrageous flirt. Every woman on the set had fallen under his bad-boy spell—every woman except Cat and Shelby. So naturally they were the two he had to pursue and conquer. Nick had a thing about sleeping with every woman he could. His success rate was extremely high.

Jonas hated the sight of the randy actor, although he was forced to admit that Nick Logan was a dynamic presence on-screen, and the dailies were excellent. Merrill was delighted with the way everything was going. He sent Cat early morning memos with his comments after he'd viewed the dailies. She found herself looking forward to his notes; they were to the point and insightful. As crass and overbearing as Merrill was, he definitely had an eye for detail.

The movie was progressing well. Her personal life was not. Somehow Jump had gotten hold of her new cell phone number and was bombarding her with calls begging her forgiveness. She hung up on him every time, but he kept on trying.

Shelby, who'd started work on the movie, was sympathetic. "Keep on changing your number until he gives up," she suggested, as they stood by the Kraft service setup, enjoying a mug of coffee and a short break.

"Why *should* I?" Cat said defiantly. "Why can't *he* accept the fact that it's over?"

"Perhaps he needs closure," Shelby said gently.

"Screw closure!" Cat snapped. "He should've thought about that when he was banging his old girlfriend."

"What're you two gossiping about?" Nick inquired, sneaking up behind them.

"Women don't gossip," Shelby said crisply. "That's a male thing."

Nick furrowed his thick eyebrows. *"What?"*

"I agree," Cat said, reaching for an apple. "Men are the biggest gossips of all."

"Bull," Nick said.

"True," Cat said.

"You two live in a fuckin' dream world," Nick countered, perplexed because his particular brand of charm didn't seem to be working on either of them.

"How many times a day do you use the F-word?" Shelby asked.

"Not as fuckin' many as Colin fuckin' Farrell," he retorted.

"Good-bye," Cat said. "I'll see you on the set."

Nick watched her walk away. "Hot stuff," he remarked. "Perfect ass."

Shelby shook her head disapprovingly.

"What?" Nick said. "It's fuckin' true."

Later that day Jump turned up on the set. Cat was shocked; she'd thought he was safely in Australia, still on tour. Now here he was with his long hair tied back in a ponytail, his many tattoos, and a determined expression.

She was in the middle of working on a scene between Nick and Shelby, and she was not about to stop. Jonas ran interference, persuading Jump to wait in a chair way back from the action.

"Tell her I'm stayin' here until she's ready to talk t' me," Jump insisted. "Okay, mate?"

"I'll do that," Jonas said, wondering what she'd ever seen in this tall, scruffy-looking, would-be rock star.

"Last chance," Lola said.

"Last chance at what?" Linc responded.

"Well, since wifey is obviously out and about," Lola said, waving a *People* magazine in front of his face, "I don't see anything wrong with us having dinner and going over the script. I'll bring my publicist, you bring yours. We'll make it a cozy foursome."

"What's that crack about my wife?" Linc asked.

"You haven't seen it?"

"Seen what?" he asked impatiently.

"Mrs. Linc Blackwood and mystery man lunching at Jerry's Deli in the Valley. Seems to me they were caught off guard."

"What the fuck are you talking about?"

Lola handed him the magazine, folded

back to the Star Tracks page. There was a photograph of Shelby, hair tied back in a ponytail, big sunglasses, slacks, and a shirt. She was not looking at the camera; apparently she was not even aware there was a camera pointed in her direction. She was glancing up at the man with her, a man who had a protective hand on her arm as they exited the deli.

Linc stared at the photograph in disbelief. The man was Pete. "Fuck!" he snarled.

"Trouble in paradise?" Lola inquired.

"What?"

"I was simply . . . commenting. Who *is* the mystery man?"

"Nobody," he said, inwardly fuming.

"Well," Lola drawled succinctly. "For nobody, he sure ain't bad looking."

Linc didn't say a word. He turned his back and abruptly walked away.

Lola gave a small triumphant smile. Obviously the photograph had not pleased Mr. Blackwood. Obviously *Mrs.* Blackwood was playing her own little game. This was working out even better than she'd planned.

Jenny approached, cell phone in hand. "It's your sister again."

"Oh Lord," Lola said, rolling her eyes. "What did you tell her this time?"

"That you're busy working. It's her third call today. She *insists* on speaking to you."

"Why can't they leave me alone?" Lola grumbled, taking the phone. "What's up, Sis?" she asked, not in the mood for a lecture, which she had no doubt was forthcoming.

"What's *up?*" shouted a frustrated Selma. "Don't you answer your messages? I've been trying to reach you for days. Mama's about to have a cow."

"Why's she having a cow?"

"Why do you think? You and Tony Alvarez, of course."

"Listen, Selma," Lola said firmly, "it's time everyone realized that I make my own choices."

"Not if Mama has her way."

"Tony's a great guy," Lola insisted. "And I wish you'd all stop criticizing him."

"Tony's a drug addict. He's always in the newspapers getting arrested for possession and stuff like that."

"Selma, please don't speak about things you know nothing about. Tony's on probation, he was arrested once. It wasn't as if he was even using himself; he was holding a small amount of cocaine for a friend."

"*All* drug addicts say that."

"What're you—an expert?"

"Mama says—"

"Shut *up,* Selma. I don't have to explain anything to anyone."

"What about poor Matt?"

"What *about* him?"

"Mama had him over for dinner the other night."

"Why?"

"She felt sorry for him."

"I do *not* want Mama entertaining my soon-to-be-ex-husband," Lola said furiously.

"She likes Matt."

"She might like him, but she'd better understand that he's not part of our family anymore."

"The way you're speaking, it seems *you're* not either."

"Oh God, now you're beginning to sound like the rest of them."

"No, I'm not."

"Yes, you are."

"Please call Mama."

"I guess none of you realize that I'm on

the set working, and that making phone calls is most inconvenient."

"Lucia—"

"Okay, okay, I'll do it now."

"It's your *mother,*" Selma chided.

"I'm doing it," she said, clicking off the phone and handing it to Jenny. "Get me my mom."

Claudine sounded cold. "What you doing with your life, girl?" she demanded. "Didn't I teach you anything? You go back with this man who's bad news. Your father knows it, I know it, we *all* know it. Everyone except you."

"Mama, chill. I know what I'm doing."

"No, daughter, *you* chill," Claudine responded. "You have no idea what you're doing."

"I knew what I was doing when I bought you the house, didn't I?" Lola snapped.

"Lucia," Claudine said sternly, "if you throw this house in my face one more time, we'll move out and *you* can come live in it. Do you understand?"

She sighed. Movie star or not, there was no arguing with Claudine. "Yes, Mama."

* * *

Linc took the *People* magazine and studied it. It really *was* Shelby with Pete. Yes, Pete, his old enemy. Well, not exactly enemy, but rival for her affections. Not even rival, because when he'd come into her life and stolen her away from Pete, it was not a problem. Now here she was, cool as can be, walking out of a deli with the prick. Jesus Christ! Women were not to be trusted.

He marched to his trailer. Norm, his publicist, materialized, falling into step beside him.

"Get lost, Norm," he grunted.

"I need to talk to you about the *Newsweek* story," Norm ventured.

"Not now," he said, slamming his way into the trailer, locking the door, and opening the closet.

Stashed in the inside pocket of his jacket were a couple of glassine packets of cocaine. He opened one, tipping the seductive white powder onto the countertop. Then he arranged it into several neat lines, and snorted them one by one.

His anger level was so elevated that the drug did not have the desired effect.

What he needed was a drink.

Shelby was due to arrive in New York the

following afternoon. Should he call her now and have it out with her on the phone? Or should he wait until he could do it face-to-face?

Yes, he'd wait. Women lied over the phone. Women could be such devious bitches.

His throat was parched. The coke was definitely not giving him his usual high.

Fuck! How could Shelby do this to him?

He left his trailer and searched out Norm. "Why is there no booze in my trailer?" he demanded.

"Mrs. Blackwood said that—"

"I don't give a flying fuck what Mrs. Blackwood said. Go buy a couple of bottles of scotch and vodka."

"If that's what you want."

"Yeah, that's what I want," he said belligerently. "And in future listen to me, not my wife."

"I'll do that," Norm said, gritting his teeth.

"By the way, how come Lola Sanchez gets to show me fucking *People* magazine?" Linc griped. "What were *you* doing—sleeping on the job?"

Norm visibly blanched. He hated it when Mr. Macho Movie Star was in one of his foul moods. "Have they written something you don't like about yourself in *People?*" he asked nervously.

"It isn't about *me,* it's about Shelby."

"I'm not her P.R."

"Isn't it your job to stop shit from appearing?"

"How can I stop something I don't know about?"

"Buy the fucking magazine, then come see me," Linc said, heading back to the set.

Lola was waiting to shoot the next scene. She was clad in a peach-colored peignoir with dramatic cleavage. "I'm so sorry," she said, placing a sympathetic hand on his arm. "I didn't mean to upset you."

"What makes you think I'm upset?" he answered evenly. After all, he was an actor—he could play the game when he had to. "Hey," he added. "How about us going over the script this evening?"

"Fine with me," she purred. "Tony doesn't get back until tomorrow."

"Then tonight's the night, huh?" he said, giving her the full-on macho sexy look.

Lola met his gaze. "Yes, Linc," she murmured, noticing a slight residue of white powder under his nose. "Tonight *is* the night." She reached up and gently brushed the powder away.

"What're you doing?" he said, taking a step back.

"You had a little . . . makeup there."

"Thanks."

"No problem."

"By the way, forget about the publicists, it'll be you and me. Nobody else."

"What about the paparazzi?"

"Fuck 'em."

Shelby was busy. Not only was she working on *Caught,* she was also continuing to do press for *Rapture* and dealing with the accelerated interest in her career. Her agent was on the phone constantly.

"It's all happening, Shelby," Ed said. "When you get back from New York I'll come to the set; we'll have lunch and discuss everything."

"I'm back Monday," she said, "in time for work on Tuesday."

"Your schedule's about to get even busier."

"That's impossible!" she joked.

"Are the press reps at the studio sending you all the reviews?"

"I'm scared to read them."

"Don't be," Ed assured her. "They're sensational. When's the premiere again?"

"Wednesday."

"Do you need an escort, or is Linc flying in?"

"He can't, he's on call every day."

"Can I take you?"

"That would be perfect, Ed."

She'd worked all day and now she was packing, ready for an early morning flight on Merrill's plane. She was longing to see Linc; separations were not good for any marriage, especially now, when Linc had given up drinking and probably needed her support, although he did still seem to be enjoying making his movie, which was a relief.

Shelby knew that all the attention she was getting could be hard for him to take. It was only to be expected, especially since Linc might view her enormous success as a threat to his masculinity. Brenda had warned her to tread cautiously around him. "As you know, Linc suffers from low self-esteem," Brenda had said. *"Your* job is to build him up, make sure he knows how much you love and admire him. Always keep in mind that he's a man first, a movie star second."

"I always put Linc first," she'd replied.

Shelby had a strong hunch that ever since Brenda had counseled Linc a couple of times, the therapist had developed a secret crush on him.

"Then double your efforts," Brenda had said. "You have to remember that he's in an extremely fragile state at the moment. He's stopped drinking, he's making a new career move. He needs you to be supportive and there for him."

Shelby understood what Brenda was saying, but she also thought, *What about me? When am I the one who gets support and love?* Linc never gave much thought to *her* needs.

That was the difference between Linc and Pete, Pete always seemed to put her first.

She'd still not mentioned to Linc that she'd seen her old boyfriend. She'd decided that the best way to handle it was to tell him in a casual way. "Guess who's working on my movie?" she'd say. And perhaps she wouldn't add that they'd gone out to lunch or shared a late night hamburger.

After all, what could she possibly gain by doing so? Only Linc's jealous wrath—and when he was angry, watch out. He could be incredibly vitriolic and possessive. She dreaded his outbursts.

Later that evening her private line rang. She did not pick up, deciding she would do so only if it was Linc. It wasn't. It was Pete again.

"I'm calling to wish you a safe trip to New York," he said, as she listened in on her answering machine. "While you're gone, I'll be working out your car stunt. You'll be great, no need to be anxious." A beat, then: "I'll miss you, Shelby. So . . . if you feel like calling, you've got my cell number. I'll see you next week."

She sighed, realizing that much as she liked being with Pete, it would be like waving a red flag in Linc's face if she continued hanging out with him.

No more Pete. She was starting to enjoy his company far too much.

CHAPTER
24

"Why are you stalking me?" Cat demanded, hands on hips, green eyes blazing.

"I'm not *stalking* you," Jump responded with a sulky scowl. "You're my freakin' *wife.*"

"Oh, *c'mon,*" she said, glaring at him. "You're supposed to be on tour in Australia; now you show up in L.A., creeping around the set while *I'm* trying to work."

"You're finished for the day, aren't you?"

"A director never finishes," she said

grandly. "I've got dailies to view, notes to go over, decisions to make for tomorrow."

"Yeah, an' you gotta eat too. Let's go to your place, order Chinese, an' talk."

"You're not getting it, are you?" she said, staring at him in exasperation. "There's *nothing* to talk about. I caught you screwing around on me. We're *over.*"

"You're such a wanker," he said, fidgeting with one of his gold stud earrings. "I dipped it in another bird. Big freakin' deal. I was stoned, didn't know what I was doing. You gonna keep punishin' me for that?"

"This is no punishment, Jump," she said, wishing he'd get lost. "I don't want to be with you anymore. It's as simple as that."

"After everything we've been through together?"

"What exactly *have* we been through?"

"If it wasn't for me," he said accusingly, "you'd be sitting in some New York pisshole stoned outta your skull with a bunch of losers."

"Oh," she said, narrowing her eyes. "Is that what you think I'd be doing?"

"You were a major druggie, Cat. The only reason you gave it up was 'cause *I* forced you to."

"Are you saying that if you hadn't come along, I wouldn't've accomplished anything?"

"That's the road you were heading down, darlin'."

"Go away," she said wearily. "Talk to my lawyer."

"Quit with the lawyer crap," he said, grabbing her roughly by the arm. "You an' me gotta work this out together."

"Don't *touch* me," she shouted, struggling to free herself.

They were standing outside her trailer. Most people had gone home, except for Nick Logan, who came bopping along at just the wrong moment. "Having trouble?" Nick asked, sizing Jump up.

"No," she said, glaring at Jump, who immediately let go of her.

"Yell if you need anythin'," Nick said, still eyeballing Jump, "I'll be in my trailer for another hour. Got lines to learn."

"Who the fuck is *that?*" Jump growled.

"None of your business," Cat responded.

"Jesus, you've turned into a tough little cunt."

"Oh very nice, the C-word."

"You're exactly like your freakin' mother."

"You don't even *know* my mother," she responded scornfully.

"Nor do you," he shot back.

"Get lost, cheater."

"I will. I'm at the Sunset Marquis. When you stop with the divorce rubbish, gimme a call." He strode off.

"Don't wait by the phone," she yelled after him.

A few minutes after Jump left, Nick emerged from his trailer. "Want me to have him whacked?" he inquired, all business.

"Excuse me?" she said, raising an eyebrow.

"I can arrange it, you know," he said matter-of-factly. "I got connections."

"Really?" she said, disbelievingly.

"Yeah. Last year I did a mafia movie, an' the dudes with the broken noses promised me a favor, which I aim to collect."

"You're nuts," she said, shaking her head.

"That's what everyone says," he said, squinting at her. "Personally I think it works for me."

"Don't be so sure."

"You're liking what you see on the screen,

aren't you?" he said, fishing in his pants pocket for a cigarette.

"You smoke too much," she admonished.

"An' *you* don't get enough sex," he responded, lighting up.

"Good night," she said, heading toward the parking lot.

"You seein' dailies?" he asked, loping along behind her.

"I am."

"Mind if I tag along?"

She hesitated for a moment, then thought, *Why not?* After all, he'd rescued her from what could've been a nasty physical fight with Jump. "I suppose so," she said.

"I'll ride with you," he said, dragging on his cigarette.

"I thought you had lines to learn."

"They'll wait."

"Oh, thanks," she said tartly. "Our movie should be your priority."

"I'm a fast study," he said, winking at her.

"That's encouraging."

They reached her red Mustang.

"Nice wheels," he said admiringly.

"Rented."

"I should warn you, I'm a backseat

driver," he responded. "So maybe *I* should drive."

"Too bad. I *give* direction, I'm not good at taking it."

"Okay, blondie," he said, sliding into the passenger seat. "Since this is our first date, I'll let *you* drive."

"You'll *let* me?" she said, raising an eyebrow.

"Sure," he said, exhaling smoke. "Ain't life grand?"

Back at his hotel, Linc was acting like a caged animal, pacing up and down, muttering under his breath. He was furious, and his pride was hurt. Of all the people for Shelby to be photographed with, she'd had to pick on that asshole Pete. How would it look to his buddies? They all knew what a pussy hound Pete was, and Shelby was his *wife* for crissakes.

He swooped on the phone, called room service, and ordered a couple of bottles of scotch. Then, since Shelby was arriving tomorrow, he thought better of it, instructed them to hold the order and send up half a bottle instead, and plenty of ice.

When the booze arrived, he filled a glass

and gulped it down without so much as blinking.

It was as if he had a hollow leg; first the coke had had no effect, now the same with the booze.

Maybe *sex* was what he needed. Maybe if he jammed it into Lola Sanchez he wouldn't feel so bad about Shelby and her indiscretion that made *him* look like a fool. Fuck her! Miss Sweet and Innocent. His proper English lady wife. And there she was on-screen with her tits hanging out, *and* now she was stepping out with an old boyfriend. Christ! What next?

It occurred to him that the anger he was feeling was not all about the dumb photo in *People.* His anger went deeper than that. Truth was, he was furious about Shelby taking it all off on-screen. A fury he'd kept under wraps until now. He was *married* to her. She was not some little hooker happy to flash the world. Her behavior on and off the screen was so fucking disrespectful.

He made a quick decision and called Lola at her hotel. "I'll meet you at the restaurant," he said.

"What a gentleman," she admonished. "I

suppose my bodyguard will have to escort me."

"Hey—I was gonna take a shower, that's all." Her silence indicated she was pissed. "Never mind," he said, "I'll come by your hotel."

"What restaurant are we going to?"

"Mario's."

"Where's that?"

"It's a small Italian place in the Village."

"Somewhere we won't be seen?" she said lightly.

"Listen carefully," he said, his voice rising, because he was in no mood to put up with *her* shit. "I don't *give* a rat's ass if we're seen or not."

"Hmm . . . ," she said knowingly. *"I get it. Your wife's in People with a good-looking guy, so now you want to get back at her."*

"What's with the good-looking-guy crap?" he said, steaming. "The asshole's a stuntman; he looks like shit."

"Oh, *sorry.*"

"I don't wanna talk about it, okay?"

"That's fine," she said, loving that he was so aggravated. "We can talk about me instead."

"I'm on my way."

"What happened to your shower?"

"How about I take it with you later?"

She put down the phone. "How about you've got no chance," she murmured, laughing to herself.

Linc got his usual big welcome at Mario's, a small family restaurant he'd been going to for years. Mama Mario adored him; he was one of her favorite customers.

"Ah, Signor Linc—so handsome," Mama Mario crooned. "Why you no marry one a my daughters? I tell you many times." She took a look at Lola, then turned back to Linc with an accusing expression. "Where's your *bella* wife?"

"This is Signorina Sanchez," Linc said. "We're making a movie together."

Mama Mario made a disapproving sound in the back of her throat before reluctantly leading them to a corner table.

A waiter came rushing over with menus. *"Mi scusi,"* Mama Mario said. "I go see other customers. *Buon appetito."*

"So," Linc said, ordering a double scotch on the rocks. "What's the deal with you and Tony Alvarez?"

"I told you before," Lola said, sticking to Evian. "He's helping me get over Matt."

"Yeah?" Linc said, giving her the macho sexy stare he'd perfected over the years. "And how's he doing that?"

"Tony's an old friend," she answered casually.

"Hey, sweetie, it's *me* you're talking to. I know all about old friends." He took another hearty swig of scotch and leaned across the table. "Are you fucking him?"

"Linc!" she said, managing to look affronted. "We don't know each other well enough for you to ask me those kinds of personal questions."

His hand slid under the table and onto her knee. "It's about time we got to know each other better."

She promptly removed his hand.

"You're not getting shy on me, are you?"

"I think you're forgetting you're a married man."

"So what?" he said carelessly. "You're a married woman."

"*I'm* getting a divorce," she reminded him.

"Hey," he said ruefully. "The way things are going, I might soon be joining you."

"I thought you and your wife were so blissfully happy?"

"Yeah, yeah," he said, draining his glass and signaling the waiter to bring him another drink. "Shelby's the best. Only she's in this movie with her tits all over the screen, an' I don't like it."

"I saw the film in Cannes," Lola said.

"How d'ya think seein' my wife like that makes *me* feel?" he complained. "What would *she* do if it was me up there with my dick hanging out?"

"If it was worth seeing, I'm sure the women in America would be very happy."

"It's worth seein', all right," he boasted, with a drunken leer.

"Lucky you," Lola murmured.

After dinner the booze began to kick in big time. "You got great tits," he said, attempting to grab a feel. "I like that in a woman."

She fended him off with a sharp slap.

Reducing Linc Blackwood to rubble was going to be too damn easy. The man was a pathetic drunk. A has-been stud.

Perhaps that was punishment enough.

*   *   *

The moment Cat walked into the screening room with Nick she could tell that Jonas was pissed. Usually they met up, watched the dailies together, took notes, then compared them. Tonight Jonas obviously realized things were different.

"Hey, man," Nick said, oblivious to any atmosphere. "I gotta take a piss. Save me a seat."

"What's *he* doing here?" Jonas asked as soon as Nick left to visit the men's room.

"He caught me on my way out," Cat explained.

"I thought we agreed we weren't going to have actors see the dailies."

"Nick says it helps him with his performance."

"So *you* said yes."

"Don't be so uptight. He's an okay guy."

"Yesterday you were calling him a lech."

"He's a lech, too. A leg-over merchant as they say in England."

"How's he getting back to his car?"

"Dunno," she said vaguely. *"You* can drive him."

"Forget it."

"What's up with you?"

"Nothing."

"Actually, Nick saved me from Jump. My dear almost-ex was being a major pain."

"I told you *I'd* stay and run interference," Jonas reminded her.

"No need. I handled it."

"With Nick's help."

"Yes, Jonas, with Nick's help. Do you mind?"

"Where's Jump now?"

"Back at his hotel. Can you imagine?" she added indignantly. "He had the balls to inform me that I'd be nothing if it wasn't for him."

"He's only saying that to irritate you."

"Well, it worked."

Nick returned and sat down next to her. Cat gave the signal for the projectionist to run the film.

She hunched forward in her seat, watching intently. On-screen Nick was a powerful presence, with his intense eyes, sexy mouth, and a brooding quality that worked well for his character.

She felt chills. The movie was going so well. How had she gotten this lucky?

When the lights went up, Nick lit a cigarette and glanced over at Jonas—the only other person in the screening room. "How about I buy you guys dinner?" he said. "I got a permanent table at Ago."

"I can't," Jonas said, still uptight.

"C'mon, man. We'll chug a coupla beers and—"

"I've got work to do," Jonas interrupted. "So do you," he said, staring pointedly at Cat.

She hated people telling her what to do. Jonas might be the big brother she'd never had, but that didn't mean he was free to boss her around. Besides, tonight she fancied hanging out. "I think I'll go grab a plate of pasta with Nick," she said, infuriating Jonas even further.

"Hey, Jonah, why don't you make the cut?" Nick asked.

"It's Jonas."

"Sorry, man."

"Are you sure—" Cat began. Before she could finish, Jonas had made a fast exit.

"Somethin' I said?" Nick remarked.

"He's got work to do. Jonas is very conscientious."

"Seems like a good dude."

"He is."

"Kinda buttoned up."

"Not really."

"Yeah. Really."

"Hmm . . ."

"You happy with the dailies?" Nick asked as they walked out of the screening room.

"Are you?" she countered.

"Never like watching myself."

"You told me it helps you with your performance."

"I was lying."

"Why?"

"'Cause I fancied spending time with you," he said, casually throwing his arm around her shoulders.

"You're crazy."

"Never said I wasn't."

"Try and keep the bullshit charm for in front of the camera."

"How about this time *I* drive?" he said as they approached her car.

"No way."

"Hate to tell you this, blondie, but you drive like a girl."

"Flattery's gonna get you all the way to nowhere."

"Okay," he said, with a half grin. "You win. But this is only a skirmish—when it comes to the battle, I got you beat."

"You think?"

"I *know.*"

By the time they were through with dinner, Linc was so bombed that he could barely stand up. Lola remained stone cold sober. No alcohol was coming between her and her looks, not unless it was the best Cristal champagne, and even then she indulged only in a glass or two.

Linc was all over her, pawing and touching, his hand attempting to creep up her skirt. She slapped him off like a particularly annoying puppy, which failed to stop him from trying. She intimated that if he came back to her hotel things would heat up. He was hot to trot.

Mama Mario would not allow him to pick up the check. "You be back soon with your *bella signorina* Shelby," she said, throwing another disapproving look Lola's way.

"We were rehearsing a scene," Lola offered. "You shouldn't read anything into it."

"Ha!" the older woman sniffed.

As soon as they walked out of the restaurant, the paparazzi sprang into action. Earlier, Lola had issued instructions to Big Jay to let everyone know where she was and with whom.

"I wonder who called them?" she asked innocently.

As the cameras began flashing, she turned to Linc, took his face in both her hands, and planted a big kiss on his lips. "Thanks for dinner," she whispered. "It was nice, even though we didn't get to discuss the script. I *love* that you found time to listen to my problems. You're *such* a sweetheart." Then she kissed him again.

She knew perfectly well what the photos would look like when they appeared. Nobody would hear the dialogue, they'd simply view the action.

"Put him in a cab," she said to Big Jay, ducking into her limo while the paparazzi continued to flash.

Linc started to follow her.

Big Jay blocked his way. "Ms. Sanchez says you should take a cab," Big Jay announced.

"What the fuck," Linc mumbled, unsteady on his feet. "Shit! I'm not feeling great; those fuckin' flashbulbs are ruining my eyeballs. What th' fuck's goin' on?"

Big Jay hailed down a cab, told the driver

where to go, and bundled Linc into the backseat. Then he joined his boss in the limo.

"Some stud," Lola murmured. "Blood-shot eyes and boozy breath. Oooh, I'm *sooo* unhappy I didn't end up with him."

Big Jay stared straight ahead. He knew better than to comment.

Shelby always set two alarms in case one failed to go off. She had a fear of being late and missing her call. Not that she had a call today, but she did have to be at the airport in time to catch Merrill's plane. He'd told her yesterday that he might be on it. She didn't mind; after all, it was *his* plane.

She'd finished packing the night before, so after dressing in a comfortable tracksuit, she was ready to go; all she needed was her sunglasses and carry-on bag.

Downstairs in the kitchen, her house-keeper had fixed her a plate of scrambled eggs.

"I'm not hungry, Lupe," she said apologetically.

"That's all right, Miss Shelby."

"Is my car here yet?"

"It's outside."

"Thanks. I'll see you in three days," she said, walking out the front door.

Standing in the driveway was Pete.

"What on *earth* are *you* doing here?" she asked, perplexed.

"Driving you to the airport," he said, with a big friendly smile.

"You're doing *what?*"

"Driving you to the airport," he repeated.

"And why would you be doing that?"

"I know you're nervous about flying," he said, pulling up the collar of his weathered leather jacket, "so I figured it would be a nice thing to do."

"Uh, listen, Pete," she said, quite taken aback. "It's a thoughtful offer; however, I can't take you up on it."

"Why not?"

"I don't know quite how to put this," she said hesitantly, "because I *do* think you're a great guy. Only here's the thing—Linc would not be happy about this."

"He wouldn't?"

"No, he wouldn't. And—"

"Shelby," Pete interrupted, his rugged face quite serious. "There's nothing going on between us. We both know that."

"Yes, *we* both know it. How about everyone else?"

"I thought it would be a gesture you'd appreciate," Pete said, managing to look hurt.

"I *do* appreciate it, Pete, but I can't risk upsetting Linc."

"I don't see him anywhere."

"I'm honest with my husband. I wouldn't lie about anything."

"You mean he'll ask who drove you to the airport?"

Shelby frowned. Pete might be a great guy, but this whole scene was getting to be too much of a good thing and she had no desire to lead him on. "Where's my car and driver?" she asked, deciding she'd better put a stop to it before it went any further.

"Now you're *really* going to be mad," he said sheepishly.

"Why?"

" 'Cause I sent your driver away."

She was silent for a moment, trying to remain calm and not get too angry, because she knew that Pete meant well. However, he'd now crossed the line, and it was time for her to do something about it.

"You're giving me no choice, are you?"

she said evenly, aware that if she didn't go with him she could miss Merrill's plane.

"That wasn't my intention."

"Look," she said, taking a deep breath, "when I get back, the only place we should see each other is on the set. Unless you and Linc resume your friendship, that's it. I hope you understand."

"Got it, Shelby," he said, suitably abashed.

"Good."

CHAPTER
25

Friday morning Cat awoke late. They were night shooting, so she had the luxury of not having to get up at dawn. She'd gotten home around 1 A.M., turned off her phone, and settled in for a long sleep.

Spending time with Nick and his friends had been interesting. Nick had not been all over her as she'd expected; instead he'd practically ignored her, chatting up a couple of girls at the table. One of them was Petra Flynn, a busty blonde who starred in her own TV series. The other was a sultry brunette, currently appearing at a small theater in Santa Monica. Nick was obviously into actresses.

Cat spent the evening getting to know some of his other friends—a mixed group of writers and actors. When she'd left, Nick barely seemed to notice her go. Not that she cared; he was the star of her movie, that's all. Yes, he'd been paying a lot of attention to her on the set, but that was only because there was nobody else around except Shelby for him to flirt with. And Shelby made it very clear up front that their relationship was strictly professional. Nick understood; he wasn't into chasing married women when they were still with their husbands.

Cat yawned and checked her voice mail. There were several messages from Jump. "I'm flying to New York," he said, sounding angry. "An' if you refuse to talk to me, I'm throwin' every freakin' thing of yours out onto the street. Got it?"

What a jerkoff. Why couldn't he accept that they were over?

She picked up the phone and reached him at his hotel.

"What?" he mumbled.

"It's me."

"Knew you'd finally call."

"I got your charming message. You know I don't have time to go to New York right now."

"You'd better," he threatened. " 'Cause I mean what I say."

"You can't throw my stuff out."

"Who's gonna stop me?"

"My lawyer says it's to your advantage if you cooperate."

"Fuck your lawyer."

"What happened to your Australian tour? Why are you back?"

"The tour's finished. If you weren't so busy with your own selfish crap, you'd know that."

"There was a time I *used* to worry about you," she reminded him. "Don't forget that I flew to Australia to surprise you. And didn't *that* turn into a memorable night?"

"Here we go again," he groaned. "Same old shitty song."

"The lease on the loft is all yours if you want it," she said abruptly. "Send me the papers to sign."

"That's all you're into now, isn't it?" he scoffed. "Papers and freakin' lawyers."

"You know what, Jump? Why don't we try to be civil about this?"

"Take civil an' shove it," he said, slamming down the phone.

He was not taking this well, which wasn't fair, because it was all *his* fault. If she hadn't caught him dicking around, none of this would've happened.

She padded into the kitchen and put on the coffee. Her mind flashed on Nick. If she was truthful she'd have to admit that she *was* attracted to him.

Hmm . . . Nick Logan was *not* a good idea. Nick Logan was a heartbreaker who'd probably make Jump look like an amateur, and that's exactly what she didn't need.

Besides, she had no time to get involved.

She called Jonas and asked him what he was doing.

"Working," he said, sounding cool.

"I thought you might want to get together for breakfast. We could go over our notes from last night."

"Now?"

"What's wrong with now?"

"Correct me if I'm wrong, but didn't you ask me to keep you away from Lover Boy?"

"Who's Lover Boy?" she replied, fully aware who he was talking about.

"You know who."

"Jonas," she said lightly, "if I wasn't sure you were straight, I'd *definitely* think you fancied him."

"That's not even remotely funny."

"Can we go get something to eat? I'm starving."

"We're on location at Paradise Cove today."

"I know, so I was thinking about brunch at the Ivy at the Shore. Then we can go over to the location early."

"I'll meet you there."

"Can't you pick me up?" She couldn't resist a small dig. "That way I won't be tempted to go off with Lover Boy, will I?"

"Fifteen minutes."

"Make it ten."

"You're impossible."

"See ya."

"Get me the *Post* and the *Daily News*," Lola ordered Big Jay over the intercom. "Now please."

Big Jay immediately took off.

She couldn't wait to see what the morning news would bring. She was lying in bed thinking about the previous night's dinner with Linc. He'd been *so* drunk. She'd heard that he was a drinker, but it wasn't until last night that he'd exhibited his addiction.

She stretched and leaned over to switch on the phone. It started ringing right away.

"There's a Miss Margolis on the line," the hotel operator informed her.

"Put her through."

"Have you *seen* the papers?" Faye rasped.

"No, Faye," she said faintly. "I only just opened my eyes."

"Your picture's on the front pages again."

"That's impossible," she said, yawning. "Tony's in New Orleans. He doesn't get back until today."

"I'm not talking about you and Tony," Faye said grimly. "It's you and your very *married* costar."

"My costar?" she said innocently.

"Linc Blackwood."

"Me and Linc?" she said, feigning surprise. "You must be kidding? Could it be they sneaked a photographer onto the set while we were working?"

"No, Lola," Faye said brusquely. "Apparently you were out to dinner with Mr. Blackwood last night. They have the two of you kissing outside the restaurant. That touching scenario is all over the front pages."

"Oh, no," Lola said, pretending to be dismayed. "We might have exchanged a friendly peck on the cheek. I never saw any photographers."

"Don't bullshit a bullshitter," Faye growled. "This is a real kiss. And it's *not* good publicity, especially after last weekend's press."

"I thought all publicity was good publicity," Lola said, tongue in cheek. "Y'know, as long as they spell my name right."

"May I remind you that you're *supposed* to be getting a divorce," Faye said. "First you're caught with Tony Alvarez, now it's Linc Blackwood. This kind of publicity makes you look like a tramp."

"*I* think it enhances my reputation," Lola said.

"*What* reputation?" Faye responded sourly.

"Aren't I the Latina sex bomb that every man wants to sleep with?" she said with a knowing laugh. Big Jay knocked on the door. "Come in," she called. He entered the room and handed her the papers. "I'm looking at the photos now, Faye. I'll get back to you."

"Do that," Faye said in her smoke-enhanced voice. "The press are driving me crazy for a statement."

"Tell them this. Linc Blackwood and I are merely costars. We were discussing our script."

"I'm sure they'll believe *that,*" Faye said curtly, and hung up.

Lola checked out the papers. There she was on the front page of both of them. The *Daily News* ran a headline that screamed, LA LOLA! DOES IT AGAIN! The *Post*'s headline was LOLA AND LINC TOGETHER? WHERE'S SHELBY?

She studied the pictures. The kiss worked perfectly. Linc's eyes were closed; the man certainly looked like he was having a fine time.

She wondered how he'd feel when he got an eyeful of these photos. Not too happy.

Ha! His wife had some innocent picture in *People,* and here *he* was on the front page of the *Post* and the *Daily News,* kissing Lola Sanchez. She didn't give his marriage much chance.

Mission accomplished.

So why didn't she feel better about it?

Because he'd been too easy, that's why. Where was the satisfaction in bringing down a guy who was obviously a total screwup?

It was all his wife's fault. He was pissed about her movie, pissed about her brilliant reviews, and pissed that her photo was in a magazine with another man. *That's* why he'd turned into a falling-down drunk.

He certainly wasn't the man he'd been six years ago. The macho movie star stud she would've done anything for. The man who'd obliterated her chances of ever giving birth.

Maybe Shelby Cheney didn't *want* to stay married to Linc Blackwood; that was a thought.

The phone rang again. This time it was Tony. "Hey, baby," he crooned, sending shivers down her spine.

The sound of his voice made her realize how much she missed him. "When are you coming back?" was her first question.

"Not soon enough," he said calmly. "I guess you've seen the New York papers?"

"Yes, I know, it's so ridiculous, Tony. There were ten other people with us. Linc was drunk, he grabbed me outside the restaurant, and *that's* what ends up in the papers. You know how those things go."

"Shit happens, baby," he said, not sounding at all upset.

"You're not mad?"

"Why should I be? I had a girl here."

"You did?" she said, shocked.

"Yeah. It wasn't happenin' for me, so I put her on a plane back to L.A."

"What girl?" Lola asked, suddenly furious.

"The foxy chick I was about t' get engaged to when you came runnin' back."

Now she was totally outraged. "Are you telling me she was in New Orleans with you?"

"Sure, baby."

"You left *my* bed to fly to New Orleans to be with some *puta?*" Lola yelled, stunned that he would do that. "I can't *believe* you'd be with another woman."

"So you're sayin' it's fine for your photo to be all over the papers with another man? But me—I gotta keep it down, huh?"

"I explained to you what that was all about."

"This our first fight, baby?" Tony said,

laughing. " 'Cause if it is, I think it's turnin' me on."

"Get your ass *back* here," she said, quickly backing down. "I'm working this afternoon, but tonight I'm all yours."

"An' that's exactly the way it *should* be," said Mr. Sure of Himself.

Linc didn't remember a thing, not one fucking thing. He staggered off the bed, fully dressed, red-eyed and sick to his stomach. He just about made it into the bathroom, where he caught sight of himself in the mirror. As usual, after a major bender he looked like crap.

Drinking fucked up his mind, his body, *and* his soul.

Christ! What happened last night? As far as he could recall, he'd taken Lola to Mario's, Mama Mario had been all over him, and that was it. The rest was a blank. He couldn't remember a goddamn thing.

Blackouts were dangerous shit.

It was all because of Shelby and the stupid photo of her in a magazine with some asshole she'd gone out with years ago. Why had that upset him so much?

Because the asshole was Pete, that's

why. And Pete was desperate to fuck with him.

He made his way into the living room and picked up the call sheet from the desk. One o'clock. By one o'clock he had to be looking human. *Yeah, lots of luck.*

What time was Shelby arriving from L.A.? He'd forgotten. Maybe five or six, something like that.

He spied an empty bottle of scotch and a dirty glass. He called maid service and ordered them to send somebody in to clean up. Then he forced himself back into the bathroom and stood under a cold shower for ten minutes.

By the time he emerged, he was ready for his first snort of coke.

Getting high meant he'd feel better, and it sure beat the hell out of drinking.

No more drinking.

Carefully he laid out the white powder and snorted a couple of lines. Without warning his nose started to bleed. He hurried into the bathroom and grabbed a damp washcloth, holding it to his nose.

Jesus Christ! What was happening to him? He was falling to pieces.

As soon as the bleeding stopped, he

paged his dealer and told him to come right over. Then he called room service and ordered eggs, bacon, and a Bloody Mary to take away the fuzziness.

A half hour later the room service waiter delivered breakfast.

The sight of food made his stomach turn; the only thing he could manage to get down was the Bloody Mary.

Soon after that his dealer arrived, a smarmy real estate agent with a know-it-all attitude. Linc wanted him in and out, but the man always attempted to stay around and talk. Unfortunately, he had to deal with him personally; it was safer that way.

They exchanged pleasantries, money, and coke, and after the guy left, Linc went into the bedroom and lay on top of the bed until it was time to leave for the studio.

Lola greeted him in the makeup trailer. "You're late," she said in her low-down, throaty voice. "And Tony is pissed about our photo."

"What photo?" he said, not in the mood for light conversation.

"You haven't seen the newspapers?" she said, drawing him over to a corner where they couldn't be overheard.

"No, I haven't seen the goddamn newspapers," he growled. "What's the deal?"

"I've no idea who alerted the photographers, but they were there when we left the restaurant last night. And let me remind you—*you* were feeling no pain. You pulled me into a clinch in front of them." A long beat. "It upset me, Linc. That's why I had Big Jay put you in a cab. You were impossible. I couldn't deal with you."

"You put me in a cab?" he said, hardly believing she would do such a thing.

"I had to."

"Great! I was suffering from some kind of twenty-four-hour *flu,* an' *you* put me in a cab. Thanks a lot for caring."

"It wasn't the flu, Linc. You drank too much."

"I hardly drink, Lola," he said, stone-faced.

"Last night you did. Tony's furious about the photo; he's threatening to beat you up."

"I could throw Tony Alvarez in a grinder and make mincemeat out of him."

"You can't blame him. Tony's a Latino man and I *am* his woman."

"Jesus Christ!" Linc groaned, his head pounding.

Everything was going from bad to worse, and the last thing he felt like doing was acting. Light romantic comedy was not his genre. He wanted to get back to doing what he excelled at. Action adventure. At least in action movies he didn't have to endure endless close-ups and turn on the charm.

"I'll see you on the set," Lola murmured.

Bitch! They were all bitches.

CHAPTER
26

Merrill Zandack was in a talkative mood. Shelby had hoped to have time to herself on the plane, but when the host was aboard, conversation became a necessary occupation—one of the hazards of flying privately.

The moment she got on board, Merrill invited her to join him at the round table he always sat at. She could hardly refuse, in spite of the heavy cigar smoke swirling around him, which made her feel slightly sick. After takeoff, he handed her a stack of press reviews of her movie *Rapture* in a leather folder embossed with her name and the date. "Had 'em put together in case you haven't seen them all," he said.

"How thoughtful of you, Merrill," she said, accepting the folder. "You shouldn't have."

"I know how most producers treat the actresses in their movies. Your P.R. shows you this, the studio shows you that. Problem is you never get to see everything. Read and learn."

"Learn what?" she asked curiously.

"Learn that you're at the peak of your career, the place every actor dreams about—the big one."

"The big one?"

"Yeah. For Tom Cruise it was *Risky Business.* Julia Roberts—*Pretty Woman.* For you it's *Rapture.* From here on out, every other movie you make, you'll have to live up to your performance in *Rapture.*"

"Wonderful," she said dryly. "Why does that make me feel so depressed?"

"It's not a bad thing, Shelby," he said, indulging in a short coughing fit. *"Caught* is the right kind of movie for you to do now. Halle Berry followed *Monster's Ball* with a

Bond movie; now *that* was an excellent choice."

"Are you saying that I can never live up to my performance in *Rapture?*"

"No, I'm sayin' that you gotta take advantage of this time. You're married to a famous man, you gotta make sure he doesn't try to hold you down."

"Linc would *never* do that," she said confidently. "He encourages me."

"You say that *now*. But I *know* what's likely to happen."

"You do?"

"There's gonna be professional jealousy," Merrill said, nodding to himself. "It's only human nature."

"Not between me and Linc."

"I've been in this business a long time, kiddo. When husband and wife are both actors, an' one does better than the other, it *always* gets tricky."

"Linc's not at all jealous of me."

"He's never had to deal with you being more successful than him."

"I'm *not,*" she said, frowning.

"Wait until you get your nomination," Merrill said, blowing a stream of acrid smoke into the cabin.

"*What* nomination?" Shelby asked, perplexed.

"You heard it from me first. You'll get nominated for *Rapture,* that's a given."

"It would certainly be a great honor; however, I'm not at all sure."

"Wanna bet money on it?"

"I don't bet, Merrill."

"Be smart—listen to what I'm telling you. Watch out."

"For *what?*"

"For Linc, goddamn it. He's your biggest enemy right now. One way or the other he'll try to sabotage you."

She'd had enough. The last thing she needed to hear was Merrill Zandack's view on her husband's behavior.

"Will you excuse me, Merrill?" she said, getting up from the table. "I think I'll try and take a nap. Do you mind?"

"Unhappy with what I'm saying, huh?" he said, his double chins bobbing up and down. "Can't say I blame you."

"It's not that," she said, making excuses. "I'm tired. I've had an incredibly busy week."

"Read your reviews. It'll make you feel better."

"Thanks," she said, moving to a seat as far away from him as possible.

After an early lunch at the Ivy at the Shore, Jonas seemed more like himself.

"You were *very* uptight last night," Cat remarked, nibbling a chocolate chip cookie. "Did you have a problem?"

"No problem."

"Maybe you miss being Merrill's assistant," she teased.

"That's a given."

"There's no way you can go back to your old assistant job. After we wrap you must insist to Merrill that he put you on all his future movies."

"You think he'd do that?" Jonas asked tentatively.

"Why not? After all, I'm sure he calls you twice a day to check up on me. Am I right?"

"Of course he does."

"And what do you tell him?"

"That you're a genius."

"Thanks," she said, with a mischievous grin. "Exactly what I wanted to hear."

"Did you speak to Jump this morning?"

"Yeah, his latest threat is to throw all my stuff out onto the street."

"What're you doing about that?"

"A few months ago my girlfriend Luanne was staying at our loft with her baby. I'll call her, ask her to do me a favor and pack up my stuff."

"Sounds like an idea."

"I guarantee Jump'll claim all our CDs and books, which is a drag 'cause *I* bought most of them."

"Perhaps you've heard of Tower Records and Book Soup?" he said offhandedly. "Not to mention Amazon?"

"You're so practical, Jonas. That's what I like about you."

"So now it's my practicality you like?"

"Nothing wrong with being practical," she said, taking another chocolate chip cookie. "Now, all we've got to do is find you a girl-friend, 'cause all work and no play—"

"You can talk," he interrupted.

"I've no time for a guy."

"That makes two of us."

"What? *You've* no time for a guy either?"

"She's such a joker."

"I try to keep it real," she said, signaling for the check.

They left the restaurant and drove to the location early. Cat stood around conferring with some of her crew who were already there. Then she went into her trailer and continued working on her storyboards.

After a while there was a knock, and Nick put his head around the door. "Hey," he said, all tousled hair and cocky grin, cigarette glued to his bottom lip. "Didja enjoy yourself last night?"

"You've got some interesting friends," she offered.

"Yeah, I do, don't I? We all moved to L.A. at the same time. I was the one who got lucky, which means that right now *I'm* the one pickin' up everyone's tab. The second they make it, it'll be their turn."

"Sounds fair."

"What didja think of the girls?"

"Lovely," she said, vaguely sarcastic. "Which one got unlucky? Oops, sorry! I mean lucky."

"Both of them," he boasted.

"Did you have enough to go round?"

"Seems like you haven't heard about my reputation," he said with a knowing wink.

"Is it as big as you seem to think it is?" she retorted.

"Wanna find out?"

"No thanks."

He chain-lit another cigarette. "How long you and your old man been split?"

"Not that long. Why?"

"You caught him with another girl, right?"

"I'm not sharing the details."

"You gotta be feeling *way* horny."

"Excuse me?"

"I *said,* you must be feeling horny."

"Y'know what, Nick?" she said impatiently. "I'm trying to work here."

"Got it," he said with another jaunty wink. "See you on the set."

Somehow Shelby harbored a romantic fantasy that Linc would be at the airport to meet her. Unfortunately, her romantic fantasy was exactly that—a fantasy. There was no Linc. Instead there was a car and driver who delivered her to the hotel.

Flying always made her anxious; she was tired, and hoped that Linc had not made any plans for that evening.

The manager of the hotel was waiting in the lobby to greet her. "We are delighted you will be staying with us this weekend, Ms. Cheney."

"Please call me Mrs. Blackwood," she

said as he helped her with her hand luggage.

"Certainly, Mrs. Blackwood. Your husband is enjoying his stay with us. I hope you will too. We do our best to please."

"I'm sure you do."

"If you're ready, I'll escort you up to Mr. Blackwood's suite."

The suite was large and luxurious. Linc wasn't there; he was probably still working. Shelby didn't mind because she wanted to take a shower and freshen up before she saw him.

A knock on the door brought a bellboy with flowers and a huge basket of fruit.

For a moment she thought the flowers were from Linc, but the note accompanying them was a welcome gesture from the producer of *Rapture.*

She tipped the bellboy and began to unpack. When she'd finished, she took a shower and put on a simple white dress, one of Linc's favorites.

For a moment she thought about calling his cell phone, then decided not to bug him. When Linc was working, he hated being disturbed.

He'd be there soon enough, and she'd be waiting.

"I'm coming right up," Tony announced.

"I thought we were on our way out," Lola responded. "I'm all dressed and ready."

"No, I wanna come up," Tony said insistently.

She'd recently got off the phone with her mother, always a downer. Mama was so damn critical of her relationship with Tony. It almost made her want to marry him and *really* piss the family off. Not that he'd asked her since they'd gotten back together. But if she really wanted him to, he would.

Hmm . . . Mrs. Tony Alvarez. Sounded good. Or how about Lola Sanchez Alvarez? Even better.

She checked herself out in the mirror. She had on a tight scarlet dress plunging in the front, Jimmy Choo stilettos, ruby chandelier earrings, and her hair was wild and sexy, the way Tony liked it.

Big Jay hovered in the lobby of her suite. "Mr. Alvarez is on his way up," she informed him. "When he gets here, make yourself scarce."

"Sure, Ms. Lola, I'll be outside if you need me."

"Thanks, you always know what I want, don't you?"

Big Jay let loose with a rare smile. He'd been Lola Sanchez's personal security for two years and he savored every minute. Who wouldn't?

Tony entered smiling, looking sharp in a white suit and black shirt. "Music, babe. I'm in the mood for Marc Anthony."

"I'm *always* in the mood for Marc Anthony," she said, smiling back at him.

"You, my sexy little witch, look *hot.* Guess who was on my mind in New Orleans? An' believe me—there's some freako babes in that city."

"Not to mention the imported babe you had with you. You're such a bastard!"

"I kicked her to the curb *real* fast."

"I should hope so."

"C'mere, Lola Lola, lemme take a long look at you." She sashayed toward him. "Get me vodka," he ordered.

"Do I *look* like the room service waiter?" she asked imperiously.

"Get me one of those bottles from the minibar."

"Why?"

" 'Cause I'm gonna suck it off your fine nipples, baby. Go to it."

"Tony!" she exclaimed. "I'm all dressed and ready to go out. I thought we were planning to salsa the night away."

"We're gonna salsa the night away, all right," he said with a wolflike grin. "Only first I gotta have those nipples in my mouth, so go fetch the vodka. Go, girl, go!"

"No, Tony," she said stubbornly. "You'll spill it on my dress."

"Do it!" he said darkly. "That's an order, woman."

There was something exciting about a man who wouldn't take no for an answer. She did as he asked, fetching a miniature bottle of vodka from the minibar.

As she walked back toward him, she realized that she was already sexually aroused. Tony had a way of turning her on like no other man.

He took the vodka from her, and with a practiced flick of his wrist undid the halter on her dress, peeling it down until her breasts were exposed.

"You're such a *bad* boy," she said, catching her breath.

"You got the finest tits in the world," he said admiringly. "Take everythin' off."

She didn't need asking twice. Wriggling out of the tight material, she placed her dress carefully on the back of the couch.

The shades were not drawn. She didn't care who was watching, it was all good.

Naked, apart from a black lace thong, she pressed her body against his.

"You're somethin', babe," he said, thrusting his fingers into the delicate sides of her thong and pulling it down. "Look at you with your shaved pussy and your big juicy tits. You do it for me, babe. Every time. I wanna see you in nothing but diamonds and high heels. My baby was made for Bling Bling. That's it." Grinning, he opened the bottle of vodka with his teeth. Then slowly he began pouring the cold liquid over her bare breasts, sucking and licking it off.

She came almost immediately.

Tony Alvarez was surely the sexiest man in the entire world.

CHAPTER
27

Linc did not trust himself to go back to the hotel. They'd finished filming for the day, but he had no urge to leave his trailer. Instead he snorted a few more lines of coke, before deciding that one drink was a necessity. Too bad if Shelby discovered he'd been drinking; she was hardly in a position to criticize.

He hoped she hadn't seen the New York papers. Tomorrow they'd be old news, somebody's cat litter.

He was still furious about the photo in

People and about her movie, which everyone seemed to be talking about. And he hadn't forgotten the *USA Today* story where she'd trashed him.

The more angry he became, the more he felt like another drink. After a couple of scotches and a swish of mouthwash, he finally got into his car and had his driver take him to the hotel.

When he entered the suite, he discovered Shelby asleep on the couch.

He stared at her for a moment, unable to take his eyes off her. She was so beautiful all curled up and innocent.

Shame she was such a devious bitch.

He didn't know whether to wake her or let her sleep. Jesus! She had his stomach tied up in knots.

Was this what love was all about? If it was—you could shove it.

"What're you doing tonight?" Nick asked.

"Why?" Cat responded.

They were sitting around on the beach while her cinematographer was busy setting up the next shot.

Nick picked up a handful of pebbles and

began hurling them at the sea. "Thought you might fancy goin' back to Ago."

"Maybe," she said tentatively.

"Should I take that as a yes?"

"Hmm . . . I'm not sure that watching you put the moves on a couple of babes is my idea of a thrilling time."

"No big deal," he said offhandedly. "The offer's there if you want it. We get together every night, usual table."

"Every night?"

"Yeah, it's like my hangout," he said, scooping up more pebbles. "By the way, my friend Max was kinda into you."

"Which one was Max?"

"The dude with the glasses. He writes for *Rolling Stone.* He's envious of you, thinks you pulled a lucky break."

"Of course he'd think that," she said scornfully. "Hard work and talent had absolutely nothing to do with it."

"He was quite into your movie too—the one you did before. What was it called?"

"Wild Child."

"Never got around to seeing it myself, but the word on it was seriously good."

"I'm surprised you accepted me as your director if you hadn't seen my movie."

"I trust Merrill's judgment. He gave me my first break."

"Did he also force you to give him a blow job?"

Nick threw her a quizzical look. *"What* did you just say?"

"Nothing," she said, grinning. "It's an inside joke."

"Oh yeah, I heard the rumor. He makes all the females in his movies give him blow jobs before they get the job, right?"

"That's what they say."

"How about you, then?"

"Get serious. Do I *look* like the kind of girl he'd come on to? My movie was called *Wild Child;* that should give you a hint."

"All about you, was it?"

"There were pieces of me in it, yeah."

"So, uh, Cat—tell me," he said, rubbing his stubbled chin. "What kind of a wild child *were* you?"

"You name it, I did it."

"You were a raver, then?"

She smiled mysteriously. "Wouldn't *you* like to know."

The script supervisor interrupted them, conferring with Cat about a problem with a line of dialogue. Cat jumped up, solved the problem, and began walking back toward the action.

Nick got up and followed her. "You gotta come tonight," he urged. "We'll make it a party. Bring Jonah if you want."

"It's *Jonas*," she corrected.

"Is he a fag?"

"Why would you ask that?"

"He's always so kind of, y'know, neat and groomed."

"Jonas is not gay."

"You screwed him, then?"

"None of your bloody business."

"God," he said amiably. "You're a cranky one today."

"You shouldn't ask so many personal questions."

"Sorry, I'll get myself in front of the camera an' see if I can nail this scene for you."

She watched him walk ahead of her with his cocky strut. He was immediately joined by the makeup girl and one of the female P.R.'s.

Popular stud, Nick Logan. And didn't he know it.

She was worried about her possessions in New York; the problem was that Jump was spiteful enough to follow through on his threat. He hated not getting his own way.

Since she still had a few minutes before they were finished setting up the camera tracks, she called her girlfriend Luanne.

"Where are you?" Luanne asked, happy to hear from her.

"In L.A., directing a movie."

"That's cool."

"The not so cool part is that Jump and I have split."

"Crap!" Luanne exclaimed. "What happened?"

"I'll tell you when I see you. Here's the thing—Jump's on his way back to New York, and he's threatening to dump my stuff on the street, so I need a favor."

"Go ahead."

"Can you organize professional packers to box up my clothes, manuscripts, and other stuff? I'll e-mail you a list, then have them ship everything to me in L.A."

"Of course," Luanne said. A long beat. "Did you catch Jump with another woman?"

"What makes you think that?"

"Well . . . when I stayed at the loft, I put in a nanny cam—one of those small hidden cameras that keeps an eye on Nanny while she's watching the baby."

"So?"

"When I moved out I forgot to take the camera. You were in London and Jump had gone off to Atlanta for a gig. There were a few days in between me leaving the apartment and coming back for the camera."

"Go on."

"I played the nanny tape, and on it was Jump banging some blonde." An awkward pause. "Sorry."

"Why are you telling me this now?"

"I didn't think it was fair to mention it before."

"What if I caught *your* husband banging some blonde?" Cat said vehemently. "Would *you* think it was fair for me *not* to tell *you?*"

"I was waiting until I saw you."

She sighed. It wasn't Luanne's fault; no good blaming her. "Thanks for telling me anyway," she said. "It simply confirms that I'm doing the right thing."

"I'm *really* sorry, Cat."

"Yeah," she said ruefully. "So am I."

* * *

Sex with Tony seemed to get more amazing every time. No games. Just mind-blowing sex with one hugely sexy Latino man. God! He turned her on big time!

By the time Lola redid her hair and makeup it was almost midnight.

They left the hotel, settled into Tony's limo, and set off for a tour of the salsa clubs, neither of them feeling any pain.

Tony broke open a bottle of Cristal in the car and poured two glasses. "Got a question," he said, handing her one.

"What?" she asked, taking a sip of champagne.

"Didja sleep with that Linc Blackwood dude?"

"Did *you* sleep with that *puta* you flew into New Orleans?" she countered.

"You first," he said, dark eyes ever watchful.

"No." A long pause. "I could've, but I didn't."

"Me neither," he said, clinking glasses with her. "Here's the deal, baby girl—you've damn near ruined me for other women."

"I have?" she said, delighted.

"Yeah, babe. You're the shit, an' that's the way it is."

She leaned forward, cupping his face in her hands, her tongue flicking lightly over his lips before grabbing his crotch with her right hand. "Mine," she said fervently. *"All mine. You stick it in anyone else, Tony Alvarez, and I swear to God I'll cut it off."*

"Oooh, scary, woman," Tony said, throwing his head back and roaring with laughter.

"Yes, I am. And don't you *ever* forget it."

"Wake up," Linc said, not so gently pushing Shelby's shoulder.

She slowly uncurled her body. "Oh," she said, yawning. "I must've fallen asleep. I wasn't sure what time you'd be back, so I put on the TV and that was it. Instant sleeping pill."

He noticed that she had on one of his favorite dresses and her hair was loose around her shoulders. She looked so damn beautiful.

She reached her arms up to bring him closer so she could kiss him. He responded. "I missed you," she murmured. "I'm so happy to be here."

It was quite apparent that she had *not* seen the New York papers.

He pulled her up, holding her close to him for a minute.

"I've decided that separations are no good," she said. "In future I'm turning down any movies that take me away from you."

He didn't believe her; she was merely saying that to appease him. She'd probably seen her photo with Pete in *People* and was wondering what kind of lies to feed him.

Her lips were soft against his. Arousal was automatic.

Details of last night began coming back. Lola Sanchez was a prize prick tease. She'd gotten him hot and drunk in the restaurant, then left him high and dry. Typical female behavior. He hated all of them.

"Love you," Shelby whispered. "Missed you."

Yeah. Sure you did. Especially when you were out with Pete.

Without saying a word he went for her breasts, caressing them roughly.

She was startled. "Can't we wait until we're in the bedroom?"

"No," he said abruptly. "I've waited long enough." Then he did the unthinkable. He ripped her dress—the dress that he liked so much—off her body.

Now she was shocked. "What's the matter with you?" she protested.

"Can't I miss my own wife?" he said, pushing her down on the couch, unzipping his pants, and mounting her. No foreplay, no kissing, just straight to it. Something like her big sex scene in *Rapture.*

She had a strong urge to fight him off, tell him he had to wait. But he was giving her no choice as he plunged inside her.

Furiously he went at her, desperately trying to rid himself of the anger that surged through him.

When he was finished, he zipped up and walked into the bedroom.

Shelby lay there, feeling used and abused, trying to figure out what had just happened. Then it occurred to her that, of course, he'd been drinking.

A feeling of dread enveloped her. Slowly she got up, went into the bathroom, and put on a terry-cloth robe she found hanging behind the door.

"What's going on, Linc?" she asked, wrapping the robe tightly around her as she confronted him in the bedroom. "What was *that* all about?"

He was sitting on the edge of the bed

smoking a cigarette. She glanced around to see if she could spy any booze. Nothing visible. Oh, God! Why had she thought he could be trusted?

"*You* tell *me*," he said, his voice hard.

"About what?"

"Isn't there something I should know?"

Instantly she realized that somehow or other he'd found out about Pete. Damn! She should have told him herself.

"Nothing I can think of," she said, adding a casual "I've been busy filming, doing press, that kind of thing." A short pause. "Oh yes, and guess what? There's an old friend of yours working on my movie. Actually, he's an old friend of *ours*."

"Yeah? Who?" Linc said, his eyes cold and distant.

"Pete," she answered. "He sends you his best regards. Can't wait for us all to get together."

"Can't wait, huh?"

"That's right," she said evenly.

"What's he *doing* on your movie, Shelby?"

"Actually he's the stunt coordinator."

"Big coincidence," Linc said with a bitter

twist to his words. "Wonder how he got *that* job."

"You always used to say that Pete was one of the best stuntmen in the business."

"Then I suppose you didn't have to put in a good word for him?"

"What *are* you talking about?"

"I'm *talking* about the photo of the two of you in *People.*"

"There's a photo?" she said, truly surprised.

"Seems you didn't realize you were being watched coming out of Jerry's Deli all tight and cozy together with *his* arm all over you."

"Oh."

"Yeah. Oh." An ominous beat. "What the *fuck* were you thinking? You've made me look like the biggest jerk walking." Another long beat. "Did you screw him?"

"How dare you," she said, blushing a deep red.

"How *dare* I?" he yelled. "What the *fuck* am I *supposed* to think?"

"He's coaching me to do a car stunt; we were discussing it. Lunch was perfectly innocent."

"I don't get you," Linc said harshly.

"What don't you get?"

"You know me well enough, right?"

"Yes."

"Exactly how *did* you *think* I'd react?"

She did not wish this conversation to go any further, but it seemed like she had no choice.

"I had no idea there'd be a photo in a magazine," she said, hoping to put an end to it.

"No idea, huh?" he sneered. "You're starring in a high profile *porno* movie, and you have no idea that the paparazzi might be following you?"

"*Rapture* is not a porno movie, Linc."

His voice got louder. "You're stupid, Shelby, you know that—you're really fuckin' *dumb*. First the *USA Today* piece, now this. Goddamn it, you're an *idiot*. And you're making *me* look like one too."

Now she knew for sure that he'd been drinking. He *never* insulted her and called her names unless he was drunk; it was only then that his venom bubbled to the surface and he turned mean and verbally abusive.

She couldn't stop herself from asking, although she knew what his answer would be. He'd deny it. He always did. "Are you drinking again?" she ventured.

"Fuck you!" he screamed, losing it altogether. "Do I *look* like I'm drinking?"

Yes, you do. Your eyes are bloodshot, your skin is blotchy, and you look horrible.

She was silent. His rages could get out of control. He'd never hit her, but Brenda had warned her that it *could* happen one day.

"If I *was* drinking, which I'm fuckin' *not, you* would've driven me to it," he said, giving her a hate-filled glare.

"I'm sorry," she said quietly.

"Here's what you're gonna do," he said, his voice rising again. "You're gonna walk off the goddamn movie."

"I can't do that."

"Call L.A., tell 'em you're not coming back."

"That's impossible," she protested. "I've already shot several days."

"Do it, Shelby," he said harshly. "Or get the fuck outta my life."

"You're being unreasonable."

"I'm being unreasonable?" he yelled. "Screw *you."*

"Linc," she said, close to tears, "if I walk off the movie, it'll ruin my career."

"Then *don't* walk," he said, his eyes glittering feverishly. "Tell 'em they have to fire Pete. And they'd better do it right now."

"What?"

"That's the way it's gonna be. Either *you* walk, or *he* gets booted." Another ominous beat. "Am I making myself clear?"

CHAPTER
28

Lola was well aware that every man in the Latin supper club was lusting after her as she sensuously danced with one of the professional dancers who were on hand to accommodate the patrons.

Tony was sitting back in a leopard-print booth with his cronies, swigging champagne, while enjoying the show. She couldn't help noticing that several women were paying plenty of attention to him. It didn't bother her. He was hers, all hers.

She swiveled her hips to the salsa sound,

feeling sexy, hot, and totally satisfied. Her body writhed to the pulsating beat of the music. She was controlled, yet out of control at the same time. *I should've been a dancer,* she thought. *I've got it down.*

Tony waved. He was laughing, having a great time as he watched her dance just for him.

Then into the club walked Tyrell White, an ex–world champion heavyweight boxer. Tyrell spotted her immediately; they'd met briefly once. Enough for him to come over and attempt to join her on the dance floor.

Shoving the professional dancer out of the way, he began grinding his crotch into hers.

Before she had time to react, Tony was on his feet, forcing his way through the other dancers until he reached her.

"Back off, jackass," Tony yelled, his eyes dark and dangerous. "This is my lady."

"She ain't nobody's lady," Tyrell sneered. "She's a piece a ass, an' *I'm* dancin' with it."

Tony hauled back and slugged Tyrell, who immediately retaliated with a right hook that sent Tony flying to the ground.

Lola started screaming at Tyrell, and within seconds a general fight broke out.

Tony's bodyguards were quick to grab him, hustling him out of the club. Big Jay was right beside them. He lifted Lola up as if she were a rag doll, spiriting her from the club.

Once outside, they all piled into Tony's limo, while the flashbulbs popped. The car shot away from the curb, tires squealing.

Tony was angry and cursing, his lip gushing blood. "I'm gonna kill that sonofabitch," he shouted, as Lola attempted to tend to him. "You hear me? I'm gonna *kill* that dumb mothafucker. Nobody messes with Tony Alvarez's woman. *Nobody!*"

"Calm down," Lola said soothingly. "I'm sure he didn't mean it."

"Didn't mean *what?*" Tony screamed.

"Maybe he thought I was alone."

"Jesus holy *Christ!* Whose side are *you* on?" He shoved her away, snatched a wad of Kleenex, and pressed it to his split lip. "That prick's gonna regret he was ever born. You fuckin' *hear* me?"

"Forget about it," Lola said. "It's over."

"Yeah," Tony growled, "you'll *see* how over it is."

*   *   *

Cat had a choice. She could go back to her apartment alone and work, she could hang out with Jonas, or she could join Nick and his friends at Ago.

She was still reeling from the information Luanne had told her over the phone. It meant that even before she'd caught Jump in Australia, he'd been screwing around. Maybe he'd been doing it throughout their entire marriage. What a depressing thought *that* was.

It was crazy the way you could live with someone and not really know them at all. She'd always thought Jump was a straight-up kind of guy, even though he was a rock 'n' roller. She hadn't imagined him poking every skanky groupie who passed his way like the rest of his band. How naive was *she?*

By the time she called "Cut" for the last time that day, it was late. When Jonas caught her on her way out and asked her if she was up to grabbing a bite, she said no. But on the drive home, after listening to several tracks of an Eminem CD, she soon began feeling energized.

There was no food in her apartment, and she had to eat, didn't she? So instead of driving home, she headed for Ago, deciding she'd have a quick snack.

Nick wasn't there when she arrived. The maître d' escorted her to his regular corner table on the outdoor patio.

Some of the faces at the table were familiar, plus a few new ones she didn't know.

A pretty, dark-haired girl wearing huge, owl-like glasses and what appeared to be painter's overalls extended her hand. "I'm Amy," she said. "And you are?"

"Cat Harrison."

"Oh yeah, you're the girl who's directing Nick's movie, right?"

Cat nodded.

"Nick was talking about you the other day," Amy said. "Mentioned you were hot, forgot to mention you were so young."

"Said I was hot, did he?" Cat said, quite amused.

"Hey—we all know Nick. If it walks and breathes, he thinks it's hot."

"What time does he usually get here?" Cat asked, keeping it casual. " 'Cause I gotta eat and run."

"It depends."

"What do *you* do?" Cat asked, wondering if Amy was one of his army of girlfriends.

"Comedian—stand-up,"   Amy   said. "Y'know, I like to get up there in front of an attentive audience and piss men off." She giggled. "You should *see* their faces when I talk about the size of their dicks and all that shit."

"Sounds like I should come see you," said Cat.

"Feel free. I'm at the Improv next week. Nick's putting together a group, maybe you'll tag along."

"Yeah," Cat said, nodding. "I might do that."

By the time Nick arrived, she'd already eaten and was ready to leave. He turned up accompanied by a busty bleached blonde in a tight pink minidress, who looked like she'd recently made a daring escape from the Playboy mansion.

"What the hell is *that?*" Amy muttered.

"I see you've got a new one tonight," Cat remarked, standing up.

"Makes a change," Nick said, running his hands through his unkempt hair. "Where're *you* off to?"

"I ate, had fun—good night."

"Is that it?" he said, looking perplexed.

"That's it," she said, checking out his date one more time.

"Meet Mindy," he said, putting his arm around the girl in the pink leather dress and squeezing tight. "Mindy's an old friend. Used to be a stripper at Scores in New York. That's where we met."

"Cozy," Cat said. "Was she naked at the time?"

"Mindy's tryin' to make it in porno out here," he said, ignoring her crack. "I think she's got a good chance, don't you?"

"I'm sure she'll be very successful," Cat said, wondering if he was serious. "See you Monday," she added, walking out.

Abandoning Mindy and her dreams of porno stardom, Nick followed Cat to the parking lot. "What're your plans for the weekend?" he asked, scratching his stubbled chin.

"Sleep and work."

"Wanna catch a movie?"

"Don't think so."

"Wanna meet here tomorrow night?"

"No thanks."

"How come no thanks?"

"It's not my scene."

"What's not your scene?"

"Busty blond bimbo strippers looking to be porn stars. I have nothing to say to them."

"Don't tell me you're jealous?"

She laughed derisively as her car arrived. "Get a life, Nick," she said, handing the valet five dollars and jumping into her car.

"I'll call you," he yelled as she revved the engine and drove off.

She didn't head home. On a sudden impulse she drove straight to LAX and bought a ticket on the red-eye to New York. Who needed Luanne when she could handle Jump's threat herself? Plus she was desperate to see the videotape that Luanne was holding.

She was so glad she'd found out about Jump before she'd gotten pregnant or something ridiculous like that.

Her husband was a serial cheater.

Not good news.

And *definitely* not for her.

Shelby couldn't sleep all night. Linc had given her an ultimatum and she was not good with ultimatums. One meaningless photo in a magazine, and he was acting as if she'd run off to Acapulco with Pete and indulged in a weeklong affair.

She planned to call her therapist and ask her what she should do, but unfortunately Brenda had recently changed her home number, and she did not have the new one with her.

Linc's ultimatum was totally unreasonable; she was sure Brenda would agree.

Linc had not come to bed; he'd stayed in the living room watching TV all night, probably drinking himself into a stupor.

One thing was for sure, she had no intention of walking off her movie, and even less intention of requesting that Pete get fired.

Linc had put her in an impossible situation. She absolutely refused to comply with either of his ludicrous edicts.

The following morning when her alarm went off, she slipped out of bed, put on a tracksuit, and took the elevator to the tenth floor, where another suite had been booked for the stylist and hair and makeup people who were getting her ready for the *Rapture* press junket.

Kara, the studio publicist with the crinkly red hair and funky tinted glasses, was waiting to greet her. "This won't be too bad,"

Kara assured her, far too cheerful for 7 A.M. "You waltzed through the last one."

"It's always difficult," Shelby replied, settling into the makeup chair. "I dread every interview—it's such an unnatural thing to have to do, talking about myself for eight straight hours."

Spying a copy of *People,* she picked it up, searching for the photo of her and Pete. She found it and checked it out. It was a perfectly tame photo, nothing for Linc to get so upset about.

"How about your reviews?" Kara said, handing her a cup of coffee. "Pretty impressive, huh?"

"Merrill Zandack gave them to me on the plane. I must say I'm shocked they're so flattering."

"Don't be shocked. You're *fantastic* in the movie."

"Thanks."

"Anyway, here's the thing," Kara said. "I'll be warning every reporter who enters the room that they cannot—under *any* account—mention the photos of Linc with Lola Sanchez."

"What photos?"

"The ones from yesterday's front pages."

Shelby looked blank.

"Oh *God!*" Kara exclaimed. "Don't tell me you haven't seen them?"

"I only flew in last night."

"I'm sure it's nothing," Kara said, obviously embarrassed. "I mean, they're making a movie together, and we all know those kind of photos happen."

"Can I see the papers?" Shelby asked quietly.

"I don't have them, but I can get hold of copies for you." A beat. "Y'know, if you *haven't* seen them, maybe it's better to wait until *after* the junket."

"I think I should know what the journalists are not supposed to mention, don't you?" Shelby said coolly.

"I'll go see what I can find for you," Kara said, scurrying from the room.

The makeup girl approached. Shelby shut her eyes and gave herself up to the process.

So, Linc was screaming about an innocuous photo in *People,* and apparently *his* photo was on the front of the New York papers with Lola Sanchez—something he had *not* bothered mentioning.

She didn't know what was going on, but

whatever it was, she was certain it wasn't good.

The limo deposited Lola back at her hotel.

"I'm not coming up," Tony said, his expression fierce.

"Please, honey," Lola begged. "Let me take care of your lip."

"No," he said, angrily shaking his head. "I'm too pissed."

"It's Friday night," she cajoled. "No early call tomorrow."

He was not to be swayed. "I'll phone you later."

"Why don't I come to *your* hotel?" she suggested, reluctant to leave him alone.

"No, Lola," he said sharply. "I gotta be by myself."

Tony had a dark side. She knew enough not to push him further.

Big Jay escorted her upstairs, and she roamed restlessly around her suite before finally going to bed.

As usual, in the morning when she removed the block from her phone, Faye was first on line.

"Are you single-handedly trying to ruin

your career?" Faye demanded, sounding hoarser than ever.

"What happened now?" she murmured, stifling a yawn.

"A *fight* in a discotheque?" Faye questioned, as if it was the most ludicrous thing she'd ever heard.

"It wasn't a discotheque, it was a club. Discos went out years ago."

"Whatever," Faye said. "There's a photo of you fleeing from a club. Once again you've made the front pages." Lola smiled to herself. *"I* can't keep up with you," Faye droned on, "and *I'm* your publicist. What am I supposed to tell the press now?"

"It wasn't our fault, Faye. Some guy hauled off and hit Tony."

"Some *guy,* Lola?"

"Okay," she said irritably. "So it was Tyrell White. The bastard *attacked* me. What was Tony *meant* to do? He was coming to my defense, Faye. Tony didn't start it."

"I'm running as much damage control as possible," Faye said wearily. "When the tabloids hit, there's *nothing* I can do to protect you. It won't be pretty."

"You'd *better* protect me, Faye," she said sharply. "You're my publicist. You must have relationships with some of those so-called journalists at the rags."

"Some of them, yes; some of them, no. I'll do what I can."

"Fine," Lola said, slamming down the phone.

Big Jay knocked on her bedroom door.

"What?" she said irritably.

"Your sister's here," he said.

"My *sister?*" she said, totally surprised.

Selma pushed past him and entered the bedroom. She was carrying an overnight bag and her cheeks were flushed. "Mama sent me to come talk to you," she announced.

"*Why* would she do that?" Lola demanded, thinking that at least it was Selma—the good sister, not the tittle-tattle star stalker, Isabelle.

"She thinks you need family near you," Selma explained. "Everyone's worried about you, even Matt."

"Matt?" Lola said, frowning. "I told the family that none of you were to have anything more to do with him."

"He's a nice guy, Sis. *You* married him, after all. We can't abandon him."

"He's not being *abandoned,*" Lola said

heatedly. "He's getting plenty of money from me. Believe me, he's in for a healthy settlement. Matt has nothing to complain about."

"It's not all about money, Lucia."

"Yes. It is."

"No. It's not," Selma said stubbornly.

What the hell was Selma doing, sticking her nose in where it didn't belong?

"Can I stay here with you?" Selma asked. "Mama's taken the kids for the weekend."

"Of course you can," Lola said, softening. "Actually, if you stop with the nagging, it's lovely to see you."

"You too, little Sis," Selma said, her face brightening.

Lola jumped out of bed and they exchanged warm hugs.

Later, when Selma was settled in the spare bedroom of the suite, Lola called Tony. He didn't answer.

Great! Now she'd have to hang around the hotel waiting for him to surface. He hadn't phoned her last night, and she was not pleased.

Most men were controllable. Tony wasn't.

Somehow it added to the attraction.

CHAPTER
29

Cat phoned Jonas from Kennedy as she strode through the airport, ignoring the admiring glances from the male population.

"I'm in New York," she announced.

"You're *not,*" he said, like she was playing some kind of bizarre joke on him.

"Yes," she answered matter-of-factly. "I caught the red-eye last night."

"Why did you do that?"

" 'Cause I need to sort things out here for myself."

"You *told* me you had everything organized," he said accusingly.

"I *did,* only something else came up."

"What?"

"Don't question me, Jonas," she said irritably. "Cover for me."

"If Merrill finds out you've left while you're in the middle of shooting his movie, he'll be seriously angry."

"I understand," she said crisply. "That's *exactly* why you're not about to tell anyone, okay?"

"Are you making *me* a coconspirator?"

"Yes."

"I don't want to be a coconspirator."

"Too bad, Jonas. This way you can't run and report everything to Merrill."

"Great! What if something happens and you get delayed—"

"Look," she interrupted. "It's all good. I'll spend the day here, and be on a flight back tonight. It's only Saturday; we don't start work until Monday. Everything's cool. Okay?"

"Why didn't you tell me you were going? I would've come with you."

"It's not like I need help, but thanks anyway," she said, spotting a cab. "I've never had someone I could rely on before."

"I'm here if you need me, Cat."

"Thanks," she said, jumping into the cab and giving the driver Luanne's address. "I'll check in later. I'm leaving Kennedy now, on my way to Luanne's."

"Do *not* get into a fight with Jump," Jonas ordered sternly. "Remember, there's nothing to be gained by losing your temper."

"What makes you think I *have* a temper?"

"I'm sure it's lurking in there somewhere."

She sat back and checked the messages on her cell. Nick had called, which didn't surprise her. Nick was one of those guys who felt it was his duty to sleep with every woman he came in contact with, and he wouldn't be satisfied until he'd closed the deal.

Too bad for him. She was not about to add herself to his considerable list.

She called Luanne to warn her she was on her way. They'd first met in their drug days, both of them zonked out of their heads. Later, when they'd cleaned up their acts, they'd remained friends. Luanne had married the wrong guy, but at least she had a gorgeous baby boy to show for it. Currently she was working as a P.R. girl at a downtown fashion house.

The cabdriver was a maniac. Cat was amazed they arrived unscathed. She paid him, and ran up the steps to Luanne's place.

"You look *great,*" Luanne exclaimed, flinging open the door. She was a flaming redhead with an abundance of freckles and a gummy smile. "I was expecting, y'know, like a haggard *My-husband-is-screwing-around-on-me* total *wreck.*"

"Yes, well, that's *exactly* how I feel," Cat said. "Pathetic, isn't it?"

"You didn't *have* to come," Luanne said, ushering her inside. "I would've dealt with everything for you."

"I had the weekend off. It seemed like a plan."

"You came so that you could see the tape, right?" Luanne said knowingly.

"Right on."

After Cat had fussed over Luanne's baby boy, she and Luanne went into the bedroom, closed the door, and viewed the incriminating videotape of Jump's indiscretion.

Cat stared at the TV screen. The images were incredibly graphic, and incredibly upsetting—especially as all the action took place on their bed.

She tried to keep it together. Crying was for sissies, and she was too tough to break down in front of anyone. Although actually watching her husband screwing someone else was pretty devastating.

"Guess *that* gives me all the ammunition I need for a fast divorce," she sighed, when it was over. "Can I keep the tape?"

"It's all yours," Luanne said, slipping the offending tape out of the VCR.

"What a bastard!" she said fiercely.

"Aren't they all?" Luanne agreed.

Later they took a cab over to the loft to deal with her move. Luckily, when they arrived, Jump was nowhere around.

"The movers are on their way," Luanne said, checking her cell phone. "They should be here any minute."

"I have no clue what to take," Cat said, looking around with a helpless shrug.

"Everything that's yours," Luanne urged. "Ship it *all* to L.A. And since he's not here, take your wedding presents too."

"You think?"

"Don't be an idiot," Luanne said. "Did *he* consider *your* feelings when he screwed that ho in *your* bed? Anyway, you're entitled to the presents from your side of the family."

"I'm not shipping TVs and stereos to L.A.," she said. "I've already bought new ones."

"Then what *are* you taking?" Luanne asked.

"Personal stuff," she said, wishing she didn't have to deal with this. "I'll start with all my manuscripts, then my paintings, and of course my books."

"Okay, girl," Luanne said encouragingly, "get packing."

Before Shelby was ready for her first interview, Kara was able to locate copies of the newspapers from the previous day. Shelby took a look at the photos and failed to understand why Linc was so angry at her. The photo of her and Pete in *People* was nothing compared to the ones of Linc and his sexy costar sharing a passionate kiss.

How could Linc be so vicious, screaming at her about something that was perfectly innocent, while all the time he was obviously enjoying a wild fling with Lola Sanchez?

She wished she could cancel the press day, go back to the suite, and confront him. But that would be totally unprofessional. *The show must go on,* she thought ruefully.

Fortunately, Russell Savage was on hand to calm her down. "Ignore all that garbage you read in the papers," he said. "They're a bunch of bottom feeders, searching for a headline. Linc's making a movie with the broad. It's all about publicity."

"You don't understand, Russell," she said, feeling lost because nobody really understood her dilemma. "He's accusing *me* of something, when it's obvious that *he's* the one doing it."

"Honey," Russell said soothingly, "I'm sure you're correct. Only right now you've got to forget about it and concentrate on selling *our* movie."

"I'm trying to," she said, realizing that as nice as Russell was, his main interest was his movie.

"You should be *so* proud of yourself," Russell said. "Mustn't let this spoil things for you."

Merrill's warning came drifting back to

haunt her. *One way or the other he'll try to sabotage you.*

Was Linc purposely trying to ruin her moment of triumph?

Determinedly she sailed through the day, charming and composed. Only once did someone dare to ask the wrong question, whereupon Kara, who could be quite feisty for such a girly-looking girl, swept the journalist out of the room so quickly that the man barely had time to catch his breath.

At the end of the day Shelby found herself dreading returning to the suite. She had *no* intention of walking off her movie, *or* insisting that Pete get fired.

It was time for a long-overdue confrontation. Linc had pushed her about as far as she was prepared to go.

Livid, because she couldn't reach Tony all day, Lola embarked on a ferocious shopping spree, accompanied by Selma. They covered Saks, Bergdorf, and Barney's. In a generous mood, Lola bought her sister anything she desired.

"I didn't come here to go shopping," Selma protested, loving every minute. "I came because Mama begged me to."

"Mama should stop trying to run my life," Lola insisted, signing an autograph for the salesgirl. "I'm a big girl. I've been out of the house for a long, long time."

"It's the family reputation she's worried about," Selma said. "Mama's upset with the things people are saying about you."

"I don't notice her getting upset when they say *good* things."

"She keeps a scrapbook of all your clippings," Selma revealed.

"She does?" Lola said, surprised.

"Yes, she clips everything, the good *and* the bad."

"Both come with the territory," Lola explained, picking up a white silk scarf and admiring it. "Look at other stars, like Madonna, Jennifer Lopez, and Britney Spears—they're on the cover of some gossip rag every day. One moment they're being called divas, the next they're supposedly into drugs and having sex with multiple men, or they're breaking up marriages. The papers make *terrible* things up. Mama has to realize that it's all a game to them."

"*I* understand," Selma said, nodding. "But surely you can see that Tony is not a good influence on you?"

"You have no idea who Tony is," Lola snapped. "You've never even met him."

"No," Selma replied, refusing to back down. "I've read all about him, though."

"We'll all have dinner tonight," Lola decided. "Then you can see for yourself what a wonderful guy he is."

"Dinner?" Selma said unsurely.

"Yes, *dinner*," Lola answered firmly. "You'll fall in love with him; everyone does."

When they got back to the hotel, Selma sat on the floor in the living room, surrounded by shopping bags.

Lola picked up the phone to check her messages, and automatically switched on the TV.

A pretty brunette newscaster was reading the five-o'clock news.

Ex–world heavyweight boxer Tyrell White was badly beaten outside his apartment last night and robbed of several thousand dollars' worth of cash and jewelry. Earlier in the evening Mr. White was involved in an altercation at a club with film director Tony Alvarez, boyfriend of Lola Sanchez. It is believed Ms. Sanchez was with Mr. Alvarez at the time. Regarding the subsequent beating and robbery, the police have no suspects at the present time.

Lola stared at the TV in total shock. Her hand flew to her mouth. "Oh my God," she exclaimed. *"Oh . . . my . . . God!"*

CHAPTER

30

The original handwritten script of *Wild Child* was the first thing Cat started searching for. It meant a lot to her, and she was not leaving without it.

"How can I help?" Luanne asked, wandering around the spacious loft.

"If you can deal with my clothes and shoes, that would be a big help," Cat said. "Although maybe I should throw some stuff away."

"This is no time to start sorting through

things," Luanne said firmly. "We must concentrate on getting everything out of here."

"Okay, okay. I'll keep looking for my manuscripts and stuff like that, while you organize my clothes."

"What about photographs, CDs, and—"

"All I want are my personal photographs. He can keep everything else."

"You're sure?"

"Absolutely," Cat said, unable to forget the graphic tape of Jump having sex in *their* bed. "I can't believe he did this to me," she said, shaking her head. "The whole time we were together I was totally faithful to him."

"And since you split?"

"*Still* totally faithful. I'm too busy directing my movie for anything else."

"You need to have a revenge fuck," Luanne said. "It'll work like a charm."

"For who?"

"You. Try it, you'll see."

When the professional packers arrived, Luanne steered them into the bedroom and put them to work packing up the clothes from Cat's closet.

Half an hour later there was the sound of a key in the door.

Oh shit! Cat thought. *The last thing I need is to see the cheating asshole.*

Instead of Jump walking in, a girl appeared. A tall, skinny redhead, wearing tight jeans, a white peasant blouse, and Cat's Fendi leather jacket—one of her most prized possessions.

"Oh," the girl said, nonplussed. "What's going on? Where's Jump?"

"Who are *you?*" Cat asked.

"Miranda," the girl said. "More to the point, who are *you?*"

"This happens to be my home," Cat said. "And *you* happen to be wearing *my* jacket."

"Excuse me," Miranda said. "This is Jump's place, and he *gave* me this jacket as a present."

"News flash," Cat said. "Jump is *my* husband, soon-to-be-ex. This is *our* place, soon to be his. And that's *my* jacket, so kindly take it off."

"I don't get it," Miranda said.

"Obviously," Cat retorted.

Luanne emerged from the bedroom. "What's the deal?" she asked, staring at the girl.

And then they both recognized her at

once—even though she'd changed the color of her hair.

She was the girl from the tape. The Jump-having-sex-on-their-bed tape.

After the press junket, Shelby went downstairs to the bar with Russell, Beck, and Kara. They sat around talking about the movie, the reviews, and the upcoming premieres.

Shelby was glad that nobody was getting into anything personal, because once she went upstairs, she knew she'd have to deal with Linc, and she was dreading it.

When she finally got up to leave, Russell took her to one side. "Look, honey," he said in a low voice. "I know things have been tough for you. But remember—you shouldn't let anyone push you around. It doesn't matter *who* it is."

"I know," she said, nodding. "I have to be strong."

"And you will be," Russell said. "There's no doubt in my mind that you've got it in you. So get rid of that goddamn English reserve—an' go for it, exactly like you did in our movie."

Kara came over and gave her a hug. "It's

been amazing working with you," she said, funky glasses slipping off her nose. "You're a real pro."

"Thanks, Kara, it was nice working with you too. I like the way you handled the journalist who got out of line."

"I wasn't about to take any crap from him," Kara said. "Who do they think they're dealing with? I might *look* young, but I've been in this business for five years."

"You're *still* a baby," Beck said, affectionately taking her hand. "Sit down and have another drink."

Kara did so. There was a twenty-year age gap between her and the actor, but it looked as if things were going well.

"How about you, Shelby?" Russell asked. "You're sure you won't stay for another one?"

"No thanks, Russ, one martini's given me enough strength to get this over with."

Russell gave her the thumbs-up sign. "Linc's a good guy. We all get caught in compromising positions. It's these damn locations. If you want your marriage to work, *never* leave an actor alone on location."

"Yeah," Beck agreed. "Location equals

temptation. The last actress I married ran off with the focus puller!"

"Don't listen to him," Russell said. "He knows nothing."

Shelby left the bar, got in the elevator, and traveled upstairs.

Once more she was exhausted from doing a day's worth of press, and a heated confrontation was not something she was looking forward to. Deep down she hoped that Linc wasn't there.

Why couldn't things be okay between them?

Why was he all over his costar?

Why hadn't she told him about Pete as soon as they'd bumped into each other?

No excuse really, except it had been so nice spending time with someone she didn't have to watch all the time, someone who wasn't constantly criticizing her. The few days Linc had spent at the Malibu retreat were useless, and they both knew it. There was nothing worse than an alcoholic who would not admit that he had a problem. Lately she'd been closing her eyes to a lot of things; now she had to be strong.

Much as she loved Linc, it was time to consider her future.

* * *

Lola finally reached Tony on the phone. "What did you *do?*" she whispered, horrified. "How *could* you?"

Tony sounded calm. "What did I do about *what?*"

"Tyrell White."

"Didn't do nothin'. Why, what's goin' on?"

"Don't snow me, Tony, I'm no fool. It's all over the news."

"What is?"

"Somebody beat the crap out of him, and *I* know who that somebody is—it's *you.*"

"You flatter me, babe. I'm sitting here in my hotel with a split lip. Haven't left the room."

"You arranged to have it done, didn't you?" she persisted, certain she was right.

"Don't even know where the dude lives," he said casually. "The guy must have a lot of enemies."

"Tony—"

"Yeah, I'm one of them, only that don't mean I arranged to have him beaten."

"Are you telling me the truth?"

"Sure." A pause. "What're you doin'? Wanna come over an' join me in the Jacuzzi?"

"My sister flew in from L.A."

"Your *sister?* I never met her. What's her name?"

"Selma. She's the nice one."

"She look like you, babe? 'Cause if she does—maybe the three of us should get our freak on."

"Don't be bad, Tony. Selma's a good girl."

"Who likes good girls? I like 'em sexy an' hot an' naughty, like you, babe."

"Selma's none of those things."

"Damn!"

"I was thinking that we could take Selma to dinner. But only if you promise to behave yourself."

"Does Selma dance?"

"Of course. She's *my* sister, isn't she? Fine dancing runs in the family."

"I'm down with that."

"You should see my mama, she used to dance professionally—she's the best."

"Maybe I *should* see your mama. I heard you can tell what a girl's gonna look like by checkin' out her mama. I'd better check out yours, huh, babe?"

"And why would you want to do that?"

"Y'know, in case we decide to spend the rest of our lives together."

"Is that a proposal, Tony?"

"You'd like that, wouldn't you?" he said, with a sly smile.

"You're such a bastard."

"An' that's what you love about me."

"Can we take Selma to dinner, or not?"

"Yeah. Get your hot ass downstairs at nine-thirty, the limo'll be waitin'."

"Thanks, Tony. And you *will* be good, won't you?"

"Baby, I'll be as good as it gets."

Lola went into the spare bedroom where Selma was happily unwrapping her packages. "We're meeting Tony for dinner," she announced.

"You've bought me far too much," Selma said, holding up a leather Gucci purse. "I'm giving half of these things to Mama and Isabelle."

"No," Lola said. "Everything's for you. *They* didn't fly out to see me, *you* did."

"Mama sent me," Selma said. "Everyone cares about you, Lucia."

"Do me a favor tonight, do *not* call me Lucia. My name's been Lola for the last five years. The *world* knows me as Lola, so why do you all persist in still calling me Lucia?"

"Because it's your name."

"It's *not* my name anymore. I'm Lola, understand?"

Selma looked unconvinced.

"Now, *what* are you going to wear?" Lola said. "You *have* to look gorgeous. After all, you *are* my sister."

"He never told me he was married," Miranda kept on repeating, looking quite crushed.

"Seems he didn't figure it was *that* important," Cat said bitterly.

"Weren't you even a *little* bit curious when you noticed a closet full of women's clothes?" Luanne asked.

"He said they were his sister's," Miranda explained. "I believed him. I had no reason not to."

"Sorry to disillusion you," Cat said. "He's a lying, cheating asshole."

"I know that now," Miranda muttered.

"I'm only here today 'cause he threatened to throw my stuff out onto the street. I guess it was that or give it all to you. I'm sure that was his plan."

"Sorry about the jacket," Miranda said, shrugging it off. "We happen to be the same size."

"You can keep it," Cat said.

"Didn't you used to have blond hair?" Lu-anne asked, staring at Miranda.

"Yes," Miranda said. "How did you know?"

"The magic of film," Cat murmured.

"What?"

"Nothing," Cat said. How could she be mad at the girl, when Miranda obviously had no idea Jump was married? It was Jump who was the serial cheater. What a jackass *he'd* turned out to be.

The packers were finished; all of her personal things were out of the apartment. Time to move on.

"Give Jump a message from me," she said to Miranda.

"After I've given him one of my own," Miranda replied. "I've never *been* so embarrassed."

"C'mon," Cat said, almost sympathetic. "It's not *your* fault."

"What's your message?"

"Tell him to *never* contact me again. If he's got anything to say, he can talk to my lawyer. That's *it.*"

"I'll be happy to tell him," Miranda promised. "Right after I say good-bye."

Outside on the street, Cat gave Luanne a big hug before hailing a cab to take her to the airport.

Mission accomplished.

She was now ready for a revenge fuck.

Once more, Linc was not in the suite. Shelby paced around, rehearsing what she would say. Either he listened to reason and stopped giving her ultimatums or she was catching a flight back to L.A. She called the airport to check on times. There was a ten o'clock she could be on if things didn't work out.

When Linc finally arrived back, he was definitely drunk. He had that glittery, mean look in his eyes, the look she'd grown to dread.

"You made a decision?" he demanded, marching into the suite. "What's it gonna be? You walking off the movie? Or does my dear old pal Pete get the boot?"

"Neither," she said, facing up to him.

"Quit the *I'm-not-going-to-do-what-my-husband-says* crap," he said roughly. "You're not a fucking feminist, you're my fucking wife. Now what's the deal?"

"I told you, Linc—neither. You cannot

continue treating me with such a lack of respect. You say things to me that nobody should say to anybody. You insult me and call me names. It's not right, and I don't intend to accept it anymore."

"You deserve it," he said, his voice filled with animosity. "Act like a moron, an' I'll treat you like one."

"Linc," she said, determined not to cry. "This is serious. I am *not* fooling around."

"Interesting choice of words," he sneered. "Fooling around."

"I wasn't going to bring this up," she said, "but how do you explain the photos of you with Lola Sanchez?"

"For crissakes," he snarled. "They're taken from the set."

"No, they're not. You're kissing her outside a restaurant."

"Are you tryin' to turn this around?" he screamed.

"No, Linc," she said, standing up to him for once. "I'm merely stating the facts."

"Do *not* fuck with me, Shelby. I want Pete off your fuckin' movie. Understand?"

"I'm not doing it, Linc."

"Yes, you *are*," he said fiercely.

"No, I'm not. And stop telling me what to do."

"Fuck you, Shelby. If you *don't* do it, I'm divorcing you. Understand?"

Suddenly she felt a calmness overcome her. It was almost as if she was in the eye of the storm, and everything seemed very clear. Linc was damaged goods, and she wasn't capable of mending him. It was time to stop trying. "If that's what you want," she said quietly.

"It fucking *is!*" he said, quivering with rage.

"Then I'll leave now."

"Good. Get the fuck out and don't come whining back, 'cause we're *over.* I've had enough of your holier-than-thou, sanctimonious shit."

"And I've had enough of you, Linc."

"Get out," he shouted. "Go flash your tits in *another* fuckin' movie. You're useless. You hear me—fuckin' *useless.*"

Tony was on a high. He greeted Selma with a courtly bow, kissing her as if she were his long-lost cousin. "You're a beauty, like your sister," he said, turning on his considerable charm. "That's some sexy dress."

Selma was wearing a slinky black cock-tail dress that Lola had purchased for her at Bergdorf. It suited her admirably. Lola had also summoned a hairdresser and makeup artist to come to the suite and minister to her shy sister. They'd managed to make Selma look quite glamorous; the result was impressive. Isabelle would be a jealous wreck.

Lola desperately wanted Selma and Tony to like each other. That way Selma could go back to L.A. and tell the family what a great guy he was.

Tony took them to a happening Cuban restaurant, one of his favorite places for dinner. They gorged themselves on pineap-ple chicken, special rice, black beans, and a full selection of delicious coconut dishes.

Lola, clad in a pale blue silk Roberto Ca-valli dress, could see that the two of them were getting along. Tony's mood was ex-tremely buoyant, and even though she was sure he was responsible for the beating of Tyrell White, she decided not to mention it again. It was over, and Tony would never admit he had anything to do with it, so what was the point?

Thinking about it made her shiver. Tony

was a wild man; it was unwise for anyone to cross him.

But he was *her* man, and whatever anyone said about him, he always would be.

Cat was in a line at the departure gate, waiting to board the United flight to L.A., when she heard a familiar voice.

"Cat, is that you?"

"Shelby!" she said, turning around. "What are *you* doing here?"

"I flew in for the *Rapture* press junket," Shelby replied. "And you?"

"I'm not supposed to be here, so you *cannot* tell Merrill. He'd be livid if he knew I'd left L.A. in the middle of the movie."

"Actually, I flew in on Merrill's plane," Shelby said.

"Lucky you. Please be *extra* sure you don't mention I was here."

The airline official escorting Shelby aboard asked if they would like to sit together.

"Certainly," Shelby said, and he went off to arrange it.

"How was your press junket?" Cat asked, once they were settled in their seats.

"It left my head spinning," Shelby replied, fastening her seat belt. "People are being so nice about the movie, I'm totally overwhelmed."

"Congratulations," Cat said. "You deserve it."

"I'm sure you experienced the same thing with *Wild Child.*"

"Well . . . I was this big discovery for ten minutes. I mean, it's not as if a lot of females get to direct movies—especially *young* ones. Fortunately for me, being a director is not like movie star fame." She wrinkled her nose. "Doesn't having no privacy drive you totally *nuts?*"

"Sometimes," Shelby replied. "Although I certainly don't have the kind of fame Linc has."

"Where *is* Linc?"

"Making a movie in New York with Lola Sanchez."

"At least you got to see him for a few hours."

"Not really," Shelby said wistfully. "We're not in a very good place right now."

"Join the club," Cat said. "My day was brutal."

"It was?"

"My girlfriend and I went up to my loft to pack up my things—I'm divorcing my husband. Anyway, in walks this girl who I'd recently seen having sex with my old man on a videotape. This same girl is wearing my favorite jacket, which *he* gave to her as a gift. How's *that* for a bad day?"

"Even worse than mine."

"I'm glad I caught him before it was too late. We've only been married a couple of years, so I haven't wasted *too* much time."

"How old *are* you?"

"I'll be twenty in a couple of months. Can't wait. Nineteen is still a teenager. I don't act like a teenager, though, do I?"

"Well . . . you don't exactly *dress* like an adult," Shelby commented.

"I'm not into that whole phony Hollywood glamour bit. Fake tits and your ass on your mouth."

Shelby laughed, glad to have something to take her mind off Linc and their disturbing confrontation.

"What is it with fake lips and boobs anyway? I think they're a bad joke—something *men* force women into getting."

"Perhaps women do it because they feel inadequate without them," Shelby offered.

"Ha!" Cat exclaimed. "Betcha wouldn't catch men with small dicks doing it."

"I'm sure they would if they could," Shelby said, smiling.

"Hmm . . . maybe you're right. Have you *seen* all those ads for penile enlargements? It's totally insane!"

"Here's what I like about you, Cat," Shelby said. "You're a true original."

"Thanks."

"It's so refreshing in a town where all the women are encouraged to emulate super-models. I hate having to go to a premiere, and I've been coerced by some stylist into wearing yet *another* designer dress. It makes me feel as if I'm selling clothes—not to mention all the borrowed jewelry."

"What's your *real* style?" Cat asked curiously.

"A tracksuit and sunglasses to hide the bags," Shelby said wryly. "I never wore makeup when I lived in England, not unless I was working. Linc always used to tease me about it. He says I'm not movie star material."

"Nothing wrong with being your own person. Look at me."

"You're right. I should be recognized for

my acting skills, not for the designer dresses I wear."

"You're so English," Cat remarked.

"Is that a bad thing?"

"I meant it as a compliment. I can't get over how good you are as my edgy American cop, yet off the set you're this perfect English lady."

"There's nothing perfect about me," Shelby assured her. "I'm actually quite ordinary."

"No," Cat said, shaking her head. "That's one thing you're *definitely* not."

Tony and Selma seemed to be getting along famously, although Lola sensed unrest in the air, because every club they went to, she found herself getting bothered by fans, and she was worried that if another man came on to her, Tony might lose it again.

"It's Saturday night," Big Jay informed her in a hoarse whisper. "Not wise for you to be out in public on a Saturday night."

Big Jay didn't speak much, but when he did he was always right on.

"Let's go back to the hotel," she suggested to Tony. "We can have drinks in your suite and party there with all your friends."

"Nah, I like to stay where the action is. I wanna watch you do your thing, babe. Get up an' dance."

"Not without you, Tony."

"Dance with your sister, then."

"Selma's too shy. Besides, that's asking for trouble—two women by themselves on the dance floor. You saw what happened last night."

"Yeah," he said with the shadow of a smile. "And Tyrell got his, didn't he?"

"Yes," she answered sharply. "And *you're* responsible."

"Why you keep on sayin' that?"

"'Cause it's true. You can deny it all you want, but I know you too well."

He picked up his glass of champagne. "You *sure* your sister doesn't swing?"

"Selma is a married woman," she answered primly.

"The Sanchez sisters," Tony said, grinning. "How about the Sanchez sisters and Tony Alvarez? Some fuckin' trio, huh? Four beautiful boobs, two beautiful—"

"Tony!" Lola said, stopping him short. "This is my family you're talking about. You want a threesome, call up that *puta* you sent back to L.A."

"Oh, yeah? If I get her here you'll do a threesome?"

"Grow up!" she said, brown eyes flashing. "You know I'm a one-man woman."

He grinned again. "I'm teasin' your ass, baby. I like watchin' you get all fiery an' excited."

One of Tony's friends, Chico, a wiry-looking record producer, moved in on Selma and asked her if she wanted to dance.

"No, thank you," Selma said.

"Go ahead," Tony encouraged. "You're in New York, have yourself a time."

Selma glanced at Lola unsurely. Lola nodded her approval. The Sanchez women were known for their skills on the dance floor, so she wasn't about to deprive her favorite sister from having a good time. If she wanted to dance with Chico, then she should go ahead and do so. Frankly, she considered Selma's husband an extremely dull man who probably *never* took her dancing.

Once Selma and Chico hit the dance floor, Lola persuaded Tony to get up and join them. She wasn't about to do any more exhibition dances for him, not in public any-way, and certainly not on a Saturday night.

As soon as she and Tony began to dance, the crowd cleared, forming an admiring cir-cle around them.

Lips parted, head back, Lola got into it as the throbbing salsa sound swept her to another place. Tony pulled her close, and they danced as one, his body hard against hers. She was utterly turned on.

By the time they left the club they were a happy group. To Lola's delight, Selma and Tony had definitely hit it off. She could tell that her sister liked him. What was there *not* to like? Tony was handsome, charming, a true Latino sexy man. Now Selma could go back to L.A. and report to the family what a great guy he was.

They exited the club laughing.

Throwing his arm around Lola's shoulder, Tony leaned close, whispering what he planned to do to her when they got back to the hotel. Selma was busy talking to Chico.

The gunshot fire came out of nowhere, a rapid blast of bullets.

Tony automatically flung Lola to the ground, his body covering hers. Big Jay fell on top of them, shielding them both.

There was much confusion and noise and screaming.

Lola could barely breathe. She struggled out from under Tony and saw Selma fall.

Tony's bodyguards were busy pulling guns and firing back. But they were too late; the car holding the gunman sped away.

"They've shot my sister!" Lola screamed. "Oh . . . God . . . THEY'VE SHOT MY SISTER!"

CHAPTER
31

Shelby and Cat spent the rest of the flight back to L.A. getting to know each other. Even though there was an eleven-year age gap between them, they found they had plenty in common. Cat talked about her drug days, meeting Jump, and how cool she'd thought he was.

Shelby talked about her early days in England, her move to America, and how overwhelming it was for her when she'd first met Linc. "He's an amazing man when he *wants* to be," she said wistfully.

"I remember seeing him in movies when I was a kid," Cat said.

"He's not *that* old," Shelby said with a slight smile. "He's only in his forties."

"I know," Cat said. "Although it seems like he's been around forever."

The flight attendant came by and served them a light snack. Then the attendant asked Shelby if she'd mind signing an autograph for her niece, who happened to have the same name as her.

"I'm not sure I can live with Linc anymore," Shelby confided when the flight attendant finally left. "He has a drinking problem, and it's getting to be too much."

"Have you told him?" Cat asked, nibbling a cheese cracker.

"I've tried to. He doesn't seem to hear me. Yesterday he informed me that I had to walk off your movie or have Pete fired."

"Pete," Cat said, shocked. "Our stunt coordinator?"

"That's right."

"Why would he want to get *Pete* fired?"

"Because Pete and I used to go out way before I met Linc. I didn't bother mentioning to him that Pete was on our movie, so when he saw a picture of us together in *People,* he went berserk."

"Ha! Those paparazzi shots can cause *big* trouble."

"I had no idea we were being photographed," Shelby explained. "Pete and I were having lunch; it was nothing more than that."

"It's all about publicity when you're famous," Cat remarked. "You can forget privacy."

"I suppose so."

"All those crap TV shows, the tabloids, and the magazines. You think the people who run them care about celebrities' feelings?"

"No."

"Here's the thing. A person can be in an awesome marriage or relationship—they don't care—they'll go right ahead and publish a rumor that you've been seen out with someone else, which creates a big mess. And that's *exactly* what they're hoping for."

"I agree."

"Man! I'm *lucky* I'm not in the public eye."

"Actually you are," Shelby pointed out. "You're a young girl directing a big movie, a gorgeous Cameron Diaz–style blonde, so you *will* get noticed and written about."

"Gee, thanks. I can't wait."

"Maybe you should've been an actress."

"Are you saying that all good-looking women should be actresses?" Cat exclaimed. "How sexist is *that!*"

"You know what I mean."

"Well, anyway, here we are," Cat sighed, helping herself to another cheese cracker. "Both of us about to get divorced."

"I didn't *say* I was getting a divorce," Shelby said quickly.

"It sounds to me that's what you have in mind."

"It's complicated," Shelby said unsurely. "I have to talk it through with my therapist."

"I'd *never* go to a shrink," Cat said, snatching up a handful of peanuts. "All they do is look bored and try to make you cry. They're all sort of the Barbara Walters of the doctors' brigade."

"I gather you've had experience."

"Oh yeah, when I was fourteen my dad thought it was a cool idea. How dumb was *that?*"

"Therapists *can* be helpful," Shelby said gently. "It's not general knowledge, although it's been written about in some of the more in-depth articles about him—but Linc suffered an extremely violent childhood."

"What happened?" Cat asked curiously.

"I don't want to get into it now," Shelby said evasively.

"I can't stand people who blame everything on their parents," Cat said, wrinkling her nose. "I could've been a total fuckup because of *my* parents. I mean, even though they were rich and kind of spoiled me, I never got any real love and attention from them. So I became a druggie at fifteen, living mostly by myself in New York, until Jump came along and rescued me. It's only now that I've finally taken control of my life."

"And a very good job you've done," Shelby said. "I have to say you're extremely mature for your years."

"Yeah, I'm an old soul," Cat said, grinning. "That's what everyone tells me."

At LAX they were greeted by airline personnel waiting to meet Shelby. Several lurking paparazzi hovered outside the terminal. Cat tried to distance herself from Shelby, which made the photographers notice her, and wonder who she was.

"Shit!" she muttered. If Merrill saw photos of her at the airport he'd be pissed. Although how could he be pissed when she was already back in L.A.?

They shared a car from the airport into town.

"See you Monday on the set," Cat said, when Shelby dropped her off.

"I'll look forward to it," Shelby replied.

Cat couldn't wait to get back to work. It was as if a heavy weight had been lifted from her shoulders. She had her stuff—no more connections. Jump was history.

It was a delightful feeling of freedom.

Lola rode in the ambulance to the emergency room. Selma was lying on a stretcher, unconscious. She'd been hit by two bullets. One had grazed her temple and the second was lodged somewhere near her thigh.

The entire evening was a nightmare—the shooting, the police, the crowds of gawkers who came out of nowhere, the flashing cameras that wouldn't quit.

Big Jay had been hit in the shoulder, although it didn't seem to have affected him too much; he was still on his feet. Tony was unscathed; so was Lola.

"Want me to come with you, babe?" Tony had asked as she'd climbed in the ambulance.

"No," she'd said, barely able to look at him. *Didn't he understand? It was all his fucking fault.*

The ambulance men were very kind. They allowed her to sit next to Selma, keeping a tight hold on her hand.

"Will she be all right?" she kept on asking.

"Can't tell until the doctors take a look at her."

"She's *got* to be all right," Lola insisted. "She's *got* to. This all happened because of me."

"How's that?" one of the attendants asked.

"She came to New York to be with me. If I hadn't taken her out tonight, this never would've happened."

"Mustn't blame yourself," the attendant said. "Violence is everywhere. You have no idea how many gunshot wounds we handle each day."

"I don't want to know," she said, her eyes filling with tears. "This is my *sister.* And she *will not* die, because *I* won't let her."

There was more chaos outside the emergency room. The paparazzi were everywhere and the flashing cameras wouldn't quit—the photographers were like rabid bees, buzzing around, getting in everyone's face.

Lola wanted to kill them all. What a bunch of lowlifes. Why did they feel they had the right to intrude on such a private moment of tragedy?

Pale and serious, she rushed in beside Selma's stretcher, still clutching onto her hand.

Doctors hurried forward and immediately took over.

Lola knew she had to call her mother before she heard it on the news.

She slumped against a wall, desperately trying to control herself. With shaking hands she took out her cell and punched in the number.

"Mama," she managed, choking back sobs. "Mama, get on a plane and come here at once. I'm . . . so . . . sorry. There's been an accident. Selma's been shot."

Monday morning, the news on the set of *Caught* was all about the Lola Sanchez scandal in New York. A shooting involving celebrities was always a hot topic.

"Lola's sister is in a coma," someone said.

"She's dead," someone else said.

"The bullet was meant for Tony Alvarez," someone else offered.

Stories bounced back and forth.

"My cousin's best friend is a bartender at the club they were at," the continuity girl confided. "Apparently Lola dissed some guy in the club, and he came back with a gun. The bullet was meant for *her,* not Tony."

When Shelby first heard about it, she was worried that Linc might have been involved. Unwilling to call him, she contacted his publicist, Norm, who assured her that Linc was not there.

"How's he doing, Norm?" she asked, hoping the news was good.

"You know Linc," Norm replied, noncommittal as usual.

"Yes, I'm afraid I do," she said quietly. "And I also know he's drinking again. So, for the time being, I won't be in touch. If you *should* get any press inquiries, as far as you know everything between us is fine."

"Of course, Shelby, I won't say a word unless I hear it directly from you."

"Let's keep it that way. We both know how the press will jump on it if they think there's any sign of trouble."

Norm hung up the phone and wondered if he should give an exclusive to Liz Smith in return for a future favor. Then he decided no, Shelby was a nice woman, and he still had *some* principles, even after years of being a P.R. to the rich and famous.

Shelby tried not to dwell on the scene between her and Linc in New York. Instead she threw herself into her work. When she spotted Pete coming toward her she was cordial toward him.

"Did you see our picture in *People?*" he asked, sounding kind of pleased.

"Yes, I saw it, and so did Linc."

"Hope it didn't ruin your weekend in New York."

"My weekend was okay," she said guardedly.

"Only okay?"

"Pete, I think it's best if we keep our distance."

"I know that, Shelby. However, I *do* need to talk to you about the car stunt."

"As long as it's all about work."

"You're still upset about me driving you to the airport, aren't you?"

"Yes, quite frankly I am."

"Linc was pissed—is that what I'm hearing?"

"I repeat," she said coolly, "let's stick to work."

"Fine. I was thinking we should try a few practice runs."

"Very well. Schedule it. I'll be there."

And even though she was filled with sadness, she managed to carry on.

Still in a drunken, stoned haze, Linc was having a fine time. Now that Shelby was no longer on his case, he could do whatever he wanted, which involved a lot of cocaine and plenty of heavy drinking. No more behaving like a man with no balls.

Over the weekend, he called up a few buddies from his single days and hung out with them. It was just like old times. The poker game in his suite, several pretty girls hanging around, plenty of booze, plenty of food, plenty of anything he wanted.

Why had he thought *marriage* was so great? This was the life.

Monday morning he awoke with a massive hangover. Christ! The jackhammers were back, pounding his head to shit. Fuck! He had to get sober for work.

Where was Shelby when he needed her? He was still mad at her, but that didn't mean he couldn't miss her.

How come she hadn't walked off her movie for him? *Bitch!* She was probably screwing Pete, and *that's* why she'd run back to L.A. so swiftly.

He was determined that *he* was not going to be the one to give in. She would have to come begging for his forgiveness.

Knowing Shelby as well as he did, he was sure he'd hear from her soon.

"I hear you went to New York," Nick said, blowing smoke rings into her face.

"Who told you that?" Cat asked, waving the smoke away.

"Word gets around," he said, giving her a lazy stare. "I might've gone with you if you'd asked."

"Didn't need company, thank you," she said curtly. "Besides, I wouldn't dream of dragging you away from your overactive love life."

"Love life?" he said, raising an eyebrow. "Listen, I'm into *casual* fucking—anything wrong with that?"

"You're so crude."

"What's crude about casual sex?" he said, genuinely perplexed. "You should try it sometime—you might even get into it."

"Not with you I wouldn't," she answered quickly.

"Why's that?" he asked, shooting her a quizzical look.

" 'Cause you're probably riddled with the clap or some other unspeakable disease."

"Charming," he said, the perennial cigarette dangling from his lips. "Aren't *you* a lady."

"Right back at you."

Entertainment Tonight was visiting the set that afternoon with a full crew. The handsome and personable Mark Steines was conducting the interviews. Shelby had already done her turn; now it was up to Nick.

"Watch your language in front of the cameras," Cat warned him.

"Jeez!" he complained. "You're nineteen, for fuck's sake. You sound like you're forty-three."

"It would be nice if they could *use* your

interview," she retorted. "If every other word is 'fuck,' it'll be a wrap."

"No way. They'll bleep me out like they do on *The Osbournes.*"

"Excuse me, Cat," Jonas said, appearing out of nowhere and shooting Nick an unfriendly look. "When you've got a moment, Mr. Zandack wants you to call him."

Man! What was *that* about? Had Merrill found out about her trip to New York?

"I'll call him later."

"He's still in New York and he's anxious."

"Okay. *Soon,*" she said impatiently.

"What about you, Cat?" Mark Steines asked, strolling over. "Can we get *you* in front of a camera?"

"I don't do interviews," she said, grimacing. "Besides, I'm too busy."

"How about a few sound bites?"

"You know me," she said awkwardly. "I prefer the other side of the camera."

"Sometimes we actually even interview directors," Mark said, smiling. *"Especially* beautiful ones."

"I'll wait until the movie comes out. You don't mind, do you?"

"As long as *E.T.* gets first shot."

"It's a promise."

She stayed behind the TV camera, watching Nick as he sat for his interview. He had a peculiar charm that worked on both men and women, and he said "fuck" only three times.

She shook her head. Nick Logan was quite a character.

Hmm . . . Character or not, she had no intention of getting to know him any better.

As she kept on reminding herself, Nick Logan was one vice she *didn't* need.

CHAPTER
32

A week later, when Selma still hadn't regained consciousness, Lola realized they were in deep trouble. She'd spent every day by her sister's bedside, holding Selma's hand and praying. Several years earlier, much to her family's dismay, she'd abandoned the Catholic Church. This had happened after her second abortion. Abortion and keeping the faith did not seem to go hand in hand.

Now she wondered if giving up her religion had created bad karma. Was Selma in a coma because of her? Suddenly she re-discovered her faith with a vengeance. If praying would help bring Selma back, she was there.

Mama and Isabelle flew to New York to-gether. The two of them were inconsolable; they kept a vigil at Selma's bedside, pale and consumed with worry.

Lola was suffused with guilt. She knew they blamed her. And in turn, she blamed Tony. If he had not taken it upon himself to have Tyrell White beaten up, then Tyrell White's people would never have come back with guns. She was sure that's the way it had gone down. A vendetta. Two macho men with shit for brains.

It was an ongoing nightmare. Over the last few days she'd spent several long hours at the police station with her New York lawyer, being questioned about what had taken place.

"I didn't see anything," she'd said.

"Did Mr. Alvarez shoot back?"

"He doesn't have a gun."

"His bodyguards were armed. They re-turned the fire, didn't they?"

"I know nothing about that," she'd said.

Faye was in full *I-told-you-so* mode.

The publicity was insane. Lola had never thought the day would come when she didn't want to be on the front pages. That day was definitely here.

Elliott Finerman had come through for her; he'd rearranged the schedule on *New York State of Mind,* allowing her a week off. The delay on the movie was costing a fortune, but Elliott didn't complain. She had not expected him to display so much compassion; it was quite touching.

Unfortunately a week wasn't enough. She needed to be with Selma until she regained consciousness.

According to the doctors, they were not sure that would ever happen.

Lola refused to believe their words of doom. She sent Jenny out to buy every book she could find on comas, while Isabelle combed the Internet for information. Between them they decided the doctors were wrong. Selma could wake up tomorrow, or in two years. It might be a miracle; however, miracles *did* happen.

The people at the hospital were extremely caring and considerate. They gave her a private room next to Selma's, where she sat every day with her mother and Isabelle. They didn't say much, although sometimes they hugged one another and wept; it relieved the tension.

She had not seen Tony. She did not *want* to see Tony. She blamed him for everything, although she could not summon up the strength to tell him.

When he called, she was curt. "I can't see you," she said. "I have to stay at the hospital."

"Can I do anything?" he asked. "You have to eat. Come over to my hotel and we'll eat together."

Was he *insane?* Did he actually think she would go to his hotel and have sex with him while her sister was lying in the hospital? He could forget it.

In spite of his injury, Big Jay was back at work, his arm in a sling. "It's nothing," he said. "If I could find the shooters, I'd crush 'em like little bugs."

She'd never heard Big Jay be quite so eloquent. He stayed at the hospital with her, hiring extra guards to sit outside Selma's room.

The paparazzi were everywhere. This was a major story for them—a story that contained every element: a shooting, a hot romance, a gorgeous movie star, a famous druggie film director, a girl in a coma.

God, how Lola hated them!

Staying in New York was a hardship for both Claudine and Isabelle, and although Lola did not want Selma taken away from a place where she could be with her, she knew her family had to leave, while *she* had to get back to work.

With Elliott Finerman's help, she conferred with the administrators at the hospital about arranging for an air ambulance to fly Selma to a facility in L.A.

Eventually arrangements were made, and her mother and Isabelle left with Selma.

Lola went to the airport to say good-bye. They were all hugging and crying. It was a sad scene.

"I'll be back as soon as I finish this movie," she assured her mother.

"I know you understand why this is best," Claudine said, her face somber. "Your papa is alone, Isabelle has her children to care for, and Selma's children need their family close."

"Anything I can do, Mama, anything at all, you know I'll be there."

"Yes, Lucia, we all know that," Claudine

said, hugging her youngest daughter. "This is God's will," she said quietly. "You cannot blame yourself."

"But Mama—," Lola said, her face streaked with tears.

"No, Lucia," Claudine said sternly. "Guilt is not good. Go to church, talk to the priest, he will help you. You must recover your faith, my daughter. You will see—things will be good again. Selma *is* going to recover. We'll all pray for her. Your strength will come from prayer."

When they left, Lola was devastated. She returned to her hotel feeling empty and alone. Her entire world of money and fame and stardom had been turned upside down. She would give it all up for Selma to recover.

Was she being punished?

For what?

She wasn't sure of anything anymore.

The weekly tabloids made the New York papers look tame. *Truth and Fact* hit the stands with a headline that screamed, LOLA CAUGHT WITH MARRIED COSTAR! And next to it there was the infamous photo of Lola and Linc kissing outside the restaurant.

Inside the magazine there was a huge

double-page spread of pictures. And an-
other headline. IS RECENTLY SEPARATED LOLA
SANCHEZ FALLING FOR HER MARRIED COSTAR, LINC
BLACKWOOD? AND WHERE IS MRS. BLACKWOOD,
THE BEAUTIFUL SHELBY CHENEY?

There were numerous pictures accompanying the story. Shelby didn't want to read
it, but people kept on coming up to her on
the set with a copy, saying, "I know you
don't want to see this, but maybe you
should."

Why would they do that? Why couldn't
they ignore it? Or throw the damn magazines in the trash?

She refused to read it, but seeing the
photos and the headlines upset her anyway.
She was sure the story would make its way
into the English papers. Her parents would
be mortified.

Since walking out on Linc in New York
she had not heard from him. She was surprised and hurt. She'd expected him to be
on the phone as soon as he sobered up,
begging her forgiveness as usual.

Maybe this thing with Lola Sanchez was
true. Maybe he *was* having an affair with the
Latina sex bomb, and *that's* why he'd been
so bitter about her and Pete, because he

wanted to make *her* the guilty party so that he didn't have to face up to his own guilt.

She was horribly conflicted. Earlier in the week she'd attended the premiere of *Rapture*—once again it was a triumph. The audience actually stood and applauded. All the reviews were fantastic, except for a snide comment in the *Wall Street Journal.*

She was ecstatic about her career, and deeply depressed about her marriage.

What did she really want? A fabulously successful career, or Linc?

It seemed like she had no choice, because Linc was not giving up his drinking; therefore he was not part of her future.

She spent many long hours with her therapist, who seemed to think the split was inevitable. "Linc is a very damaged man," Brenda repeated over and over. "He is filled with guilt and shame about what happened in his childhood. Drinking helps him to forget. He feels *safer* when he's drunk. Marriage is turning out to be too big a responsibility for him to handle."

Pete was around the set a lot. He went out of his way not to approach her unless it was to talk about the upcoming stunt.

Sometimes she found herself watching

him from afar. He wasn't Linc, but he was certainly a handsome man, in a rugged, outdoorsy way. She remembered the time they were dating. He'd treated her like a queen. And yet . . . she'd left him for a movie star, a man with charisma to spare. A man who obviously preferred alcohol to her.

Fortunately she had her work to throw herself into, and she liked hanging out with Cat. They giggled like a couple of girlfriends about Nick Logan and his pursuit of every woman on the set. Almost every day Nick had a different girl come to his trailer for lunch. The crew took bets on whether it would be a blonde, redhead, or brunette. He seemed to favor no particular color, although they all had spectacular bodies.

"I've been watching him," Shelby remarked. "He definitely has a thing for you."

"Don't be ridiculous," Cat said, frowning. "I could eat him up and spit him out. He's a womanizing jerk."

"So . . . we think he's a jerk, do we?"

"Good description," Cat said. "I mean, in an unruly, puppy-dog sort of way."

"I think you like him," Shelby teased.

"I do *not,*" Cat protested—a bit too vehemently.

Shelby found Nick was friendly and professional toward her. If it wasn't for her problems with Linc, she would be having a good time on *Caught.* Her role was challenging and exciting—she'd never played such a tough character. In a way it was exhilarating.

The day of the car stunt, Pete was very much in charge. He issued instructions at a rapid-fire pace, while everyone listened intently. Pete had a great reputation as one of the best stuntmen in the business. Shelby had to drive the car—a Jaguar—while being chased by Nick in another vehicle. The stunt part was executing a sudden stop and completing a 180-degree turn without the car spinning out of control.

They'd rehearsed it for a week, and she was hoping she had it down. Pete, directing second unit, rode with the camera crew on a truck behind them.

Her heart was pounding. She didn't want to let Pete down. She *could* do it, *had* to do it.

"Action!" Pete yelled, and Shelby took off.

The stunt worked perfectly. Shelby was ecstatic. Pete hopped off the truck and ran toward her, helping her out of the car. "You're the greatest!" he said, beaming. "I'm so proud of you."

"Thanks to you," she murmured.

"One take, Shelby," he said, turning to the rest of the crew. "Let's hear it for our girl!"

The applause was gratifying.

"I think you gotta come to my movie premiere with me tonight," Nick said, smoking as usual. "It's a big deal."

"It is?" Cat said.

"I *gotta* go, an' I don't fancy doin' it alone."

"Take one of your many girlfriends," she suggested. "You've got enough of them to choose from."

"I wanna take you," he said, giving her a moody stare.

"Why?"

" 'Cause it'll be dynamite publicity for *our* movie. We'll get outta the limo, an' here I am with this knockout blonde, an' everyone's gonna say, 'Who's the fox?' An' *I'm* gonna say—she's the director of *Caught,* the movie I'm making."

"What makes you think we need that kind of publicity?"

"We don't, but it'll be fun."

Fun? Hmm . . . She hadn't experienced a lot of that lately. Although when she'd called Merrill back, the conversation had been pretty damn good. Before she could say a word, Merrill had started raving about the dailies. "I showed them to people here," he said. "They love you, they love your work. We got plenty of backers, kitten. When do I get your next script?"

She'd given no thought to what she planned to do next. Maybe take some time off and go island hopping, read some books, generally veg out.

"I'll get back to you, Merrill," she'd said.

"Do that, kitten. It's you and me all the way."

It was nice to know that somebody was waiting for her next project, although she was wise enough to realize that if *Caught* failed horribly at the box office, she'd be yesterday's news.

"What're you thinking?" Nick asked, still waiting for her answer.

"I *hate* that question. Like I'm going to tell *you* what *I'm* thinking."

"Why not?"

"Okay, I'm thinking you're an asshole—does that satisfy you?"

"Y'know, there's something about you," he said, grinning. "You're kinda like old and young at the same time. It's the sexy bod and the old mouth."

"Old mouth?" she said, frowning again.

"Y'know what I mean." He chain-lit another cigarette. "So—you comin' to my flick?"

"Why are you always asking me to go places when you have a million babes who would happily go with you at the drop of their knickers?"

"Knickers!" he exclaimed, laughing. "That's a nice old English word. Didn't know you were English."

"I lived there for a while."

"You did?"

"Yes."

"I don't know much about you, do I?"

"I don't know much about you either, and I'm not sure I want to, so don't sweat it."

"You coming with me, or not?"

"What's the movie?"

"*Trucker.* Big-time action. You'll get off on it."

She sighed. "I dunno . . ."

"For fuck's sake," he snapped. "Stop givin' me this *I'm-not-sure* crap."

"Okay," she said, making a snap decision. "Your charm has convinced me. Only no hands on."

"What does *that* mean?"

"I'm not one of your conquests. I'll go with you 'cause you're right—it'll be great publicity for our movie."

"Jeez!" he grumbled. "You sure as shit don't make it easy."

"What time?"

"I'll pick you up at seven. Wear something sexy."

"Shove it up your—"

"Okay, okay," he said, holding up his hand. "I get it. Wear whatever you want. See ya later."

CHAPTER

33

"I got somethin' to tell you that'll shock the shit outta you," Freddy Krane announced. He was back in town and visiting the set.

"What's that?" Linc asked, high on coke and feeling no pain, even though he was in the middle of working.

"Lola Sanchez," Freddy said, a triumphant gleam in his eyes. "A coupla nights ago I was havin' phone sex with that model broad, Allegra. So I'm pullin' the old pod, an' all of a sudden, whammo! I realize

I'm sittin' in the same bed you fucked Lola in."

"I didn't fuck her," Linc said, frowning.

"Sure you did. Only you've forgotten about it."

"I have?"

"She's changed, but Freddy never forgets a face, so I did some checking."

"I've no idea what you're talking about."

"Keep listenin'. A few years ago at one of my parties I hired a Latino DJ who'd been recommended. He brought his girlfriend with him."

"So?" Linc said, not even vaguely interested in Freddy's ramblings.

"She was a hot-lookin' piece, turnin' on the sexy dancin' for us. So I sent one of my girls to bring her over."

"You did, huh?"

"Over she comes, this hot little Latina chick, an' that's the last I saw of her, 'cause *you* took her inside an' spent the night with her in *my* bed. I couldn't even sleep in my own freakin' bed! So in the mornin' when I come in—you're gone and she's still there, naked as a *Playboy* spread, an' sexy as all get-out."

"Who are you talking about?"

"Lola Sanchez, schmuck! Course, her name wasn't Lola then, but it was her. I had one of my assistants track down the DJ from that night. The dude's now producing records in L.A. I spoke to him personally— asked him if he played a gig at one of my parties, and was the girl with him Lola. He told me yes."

"I'm still not getting you," Linc said.

Freddy shook his head in disgust. "What are you, stoned?"

"Who understands *what* the fuck this story is about?"

"*You* were *screwing* Lola Sanchez, only that wasn't her name then. She was just some sexy Chicana chick tryin' to get herself noticed. You nailed her in *my* bed, spent the night with her, then passed her on to me. Unfortunately she didn't want anythin' to do with me. End of story. Now, six years later, here we are."

"Holy shit!" Linc said, finally getting it. "You *sure?*"

"Course I am," Freddy agreed, chuckling. "I got a memory like a freakin' elephant— 'specially when it comes to women. If I've seen 'em naked, you can *bet* I'm gonna remember 'em."

"But you *didn't* see her naked. According to you it was *me* who spent the night with her."

"Why d'you think she hasn't mentioned it to you?"

"Maybe she's embarrassed."

"She's *pissed* at you, man. You screwed her all night, then dumped her. Bet you never even called her—did you?"

Linc shrugged. "Who remembers?"

"You shoulda called, sent a flower or somethin'. *I* would've, only she didn't want *me,* she wanted *you,* the big movie star. Marched outta my house all bent outta shape."

"You think it *was* Lola?"

"I *know* it was."

"What should I do?"

"Get her into bed again, then tell her you remember while you're screwin' her. *That'll* give her the come of the century."

"Anybody ever mentioned you're a dirty old man?"

"No shit?" Freddy said, yawning. "Where's Shelby?"

"In L.A."

"Wasn't she supposed to be here?"

"She flew in for a day, then she had to get back."

"Something goin' on with you two?"

"Nothing I want *your* big mouth to know about."

"Okay, dinner tonight with Allegra. An' this time—the three of us. Let's get a party goin'. Why waste a sure thing?"

Lola was nervous about returning to the set. Her mind was elsewhere; it was certainly not on emoting in front of the camera in a sexy dress, flirting with Linc Blackwood, and making it work for the romantic comedy they were shooting.

She was well aware that she had to get back to work, because if she didn't, it would mean career suicide. Elliott Finerman had been helpful up until now, but he would not continue to be so understanding. They'd already shot half the movie, so she had no choice.

"You must check with the hospital every hour," she instructed Jenny. "I have to know what's going on."

Tony kept on calling. She refused to accept his calls. In one of her prayer sessions she'd made a pact with God—if she was good, God would save Selma and bring her out of her coma.

Being good meant not seeing Tony. Tony unleashed her wild side, and it was because of her reconnection with him that a tragedy had taken place.

Matt phoned to offer his sympathies. She was touched to hear from him; the once-boring Matt now seemed like a nice, caring person—and even more important, Selma liked him.

"Lola, are you okay?" he kept on asking her.

"Yes," she answered.

"Can I come to New York?"

"You know," she said, thinking that she was still married to Matt, therefore he *should* be by her side, "that might be nice."

"I'll hop a plane today."

Now what was she to do about Linc Blackwood? She'd probably broken up his marriage with their photos all over the front pages, and maybe that was punishment enough. Revenge was not something that went hand in hand with religion and prayers.

She struck another bargain with God. If he made Selma better, she would forgive

Linc Blackwood for the past, and not pursue revenge against him.

Matt must have jumped on the next plane, because before she knew it, he was there. Tall and white-bread and boring, he'd shaven his stupid goatee and was thrilled to be back by her side.

She clung to him because she had to cling to someone and in her mind Tony Alvarez was now the enemy.

Matt was one happy man. He had his wife back, and that's all he cared about.

"Can we at least celebrate your success?" Pete asked.

Shelby's cheeks were flushed. She felt that she'd conquered a fear, considering she'd always been slightly scared of driving. In fact, she'd only learned to drive when she'd first moved to L.A.

Now she was actually doing car stunts in a movie. It was quite an achievement.

"I . . . I don't know," she said, not sure she should encourage him.

"Look," Pete said. "I *know* things aren't going well with Linc."

"How do you know that?" she asked quickly.

"It's all over the tabloids, Shelby."

"That's why I can't be seen with you," she said. "If we were photographed together it would only make things worse."

"You could come to my house," he suggested. "There's no photographers hanging out there."

"And what if they caught me coming *out* of your house? That would look terrible."

"It's not as if we're doing anything, Shelby," he said patiently.

"I know that."

"Look," he said. "We *should* celebrate. However, if you feel it's inappropriate, tell me, and I'll stop bugging you."

Linc hadn't phoned, and she did not relish the thought of sitting in her big mansion by herself for one more night. She was lonely by herself in America, with no family and hardly any friends.

Oh yes, plenty of people were calling to congratulate her on the enormous success of her performance in *Rapture,* but there wasn't anyone she was close to. Cat was the only person she'd developed any kind of relationship with.

And here was Pete. Good solid Pete. And

he wanted her to come to his house, and she wanted to go.

"Okay," she finally said. "Your house it is."

"There'll be nobody around," he promised. "And I'll barbecue for you—how's that? Remember how you always loved my burgers?"

"Do I! They were delicious."

"You used to wolf down two if I remember rightly."

She smiled at the memories. They'd spent one glorious summer together and had a very good time, although they'd never consummated their relationship.

"We can go right from the set," he said.

"It's not a good idea for people to see us leaving together."

"You know where my house is—drive yourself over. I'll be waiting."

"I think that's best."

"Whatever you want, Shelby."

"Pete," she asked curiously, "do you have a girlfriend?"

"Why?"

"I, uh . . . thought if you did, she might like to join us."

"Am I making you nervous, Shelby?" he

said, giving her a penetrating look. " 'Cause that's not my intention."

"No," she said quickly. "I'm simply a little confused right now."

"The truth is I have several girlfriends, but I'm not asking any of them to join us. It's dinner alone together, for old times' sake. How's that?"

"Sounds nice."

"Do you need to go home first? Or will you come straight from the studio?"

"I don't have to change clothes or anything; after all, it's not as if this is a date."

"Right," he said. "I'm leaving in ten minutes, so I'll see you when you get there. Drive carefully, Shelby. Me and the dogs'll be waiting."

"Wear something sexy," Nick had said.

Oh yeah, sure, like she was about to dress up for *him*. Ha! Was *he* going to wear something sexy for *her*?

What did he consider sexy, anyway? She had on the tightest jeans known to man and a cutoff Abercrombie & Fitch island tee shirt that exposed her midriff and pierced navel. Wasn't *that* sexy?

Her stuff had recently arrived from New

York, and there were boxes piled all over her apartment. She riffled through some of her clothes, searching for a suitable outfit for the premiere.

Look at you, she thought. *Getting all excited about a date with a womanizing little prick. Or big prick.*

Yeah, she giggled. *He has the big-prick cocky attitude.*

What was it about men? Why did they always have to tie you up in knots? It wasn't as if she even *liked* him.

Well . . . maybe a tad.

She finally settled on an off-the-shoulder white ruffled blouse and skintight black leather pants. Then she added lots of silver Gypsy jewelry she'd inherited from her grandmother.

She ran her hands through her short blond hair, spiking it up even more, and added plenty of kohl around her eyes, giving her the fashionable heroin-chic look. A touch of lip gloss and she was ready.

Why am I doing this? she thought.

Because I want to, that's why.

The downstairs buzzer started ringing, making it too late to back out now. Two minutes later Nick slouched his way into her apartment.

"I thought we had to leave," she said.

"Tidy, aren't you?" he said, regarding the stack of half-unpacked boxes littered all over the floor.

"I'm trying to find the time to unpack properly," she answered. "Why? Are you doing a photo shoot for *Architectural Digest?*"

"S'matter of fact—"

"Shut *up.*"

"Cool apartment," he said, checking out her CD collection. "I'm stuck in a friggin' hotel. I gotta get myself a place out here."

"Do you have a home anywhere?"

"I kinda live like a Gypsy. Friends' floors, that kinda deal."

"You're a movie star," she pointed out. "A house is a good investment."

"Does that mean you'll help me look?"

"No," she said firmly. "Wives and fiancées are the people who help guys look for houses. *Not* the director of your movie, who happens to be doing you a huge favor by accompanying you to your premiere."

"God, you're a hard nut," he complained. "Your husband must've treated you real bad."

"It's not important," she said.

"Anyway," he said, checking her out with an appraising eye, "you look pretty hot."

"Oh," she said, slightly flustered. "Thanks."

"How about me?"

She gave him an exaggerated once-over. "Hmm . . . let me see. A comb wouldn't be a bad idea."

"Can't let the fans down," he said, mocking himself. "This is how they like me."

"They do?"

"You should *see* some of the letters I get—naked pictures, offers of anything I want. It's a wild trip. Come to my trailer one day and read my fan mail."

"What a *great* idea," she said sarcastically. "I've got nothing else to do with my time."

"Got any joints lying around?"

"No, I gave up recreational drugs."

"Gave 'em up?" he said, shocked. "Why would you give up weed?"

"I told you," she said patiently. "I used to be a druggie. Now I don't do anything. It's better for me not to be tempted."

"Fuckin' boring. C'mon, blondie, let's hit the road."

CHAPTER
34

Allegra, the tall, skinny model with the strong Australian accent, was quite happy to see Linc again.

"Are you getting a divorce?" was her first question.

"No," he responded sharply.

"The *Enquirer* says you are."

"Believe the *Enquirer*," he said shortly. "Don't believe me."

Why had he said he would come out with her and Freddy again? He couldn't take the accent, although Freddy had assured him she was a wildcat in bed.

Allegra preened like an exotic bird. "I'll be on the cover of the next *Sports Illustrated,*" she boasted. "Do you *know* what an honor that is? Of course," she added—in case they didn't know—"I've been on the cover twice before."

"Sure, honey," Freddy said, groping her almost nonexistent ass.

Lola was due back on the set tomorrow. Linc had been racking his brains trying to remember more about the night he'd apparently spent with her in Freddy's bed. Before Shelby, there had been so many one-night stands—at least three women a week. Fortunately or unfortunately, they were all a blur; no way could he single out Lola.

Freddy was in rare form. First they went to a Russian restaurant, where they feasted on borscht and blini with caviar, washed down with several shots of Russian vodka. Then they dropped into Elaine's for drinks, where Freddy proceeded to regale Elaine with outrageous stories about his last movie—an action adventure shot in Cambodia, and according to Freddy, starring the asshole of action adventure heroes. "This jerk was such a hero," Freddy revealed, "that he used to stiff all the hookers *after* he'd fucked 'em."

Elaine gave Linc a look as much as to say, *Can* you *shut him up, or should I?*

After dinner Allegra wanted to make the rounds of her favorite clubs.

"Didn't we do that last week?" Linc asked.

"So we'll do it again," Freddy said.

Yeah, Linc thought. *Why am I hanging back? I've got a wife who's screwing some fucking stuntman in L.A., and I'm in New York like a schmuck, not even getting laid.*

He took another look at Allegra, although the thought of a threesome with Freddy was pretty gruesome.

Then he downed a couple of straight scotches and suggested they visit a strip club.

"Yes!" Freddy said.

"I *have* been known to get it on with girls," Allegra promised, sloe eyes gleaming. "Does that send shivers up and down your spine, boys?"

In bed with Matt, Lola felt comfortable and safe. Matt was not exciting, but at least he didn't go around beating people up and getting her sister shot in return.

"I missed you so much," Matt said, his hands all over her. "I was shattered when your lawyer told me I had to leave the house. You broke my heart, Lola. But we're here together now, so I won't dwell on it."

They'd recently finished making love. Apart from the size of his dick, Lola considered Matt incredibly dull in bed. He got on, pumped away, and got off—in more ways than one. He wasn't even capable of giving good head.

She didn't care. If this was her punishment, so be it. Her only concern was for her sister's recovery.

"Can I come to the set tomorrow?" Matt asked. "You might need my moral support—it being your first day back since the shooting."

"You can come everywhere with me," she said, resigned to her new situation. "I feel safe with you around."

"That's the way it should be." A long pause. "I have to ask you something."

"What?"

"Was anything going on between you and Tony Alvarez?"

"Nothing," she answered without blink-ing.

Damn! Now she'd lied. She had to *stop* lying.

"Actually, that's not true," she said, hastily correcting herself. "Tony and I did get together a couple of times, only I soon realized it wasn't the same as being with you."

There, she'd corrected that lie.

Sorry, God. I'll try to do better. But believe me, it's not easy.

Pete's dogs raced out to greet Shelby. There were three of them—a golden re-triever, a black Lab, and a police dog incon-gruously named Pudding.

She bent down to fuss them. They licked her face, barked, and jumped up at her.

"The guys remember you," Pete said, emerging from the house wearing jeans and a work shirt with rolled-up sleeves. "I made it here ten minutes before you, just in time to make you a glass of your favorite sangria *and* get the barbecue fired up."

"The dogs seem to be in great shape," she said, straightening up.

"Looks like they missed you. Remember

when we used to take them to the dog park?"

"Oh, yes. I loved going there," she said enthusiastically.

"How come *you* don't have dogs?"

"Linc's allergic."

"That's a new one."

"He is."

"Come inside. I got something to show you."

She followed him through the cluttered house into the warm and cozy kitchen. He took her hand and led her over to a basket containing a tiny golden puppy. The other three dogs trotted eagerly behind them.

"Oh my!" she exclaimed. "This is the sweetest little thing I've ever seen."

"Found it wandering around the canyon. I brought it in before it got eaten by coyotes."

"What's its name?"

"Haven't named it yet. Thought *you* could do the honors."

Gently she picked up the golden ball of fluff. "Hi, little guy," she said, scratching it under the chin. The puppy gazed up at her. "I think I'm in love!" she exclaimed. "She's so adorable!"

"It's a he," Pete said, handing her a glass

of sangria. "There's supposed to be a beautiful sunset," he added. "Let's go see if we can catch it."

They went out to the backyard. There was no swimming pool, just an old hammock and a jumble of wild rosebushes. It was so unlike all the polished Beverly Hills and Bel Air mansions she'd gotten used to.

"I love this house," she said warmly. "I especially love the view of the city at night."

"Yeah, there's something magical about it. It gets me every time," he said, going over to the barbecue. "I hope you're still a meat eater."

"I'm English, of course I eat meat."

"That's good, 'cause I'm making Omaha steaks, baked potatoes, and hot dogs."

"Sounds like a man-sized meal."

"You got it," he said, smiling. "And, to go with everything," he added, activating an outdoor speaker, "your favorite James Taylor song."

"You remember everything," she said, smiling as "You've Got a Friend" filled the night air.

"Yes, Shelby," he said, looking into her eyes, "I remember absolutely everything."

*   *   *

The onslaught of flashbulbs was startling. Cat was not used to this kind of relentless attention.

Nick flung his arm around her shoulders in an all-encompassing way so that she couldn't escape.

Fans were lined up on each side of Grauman's Chinese Theatre, screaming his name. The TV cameras were stationed in a long line down one side of the red carpet, the photographers along the other.

A harassed publicity woman approached them. "Mr. Logan, this way."

"You're coming with me," he whispered to Cat.

"I'm not," she protested. "I'll wait inside."

"I said you're coming with me," he hissed, not loosening his grip.

So much for anonymity, she thought, as he dragged her down the press line, chatting amiably to all the TV crews, introducing her to every one of them.

"I wish you hadn't done that," she said when they finally made it inside the theater.

"You could've run," he said, groping in his pocket for a chewed-up toothpick.

"How could I run with your hand on the scruff of my neck?"

"You're gonna get plenty of attention anyway," he said. "Don't think you can avoid it."

He was repeating what Shelby had said. Was celebrity inevitable simply because she was young and not bad looking?

In the lobby he introduced her to a few of the cast members from his movie and to the director.

She felt humiliated because she was sure they were all looking at her as if she was another one of his conquests. *I must have been crazy to come to this,* she thought. *Stark raving crazy.*

After the movie—a salute to violence—there was a big party.

Nick said, "We only have to stay five minutes, then we can leave."

"But I'm hungry," she protested.

"We'll join the gang at Ago."

Not only had she been exposed to the world as another one of Nick Logan's girlfriends, now he wanted to show his friends that she'd gone out with him.

"You know what?" she said. "I'd sooner go someplace else—maybe Chow's."

"Why?" he said. "Everyone's at Ago."

"How come they didn't come to your premiere?"

"You think they'd come to a shitty movie like that?" he said, abandoning his tooth-pick and reaching for a cigarette.

Oh great! *She'd* had to endure his movie, and they didn't have to.

"Anyway," he added, lighting up, "we'll toss a coin."

He tossed. She lost. She was sure that he cheated.

By the time they arrived at Ago, his table was packed.

"Do you really pick up the check for all these people every night?" she whispered.

"I can afford it."

"It must be costing you a fortune."

"It's them or the tax man. I'm a generous soul."

"So I've noticed."

Amy, the pretty stand-up comedian with the oversized glasses, was there. Nick greeted her with a great show of affection.

She must be an old girlfriend, Cat thought.

"Didja meet Amy?" Nick asked.

"Yes," Cat replied. "I was planning on catching your act at the Improv, right."

"She remembers," Amy said. "This one's a keeper."

Nick gave Amy another kiss and a hug. Cat frowned. What did he think—that they were going to get involved in some kind of bizarre threesome?

"I think I'll take off," she said. "I've got to be up early, and it's getting late."

"No," Nick urged. "You're staying to eat. She's staying, Amy—right?"

"Whatever you say, Brother dear."

Brother dear? Was that a term of affection, or was she actually his sister?

"Are you brother and sister?" Cat asked.

"Yup," Amy said, grinning. " 'Fraid so."

"Oh," Cat said, and immediately thought that Amy would be the perfect girl for Jonas.

"My steak was delicious," Shelby said, pushing her plate away. She was sitting comfortably on an outdoor chair in the backyard of Pete's house, nursing a second glass of sangria.

"You haven't finished."

"I can't. This steak was big enough for a three-hundred-pound truck driver."

"I'll give the rest to the dogs," Pete said, picking up the plates.

"Expensive dogs," Shelby remarked as the dogs came bounding over.

"I believe in looking after my animals."

"I can see that."

"Unconditional love," Pete said, patting the black Lab. "That's what I get from these guys."

"You were telling me about your love life earlier," Shelby said. "Can I hear more?"

"Why?" he said. "It's boring."

"No. I'm fascinated."

"Sadist!"

"Come *on,* Pete."

"Okay," he said, matter-of-factly. "After Liz the actress, there was Janet."

"And what was wrong with Janet?" Shelby asked good-naturedly.

"Janet was okay, except she was desperate to get married."

"And you didn't want to?"

"After I get to know someone, maybe. Janet wanted to get married after we'd only been together three weeks."

"So Janet had to go?"

"Right. Then after Janet there was Clarissa, the hairdresser."

"And *her* problem was?"

"Sex maniac. She wanted it three times a

night." He gave a self-deprecating grin. "Now, I like sex as much as the next man, but three times a night, forget it."

Shelby smiled. "It certainly seems you've been busy since we broke up."

"We never broke up, Shelby," he said, correcting her gently. "You ran off and married one of my best friends."

"I wish you wouldn't keep reminding me."

"I wish *you'd* face up to the fact that Linc is not making you happy."

She flushed. "How can you say something like that?"

"It's obvious, Shelby. I see the tabloids. Linc's a player, he always has been. He likes booze, women, and—" He stopped abruptly.

"Booze, women, and *what?*" she challenged.

"I'm sure he's not into it anymore."

"Into *what,* Pete?"

"He was, uh, always kind of a cocaine freak."

"Don't be ridiculous," she said scornfully. "If I'd *ever* suspected that Linc took drugs, it would've been the end of us."

"He probably stopped when he met you," Pete said, wishing he hadn't mentioned it.

"It's time to go," she said, standing up. "This was nice. You'll make some lucky girl a wonderful cook."

"I have other talents, too."

"I'm sure you do," she said, petting the puppy.

"I'll walk you to your car."

They went through the house out to the front.

"There's something I think you should know before you go," Pete said, standing by her car.

"Yes, Pete. What?" she said, finding her keys.

"It'll sound corny, but there's no other way to say it."

"Go ahead."

"I love you, Shelby," he said quietly. "I always have and I always will. And you know what? I'm sorry, but there's absolutely nothing I can do about it."

CHAPTER 35

Linc had never been to a strip club with a woman before, and Allegra was into it. The moment the girls began strutting their stuff, Allegra jumped up—all six feet of her—whistling as if she was a randy guy out on the town looking to get laid.

"Gimme money," she kept demanding of Freddy.

He obliged, bringing out his considerable bankroll.

Snatching a handful of cash, she immediately began sticking twenty-dollar bills into the girls' G-strings.

"Let's get us a private room," she shrieked. "I'll pick out three girls, one for each of us."

"Oh Jesus," Linc groaned. He wasn't thinking straight; the booze was clouding his brain. "I dunno if I wanna do this."

"For crissakes," Freddy complained. "You're turnin' into an old fart."

"I got a reputation to protect."

"What friggin' reputation?" Freddy exploded. "You're all over the goddamn papers with the Latina sex bomb. Shelby's dumped you, so relax, have yourself a ball."

Yeah, that's what he should do—have himself a ball. Although Shelby hadn't dumped him. He'd told *her* to fuck off.

What a mistake.

No. It wasn't a mistake. He was free now. He could do whatever he felt like without having to listen to her sanctimonious nagging.

Allegra spent fifteen minutes picking out girls to accompany them to the private room. She selected three different types—a sinuous black girl, a Southern redhead with huge knockers, and a petite Asian.

On their way to the private room, Allegra was whooping and hollering, causing other patrons to stare and recognize Linc—which pissed him off.

"This is fuckin' ace!" she yelled in her loud Australian accent. "You guys are fan-fuckin'-tastic!"

Finally they settled into a private room.

One of the strippers had a key, and Allegra ordered her to lock the door. "I've been here before," Allegra offered, winking jauntily at the guys. "We gotta have our privacy."

Linc sat back, ready to enjoy his first lap dance in a while.

"I'll take the one with the big tits," Freddy roared.

"Fake," Allegra pointed out in a bitchy tone.

"You think I give a fast crap?" Freddy chortled, waving a wad of bills at the red-head.

The black girl was all over Linc, humping and grinding while brushing her pointed breasts against his mouth as she straddled him.

Halfway through her routine she did something that turned him off, so he shoved her away and clicked his fingers for the delicate Asian with her china doll features.

"Looks like I'm stuck with *you,*" Allegra said, attempting to kiss the black girl on the mouth.

Soon everyone was going at it. Dry humping, heaving, and groaning.

Before long, Linc found himself getting a blow job, although it was strictly against the club's rules. Any kind of fucking or sucking was against the club's rules. But who gave a shit?

The Asian girl was into it—a regular little suction pump.

Linc leaned back like a king, allowing her to service him. Hookers and strippers were the best. A man didn't have to buy them presents or take them out to dinner. No foreplay. No declarations of love. And no recriminations in the morning. Merely a businesslike exchange of cold hard cash. It suited him fine.

By the time they left the club he was completely wasted. Allegra was all over him, while Freddy had paired up with all three strippers.

"Everyone back to my place," Freddy announced.

"I'm on!" Allegra said, before whispering in Linc's ear, "Or we could dump him and have our own party at your hotel. I can do things you've only ever dreamed about!"

God! He was *so* fucked up. Drink, drugs, women—he was back to his old ways big time.

What was so bad about that? At least he didn't have Shelby watching him like the town detective.

Outside the club, two paparazzi came darting out of nowhere. *Flash! Flash! Flash!*

For a brief moment Linc was blinded, then he lashed out, grabbing one of the photographers, wresting his camera away from him, and smashing it to the ground. The photographer was livid; he lunged at Linc, who managed to kick him in the groin. Within moments they were fully involved, while the second photographer snapped away.

The club bouncer emerged from inside and separated them.

"You'll be sorry for this," the photographer yelled, picking up his broken camera. "My friend got it all, buddy. You fuckhead movie stars think you can get away with anything. Forget it, cocksucker." Then the two photographers began running off down the street.

"Shit!" Freddy mumbled, attempting to bundle the three strippers into his limo. "What didja hafta do that for?"

"He deserved it," Linc answered, rubbing his jaw where he'd received a glancing blow.

"Come on, mate," Allegra said, pulling him by the sleeve of his jacket. "Let's go get it on."

Why not? Why the hell not?

Only a few hours later, Linc sat in the makeup trailer, scowling and hungover.

"What am I supposed to do with you today?" the makeup girl bitched. "Your skin's like sandpaper, your eyes are superbloodshot. Lean back, Linc, I'll try putting Visine in them."

"Leave my eyes alone," he muttered. "I feel like crap as it is."

"You *look* like crap," the makeup girl scolded. "Relax, while I do my best to make you look human."

Lola entered the makeup trailer with Matt right behind her. "Well," she said, flopping into one of the makeup chairs, "I see you've taken over the front-page spot."

He'd already viewed the damage. The *Daily News* carried a photo of him with Allegra, whereas the *Post* had a picture of him kicking a photographer.

"Jesus, Lola," he groaned, then he spotted Matt. "Hey," he muttered.

"Hey," Matt responded.

There was an uneasy silence.

"Matt and I are back together," Lola said, breaking the silence.

Linc peered at her through the mirror. Was it true? *Had* he slept with her?

Freddy was probably wrong. If he'd screwed Lola Sanchez, it would surely be something he'd never forget.

Damn! He simply couldn't remember.

"I'm fixing you up," Cat announced.

"Excuse me?" Jonas replied.

"I *said* I'm fixing you up. I've found the perfect girl for you."

"If I was interested in the perfect girl, I'd go find her myself," Jonas said. He hated it when Cat got busy with his love life. He didn't need any help; unbeknownst to Cat, he and the continuity girl had been hitting it off quite nicely.

"How would you do that?" Cat asked, hitching up her low-rider jeans. "You never *go* anywhere, you work *all* the time."

"Something wrong with that?"

"Forget about it. This girl is great and we're all going out."

"Who's *we?*"

"You, me, her, and Nick."

"Nick?"

"Coincidence. Amy is Nick's sister, and she's interesting *and* pretty. She's also a stand-up comedian, isn't that wild?"

"A stand-up comedian?"

"Yeah, she's funny. You like funny, don't you?"

"I do *not* need fixing up."

"Too late. We're all having dinner at Chow's tonight."

"You can't go ahead and make arrangements for me," Jonas protested. "I'm not going."

"Oh yes you are. You *work* for me."

"Since when do I work for *you?*"

"Well, you work for Merrill Zandack and *I* do too, so it's all in the family. Anyway, I need to discuss postproduction things with you, and there's never time on the set. Chow's, eight o'clock. You be there, Jonas, otherwise I'll definitely assume you're gay." She hurried off before he could object further. Amy was perfect for Jonas, even though Nick kept on insisting that Jonas was gay.

"I'm telling you, he's *not,*" Cat assured him.

"He's either gay or the dude's got a major crush on you," Nick said.

"Don't be crazy. We're like brother and sister."

"You haven't seen the way he watches you on the set."

"He's watching me *work,* Nick. He's Merrill's spy, it's his job to keep an eye on what's happening."

"You're a fuckin' girl, you don't get it. I know these things."

After his premiere, Nick had attempted to invite himself up to her apartment.

"No way," she'd said, blocking him in the lobby of her building.

"Why?" he'd said, giving her his famous bad-boy look. "Don't you fancy gettin' laid?"

"Not by you."

"Jeez!" he'd complained. "Are you telling me I've wasted an evening?"

"Oh *pul-eeze. Get over* yourself."

Actually, she'd been quite tempted. She hadn't had sex in so long it was a joke.

Then she realized that she had to be smart. Sex with Nick Logan could turn out to be a major mistake.

Although . . . maybe when they wrapped.

Yeah. Why not? After all, it wasn't as if she was a nun.

"Your father and I are flying in," Martha Cheney informed her daughter over the phone.

"You are?" Shelby said, quite startled at the thought of her parents descending on her.

"Yes, dear. Your father needs a break."

"He does?"

"Is it convenient if we stay with you?"

"Of course. Although you *do* know that I'm in the middle of filming, so I won't be around too much."

"We *were* planning on driving to the south of France, but there've been so many robberies there lately that your father feels we shouldn't risk it. Besides, we'd rather spend time with you. I promise we won't get in your way."

"I'm sure you won't," Shelby murmured.

Since the success of *Rapture,* things had definitely changed. Occasionally there were paparazzi lingering outside her house, and many stories about her and Linc in the tabloids. It seemed that their marriage had become public fodder. The story about Linc being with Lola Sanchez must have hit the English papers, so now her parents were concerned. Hence their upcoming visit.

"When will you be here?" she asked.

"At the end of the week," Martha replied.

"You don't *have* to do this, Mum. I'm okay, really I am."

"Darling, you're our daughter," Martha said. "We want to be there for you."

Shelby realized there was no point in trying to put them off. Martha Cheney was a very determined woman.

She hung up the phone and started thinking about the previous evening and Pete's declaration of love. He'd caught her off guard, and she hadn't known how to respond.

"I needed to share my feelings with you, Shelby," he'd said. "If you and Linc don't make it, you have to know that I'm here for you."

"I appreciate it, Pete, only I can't think about getting involved with anyone else at this time."

"I know," he'd said. "I can wait."

Pete was a very special man, and the knowledge that he still loved her was quite an ego boost.

Soon she got in her car and drove to the studio. When she arrived, the second assistant informed her there was a surprise waiting in her trailer.

"What?" she asked.

"You'll see."

She opened the door of her trailer, and there, in the middle of the floor, was a basket containing the adorable golden puppy from last night. Next to the basket was a glass bowl filled with apricot roses—her favorite color.

She opened the attached note.

He pined for you all night.
So did I. He needs a safe haven—
so do I.

  Love always,
  Pete.

She didn't know how to react. It was such a sweet and thoughtful gesture. So genuine.

She picked up the puppy and it immediately began licking her face.

She reread Pete's note.

If Linc didn't get it together soon, she *would* move on.

CHAPTER

36

Lola was desperate to get back to L.A. so that she could take her turn sitting by Selma's bedside. Her day was spent either working or on the phone. She called Mama at least three or four times, and after work she spoke first to Isabelle, then Selma's husband *and* her two children.

Matt didn't complain. He was so relieved to be back with her that he didn't dare say anything that might cause her to throw him out again.

Most days—since he had nothing else to

do—he followed her to work and hung around the set. He was determined to watch out for Linc Blackwood. He'd seen the newspapers, he knew about the rumors.

Lola's heart was not in the movie. She was well aware that her performance had become lackluster, although Elliott Finerman had not complained.

One day, when they were shooting on location at a restaurant in Tribeca, Tony Alvarez turned up.

Fitch Conn welcomed him to the set and was all over him like a cheap suit. Tony Alvarez was a cult figure in the directing world; his movies were cutting-edge, and other directors admired his style.

Lola was shocked to see him; it had been weeks.

"Hey," Tony said, walking straight over to her, his intense, dark eyes burning into hers.

She automatically drew back. "Tony," she said nervously, "what are *you* doing here?"

"You won't take my calls, you don't phone *me*. Why you *think* I'm here?"

"I . . . I've been so busy," she said, thinking how handsome he looked, in a black silk tee shirt and perfectly creased pants. "This film is taking up all my time. As soon as it's over, I'm flying to L.A. to be with Selma."

"How's she doing?"

"She's still in a coma."

"That's real messed up."

Her eyes darted around to see where Matt was. She did not want them coming face-to-face; that would *not* be a good idea.

"Well, Tony," she said in a strained voice, "it's nice of you to visit, but as you can see—I'm busy, so maybe we should do this another time."

"Are you handin' me bullshit?" Tony said in a low, angry voice. "You got a short memory, Lola. You *swore* when we got it back on, there'd be no more walkin' out. You *swore* you were tellin' the world about us. An' now, 'cause there's a little trouble, you run."

"I would hardly call my sister getting shot a *little* trouble," she said, her brown eyes flashing.

"I took care of that problem," he said ominously.

"Took care of *what?*" she asked, shivering.

"You'll hear about it."

"Do you know that I've been questioned

by the police several times? How do you think *that* makes me feel?"

"Ignore that crap."

"They wanted to know if you carried a gun."

"What did you tell 'em?"

"The truth. That *I* don't know." She sighed deeply. "I am not happy about any of it."

"Scared it'll hurt your career again, huh?" he said mockingly. "Is it your fuckin' *lawyer* advisin' you to stop seein' me?"

"It has nothing to do with my career this time," she answered quickly. "I don't know if you can understand this, but I feel that what happened to Selma is our fault—you *and* me. So . . . it's better if we don't see each other anymore. We create too much turmoil."

"You can be a cold bitch when you turn it off."

"Calling me names now, Tony?"

"I'm saying it like it is. You professed your love for me. One smell of trouble and you're gone. What kind of loyalty is *that*?"

"I'm trying to explain how I feel."

"No, baby," he said forcefully. *"I'm* explaining how *I* feel. I wanna be with you, only you got the wrong dude if you think you can treat me like a piece of shit. If you *don't* wanna be with me—you'd better say it now."

Lola bit down on her lip. The very sight of Tony was an emotional experience. He still sent tingles up and down her spine, making her weak with desire. How *could* she give him up?

Because she had to, for Selma's sake.

"Are we finished?" he demanded, his dark eyes staring into hers. "Is this for real?"

Before she could answer, Matt appeared. Obviously furious at seeing Tony, he possessively took her arm. "Is everything all right?" he asked in an uptight voice.

"Who the fuck is *this?*" Tony growled.

"For your information, *I'm* Lola's husband," Matt said.

Tony laughed derisively. "So *you're* the jerk she kicked to the curb so that she could be with me."

Matt took a step toward him.

Lola held him back. "No, Matt," she ordered. *"Don't."*

"Leave my wife alone," Matt said. "She doesn't want to see you."

"Who the *fuck* d'you think *you're* talkin' to?" Tony raged.

"You," Matt responded. "And you'd better take notice."

"Or what?" Tony jeered.

"Or you'll regret it."

"Are you *threatening* me?" Tony said. "You got any idea what happens to people who *threaten* me?"

"Tony," Lola said, becoming alarmed, because Matt had no idea what kind of man he was dealing with. "Please don't."

"Don't *what*, Lola?" Tony said, playing with her. "Don't tell this dumb prick about our life together? About how *hot* an' steamy the sex is between us? Or how many times you've complained about the asshole you were married to? Now he's standing here *threatenin' me.* Jesus holy *Christ!* Go back to him, live your dull life, 'cause *I'm* outta here. An' baby, don't *ever* come beggin' me to take you back again. This time it's *finito.*"

She watched him walk out, and later, on the evening news, she was horrified to see a report of Tyrell White's mysterious death. He'd fallen from a nineteenth-floor hotel window. The newscaster called it a tragic suicide.

Lola shuddered. Tony Alvarez was an extremely dangerous man.

Linc informed Allegra she could not come to the set.

"Why not?" she demanded.

"Because I don't want you there. It's distracting."

Allegra scowled. She was a woman used to getting her own way. Especially as she now considered herself Linc's girlfriend.

He didn't know how it had happened.

Well yeah, actually he did. Sleeping with her was a start, and Freddy leaving town was a second.

Allegra had no intention of going anywhere without her new movie star boyfriend. She was into booze, drugs, and other girls. In fact, she was into anything Linc wanted. When it came to drugs and drinking, she made *him* look like a Boy Scout.

She had long, jet-black hair, slanted gray eyes, and Slavic cheekbones. Her body was long and lean, her small breasts all nipples. If only she would keep her mouth shut and not talk so much, she'd be quite beautiful—in a tall, skinny, supermodel way.

However, Linc didn't want a girlfriend. He wanted his wife back, by his side, so that she could protect him like she always had. He felt his life spiraling out of control, and it wasn't a good feeling.

Sometimes he thought about Shelby. Drunk, he hated her guts. Sober, he loved her beyond reason.

Most of the time he was totally out of it, barely able to remember his lines.

Elliott Finerman was furious. The dailies were shit. Linc was looking worse every day, and Lola was merely going through the motions. When Elliott tried to talk to him, Linc told him to fuck off.

Elliott Finerman could not believe the two stars he'd gotten stuck with. A dazed Lola Sanchez and a stoned Linc Blackwood. A fine romantic comedy *this* was turning out to be.

Linc had his routine down. First thing in the morning a couple of snorts of coke. For breakfast, two Bloody Marys. Lunch, more Bloody Marys and more coke. Then at night, whatever took his fancy.

Occasionally he experienced a lucid moment or two when he realized he was running on empty. He knew it was bad. Very bad. But he was unable to stop his self-destructive behavior.

Unasked, Allegra had moved her stuff into his hotel suite. A few nights after she'd moved in, Linc experienced a horrific nightmare. He awoke screaming, his body bathed in a cold sweat.

Allegra did not stir.

He got out of bed, made his way into the bathroom, and splashed his face with cold water.

Jesus! It was the same nightmare he'd experienced over and over again as a child. For years he'd suffered from vivid dreams, then one day they'd stopped. Now the nightmare was back.

His hands were shaking as once more he pictured the scene. His father was a brutal man, but never as brutal as that particular night when he'd picked up a cast iron frying pan, smashing it across his wife's face repeatedly, until she'd dropped to the ground covered in blood.

After killing her, his father had calmly taken his gun and, in front of Linc and his sister, blown his brains all over the kitchen wall.

The images were scorched into Linc's mind forever.

Some things a man never forgets.

Cat found there was no escape from Nick. Since she was directing him in a movie, they were constantly together. Making movies creates a very intimate situation, and Nick was always there—watching her, laughing with her, teasing her.

Somehow it was becoming extremely comfortable being with him, and quite a kick to be working with someone who was totally on her wavelength. Nick got it. He was an instinctive actor with talent to spare. And on the screen he and Shelby were dynamite together.

How did I get so lucky? Cat asked herself every morning when she got out of bed. *How am I directing a big movie with two major stars? And they're both a dream to work with.*

Nick was hot to take things further, while her thought was, why complicate matters? She might look like a total raver; however, her raving days were in her wild-child past. Now she was interested in a relationship that meant something, not a few-weeks stand with an admitted carouser.

On the other hand, as Luanne had suggested, a revenge fuck was not completely out of the question—although she was fearful that if she slept with Nick, it might upset the delicate balance between actor and director.

She decided to stick to her original decision and wait until the movie wrapped.

The fix-up between Amy and Jonas couldn't have gone better; they seemed to like each other. According to Amy, they'd even been out a few times since, without the watchful eyes of Nick and Cat all over them.

"Okay, so you're right," Nick informed her. "Jonas is not gay."

"I told you," Cat responded.

"Apparently he's getting real cozy with Sis."

"Does that mean—"

"Yeah, she's into him."

Cat was happy for Jonas. Amy wasn't a Hollywood starlet type, she was a smart girl with brains and a dry sense of humor, exactly the kind of girl Jonas needed.

Nick had stopped inviting a parade of nubile girlfriends for lunch in his trailer. He now spent the lunch break with Cat, or he sat around with the crew swapping dirty jokes. Most nights they grabbed a plate of pasta or a burger, and went to bed early. Not together, although Nick refused to give up. "We *gotta* do the nasty," he kept on urging her. "This is turning into a freakin' joke. I'm developing a relationship with my right hand I haven't had since I was ten!"

"Didn't I tell you?" she answered casually. "I've decided it'll be your wrap present. How's that?"

"Hmm . . . ," he said. "How many weeks we got left?"

"Not many," she said. "Think you can wait?"

He grinned his irrepressible grin. "I suppose I can try."

"She did *what?*" Lola shouted excitedly over the phone.

"She moved a finger," Isabelle repeated.

"That's *fantastic!*"

"Yes," Isabelle agreed. "The doctors say it's an excellent sign, so perhaps she *will* come out of this coma after all."

"I couldn't be more thrilled," Lola said. "I

only have two more days on the movie, then I'm on a plane. I'll be able to sit by her bedside, sing to her, tell her stories. I've been reading so much about what to do for people in comas. We must be there for her every second. You understand that, don't you?"

"Of course *we* understand it, Lucia," Isabelle replied, a touch frosty. *"We've* been doing it every day."

"Yes, I know. I can't wait to see you all." She ran into the living room of the suite, where Matt was watching TV. "Matt!" she yelled. "Can you believe it?"

"What?" he said, eyes fixed firmly on a college football game.

"Selma moved her finger. Isn't that great news?"

"Great," he agreed, stuffing his mouth with a handful of corn chips.

"I think I'll start getting things together. The moment we wrap, we're out of here, okay?"

Matt barely moved his eyes from the TV.

Lola was psyched; her bargain with God was working. She'd given up Tony in exchange for him bringing Selma back to life; now it was starting to happen.

She summoned Big Jay to fetch her suitcases from downstairs in the storage room of the hotel, then she called Jenny to come up to the penthouse and help.

Jenny arrived five minutes later. "Can I put on the TV while I pack?" she asked. "There's an interview with Nick Logan coming on *E.T.* He's *such* a hottie."

"Got a crush, have you?" Lola asked.

"You bet," Jenny said, blushing.

"Okay, go ahead," Lola said.

Jenny switched on the TV, then she began removing Lola's designer gowns from the closet, carefully laying them out on the bed, ready to fold into special plastic bags before she put them in the suitcases. When the Nick Logan interview started, she stopped everything.

"Hmm . . . ," Lola said, taking a peek at the TV. "Nick Logan looks like he could use a shower."

Jenny giggled. "That's part of his charm; it's that grungy bad-boy thing."

"I didn't know you liked bad boys," Lola teased.

"Oh yes," Jenny said. "And tomorrow they're advertising an interview with Shelby Cheney; she's in the movie with him."

"Wonderful," Lola drawled sarcastically. "Can't wait."

"Should I turn the TV off?" Jenny asked.

"No, leave it on. Let's see what Britney and Justin and all of them are doing today," Lola said, opening drawers full of unworn cashmere sweaters. "I have to live vicariously now. Matt never cares to leave his precious sports. Not that I *want* to go out."

"Oh look!" Jenny exclaimed.

"What?"

"Isn't that Tony Alvarez?"

Lola glanced quickly back at the TV. Sure enough there was Tony, strolling into some L.A. event with a girl on his arm. A very young, very pretty girl.

"Turn the sound up," she ordered.

Jenny did so, and they both listened as Jann Carl spoke.

"Attending the *In Style* party in L.A. for pediatric AIDS, film director and one-time fiancé of Lola Sanchez, Tony Alvarez, announced his engagement to up-and-coming Puerto Rican singer Maria Estevan. Maria's first album, *Lost,* comes out early next year. Tony Alvarez is currently in pre-production on his next movie, *Manic,* starring Nick Logan and Lara Ivory."

Lola stared at the TV in shock. He'd done it. He'd actually done it. The bastard had gone and gotten himself engaged.

Who was the little tramp anyway? She looked about twelve years old, with her brown curly hair and slight build. No boobs. No ass. Not sexy at all. Nothing like Lola Sanchez.

How could he do this to her? How *could* he?

She knew why. She'd rejected him, and this time it would not be so easy getting him back.

Not that she planned on doing so. Hell, no. She'd made a promise to God and it was one promise she intended to keep.

Caught was winding down, and *still* Shelby had not heard from Linc. She was devastated. They'd been married for over four years, and he'd always come back to her whenever they'd had any kind of fight.

This time there was an ominous silence, apart from the things she read in the gossip columns and saw on TV. Apparently a photographer was suing him for millions of dollars—claiming assault and battery outside a strip club.

So now he was frequenting strip clubs. Obviously he was completely out of control.

Her parents had arrived from London, which was nice. They were not the kind of parents who would question her into the ground; they were there to offer their support if she needed it.

She invited Pete over for dinner. Her mother helped out in the kitchen, and they cooked a traditional English meal of roast beef with Yorkshire pudding and roast potatoes.

Pete was a big hit; her parents warmed to him immediately.

After dinner they all sat outside on the terrace. Shelby played with the puppy, whom she'd christened Tiger, while Pete talked to her father about vintage cars and how surprised he'd be when he saw Shelby doing her car stunt in *Caught.*

Later her parents went off for a stroll around the grounds, leaving Pete and her alone.

"Thanks for inviting me this evening," he said. "The dinner was great. Those potatoes—I'm hooked."

"It's my pleasure," she replied. "My parents like you."

"Are they here because of what's going on between you and Linc?"

"They don't believe in interfering, so they haven't said anything, and I'm not volunteering any information."

"You never do," he said wryly. "Not even to me."

"Don't push me, Pete."

"I wouldn't do that. But I see everything too. Now Linc's photographed leaving strip clubs and beating up photographers with some model girlfriend by his side. I don't get it, Shelby. You should be instigating divorce proceedings. What are you waiting for?"

She nodded silently. She knew he was right, but something was holding her back. It wasn't as easy as everyone seemed to think.

The next day, as soon as she finished work, she drove over to her therapist's office.

"What do *you* think I should do?" she asked Brenda, hunching forward on the couch.

"That's not for me to say," Brenda replied in measured tones. "It's *your* decision, Shelby."

"You always *say* it's my decision," she said, wishing Brenda would be more forthcoming. "Meanwhile, I'm coming to *you* for *your* advice."

"No, Shelby, you're coming to me because you need to *talk* about what's happening. My job is to help you listen to yourself; that's what you have to do. You'll know when it's the right time for you to consider divorce. You don't need *me* to tell you."

"There's another man," Shelby blurted.

Brenda was surprised. "You haven't mentioned *that* before."

"He was my boyfriend before Linc. He's working on my movie, and . . . I think I like him."

"Enough to leave Linc for?"

"Linc's already left me, hasn't he?" she said sadly.

"Has he?"

"It's obvious."

"As I said before, Shelby, only *you* can make the decisions that affect your future."

Damn! She was getting nowhere fast. Talking to Brenda was like wading through quicksand.

On the way home she started thinking more deeply about Brenda's words. Perhaps they made sense after all. It was true—only *she* could make the decisions that affected her future.

Then that's exactly what she had to do—make up her mind. Either her marriage was over or it wasn't. And only she could decide which it was.

CHAPTER
37

At the airport, Matt trailed behind Lola, organizing her piles of luggage. She seemed to have accumulated a dozen more suitcases during her stay in New York.

The usual army of paparazzi were staked out at Kennedy. Lola was happy to pose with Matt. No more scandal; she was a good girl now.

Oh yes, and no more Tony, because the bastard had gone and gotten himself engaged to some Puerto Rican tramp. God!

How could he walk away from her as if she meant nothing to him?

No, her inner voice informed her, *you walked away from him. And it was a wise move. The man is nothing more than a dangerous thug.*

He might be a dangerous thug, but that didn't mean she was able to stop loving him.

"Over here, Lola," called one of the photographers. "Big smile."

She put her arm around Matt and posed, making Matt a very happy husband.

"Did you enjoy working with Linc Blackwood?" another of the photographers called out.

"Linc Blackwood is a real star," she said graciously. "I'm sure everyone who goes to our movie will definitely enjoy it."

Matt did not agree. He'd seen the dailies. As soon as they were settled back in L.A., he planned on resuming his acting classes. If Linc Blackwood could be a star, there was hope for anybody.

"Cut. It's a print," Cat called out.

The cinematographer gave her the

thumbs-up sign, while the actors in the scene dispersed.

"Are you okay?" Cat asked, walking over to Shelby.

"Yes, I'm fine, why?" Shelby answered, as the wardrobe woman took her jacket and handed her a robe.

"You look awfully pale."

"I *was* feeling a bit headachy this morning," Shelby admitted.

"Go to your trailer and take a break. It'll be at least forty minutes before we get to the next shot."

"I think that's a good idea," Shelby said.

"Only a few more days to go," Cat said, grinning triumphantly. "And we're ahead of schedule *and* under budget. In Merrill's eyes I'm the girl genius."

"That's excellent news," Shelby said.

"Are you bringing your parents to the wrap party?"

"I was thinking of doing so."

"Bring 'em. It'll be a blast."

"I'm not so sure. They won't know anyone. Perhaps I should take them out to dinner instead."

"With Pete?"

"Cat," she said warningly, "don't cause trouble."

"Just asking," Cat said innocently. "I mean, I know Linc is seeing Allegra—it's all over the papers—so *you* shouldn't feel guilty."

"You're a fine one to talk," Shelby responded. "What's happening with you and Nick?"

Cat grinned again. "I'll let you know in a couple of days."

"Oh, I see. It's like that, is it?"

"Yeah, it's like that," Cat said, suddenly feeling shy.

Shelby went to her trailer to rest. Tiger greeted her, tail wagging. He'd peed all over the floor, but she didn't care. She scooped him up into her arms and cuddled him, still not feeling great.

She lay down on the couch and tried not to think about Linc. Then suddenly it struck her like a flash of lightning. Oh, God! She was two weeks late, and she was *never* late. Was it possible that she was finally pregnant?

No. Not now. The timing couldn't be worse.

She started thinking back. The last time

Linc had made love to her was that fateful weekend in New York. He'd ambushed her on the couch in his hotel, almost forcing himself upon her. And he'd not withdrawn as he usually did.

How ironic if it had happened then.

She had to find out. Unfortunately, she could hardly pop into the pharmacy and buy a pregnancy testing kit, because it would be all over the news before she got home. And if she sent someone to get it for her—same deal. So she called her gynecologist and made an emergency appointment for later that day.

She cuddled the little puppy to her. If she *was* pregnant, she had no idea *what* she'd do.

"Here's the deal," Nick said, unshaven, his dark, unruly hair flopping on his forehead. "After the wrap party I've got a surprise for you, so bring an overnight bag."

"Are we eloping to Vegas?" Cat deadpanned. "Do you want to screw me *so* badly that we have to get married? I hope you've booked an Elvis impersonator. I refuse to do it unless you organize the full deal."

He laughed. "Sorry to disappoint you.

There'll be no getting down on one knee, and *definitely* no ring."

"Shame!" she said, mocking him. "I'm *so* disappointed."

"Overnight bag. Wrap party. Don't forget."

"Like I would forget. I think I'm finally as horny as you!"

"My kind of girl," he said with his usual cocky grin.

By the time Lola arrived back in L.A., stopped off at her house, and went straight to the hospital, Selma was doing more than moving her finger. Over the last few hours her eyelids had fluttered open, and she was conscious.

Lola sat by her bedside surrounded by her family, and Selma's husband and children.

"It's a miracle," Claudine kept on repeating.

No, it's not a miracle, Lola thought. *It's the result of my bargain with God.* She'd given up Tony and now Selma was on the road to recovery.

Her mother took her to one side. "We're all so happy you're back with Matt," she whispered. "He's such a nice guy, and so right for you, Lucia."

And boring! a voice screamed in her head. *And a lousy lay! And a sponger!* "Maybe," she said in her best noncommittal tone.

"No, not maybe, my daughter. Matt will always be there for you. You don't *want* a wild man like Tony Alvarez. He's no good."

I don't? she thought. *Why not? Tony Alvarez makes me feel alive.*

"Besides," Claudine continued, "Matt will make a wonderful father for your children."

What children, Mama?

She stayed at the hospital for a couple of hours, then finally went home to bed and Matt, who was naturally watching sports on TV.

Now that Selma was going to be all right, her thoughts turned to Tony. How could she possibly survive without him?

She realized that, yes, she'd made a bargain with God. But if Selma completely recovered, didn't that change everything?

She and Tony were so good together. Sure, she knew he was dangerous and capable of doing terrible things, but somehow it didn't *really* matter. He'd never done anything terrible to her.

As far as Lola was concerned, love conquered all, good *and* bad.

Early the next morning, Shelby's gynecologist called her with the news. She was a pleasant woman, young and confident.

"Shelby," she said, her tone extremely friendly.

"Yes?" Shelby said, holding her breath.

"It's as you thought."

"It's as I thought," Shelby repeated blankly.

"Yes, I'm happy to tell you that you are indeed pregnant."

On the one hand, Shelby was ecstatic. On the other, she was more depressed than she'd ever been in her entire life. How could it happen now, when things with Linc were so bad?

Maybe the news of her pregnancy would bring him to his senses. Maybe he'd give up the wild life that he'd decided to pursue, and be the husband she'd always wanted. Surely the thought of a baby coming into their lives would straighten him out? Didn't he deserve one more chance?

Without giving herself time to change her mind, she picked up the phone and called him in New York.

"Who's speaking?" the hotel operator inquired, monitoring his calls.

"Mrs. Blackwood."

"One moment, please."

Then another female voice, with a strong Australian accent and a sour attitude, got on the line. "Yes, *what?*"

"Is Linc there?"

A bad-tempered "No. Who's this?"

"Mrs. Blackwood."

Change of tone. "Oh yeah, Shelby. He's mentioned you. I'm Allegra. We live together, y'know."

"No, I didn't know that," she said quietly, her stomach sinking.

"I guess the divorce is coming up anytime soon, right? Is that what you're calling about?"

"No," Shelby said tersely. "I'd like to speak to my husband."

"You *could* speak to him if he was here, but he's not, is he?"

"Then tell him I called, and have him get back to me as soon as possible."

"He's busy, y'know."

"*What* did you say your name was?"

"Allegra. You've probably seen me on the cover of *Sports Illustrated.*"

"Not a magazine I subscribe to."

"Buy it," Allegra said in a bitchy fashion. "Then you can get a gander at your competition."

"Have Linc call me," Shelby said, uncharacteristically slamming down the phone. It wasn't often that she lost her temper, but who was this bitch? And what the *hell* was Linc doing with her?

Martha entered the room. "Your father wants me to double-check our tickets to London, darling," she said. "Daddy and I are leaving this week. You'll be all right here by yourself, won't you?"

"Of course I will," she said, attempting to calm down.

During the course of her parents' stay they had not once discussed her separation from Linc. Her parents were determined not to bring it up until she did, and she had no desire to raise the subject.

For a moment she thought about confiding in her mother, but then she realized it was hopeless. Neither of them would understand. They were both sweet people, and they'd always been caring parents, but they were totally unsophisticated.

"I've left my Saks credit card on the hall table," Shelby said. "Go there today while I'm at the studio, and buy yourself a glamorous outfit for the party. I want to be proud of you."

"Are you saying that you wouldn't be proud of me if I wore one of my suits?" Martha replied, sounding hurt.

"Your suits are lovely, Mum—for England. But you should buy yourself something sexy."

"Don't be so silly, Shelby," Martha said, pursing her lips. "Your father would be shocked."

"Wouldn't it be fun to shock him sometimes?"

"No, dear," Martha said primly. "What *is* the matter with you?"

"Nothing," Shelby said, kissing her mother on the cheek.

Nothing, except that my husband is now living with a woman in New York, and I'm pregnant, and I don't know what to do about anything. How sad is that?

"Okay," she said. "I've got to go, I'll see you later."

Gathering up Tiger, she set off for the studio.

Pete was waiting outside her trailer with two cups of Starbucks coffee. "Morning, beautiful," he said, handing her a paper cup.

"Hi," she said wanly.

"Did you sleep okay?"

"Why?"

"You look tired."

"You know, it's so rude," she said irritably.

"What is?"

"First of all Cat told me I didn't look well yesterday, now *you're* telling me I look tired. I'm sorry, Pete, but I don't appreciate it." She slammed her way past him into her trailer.

He followed her in. "You heard from Linc, didn't you?" he said.

"No. Actually I called to speak to him, and some *bitch* got on the line."

"Who was she?"

"I imagine it was his new girlfriend."

"Shelby," he said patiently, "I keep on telling you—hire a lawyer before he does."

"Why? I don't want anything from him. No alimony, nothing."

"It's not as simple as that, Shell. You have

houses, cars, investments. It's all community property."

"But if I don't want anything . . ."

"You *still* need a lawyer," he insisted.

"Why can't Linc and I work it out together? Why should a man be stuck paying the woman, unless there's children to consider?"

"Hmm . . . you're every man's dream," Pete said. "In more ways than one."

"And another thing," she said. "Why are *you* so nice to me?"

"Because, as I've told you repeatedly, I'm waiting in the wings."

"It might be a long wait, Pete."

"There's something you should know about me."

"What?"

"I'm a *very* patient man."

Their eyes met, and she found herself weakening. Pete might not have to be as patient as he thought. After her conversation with Linc's girlfriend, she was almost ready to move on.

CHAPTER

38

Cat was ecstatic. She'd actually done it. She'd finished her movie!

"How do you feel?" Jonas asked, sitting in the production trailer with her.

"It's difficult to say," she replied, drinking 7 UP from the can. "I'm kind of psyched it's over. Then I'm kind of sad—'cause I've *so* loved working with everyone. The crew, the actors—*you.* Saying good-bye is miserable. These people have become like family."

"You should do a Woody Allen or a Clint

Eastwood, and always work with the same crew."

"Don't I wish!" she said fervently. "Although somehow I've got a strong suspicion I'm not in the Woody, Clint arena yet."

"You will be."

"I do love you, Jonas," she said, jumping up and giving him a hug. "You're always so positive."

"I try."

"You succeed."

"Did I tell you Merrill's coming to the wrap party?" Jonas said. "He doesn't usually do that."

"Should we be flattered?"

"Definitely."

"Is Amy coming?"

"Of course."

"You two are going strong, huh?"

"You were right. Amy's a great girl." He hesitated for a moment. "And since I can't have you—"

"What?" Cat said, alarmed.

"Just effing with you."

"Well, *don't,*" she said crossly. "You're like the brother I never had. Do *not* spoil it."

One of the production assistants came in to go over final details for the party. Cat left

Jonas to organize it. She wanted to run home first, take a shower, and change clothes. After all, tonight was a big celebration in more ways than one.

Allegra conveniently forgot to tell Linc that Shelby had phoned him. Why should she? She wasn't his personal message service.

What did his wife want anyway? Why was she bothering him? Didn't she understand that she was now out of the picture? Linc Blackwood had moved on.

Allegra had plans. Linc had only a couple more days to shoot on his movie; his costar had already departed for L.A., and when he was finished, Allegra quite fancied a trip to the Bahamas.

He could afford it. He could afford anything she wanted. He was a movie star. *Her* movie star.

The night before, while he was lying in bed in a drunken stupor, she'd said to him, "I need to buy a few things tomorrow and my credit card is out of date. Can I borrow yours?"

"Do what you want," he'd mumbled. "I don't give a shit."

So she'd taken his black American Express card from his wallet and spent the day putting it to good use.

Allegra enjoyed all the attention that was coming her way now that she was with Linc Blackwood. Sure, she was famous in the modeling world, but being with a big movie star gave her added cachet. Most models ended up with scruffy rock 'n' rollers. *She'd* hit the jackpot.

Every night when he returned from the studio, they sat around indulging in coke or crack. After that, they took a leisurely cruise around the clubs.

Allegra introduced him to Vicodin, which calmed his raging hangovers. He was already into an assortment of heavy-duty sleeping pills. She'd also introduced him to the world of three-ways big time, because what man *didn't* like getting it on in bed with two girls? Although, Allegra made sure that every time it was with a different girl; she was very careful that Linc did not get hooked on someone else.

There were times Linc could be a mean sonofabitch, and Allegra didn't like that. He called her names. He called her dumb and a whore and stupid.

She gave back as good as she got.

A couple of times he slapped her across the face. She retaliated by kicking him in the balls.

Their relationship was becoming more violent every day. But since they were both stoned most of the time, neither one of them seemed to notice.

Allegra was no weakling. She'd grown up in the Australian outback, with four older brothers and a bully of a dad. Only the strongest made it out in one piece. And she was strong.

When Linc arrived back from the studio, Allegra had developed a yen to drop by a late night transvestite club. She wondered how Linc would feel if they brought another *man* home?

A man dressed as a woman might not bother him. Then, when he discovered the added appendage, it would be too late for him to do anything about it.

The thought amused her. Big macho movie star, Linc Blackwood, and another man sticking it up his untouched-by-human-male ass.

She laughed to herself as she put on the new eighteen-hundred-dollar Valentino dress she'd bought that afternoon with his American Express card.

As far as Allegra was concerned, she was a stunner, and Linc was lucky to be with her.

"You look lovely!" Shelby exclaimed, admiring her still-pretty mother, who'd purchased a most attractive flowered outfit from Saks.

"You don't think it's too girlish for me, do you?" Martha said, worrying.

"Not at all. Daddy will love it."

And when her father came downstairs a few minutes later, he did indeed love it. "Why, Martha," he said, "you look as pretty as the day we were married."

Martha actually blushed, and the two of them exchanged a warm smile.

It must be nice to be so in love after all these years, Shelby thought.

In love and unworldly. That about summed up her parents.

She'd miss them when they left, but it was for the best. She needed time alone to think things out. She had many decisions to make; it was certainly not going to be easy.

Linc had not called her back. Did that mean he didn't wish to speak to her?

She didn't know. She was giving him a

chance to find out about the baby. If he didn't call, it wasn't *her* fault.

"I'll go get dressed," she said to her parents. "Help yourselves to a glass of sherry. As soon as I'm ready, we'll go to the party together."

She went upstairs, her mind racing in a hundred different directions. Abortion was *not* an option. She didn't believe in it, never had—unless there was a very good reason, such as rape or incest.

Did she want to raise a baby without a father? No.

Did she have a choice? Maybe.

Because if Linc called back, a reconciliation *could* take place.

Now that she was pregnant, she would not be able to do the Bond-style movie that was upcoming in a few months. She couldn't care less; her career was the last thing on her mind.

She opened her closet, selecting an off-the-shoulder silk dress and comfortable sandals. Wrap parties were for having fun with the crew, and tonight she planned on forgetting her troubles and dancing the night away.

*   *   *

When Lola arrived home from her daily visit to the hospital, she discovered Matt sprawled in front of the TV. *Big* surprise.

She stared at him for a moment. Her dear husband gave boring a bad rap. Spending time with him was about as invigorating as lying motionless in a tanning booth—which she didn't have to do anymore on account of the fifteen-second miracle-tan spray.

"I want to go out tonight," she said, picking up a bunch of invitations stacked on the coffee table.

"Why?" Matt responded. "There's plenty of good stuff on TV."

"I don't know if you've noticed," she said pointedly, "but TV sports bore me to death."

"I thought you *liked* curling up in bed with your fashion magazines."

"How many magazines do you think I can read?"

"Vogue, Harper's Bazaar, Us—"

"That's enough," she interrupted. "Tonight we're going out. You pick," she added, throwing a bunch of invitations at him.

Reluctantly he began shuffling through them.

After a few minutes she marched over

and snatched the invitations from his hands. "We'll go to this one," she said, picking out an invite to a private reception and dinner for Raja Mestres—a Latina artist. "I adore this woman's work, she reminds me of Frida Kahlo. I might even buy a painting for Selma. Wouldn't *that* be nice?"

"You're sure you want to go to this?" Matt asked, obviously loath to shift his lazy ass.

"I'm positive. You'd better go get dressed."

She left him still lounging on the couch, went upstairs, and called Faye. She asked her to alert the host that she would be attending the party for Raja Mestres, adding a restless "I'm ready to do publicity again."

"You realize that we have a lot of damage control to take care of," Faye lectured.

"I understand."

"You understood last time," Faye scolded. "It didn't seem to make any difference."

"Please don't speak to me like I'm a child," Lola said irritably. "I pay you to look after my P.R., not to tell me how to live." Faye was silent, a bad sign. Lola knew she'd overstepped a boundary with the powerful publicist. "I'm sorry, Faye," she said, backing down. "Didn't mean to snap. I'm kind of, you know, *emotional.*"

"Aren't we all?" Faye said dryly.

"Selma actually spoke today; she's progressing so fast. I'm overwhelmed."

"I suppose we'd better start putting the pieces back together," Faye said. "Image is everything, Lola, so if you're up to it, I'll go ahead and arrange an informal press conference outside the hospital—perhaps later this week."

"I'm up to it."

"I'll tell you *exactly* what to say."

"Okay."

"And I want Matt standing beside you. *Silently.* No statement from him. He should keep his mouth firmly *shut.*"

"Yes, Faye," she said obediently. "Tell me when and where, and I'll be there."

Faye was the best in the business, and Lola had no desire to alienate her.

She needed Faye. Faye needed her. They were a perfect team.

The wrap party for *Caught* was taking place at the Sunset Room, a huge, cavernous venue in Hollywood. Cat had made sure that there was plenty of money in the budget for a lavish blowout. She believed in rewarding the crew, since they always seemed to enjoy the wrap parties more than anyone.

The club featured a restaurant on one side and an area for dancing in the back. Cat had booked the hottest DJ of the moment—Big Boy, a onetime rapper who was into the best sounds, current *and* vintage.

"I'm not into givin' out compliments," Nick Logan said.

"Good," Cat replied. "'Cause I'm not good at accepting them."

"But," he said, rubbing his stubbled chin, "somebody's gotta tell you that you look fuckin' *great.*"

"It's for the crew," she said casually. "They've only ever seen me in jeans and combat boots, bossing everyone around. So I thought—"

"You thought right," he interrupted. "I repeat—you look fuckin' great."

She'd pulled out all the stops and glamoured up for a change. She was wearing a jagged-hemmed Isaac Mizrahi skirt and a plunging Dolce & Gabbana silk jersey top with no bra.

She was delighted Nick had noticed.

Not that she cared.

Well . . . maybe just a bit.

Mustn't take Nick Logan too seriously. He was about to be her revenge fuck, then they could both go their separate ways.

She left Nick and walked around, hanging out with all the guys—her cinematographer, the camera crew, the sound guys, grips, and gaffers. Plus the union drivers—they were all there with their wives and significant others.

The music was deliciously loud and overpowering. The drinks flowed freely and the food was bountiful—spare ribs, steaks, salads, baked potatoes, lobster, and shrimp. Something for everyone.

Cat dropped by Shelby's table. The beautiful raven-haired star was with her parents. Cat sat down and chatted with them for a few minutes. She wondered when Merrill would put in an appearance, then she noticed Jonas getting busy on the dance floor with Amy. The two of them made such an interesting couple—they were a perfect fit.

Nick was dutifully doing the rounds, charming every woman in the room. His bad-boy act was extremely popular; they all fell for it.

Cat found herself watching *him* longer than she should. He certainly knew how to turn it on.

"Mrs. Cheney," Pete said, coming over to their table, "can I interest you in a dance?"

"No, you cannot," Martha replied, blushing.

"Maybe I should ask your husband's permission."

"I don't dance," Martha said quickly.

"Yes, you do, Mum," Shelby interrupted. "Go on. Live dangerously."

Pete put out his hand and pulled her to her feet, escorting her to the dance floor.

"Doesn't Mum look lovely tonight?" Shelby said to her father.

George nodded, his face serious. "Now that your mother's not here," he said, "there's something I've been meaning to mention."

"Yes, Dad?"

George cleared his throat. "We're not fools. We know what's going on. And if things don't work out between you and Linc, divorce is not a disgrace. I know we've always set you an example that marriage is forever, but if Linc is treating you badly, and I suspect that he is, you must put an end to it."

She was startled that her father had finally addressed the subject. She was also relieved.

"Don't worry, Daddy," she said, putting her hand over his. "I won't let anyone mistreat me. I'm quite prepared to deal with the situation."

"I'm sure Linc's a kind man when he wants to be," George said. "However, I couldn't help noticing the way he treated you in London on your last trip. It wasn't pleasant to watch."

"I've told you about his childhood," she said. "Sometimes it's hard for him to deal with. The tragedy colors his behavior; that's why I've always forgiven him."

"I understand, dear. Only how long can you go on making excuses for someone?"

"You're right, Dad, I *am* planning on doing something about it."

"Pete seems like a genuinely nice man," George remarked.

"He is."

"There's no reason you shouldn't move on."

"I'm so glad you understand."

"We both do, dear. And remember—we're only a phone call away. We can come back anytime you need us."

"That means a lot," she said gratefully.

She was tempted to tell him that he was going to be a grandfather, then she thought, no—it wasn't fair to reveal the news to him without her mother knowing first. She'd tell them both when the time was right.

Pete returned a flushed Martha to the table.

"You're a great dancer, Mrs. Cheney," he said gallantly.

"Call me Martha."

"Sure, Martha." He put out his hand toward Shelby. "Your turn."

"I'm not in—"

"Get on the dance floor with me right now," he said forcefully. "I saw you dancing with one of the grips, and you are *not* shutting me out. Let's go."

"Run along, dear," her mother urged, beaming.

As luck would have it, the moment they hit the dance floor, Big Boy decided to slow things down, and put on Brian McKnight's very sexy "Shoulda, Woulda, Coulda."

Pete didn't hesitate; he pulled her in close.

She did not push him away. For a few minutes she forgot about everything and gave herself up to the feeling of being held close by someone she liked—a lot.

"Did Linc call you back?" he asked.

"No."

"What did you want to talk to him about anyway?"

"If you must know—I was hoping to straighten a few things out."

"Straighten out *what*, Shelby?" he asked, exasperated.

"I . . . I need to find out if we're really over, and if he's serious about wanting a divorce."

"Shelby," Pete said gently, still holding her close, "that's not *his* decision, it's *yours.*"

"I know," she said restlessly. "But it's so difficult. Sometimes I feel absolutely lost. I wish I could just fly back to England with my parents."

"You can if you want to. You're an independent woman. Of course," he added, "I'd miss you so much that I'd be forced to get on a plane and chase after you."

She smiled up at him. "Pete, you've been a true friend to me. I appreciate it so much."

"That's what friends are for," he said, pulling her even closer.

The warmth of his body made her feel safe and secure.

She wondered how he'd feel about raising another man's child.

Merrill Zandack made his usual flashy entrance. This time he was not accompanied by one steely-looking brunette, but two of them. They hovered closely behind him like a pair of matching sentinels.

Jonas cleared a table for him to sit at. After a few minutes, Cat moved over and joined him.

"Merrill," she said enthusiastically, "I'm glad you could make it."

"As if I would miss your coming-out party," he said, waving a large Cuban cigar in the air. "You're my new star, kitten. You're very, very good at what you do, and you're young, so I've got many years left before you turn into an arrogant pain in the ass."

She wanted to say, "Like you," but she

managed to control herself. "I'm glad you like what you've seen. I should have a rough cut for you in three or four weeks."

"I'll come to the editing room," he said. "I've got an eye, you know."

"No, Merrill," she said quickly. "You've got to leave me alone until I deliver my rough cut. Then, if you have any words of wisdom, I'll be happy to listen."

He rolled his eyes in an exaggerated fashion. "The girl's already talking back to me."

"Yup," she said, grinning. "Now I can."

"When do I get your new script?" he demanded. "I'm waiting."

"Let me finish *this* project. After that we'll talk."

"Oh, we'll talk, will we?" Merrill mocked. "I suppose your plan is to surround me with lawyers and shit."

"You didn't exactly treat *me* fairly last time."

"You won, didn't you?"

"Not thanks to you. If Nick or Shelby hadn't wanted me, I would've been screwed."

He roared with laughter. "You're a good-looking girl," he said. "Ever thought of being on the other side of the camera?"

"No, Mr. Z.," she said firmly. "I've never thought of that."

And so the party continued, with everyone having a good time.

CHAPTER
39

Allegra was stark-raving-crazy mad. Linc knew that much about her. She was always on, always yelling, always bitching about something or other.

She had the longest legs he'd ever seen, a tight pussy, and a vile temper. They shared ferocious fights, which made a refreshing change from Shelby clamming up on him.

Allegra was twenty-five. He was just about to celebrate his forty-third birthday.

Some celebration, with no Shelby by his side.

He missed her desperately. Often he harbored murderous thoughts about Pete. He wanted to hang the asshole by his balls from a very high pole. Stunt *that!*

He was not pleased with Lola, either. He was almost certain she'd orchestrated those photos outside the restaurant. Could it be that Freddy was right? She'd wanted to get back at him because he didn't remember fucking her. *Bitch!* He wouldn't fuck her with someone else's dick.

Allegra waltzed into the room wearing a skimpy Valentino slip-dress, four-inch stilettos—making her six feet four—and not much else except for a few strategically placed diamonds. One was a nipple piercing—painful, but extraordinarily sexy.

"Tonight," she said, her long, jet-black hair almost covering her face as she laid out several lines of coke, "we're takin' a walk on the wild side. You up for it, *stud?*" she challenged.

"I'm up for anything you got to offer," he responded.

"Cool," she said, greedily snorting as much coke as she could.

"Yeah," he agreed, doing a few lines, then reaching for a nearby bottle of scotch, knowing it was necessary to anesthetize himself before the onslaught of whatever Allegra had in mind.

Raja Mestres was a formidable-looking woman in her early sixties—with strong, powerful features, deep scarlet lips, and a commanding attitude. Clad in a flowing embroidered orange cape over black matador pants and a black cashmere turtleneck sweater, with numerous gold bracelets and bangles jangling on her wrists, she attracted the attention of everyone at the party in her honor.

The event was taking place in a magnificent thirties-style mansion recently restored to its former glory by self-made billionaire Jorge Jobim. Everyone who was anyone in the Latin community was there, plus a scattering of Hollywood stars and art-collecting producers and directors.

Lola had not met Jorge before. She was delighted to make his acquaintance, because she'd heard that he sometimes invested in movies, and there were future projects she had in mind that would never be considered by any of the major studios.

"You are as lovely as the image I see on the screen," Jorge said when they were introduced. Rumor was that he was bisexual—with a rich-in-her-own-right older wife and a series of beautiful young boys imported from South America, and later sent back with thousands of dollars' worth of designer clothes.

"And might I say that *you* are just as charming," Lola responded. "I have heard many great things about you."

"My dear," Jorge said, kissing her hand in a courtly fashion, "come, I will introduce you to *la belleza.*"

Lola did not consider Raja Mestres a beauty. She *did* consider her a great artist, and it was an honor to meet her.

Unfortunately Raja spoke very little English, and since Lola's Spanish was limited, their conversation was short.

"Can we go now?" Matt whispered, trailing behind her.

She turned on him. "No," she said fiercely. "We only just got here. This is an amazing house. Go take a look around."

A waiter hovered, holding a tray of canapés.

"What's the score?" Matt asked the waiter.

"Lakers are winning. The game's on in the kitchen," the waiter confided in a low voice.

"Where's the kitchen?" Matt asked.

"The other side of the swimming pool," the waiter replied.

Matt turned to Lola. "Do you mind if I—"

"Go ahead," she said, glad to be rid of him. He vanished off in the direction of the kitchen. It wasn't as if he was a great escort. He stood around like a dressed extra at a funeral, and had absolutely nothing to say.

"So," Nick said, giving Cat a long, intense look. "You think we can blow this pop stand?"

"Huh?"

"Leave. Split. Get outta here."

"I have to stay until the end."

"No way," he groaned. "You know what the crew's like when it comes to free booze; they'll be here all night."

"I should hang around until at least one."

"You brought your overnight, didn't you?" he asked, raising a hopeful eyebrow.

"One toothbrush."

"No clothes?"

"Why? Are you planning a hiking trip?"

"Maybe."

"You don't strike me as the hiking type, Nick."

"Hey," he said, fishing for a cigarette, "you might *think* you know me, but here's a news flash—no way."

"I know that you love women."

"Would you sooner I loved men?" he asked, squinting at her.

She laughed. "I guess I'm gonna miss you," she volunteered.

"I *know* I'll miss you," he responded, lighting up his cigarette. "I was thinking that after you finish editing, I'll still be on location in Miami—you could come visit."

"I'm not good at visiting my men on their various locations."

"How many *men* have you had?"

"I *told* you what happened when I surprised Jump in Australia."

"That was *one* guy," Nick insisted. "One major *asshole.*"

"And *you're* different?"

"You noticed any girls around lately?"

"No."

"That's 'cause I'm attempting to make a good impression," he said, exhaling smoke.

"Oh, I see. For our one night of crazy sex, huh?"

"Who said it was gonna be one night?"

"*I* did."

"You might be so into it you'll be *beggin'* to come back for more."

"Man, you certainly have a high opinion of yourself."

"Hey," he said with a cocky laugh, "never had any complaints."

Her parents were ready to go home, and Shelby was ready to leave with them, only Pete wouldn't allow her to. "They can take your car," he said. "You can't let the crew down. Everyone wants a photo or a dance with you."

She agreed to stay, although she would've preferred to go home and check her voice mail to see if Linc had called her back. Before she consulted a lawyer she hoped to have at least *one* conversation with him.

Allegra. A cover girl on *Sports Illustrated*. Was *that* the kind of woman Linc wanted to be with now?

Obviously.

Pete guided her around the club, satisfying everyone as he organized photos, making sure to move her from group to group at a brisk pace.

"Were you ever a publicist?" she asked with a smile. "You do it so well."

"Army training," he replied. "When I was a kid I ran away and enlisted. Then they found out how old I was and threw me out."

"How old *were* you?"

"Fourteen."

"No!"

"I was a big boy for my age."

"And smart too."

"Right. If I saw something I wanted, I went for it."

"Really?"

"Yes, Shelby," he said, giving her a meaningful look. "I've always been *very* determined."

The party was a huge success, with everyone enjoying themselves.

"We're *never* getting outta here," Nick grumbled.

"Oh yes we are," Cat responded. "Ten

more minutes and we'll sneak out without saying good-bye to anyone. How's that?"

"Perfect, if you think we can get away with it."

"We will, especially if you manage to shake some of those women who've been following you around with their mouths hanging open."

"*You're* not exactly going unnoticed," he retorted. "Who knew you cleaned up so good?"

"You did."

"Oh yeah," he said, grinning. "I did, didn't I?"

Fifteen minutes later they were in his red Maserati Spyder two-seater, roaring out of the parking lot.

"Nice wheels," Cat remarked.

"Had it delivered today," he answered. "My end-of-movie present to myself. This little mother can go from zero to sixty miles per hour in four-point-nine seconds."

"Gee," she drawled. "I can't wait."

"You're not into speed?"

"I love it—when *I'm* driving."

"Shut your eyes and think of James Dean."

"Oh, *you're* a laugh a minute."

"C'mon, blondie, take it easy."

"I will if you tell me where we're going."

"You'll find out when we get there."

"I want to know *now.*"

"Control freak."

"I am *so* not."

"Oh yes you are."

"Well . . . it takes one to know one."

"Guess so." And with that he put his foot down even harder.

Allegra's idea of a walk on the wild side was just that. An after-hours private club in the meatpacking district, with entry gained by possessing a phallic-shaped key, passing through two sets of door people, and uttering two passwords. Allegra was well prepared. They sailed through.

"Jesus, what *is* this place?" Linc mumbled, feeling high and low and totally fucked up.

"You'll see," she answered mysteriously. "It's a trip. You'll get off on it."

Yeah, he'd get off all right. He was so stoned he didn't even know what day it was.

Allegra pulled him by the hand, leading him down a flight of dark steps into a dimly lit club. The air was thick with cigarette and pot smoke. A tangled mass of people were thrashing about on a crowded dance floor, while a fat black woman stood on a small stage, clutching a microphone and wailing the blues.

All around the room there were large mattresses where people lounged. They were drinking, smoking, and making out.

Linc shook his head. What was this, a sex club?

"Hey, what's goin' on here?" he managed.

"You'll get off on it, hon, I promise you," Allegra said, her voice louder than ever as she led him over to a circle of mattresses where friends of hers were indulging in an abundance of illegal substances. She shoved him down onto one of the mattresses. "Meet Linc Blackwood, everybody," she said. "Never thought I'd bring *him* here, did you?"

"Well, well," observed a harsh-faced bottle blonde in bondage black leather. "Isn't *he* quite the prize."

Before Linc knew it, hands and tongues were all over him, fast divesting him of his clothes.

He didn't have the strength to fight back. What the fuck! Who cared? The sensations were pleasant enough, the bottle blonde's tongue talented, wet, and amazing.

Somebody began feeding him mushrooms, somebody else was rubbing coke on his nipples.

"You ever smoked heroin?" Allegra whispered. "Try it. You'll think you died an' went to heaven."

Jesus! Should he be doing this in a public place? How public was it anyway? Nobody could get in, not unless they had the key or the passwords.

"Relax and enjoy," Allegra murmured, slipping off her expensive dress and leaning over him, her nipples hard against his chest.

Everything was spacelike. Linc had no idea where he was or who he was with.

Lay back and join the party, that's all he could think about. *Relax and enjoy.*

Where the fuck was Shelby when he needed her?

CHAPTER
40

"Lola," a female voice called out, "it's so *fun* to bump into you again."

Fast approaching was Petra Flynn, the blond TV bombshell Lola had met at the health spa.

For a moment she almost forgot the bountiful blonde's name, then it came to her. "Petra," she exclaimed just in time, "how *are* you?"

"Better than the last time I saw you," Petra responded, pulling her escort over, huge breasts spilling out of a low-cut red dress.

"Meet my new man," she said proudly. "Jump Jagger."

"Any relation to—"

"No," Jump interrupted, a tall, skinny rock 'n' roller with multiple piercings and tattoos.

"Jump's a rock star in his own right," Petra confided, giggling. "He's going to be huge. Oh, sorry, honey," she said, clinging to his arm. "I didn't mean you're *going* to be huge, we all know you *are* huge."

Where is Isabelle when I need her? Lola thought. *Petra Flynn is too much for me to deal with.*

Then she saw him. Tony Alvarez, walking into the party for Raja Mestres, his Puerto Rican baby-faced tramp clinging to his arm. Not only did the girl look twelve, she was also short.

Tony hadn't spotted her yet, but Lola knew it would be only seconds before he did. The magnetic force that existed between them was undeniable.

Sure enough, he glanced over and their eyes met. They shared one of those looks-across-a-crowded-room moments.

She immediately turned her head and started talking to Petra and her rock star boyfriend. "How did you two meet?" she asked, not at all interested.

"I was in New York doing a voice-over for a commercial," Petra explained, only too happy to relate the story. "And as I was walking out of the recording studio, there was Jump walking in. We literally bumped into each other. I started asking him about his tattoos 'cause I just had one put in a place that I'm not revealing to *anyone.* And he recommended a terrific guy in L.A. So I asked him if he ever came to L.A. And he said he didn't have a place here, and *I* said he could come and spend the weekend with *me.* And here we are."

"Sounds romantic," Lola murmured, although she hadn't listened to a word.

"It is," Petra agreed.

"Good for you."

"I read about your sister getting shot," Petra said, lowering her voice to a respectful whisper. "That was *so terrible.* Was she the sister I met at the spa?"

"No," Lola said, keeping one eye on Tony as he maneuvered his way across the room, slowly making his way toward her. "It was my other sister, Selma."

"How awful!" Petra exclaimed.

"I'm happy to say she's out of her coma and doing well."

"It's *incredible* what they can do at hospitals," Petra said, absently fingering one of her enormous implants.

"Hospitals don't bring people out of a coma," Lola said. "They come out of it on their own."

"What a drag that they can't do that," Petra said. "Isn't that a drag, Jump?"

"Yeah," Jump agreed. "Anywhere around here I can go take a smoke?"

Suddenly Tony was upon them. God, he had a nerve, approaching her with his girlfriend by his side. How dare he!

"Lola," he said, dark eyes sexy as ever.

"Tony," she responded, desperately attempting not to fall into them.

"Meet Maria."

"Hi, Maria, dear," she said, coolly, looking down at the girl, who was not only short but flat-chested, with no ass. *She must sing one hell of a song in the bedroom,* Lola thought sourly.

"Hi," Maria answered in a little-girl voice.

"Do you know Petra Flynn and Jump Jagger?" Lola asked, playing gracious hostess. "And no, he's not any relation to—"

"To who?" Tony interrupted.

"Mick Jagger, of course."

"Why would he be related?"

Tony was purposely being obtuse. *Go screw yourself,* she wanted to say to him as he stood there with his baby girlfriend by his side. He thought he was so smart. Well, he wasn't. Tony Alvarez was a thug, and she knew it.

"How's Selma doing?" Tony asked.

Oh yeah, like you care. "She's doing well, thank you. The doctors assure us she'll be out of the hospital within days."

"I'm pleased."

So you should be, you bastard. It was all your fault.

"Who's Selma?" Maria piped up in her thin, annoying voice.

"Lola's sister," Miss Know It All Petra said. "The one who got shot. I read about it in the *Star.* It was *horrible!* Ohmigod—," she exclaimed, suddenly realizing who Tony was. "You were *with* her, weren't you?"

"Yeah," Tony said. "I was there."

An awkward silence took place while Maria looked at him questioningly, waiting for an explanation. There was none forthcoming.

"Oh," Petra said, waving across the room. "Isn't that Ricky Martin? I must go say hello." Dragging Jump by the arm, she departed, leaving Tony, Maria, and Lola standing by themselves.

There was another awkward silence. This time Tony broke it.

"Maria," he commanded, "go look at the paintings."

"I'll wait for you," Maria ventured.

"No," Tony said sharply. "Go look now. I'll catch up with you."

Maria was too young to argue. She took off with a hurt expression.

"Dealing in juveniles now?" Lola said, arching an eyebrow.

"She's eighteen," Tony replied evenly. "Is that a bad thing?"

"Let me ask you something," Lola said. "If *I* was with an eighteen-year-old boy, would you think *that* was a bad thing?"

"Ah, but you wouldn't be," Tony responded knowingly. "You prefer your men seasoned."

They exchanged a long, lustful look.

"Have you explored this house?" he said. "The architecture is quite something."

"That's what I told Matt," she said. "He didn't seem to get it."

"Where *is* your old man?"

"Watching a ball game in the kitchen with the waiters."

"Then maybe *I* should show you around. I've been here many times before. Jorge is a close friend."

"Why not?" she said, her voice husky.

"Come," Tony said, taking her arm and leading her in the opposite direction from Maria.

Somehow, now that Selma was better, her bargain with God did not seem so important.

"What are we going to do?" Pete asked. They were sitting in his SUV in Shelby's driveway.

"Nothing right now," she replied.

"We can't go on pretending that there isn't something happening between us."

"Pete, you *know* the position I'm in."

"Yes, I do. And I also know that you shouldn't wait any longer," he said forcefully. "Linc's living with someone—doesn't that tell you it's over between the two of you?"

"I suppose so," she answered listlessly.

"Then *act* on it."

"I will."

"When?"

"Monday."

"Promise?"

"Yes, I promise."

He leaned over and kissed her on the lips, gently at first, but as the kiss progressed, things became more intense.

She found herself responding to him with a rush of passion, remembering the long, steamy necking sessions they'd indulged in way before she'd met and married Linc.

After a few minutes he backed off. "Why don't we go to my house?" he suggested.

"I can't," she responded breathlessly. "This is my parents' last night in L.A. I have to be here for them in the morning."

"You sound more like a schoolgirl than a big movie star," he said, amused.

"Aren't we *all* kids when it comes to our parents?"

"Guess so," he said, and he leaned in and started kissing her again, long, dreamy soul kisses. "When?" he asked.

"As soon as they leave," she promised, thinking that Pete was a very special man, and if Linc hadn't come along, who knew what would've happened?

"I'll wait," Pete said.

"I know you will," she answered softly, reaching for the door handle.

"Where are you going?" he asked, loath for her to leave.

"Home. I live here. Remember?"

"Can I come in with you?"

"No, Pete. My parents . . ."

"Man," he said, shaking his head. "You're making me feel like I'm back in high school."

"Sorry."

"Don't be," he said, jumping out of the driver's seat and running around to open the passenger door for her. "I kinda like it. Makes me feel young."

She stepped out of the SUV and into his arms. He kissed her again, holding her close for several minutes.

"Tomorrow," she whispered, extracting herself.

And she entered her house, wondering how he'd feel when she told him she was pregnant.

* * *

"I'm *ravenously* hungry," Cat exclaimed as Nick's Maserati sped along the Pacific Coast Highway at ninety miles an hour. "And *you're* about to get us arrested."

"For what?" he said, clicking on the CD player, flooding the night with the raucous sounds of Fifty Cent.

"Speeding, of course. *And* driving half drunk."

"I am *not* half drunk," he protested. "Had a coupla beers, that's it. Besides, alcohol doesn't affect me."

"It might not affect you," she lectured. "However, I don't think the cops would be too happy. The speed limit on PCH is probably like thirty-five. What do *you* think?"

"I think I like this car a lot," he said, shooting her a quick look. "Almost as much as I like you."

"Oh, so now I'm in competition with a car, am I?"

He laughed. "You're not in competition with anyone. You're an original. You're funny, talented, unusual, knowledgeable; now all I gotta do is find out if you're a great lay."

"Ha! *I* don't have to prove anything," she said. *"You* do."

"You wanna know if *I'm* a great lay?" he said quizzically. "I'll give you a book of references, how's that?"

"Your girlfriends write you references, do they?"

"I've had a couple of English ones write about me in the London tabs. 'Nick Logan is the greatest lover I've ever had,' and that's a direct quote."

"I know *all* about the English papers. Those girls say it about any famous guy they can lure into bed. They get paid big bucks for scoring with a celebrity—doesn't matter who it is. Jack Nicholson, Nic Cage, Rod Stewart. They always claim the guy is the greatest lover they ever had, with the biggest dick. It sells more papers."

"No shit?"

"Like you didn't know."

"I didn't," he protested.

"Yes you did."

"No. I *didn't.*"

"Where the *hell* are we going, Nick? Did you buy me a beach house?"

"Yeah, *right.*"

"Then where?"

"You'll see."

"When?"

"Stop bitchin'."

"Can we pull over and get something to eat?"

"Close your eyes and be patient."

"I *am* patient."

"No, you're not."

"It's been such an incredible night for me," she sighed, leaning back in her seat. "Finishing the movie, and then the party."

"The party was great," he agreed.

"So . . . right now I'm not into a magical mystery tour. I'm tired and I'm hungry."

"Can we add horny?"

"You *wish.*"

"Five more minutes," he promised. "How's that?"

"Okay," she said, glancing pointedly at her watch. "But I should warn you, I'm timing you."

Five more minutes, and true to his word he spun the car off the road toward a private gated estate, whereupon he entered a security code and the large gates swung open.

"Where are we?" she asked curiously.

"A friend's house. He lent it to me."

"What friend?"

"You have to know everything, don't you?"

"As a matter of fact, I do."

"A very *discreet* friend, 'cause I knew you wouldn't want to go to a hotel."

"You could've come to my place."

"Nope. We're not doing it at your apartment where you can throw me out after it's over. This is neutral territory. Not my turf or yours. Smart, huh?" he said, speeding the car up the long, palm-tree-lined driveway.

"This must be a very rich friend," Cat remarked.

"He's got a buck or two."

"It's not your mafia friend who owes you a favor, is it?"

"I didn't say *he* owed me a favor, I said *they offered* me a favor. Big difference," he said, pulling the Maserati up in front of the house. "C'mon," he said, jumping out of the car. "It's time for you and me to see if we *really* connect."

"What do you think you're doing?" Lola asked, her heart pounding, because Tony always had that effect on her.

"Locking the door," he responded.

"You can't do that," she argued.

"I can't, huh?" he said, throwing her one of his looks.

"This is obviously the master bedroom, and the windows overlook the party."

"Nobody's spying on us."

"You're sure about that?"

"Yeah, baby, I'm sure."

She wandered around the room for a moment, taking in the lush furnishings—everything in various tones of brown and beige. Then she sat on the edge of the king-size bed. "Well," she said, her heart still beating fast. "Here we are again."

"Yeah," he replied. "Here we are."

"What do you want from me, Tony?" she asked.

"What do *I* want from *you?*" he replied. "The question is, what do *you* want from *me?*"

"Nothing."

"Then why did you come in here with me?"

"Because I thought you were showing me the house."

"Last time I saw you it was a different story," he said. "Remember?"

"Nothing's changed," she replied, wishing he wasn't so damn hard to resist. "We *still* shouldn't be together."

"That's why I got myself engaged."

"Because of me?"

"Yeah. Thought it might cool things down for you now that you're back with that prick you're married to."

"Y'know, I should be going," she said, getting up and heading for the door.

Tony quickly moved in front of her, blocking her way. She attempted to dodge past him. He refused to allow her to. Then he began running his hands up and down her body.

"Tony," she said in a low husky voice, "this is impossible."

"Missed you, babe," he said, touching her breasts, before sliding his hand up the slit in her skirt and caressing the top of her thigh.

"We . . . can't do this," she said, his touch already driving her crazy. "I'm back with my husband."

"You get off on it, babe. I know you too well."

"There's people outside," she protested. "Your girlfriend, my husband. We could be seen."

"Who gives a fuck?" he said, unzipping his pants. "We got a thing goin' nobody can break. So, c'mon, baby, suck my cock. You know you do it better than anyone."

She thought about refusing, walking away, telling him to get lost.

But the truth was that she was incapable of doing or saying any of those things.

She didn't want to. Tony Alvarez was *still* her addiction of choice.

CHAPTER

41

Nick's friend's house was not a simple beach shack; it was a magnificent oceanfront mansion.

"Who does it belong to?" Cat asked, exploring the series of huge reception rooms, which all overlooked an enormous marble terrace, which in turn overlooked the beach.

"A record producer dude I know," Nick answered, going to the bar and taking out two bottles of beer. "I played a rock star in a movie. This guy did the music."

"Single?"

"Why, wanna hook up with him?" he said, handing her a beer.

"You're hilarious," she said. "I was wondering how his wife feels about us borrowing their house."

"The dude's on the loose. No wife. He's the kinda guy runs three girls at a time."

"Sounds like a pimp."

"What can I tell you?" Nick said, swigging beer. "He's a player."

"Then it's no surprise the two of you get along."

"We've shared a girlfriend or two," he admitted.

"Is this his picture?" she asked, picking up a silver frame from the top of a baby grand piano and staring at a silver-haired man with a George Hamilton suntan.

"That's him."

"Not bad looking, in an older-man sort of way."

"The dude's pushing sixty."

"I can't stand all those old geezers who think they're so hot," she said, wrinkling her nose. "All they do is chase after girls a quarter of their age. It's a total turnoff."

"At least they can still get it up."

"What's the *point* if they can only get it up with Viagra?"

"You don't believe in Viagra?"

"My philosophy is that if you can't get it up in the normal fashion, why bother?"

Now it was Nick's turn to laugh. "Tell *that* to all the old guys," he said, opening up the doors to the terrace. "I'm thinking Jacuzzi. How about you?" he said, walking outside.

"You know what," she said, following him out. "This is too over-the-top for me."

"Huh?" he said, shooting her an I-do-not-believe-that-you're-backing-out-on-me look.

"This whole cool playboy scene," she said restlessly. "Y'know—the fabulous mansion, the outdoor Jacuzzi. I feel like I'm in some cheesy TV reality show."

"Does that mean you wanna go somewhere else?"

"Yes."

"You're kidding, right?"

"No. Why don't we get in the car and drive?"

"Where to?"

"Anywhere we feel like."

"*C'mon,* Cat," he groaned. "It's late, an' we're already here."

"Don't tell me you're chicken?" she challenged.

"Me?"

"Chicken, 'cause *you're* not into taking chances."

"Who said I wasn't?"

"Then let's blow this mausoleum and hit the highway."

"You're crazier than me, you know that?"

"Actually," she said, smiling sweetly, "I never doubted it."

As Tony reached a noisy climax, somebody began rattling the handle of the bedroom door, and a loud voice said, "This is security. Open up."

"Oh, *shit!*" Tony said, zipping up his pants.

"Oh shit is right," Lola gasped, adjusting her dress. "Now everyone will see us come out. This is terrible!"

"Lock yourself in the bathroom. I'll go out first."

"Open this door now!" the security guard commanded.

"Go on," Tony urged. "Get in there. I'll handle this."

She hurried into the bathroom and locked

the door. Her hands were shaking, her cheeks flushed.

This was madness. She and Tony were over.

And yet . . . tonight she'd been powerless to resist him. Totally powerless. Her career, her family meant nothing compared to her lust for Tony.

"Pull over," Cat ordered.

"We're in the middle of nowhere," Nick pointed out.

"You're such a wuss."

"What didja call me?"

"You heard."

They were way down the Pacific Coast Highway, with high cliffs on one side and rocks and surf on the other. It was pitch-black and the roar of the ocean was fierce.

"Pull over," Cat repeated.

"Jesus!" he complained. But he did as she asked, pulling the Maserati onto the hard shoulder of the road and cutting the engine.

"Out!" Cat commanded.

"What we gonna do—take a walk?"

"You're not very adventurous, are you?"

she teased. "We're going to climb down to the beach and . . . who knows?"

"Shit, Cat. It's dark and it's dangerous."

"Oh my God! Mr. Nick Logan, big stud, is really a great big scaredy *boy!*"

"Shut the fuck up," he said, laughing—because this girl was nuts, and he liked it.

"Make me," she said, jumping out of the car, hiking up her skirt, and scrambling over the rocks, climbing her way down toward the small strip of sand.

"I'll make you, all right," he yelled, coming after her.

"Yeah? Catch me if you can!" she shouted, feeling free and exhilarated and totally alive.

This was a lot more exciting than lounging around in a Jacuzzi in some rich guy's fancy mansion.

Lola could hear loud voices, then there was silence. Was Tony coming back to tell her it was all clear, or was she supposed to wait?

She glanced at her watch and decided to stay in the bathroom—which incidentally was quite sumptuous. Black marble with touches of gold. A huge tub surrounded with gold cherub fixtures. Ornate gilded mirrors and a lounging area covered in some kind of animal fur with a TV suspended above it.

She waited five more minutes, then slowly emerged.

On her knees in the master bedroom was Raja Mestres going down on Maria—Tony's innocent little eighteen-year-old fiancée, who lolled casually on the edge of the bed.

"Oh!" Lola exclaimed.

Raja raised her head for a moment, quite unperturbed, while Maria lay there like a playful kitten—skirt around her waist, legs spread, exhibiting a small mound of silky pubic hair.

"Excuse me," Lola muttered. "I was using the bathroom. I didn't realize—"

"Iss *bueno*," Raja interrupted in her man-size voice. "You like join us?"

Maria didn't move.

"Uh, no thank you," Lola said, quite shocked, as she edged her way to the door, which was once again locked.

Raja rose from her knees and quietly let her out, locking the door behind her.

What a surreal scene *that* was. Lola couldn't *wait* to tell Tony.

* * *

The waiters were discussing the guests. Normal observations—"Didja see the rack on Petra Flynn?"

"Who's that fat stoner with the attitude?"

"One more bossy order from that skinny bitch with the diamond rock an' I'm pissin' in her drink."

"How about the ass on Lola Sanchez? I'd like to move in an' stay a week!"

Matt blended in. They'd forgotten he was there as he sat in front of the TV tossing peanuts into his mouth. He took the comment about his wife as a compliment. She *did* have a gorgeous ass, nothing insulting about *that.*

Now that they were back together he had to work on making sure that she didn't throw him out again. To be safe, he'd consulted a lawyer, making sure that next time it would not be so easy for her to dump him.

One of the waiters came running into the kitchen, slamming his tray down on the counter. "Nobody's gonna believe *this* one," he announced. "Tony Alvarez locks himself in the master bedroom with that hot Lola Sanchez piece, then security figures out somebody's in there, so *they* tell Jorge, *he* gets pissed, an' sends security to throw them out. Well, security starts hammering on the door, and two minutes later out comes Tony Alvarez and no Lola. So, I'm keeping an eye on the situation, and suddenly I notice Raja Mestres go in there with Tony Alvarez's girlfriend. Now the three of them are in there together. Then Lola Sanchez waltzes out looking mighty pleased with herself. Guess she had a good thing going with the two women."

"What're you gettin' at?" one of the other waiters asked.

"What do you *think* I'm gettin' at," the first waiter said triumphantly. "They're a bunch of lesbos."

"Isn't Lola Sanchez married?"

"Yeah. Poor guy. She's cut his balls off an' she's wearing them as earrings."

All the waiters roared with laughter.

Matt wanted the floor to open up so that he could sink into it and vanish from sight. The only good thing was that nobody had any clue who he was. He blended in, just another basketball fanatic who couldn't miss a game.

Jesus! he thought. *I married the biggest bitch of all time.*

*   *   *

Nick caught up with Cat, grabbed her, and they collapsed on the damp sand, laughing hysterically. Pinning her hands behind her head, he kissed her, his tongue exploring her mouth.

"Isn't this more exciting than that movie set you wanted us to do it in?" she gasped, escaping from his insistent lips. "We never made it to the bedroom, but I bet there were satin sheets on the bed. How cliché is *that?*"

"I'm freezing my ass off, can't see a fuckin' thing, *and* I left my smokes in the car," Nick complained. "Apart from that, this is great!"

"Glad you're enjoying it."

"What if the tide comes in an' we're trapped? You thought of that?"

"You're *such* a downer."

"And you're *such* a wild one."

"Should be. I wrote the movie."

"Oh yeah, so you did."

"Hey—I've been on best behavior the last couple of months. I've directed a big-time movie, played grown-up, been totally responsible. I'm only nineteen, y'know. I can have some fun, can't I?"

"We'll have fun all right," he said, rolling on top of her and kissing her again.

It suddenly occurred to her that Nick Logan was a sensational kisser. There was a technique to really good kissing, and Nick had it down. Of course, she was no slouch herself. Jump had never mastered the art of a great kiss.

The wind was whipping up, they were getting sprayed by the surf, and Cat knew she was ruining her outfit, but she didn't care.

Nick's hands began exploring. She retaliated, unzipping his pants and investigating the possibilities. "No underwear?" she questioned.

"Never had any use for it."

"Bingo," she laughed. "Me too!"

Now he was kissing her in earnest, his talented tongue stirring her juices. The sand was everywhere. Neither of them cared as they hastily divested themselves of their clothes.

It was as good as they both expected it to be. Better in fact. Sexy and hot and exciting—with the added element of a dangerous location, the surf pounding right next to their bodies, and the darkness enveloping them.

When they were finished, they couldn't find their clothes.

"Oh . . . my . . . God," Cat joked. "We'll have to drive home totally nude. How's *that* for an excellent story on *E.T.?*"

"Got an idea," Nick said.

"What—wrap seaweed around your dick and play merman?"

"I want *you* around my dick," he said playfully. "I want *you* around it all the time."

"Hmm . . . sounds good to me."

Giggling and laughing, they started crawling around the gritty sand searching for their clothes.

Cat retrieved her skirt and top just as a huge wave came in, drenching them both.

"We'd better get outta here," Nick said, taking her hand and pulling her up. By this time the surf was lapping around their ankles.

"If we don't drown first," Cat yelled. Spotting her sandals, she snatched them up. Then they began the precarious climb back up the rocks.

"I can see the headline now," Cat giggled. "'Girl director and boy star washed out to sea.'"

"How come *you* get top billing?"

"Typical actor! Let's negotiate."

"Move it, smart ass," he said, pushing her from behind.

"Yes, *sir!*"

Still laughing, they finally made it to the top of the rocks.

"That was insane!" Cat exclaimed, attempting to struggle into her wet clothes.

"You're insane."

"So you keep on telling me."

"I always dreamed of meeting a girl like you," he said, pulling on his pants.

"You did?"

"Or maybe it was a nightmare."

"Screw *you.*"

"Anytime, ma'am, anytime at all."

"Are you awake?"

Shelby cradled the phone. "Yes, I'm awake."

"This is Pete."

"I know," she said, decidedly pleased to hear from him.

"I wanted to tell you how much I enjoyed tonight. I hope you did too."

"Yes . . . I did."

"And Shelby—"

"What?"

"Whatever happens, I'm always here for you."

"I think I'm beginning to understand that, Pete."

"I wish you would've come back to my house."

"I'm English," she said, letting him down gently. "I prefer to wait until I'm divorced."

There. She'd said the word aloud. Divorce. *I am going to divorce Linc.*

Oh God! How can I when I still love him?

Because I have to.

"I get it," Pete said. "I'm very—"

"Patient," she said, finishing the sentence for him.

He laughed.

"Good night, Pete," she said.

"Talk to you tomorrow," he said.

After putting down the phone, she lay awake for a long time thinking about what the future held.

No more procrastinating. Her baby needed a father, a man she could depend on. And much as she still loved Linc, he was sadly not that man.

CHAPTER

42

"I have a news flash for you," Lola said, sidling up to Tony, who was standing next to Jorge.

Tony turned to look at her as if they were merely vague acquaintances, not passionate lovers.

"Hi, Lola," he said. "Did you meet Jorge?"

"Ms. Sanchez is the most beautiful woman here," Jorge said, taking her hand in his, bringing it to his lips, and kissing it once again in a courtly fashion. "Voluptuous. I *love* voluptuous women."

"Me too," Tony agreed.

Then what are you doing with that nothing little girl? Lola thought.

"How's everything, Tony?" she said, playing the game. "I don't think I've seen you since New York."

"Everything's tight, Lola," he replied. "I signed the deal for my new movie yesterday."

"Yes," Jorge joined in. "And Tony also recently announced his engagement to a delightful young lady, quite delightful."

Somehow or other Lola kept the smile on her face. Jorge must be an idiot. Didn't he know that she and Tony were once engaged?

"Thanks, Jorge," Tony joked. "If Maria was a boy she'd be exactly your type."

Jorge frowned. He did not appreciate his sexual predilections being advertised to the world.

"Where's your wife?" Lola asked, plucking a glass of wine from the tray of a passing waiter.

"Unfortunately she could not come on this trip," Jorge replied. "She is at our house in Buenos Aires. Her father is a most important politician."

"She doesn't mind you coming here alone?"

"Why would she mind?" Jorge said, his eyes lingering on Lola's cleavage.

"L.A. is known as the city of temptations," Lola said, shooting a sideways glance at Tony.

"Ah, but my wife is a *very* understanding woman, and I am a very understanding man. It is only in unsophisticated societies that people get upset when extracurricular activities take place."

"Yeah, women can get very uptight in America," Tony agreed.

More guests were arriving. Jorge politely excused himself and drifted off.

"So," Tony said, his eyes inviting her to stay. "You wanna tell me your news flash?"

"Since you don't seem bothered by extracurricular activities," she said, savoring the moment, "it's about your girlfriend."

"You got somethin' to say about Maria?"

"Only if you want to know." A long beat. *"Do* you, Tony?"

"Depends."

"Where is she?" Lola asked, taking a sip of wine.

"Around somewhere," Tony said irritably. "When I'm ready to leave, I'll snap my fingers and she'll be there."

"Ah . . . men," Lola sighed. "Their egos are so big, just like your beautiful—"

"You tellin' me or not?" he interrupted.

"I thought you weren't sure if you wanted to know."

"Stop jackin' me, Lola. Spill."

"When you left me in the bathroom without coming back to rescue me—"

"You coulda come out whenever you wanted."

"As you can see, I did. However, I waited a few minutes first."

"Uh-huh?"

"And . . . it seems someone else had the same idea as us."

"You mean somebody else was makin' out in there?"

"Yes, and one of those two people was your dear fiancée."

His face hardened. "You're shittin' me?"

"No, Tony. I'm telling you the way it is. You think Maria is so sweet and innocent, when obviously you're totally wrong."

"Who was the guy?" he said harshly.

"Ah . . . that's what makes this such an *interesting* story."

"Stop fuckin' with me, Lola. I don't like it."

"It wasn't a man," she said, sipping her wine. "It was our esteemed guest of honor."

"Raja?"

"Yes, Raja. The great artist was busily going down on your fiancée like there was no tomorrow."

Unexpectedly Tony burst out laughing. "Jesus holy Christ!" he said. "And I thought Maria was so demure."

Lola was shocked by his reaction. She'd wanted him to call the girl every name he could think of. Instead he was laughing as if it didn't matter. "You mean you're not upset?" she said.

"No way. She's got the guest of honor's tongue up her crack. Hey—maybe I can get a discount on a painting."

Lola scowled. Her news had not had the effect she'd hoped for. "You're a pervert," she said.

"No, babe," he said, still laughing. "I'm a man."

*   *   *

"You know what?" Nick said.

"What?" Cat replied.

"My turn to do something wild now."

"Thought we just did."

"Yeah, we did, and I'm wet and freezing my balls off. How about you?"

"*Look* at me," she said, shivering. "I'm like something left outside in the rain all night."

"You're still a beauty."

"Ooh, compliments," she said, grinning. "I like it."

"Here's what we're gonna do," he said, executing a U-turn and heading back along the Pacific Coast Highway. "We're drivin' to Vegas and playin' blackjack. My game of choice."

"Oh, in our wet clothes, with *you* driving seven hundred miles an hour, we're off to Vegas, so *you* can play a dumb card game?"

"C'mon," he encouraged. "You're an adventurous soul. You *gotta* like gambling."

"Can't say I've ever done it."

"I'll teach you. I'm a degenerate gambler."

"That sounds *bad.*"

"I always win."

"Why Vegas?"

"Why not?"

"I can think of a hundred reasons."

"Go ahead," he said, driving fast.

"Okay. My movie wrapped, I'm beat, and come Monday I'm locked in the editing room. I think I need to go home."

"That's not a hundred reasons," he argued. "Besides, it's Friday. We've got the whole freakin' weekend. I'll have you back Sunday night."

"I can't walk into the editing room a total wreck."

"I did *your* adventure, climbed down a freakin' cliff to make out with you, *and* nearly got swept away. Now it's *your* turn to do something for me. Here," he added, tossing her his cell phone. "Call Amy. Tell her and Jonas to come join us at the Hard Rock."

"Really?"

"My dime. We'll make it a weekend."

"You *are* crazy."

"Have you noticed that if I'm not telling *you* that you're crazy, you're telling *me?*" he said, looking more disheveled than ever. "Are we a fuckin' match made in heaven, or what?"

"Actually, yes," she admitted, thinking how right he was.

"Go ahead," he said, shooting her a grin. "Call my sister."

"What's her number?"

"Speed dial number one."

Amy answered immediately. "What happened to you two?" she yelled, music blaring away in the background. "Jonas and me are still at the party. It's a blast."

"We took off on a side trip," Cat explained.

"Hmm . . . I see."

"Anyway, your insane brother has requested that you and Jonas join us in Vegas."

"Why?" Amy said, completely unfazed. "Are you two getting married?"

"No," Cat answered, choking with laughter at the thought. "I'm not even divorced, and somehow I don't get the vibe that your brother is the marrying kind."

"Stop speaking for me," Nick interrupted. "You never know, I might marry you. Stranger things have happened."

"Ooh, I'm *so* excited," Cat drawled sarcastically. "Try not to forget that I'm still married."

"Shut *up.*"

"Anyway," she added, talking back into the phone, "hop a plane and meet us at the Hard Rock. We're driving."

"You're actually risking your life in a car with my brother?" Amy questioned. "He's a lunatic driver."

"We've risked more than that tonight."

"I'll run it by Jonas, but you *do* know that he's not a spur-of-the-moment kind of guy."

"Tell him that we're celebrating the end of our movie," Cat said. "And that I'm *begging* him to come. That should do it. Wait a sec— talk to your brother," she added, passing the phone to Nick.

"Hey, little Sis," he said, one hand off the steering wheel as they zoomed down the highway. "You gonna make it?"

"If you say so, big Bro."

"I say so."

"Having fun, are you?"

"Oh *yeah.*"

"Told you she was a keeper."

"Right as usual," he said, clicking off the phone.

"Can we stop by my apartment?" Cat pleaded. "I need to grab some clothes.

Look at me. I vaguely resemble a drowned rat."

"I'm looking at you," he said sincerely. "It's a beautiful sight."

Matt emerged from the kitchen. The party was in full swing, crowded with guests laughing, talking, and clinking glasses. A classical guitarist played inspirational music, only Matt was not in an inspirational mood. He was severely pissed as he began searching for his wife—his lovely, gorgeous, *famous* wife, his delectable, unfaithful *bitch* of a wife.

Finally he spotted her, talking to Tony Alvarez. He walked purposefully over, his bland face grim.

"We're going," he said, roughly taking her arm.

"Excuse me?" she said, shaking free.

"We're leaving," he repeated.

"I didn't say I was ready to leave."

"I want to go *now."*

"I don't think so, Matt," Lola said, her brown eyes flashing. "Go back and watch your precious ball game. I'll let *you* know when I'm ready."

"Don't talk to me like that," he said angrily. "I'm your husband. Your *legal* husband."

She could see he was angry. Taking him back had been a major mistake. Now she'd have to get rid of him all over again, and she was sure her lawyer would not do it for her a second time.

Tony was watching both of them, his dark eyes cool and appraising.

She wondered if he'd dispose of Matt if she asked him to. Tony was a dangerous man, he'd probably do it. Not that she'd ever consider asking him. The only way she'd get Matt out of her house was to promise him another settlement, exactly like she'd had Otto arrange the first time.

"Go home if you must," she said. "Send the car back for me."

"You'd like that, wouldn't you?" Matt said, glaring at Tony. "You'd like to stay here with your boyfriend."

"What did you say?" Lola demanded.

"Everyone at this party knows the deal. You were *caught* in the bedroom with him earlier."

"Hey, man," Tony said. "This is not a conversation to have in public—cool it. People are starin'."

"Like *you* give a shit," Matt said belligerently.

" 'Scuse me?" Tony said, his face darkening.

"You're a two-bit druggie loser. A—"

"Enough, Matt," Lola said quickly, putting her hand on his arm. *Enough, or you could end up like Tyrell White—falling from a nineteenth-floor window. An unfortunate suicide.* "We'll leave, if that's what you want."

Matt shot Tony a triumphant look, while Lola made a face as if to say, *What can I do?* She wanted Matt out of her life, but certainly not as the result of violence.

Unfortunately Tony was capable of anything, so to diffuse the situation, she decided to leave the party with Matt, before the two men got into a fight. A fight that Tony would surely win.

Tomorrow she'd call Tony and make everything right. Come what may, their future was together.

The phone awoke Shelby at 3 A.M. She groped for it in her sleep.

"Yes?" she mumbled. "Who is it?"

"Shelby, this is Connie."

She couldn't imagine why Linc's sister was calling her in the middle of the night.

"Connie," she said, struggling to wake up. "Is everything all right?"

"No, I'm sorry, but it's not."

"What happened?"

"It's an emergency, Shelby. A few minutes ago I received a call from a New York hospital."

"What about?" Shelby asked, starting to panic.

"It's Linc," Connie said. "He overdosed on drugs."

"He did *what?*"

"Right now he's in intensive care. Suki and I are on our way to the airport. They're, uh . . . not exactly sure if he's going to make it."

I'm dreaming, Shelby thought. *This is all some horrible nightmare.*

Then she realized this was no dream, and her world started to collapse.

CHAPTER
43

"Tell me more," Cat said, her long legs propped on the dashboard.

"Jeez!" Nick answered, racing his Maserati past a sporty Mercedes. "I've told you *everything* about myself. You give a third degree like nobody I know."

"I'm excellent at it, aren't I?" she boasted with a wicked grin. "I should've been a prosecuting attorney."

"You would've killed."

"Thanks," she answered proudly. "Are we nearly there?"

"I hope so."

"What a night," she said, yawning loudly. "I never thought I'd meet anybody who'd want to do the crazy stuff I do."

"I never met a girl like you either," he agreed. "It's a kick."

"So—may I hear the rest of the Nick Logan life story?" she said encouragingly.

"The *rest* starts now," he replied. "I'm sitting in my new car with my new girl. And I like it!"

"Hmm . . . do you think Amy and Jonas have arrived yet?"

"They've probably checked into the hotel and hit the sheets. It's some ungodly hour. Sleep seems like a plan."

"Sleep *would* be nice," she agreed, thinking how much she liked him.

"In a bed—with you next to me."

"What?" she said, lightly mocking him. "You didn't enjoy the sand?"

"I can safely say I'll never forget it."

"Nor will I. It was good, huh?"

"It sure was. Did you—"

"Of *course* I did. How about you?"

"Like *I* could fake it."

"Men do, you know."

"You've *really* been mixing with a strange group of guys."

"Yeah, I should've stuck to the classy type of person *you* hang with."

"You're talkin' about my nefarious past," he said, changing CDs.

"I am?"

"Right on."

"Thank God we're almost there," she said, checking out a passing billboard.

"When was the last time you were in Vegas?" he asked, pumping up the volume on Kid Rock.

"Don't recall ever coming here. Isn't *that* sad?"

"A Vegas virgin," he said, whistling. "Wow!"

"Let's not get carried away. When were *you* last here?"

"I sometimes fly in for the fights with some of my pals. It's a regular party scene. Booze, babes, and two monsters knocking the shit outta each other."

"Sounds delightful."

"It's a diversion."

"And you always win at blackjack?"

"I'm lucky that way."

"Gambling is an addiction, you know."

"Does that mean I'm about to get a lecture?"

"Not from me. Trust me, Nick—lectures are not my thing."

On the way home, Lola checked with her mother on the car phone.

"Selma was very talkative tonight," her mother assured her. "The doctors say that she'll be able to come home in a few days. No permanent damage."

"That's *such* great news, Mama."

"It's late, where are you calling from?"

"Matt and I were at a party. We're in the car."

"Was it a nice party?"

"Yes, Mama, it was very nice. It was for the artist Raja Mestres."

"That *is* exciting."

"I think I saw Antonio Banderas there—your favorite."

"What I wouldn't give to meet that man," Claudine sighed.

"Next time I'm invited to one of his premieres," Lola promised, "I'll take you with me."

"No," Claudine said firmly. "You'll take Matt. He *is* your husband."

Oh God, now she'd have to confront the family again when she got rid of Matt. Her problems were never-ending.

Matt was sulking in the car.

"*I'm* the one who should be giving out the silent treatment around here," she said, when she got off the phone. "How *dare* you drag me out of a party while I'm talking to my friends."

"Your *friends?*" he sneered. "Is that what you call Tony Alvarez—a *friend?*"

"Tony's a very fine director and, for your information, a *loyal* friend."

"What were the two of you doing in the bedroom?"

"He was showing me the house."

"Some of the waiters were laughing about it."

"Laughing about *what?*"

"You and him in there, then *you* with two women. What are you, a *lesbian?*"

"Oh, for God's sake!"

They traveled the rest of the way home in silence. When they arrived at the house, Lola marched straight upstairs. Her mind was in turmoil. Thank God Selma had fully recovered and would shortly be coming out of the hospital. Normal life would resume, and Lola decided that there was no way she was about to be stuck with Matt.

There was only one answer. She and Tony should get married, then *nobody* could criticize them.

How quickly could she divorce Matt? That was the question. And how much would she have to pay him this time? She was rich, but not a billionaire by any means, and getting rid of Matt was turning into a big expense.

Matt walked into the bedroom shortly after.

"No TV?" she said sarcastically, sitting on the edge of the bed, brushing her hair. "Surely you want to sit downstairs watching sports for another three hours?"

"I'm not happy," Matt mumbled.

"Nor am I," she retorted.

"*I'm* the one who's being treated like crap," he whined. "I'm your *husband,* Lola. You married me, threw me out, then took me back. You can't treat me like a dog and expect to get away with it. I *refuse* to be made a fool of by someone like Tony Alvarez."

"I'm glad *you* brought it up," she said, seizing the opportunity. "The truth is that we *never* should've gotten back together. We're not compatible. It was a big mistake."

"What?" he said, perplexed by her attitude. He'd expected to mend bridges—not demolish them.

"You heard," she answered. "You're not the man for me, and I'm not the woman for you. That's the way it is, Matt. We should both face up to it."

His left eyelid began twitching—a sign that he was nervous. "What are you saying?" he said, flushing angrily.

"I'm *saying* this is not working out for either of us. You have to go."

"Lola—"

"I'll make sure you're well compensated."

"Compensated?" he exploded. "What do you think I am—an employee?"

"You know what I mean," she said, wishing she hadn't started something that her lawyer would obviously have to finish.

He started pacing around the room. "It's Tony Alvarez, isn't it? He always manages to come between us. If it weren't for him, you and I would be fine."

"Maybe so," she answered, putting down her hair brush. "However, that's the way it is."

"That's the way it is," he muttered.

"Not only is Tony one of the most talented directors in the world," she said, deciding that since she'd started it, she may as well lay it all out, "but he loves me, and I'm finally admitting that I love him too." She was glad that she'd said it. Relieved it was out in the open. No more deception.

"You *love* him?" Matt said, his bland face turning a dark crimson. "He's *engaged* to another woman."

"Maria is only a smoke screen," she explained. "Tony and I are meant for each other."

"You honestly believe that?" he said, shocked she would say such a thing.

"Yes," she said. "I only took you back because my family begged me to. It was a mistake. I need to be with Tony, and for once I'm doing what *I* want, not what my family thinks I *should* do."

Something exploded inside him. He was filled with a fury he hadn't known he was capable of.

"You unfeeling *bitch!*" he yelled.

"Pack up and leave tomorrow morning, Matt," she said coldly. "Tonight you can sleep in the guest room."

"You'd appreciate that, would you?" he said, completely enraged. "Why don't you have your *lawyer* throw me out, like before?"

"Don't fight it," she said, perfectly calm. "I've made up my mind."

"You're *obsessed* with Tony Alvarez, that's what this is all about," he shouted. "If he wasn't around, you and I would be very happy together."

"Whatever you say," she murmured, tired of arguing. "I'm going to sleep now. I'm sorry it had to work out this way."

Shelby did not know who to turn to, so she called Pete, who assured her he'd be over immediately.

When he arrived, she was already dressed and ready to go. She'd written a note to her parents, stuck it on the fridge, and put the puppy in its playpen, where it couldn't get into trouble.

"I need somebody to take me to the airport," she said, choking back tears.

"I'll drive you," Pete said, hugging her for a brief moment. "Everything will work out, Shelby."

"This is all because I left him alone," she

said, her beautiful face pale and wan. "I should have gone back to him, done what he wanted. I could've walked off the movie. It didn't matter."

"It has nothing to do with you," Pete assured her. "This would've happened anyway."

"Not if I'd given up my career and been by his side."

In the car on the way to the airport she decided to tell him about the baby. "There's something you should know, Pete," she said in a low voice. "Yesterday I found out I'm pregnant."

"Oh Jesus! *Now* I know why you've been in such a funk about everything."

"I have to go back to Linc," she said, nodding to herself. "You're a wonderful man, and I've enjoyed our time together, but Linc is my husband and I love him, so I *am* going back."

Pete nodded, although he was dying inside. "I understand."

At the airport he informed her that he was coming with her on the plane to New York.

"It's not necessary," she said. "I'll manage."

"No," he said, watching her closely. "I'm flying with you. You can't be by yourself."

"You don't have to do that," she said softly.

"Yes, Shelby. I do."

He purchased both their tickets, and they caught the next flight out.

Later, sitting on the plane, Shelby was frozen with fear. She kept on remembering the good times *and* the bad. The happiness and despair. Life with Linc had never been dull. And now . . . What if he didn't pull through? What would she do then?

She had to stop thinking about it. The only positive thing she could do was hope that he made it.

As soon as Nick and Cat walked into the Hard Rock, the front desk alerted the manager, and he came running out to meet them and escort them to a complimentary suite, where Amy and Jonas were already settled.

Amy, clad in yellow-and-black striped leggings and an oversized tee shirt, was sitting cross-legged on the terrace eating a bowl of cereal and sliced banana. "Wow!" she exclaimed, jumping up. "What happened to *you* two? You look like you've been through a garbage dump and come out the other side."

"Thanks," Cat said, stealing a slice of banana. "Guess I'd better go take a shower."

"Lead the way," Nick said, regarding her with affection.

"Oh," Amy said knowingly, "so it's like that, is it?"

Nick and Cat exchanged an intimate look, both of them unable to wipe the smile off their faces.

"That's cool," Amy said casually. "It means you won't be too knocked over by *our* news."

"What news?" Nick asked. "And where's Jonas?"

"He's downstairs buying me a—"

"Buying you a *what?*"

"Hmm, you'd better take a look at these and have a guess," Amy said, handing them a couple of photos.

Cat and Nick viewed the photos together. They were of an overstuffed Elvis impersonator in a white suit, holding a Bible, standing under a sign that read THE ELVIS WEDDING CHAPEL. Opposite him were Jonas and Amy, hand in hand, with huge smiles on their faces.

"Don't tell me you—," Nick began.

"Yup," Amy yelled excitedly. "We *did!*"

"You did!" Cat screamed. "And you had Elvis! How cool is *that?*"

"Couldn't help ourselves," Amy said. "We got here *way* before you guys, and we had nothing to do—except gamble, which Jonas doesn't. So . . . since we were celebrating—"

"Celebrating *what?*" Nick asked.

"Merrill made Jonas a producer on his next movie."

"That's fantastic!" Cat exclaimed.

"Anyway," Amy continued. "So we kinda sorta . . . y'know, decided to get married."

"Holy *shit!*" Nick exclaimed.

"Insanity obviously runs in the family," Cat remarked.

"I'll tell you something," Nick said, indicating Cat. "If my girl wasn't already married, we'd probably be doin' it ourselves."

"We would?" Cat said.

"Yeah, we would," Nick said, challenging her to argue.

"I dunno about that."

"*I* do."

"*I* don't."

"You always have to be the boss, don't you?"

"Yeah, as a matter of fact I do."

"What you need is a man who can control you."

"And I suppose *you're* that man?"

"Looks like it."

"Children! Children!" Amy chided, as Jonas walked in.

"Hey," Jonas greeted. "You're here."

"And *I* always thought you were so introverted and careful," Cat said, shaking her head. "Obviously I was totally wrong."

"She told you," he said sheepishly.

"She sure did! I'm *proud* of you, Jonas. Get your butt over here—the bridegroom owes me a kiss."

"Here's the plan," Nick said. "We'll grab a couple of hours' sleep, then we're gonna blow this town *wide* open. We got some *major* celebrating to do. It isn't every day my little sis gets married!"

She'd been lying to him. Lola Sanchez loved Tony Alvarez. She did not love Matt Seel.

The bitch had been lying to him all along.

Matt prowled around the house while his

wife slept in the luxurious bedroom she wanted *him* out of.

Matt out.

Tony in.

It was that simple.

Goddamn spic. Matt hated his guts. If it wasn't for Tony Alvarez everything would be all right between him and Lola. They'd stay married. Probably have kids to cement the deal. And he, Matt Seel, would become a superstar.

Jesusfuckingchrist! Tony Alvarez was the devil. He'd lured Lola away with his devilish powers.

Matt walked to the bar and took a bottle of beer from the fridge. He drank it down in several big gulps, then opened another one.

Did she honestly expect him to leave again? Leave, so that she could get all cozy with the spic?

Of course, she wasn't exactly a pure American girl. She was a spic herself, if the truth was known. And the truth *was* known, she didn't try to hide it.

Lola Sanchez. The Latina sex bomb.

Lola Sanchez. Cheating bitch!

So the two spics wanted to be together and have little spic kids, was that it? While *he,* Matt Seel, a pure-born American, was left out in the cold.

He'd had enough.

Tony Alvarez was not going to come between him and his future.

No fucking way.

Cat closed her eyes and gave herself up to the moment. Nick was a skilled lover, with all the right moves. They had a rhythm going, a fantastic, wonderful rhythm. Being in bed with him was almost as if it was their first time together. Making love on the beach earlier seemed like some kind of distant crazed adventure.

This had all started as a revenge fuck; now she was in bed with Nick Logan in Las Vegas and enjoying every minute of it. They were totally compatible.

"You do know that you're fuckin' gorgeous, don't you?" he said, pumping away.

"Such a way with words," she murmured, moving out from under him so that she could get on top.

He began to laugh as she straddled him. "Always gotta be in charge, huh?" Then his laughter turned to heavy breathing as she rode him to an incredible climax.

"Jesus!" he exclaimed when they were both finished. "That was the greatest."

"Mmm," she agreed, rolling off him. "You're not bad."

"Seems like you've had a practice run or two," he said, reaching for a cigarette.

"And I've got a feeling *you've* done this before," she murmured.

"A few times," he said, lighting his cigarette. "Never with anyone like you."

"And he knows what to say, too."

"Hey, the first time I saw you I knew this was gonna happen."

"I didn't."

"You certainly did," he said, blowing smoke rings toward the ceiling. "You were trying to ward me off 'cause you were my director, so it wasn't cool to hop into bed with your main actor. Right?"

"Your ego is out of control."

"Took a lotta willpower, though, didn't it?"

"Don't flatter yourself."

"There's nothing like the real thing, huh?" he said, turning toward her.

"I thought casual fucking was your bag."

"Then I met you."

"Hmm . . ."

"Hmm, *what?*"

"Until the next one comes along."

"You're wrong, blondie. Very, very wrong."

"We'll see," she said, not prepared to believe a word he said. "Only don't sweat it, 'cause casual sex suits me just fine right now. We can make it as casual as you like."

CHAPTER
44

Something awoke Lola. She wasn't sure what it was—a noise, a bump, or maybe it was a car starting.

She sat up and glanced at the clock. It was almost six in the morning.

Hmm . . . if there was an intruder on the premises, Big Jay would've been on the case. Big Jay slept above the garage in his own apartment, and there was also a guard on duty down by the front gate.

She wondered if Matt was still asleep in

the guest bedroom. Had she been too harsh on him?

No. Why pretend? He was about to walk away with a lot of money, *and* a case of half-assed fame. Women would want to be with him simply because he was the ex–Mr. Lola Sanchez.

She clicked on the TV, switching to the security channel, where she could see the gate.

There was a car leaving the driveway. *Her* car. *Her* Bentley.

Oh *shit!* Matt had taken her Bentley again. He'd gone and taken her car. Damn! She couldn't believe his nerve; he *knew* how pissed off she'd be.

Oh well, too late to stop him now.

Did this mean that she'd have to give him another settlement *and* the Bentley? Because it was unlikely that Otto would get it back for her a second time.

Her thoughts shifted to Tony. Today she'd call him and tell him of her plan. "I think we should get married," she'd say. "Dump the *puta* and let's get serious here. I'll arrange a fast divorce, and I promise I'll *never* run out on you again."

Yes, that's what she'd say. And Tony

would forgive her, because if he *wasn't* prepared to forgive her, he wouldn't have lured her into the bedroom at the party, locked the door, and forced her to her knees.

Not that he'd had to force her. She *loved* giving Tony Alvarez head. He was the best-tasting man in the world. A prince, a king. He was *her* man. And she loved everything about him.

Was it too early to call him? Yes. Tony was a night person. When he wasn't working he usually slept until noon.

Was Maria lying next to him?

Unlikely, because after she'd told him about catching his girlfriend with Raja, he'd probably dumped her. Tony was not the kind of man who'd put up with sloppy seconds.

She got out of bed and went into the bathroom. It was almost light outside, and she didn't feel like going back to sleep. She thought about driving over to her mother's. Claudine always arose early, and sometimes she could be persuaded to fix pancakes with crispy bacon and homemade jam.

Yes, she'd go over to Mama's house, corner her in the kitchen, and tell her very calmly that she did *not* love Matt, that there was no way she was staying with him—and if Tony would have her, they were getting married.

If Claudine threw a shit fit, it was too damn bad.

Matt drove Lola's Bentley as though he was a general about to go to war.

Oh, Lola would be so angry when she noticed her precious car was gone.

He couldn't care less. After all, he was only borrowing it. He'd bring it back, because very soon she'd want *him* back.

He'd dressed all in black and found his ski mask, which he'd placed on the passenger seat. He also had on a knit cap pulled low on his forehead. His outfit made him feel powerful and invincible—like a Ninja warrior.

Whistling softly under his breath, he headed for the Hollywood Hills.

"There's no way I can sleep," Cat said, suddenly sitting up in bed. "I'm way too hyper."

"Me, too," Nick agreed. "Wanna go play?"

"It's six A.M.," she pointed out.

"So?" he said, yawning. "There's no clocks in casinos. Nobody gives a shit. I'll set you up with a bunch of dollar bills and you'll play the slots."

"Oh," she said tartly. "You think *I'm* playing the slots while *you* sit at the blackjack table having fun with the grown-ups?"

He reached for a cigarette. "You'll have fun playing the slots."

"Who do you think I am, a little old lady on a walker?" she said, jumping on top of him. "I *insist* you teach me blackjack."

"I can't believe you've never played," he said, rolling her off him.

"I used to hang out in the casinos in Cannes and Monte Carlo with my dad," she said, remembering her unconventional childhood. "It was major boring. Full of incredibly ancient people hunched over the tables. I used to sneak off to the bar and persuade the barman to slip me a drink."

"What didja have to do to persuade him?"

"Well," she said, grinning, "remember that technique I demonstrated earlier?"

He put up his hand. "Don't wanna hear where you learned it."

"It was pretty good, huh?" she said, still grinning. "Gives a whole new meaning to the word 'French.'"

"Oh *yeah,*" he said, laughing and dragging her out of bed. "C'mon, let's get dressed and go downstairs."

"Should we do anything about Amy and Jonas?"

"No. They're a honeymoon couple, let 'em sleep."

Lately Tony Alvarez had been doing a lot of thinking about Lola. She was hot, she was sexy, but sometimes her fame was too much of a good thing. Everything she did was scrutinized. Everywhere they went, people stared.

Not that he minded the staring so much—he was well known in his own right. But the constant wave of publicity that followed her everywhere got on his nerves, plus he hated being picked to pieces by the tabloids. Maybe if he *didn't* keep on getting back with Lola, they'd leave him alone.

On the other hand there was Maria. Young, pliable Maria. Not famous yet, she was always available, and certainly not as contrary as Lola. One moment Lola was leaving her husband, the next she was back with the prick. He never knew where he stood with her.

This kind of drama did not appeal to Tony, although if he made the decision *not* to see her again, he'd miss her soft lips, voluptuous body, and their very special private games.

Knowing Lola, he wouldn't have to give her up entirely. If she stayed with her husband, she'd *still* want to get together on the side.

On the way home from the party, he'd questioned Maria about Raja.

"How could I say no?" Maria had answered, all wide-eyed and exceptionally pretty. "She *was* the guest of honor, Tonee. My parents taught me to be polite."

Sweet.

"Sometimes, Tonee," she'd added slyly, "you might enjoy two girls together? I have a friend who will come over and spend the rest of the night with us."

Even though Lola had given him spectacular head in Jorge's private bedroom, he was always up for more.

"Go ahead and call her," he'd said.

Maria's friend had come to his house.

She was a Caucasian beauty with long blond hair down to the top of her thighs. The three of them had played in Tony's bed until the early hours.

Later, both girls had fallen asleep draped all over him.

He hadn't minded. Why would he?

The only problem was that Lola was on his mind, and he couldn't sleep.

Lola hurriedly put on a tracksuit and base-ball cap, then ran downstairs.

Big Jay was still not up, nor was her housekeeper.

She peeked into the den to see if Matt had collected all his personal possessions, such as his collection of sports DVDs and the script he'd been writing forever.

She noticed that her personal organizer lay open on the desk. She didn't remember opening it herself, so she walked over and picked it up. The organizer was open to the letter *A,* where Tony's address and private numbers were listed. Somebody had slashed a thick red *X* through his name.

Why would anybody do that?

Matt, of course, showing off his venom.

How pathetic.

She was about to leave the room when it occurred to her to wonder *why* Matt was looking up Tony's address. Not that Matt would ever do anything foolish. But still . . .

Returning upstairs, she checked out Matt's closet to see if he'd taken his clothes.

No. Everything was still there, hanging neatly.

Hmm . . . he'd left early in the morning without taking anything. She had a lingering feeling that something was not quite right.

Maybe she should call Tony just in case.

No, she decided, absolutely not. Tony would not appreciate being awoken so early.

She picked up the phone and called her mother instead. "Pancakes, Mama?" she asked hopefully. "I'm starving."

"For you, Lucia—of course."

"I'm on my way."

"Can I get you anything?" the flight attendant inquired. She was a faded pretty girl with tight brown curls and a tired smile.

"No, thanks," Pete said, indicating Shelby, who'd fallen asleep with her head on his shoulder. "Ms. Cheney is sleeping."

"Do you think I can get her autograph when she wakes up?" the flight attendant asked, brightening slightly.

"This is not a good time."

"It's not?"

"Ms. Cheney is dealing with a personal crisis."

"So an autograph *won't* be possible?" the flight attendant said, bristling slightly.

"I'll ask her for you."

"I'd certainly like to get one."

Pete rolled his eyes as the woman walked away. When it came to celebrities, people didn't care what was going on in their personal lives. As far as the general public was concerned, celebrities were their rightful property.

His right arm was numb, but he was loath to move it and disturb Shelby. She looked so peaceful and relaxed, and she smelled so good.

He kept on thinking about Linc. They'd once been close, and although Linc had stolen Shelby from him, he certainly did not wish him any harm.

It was difficult, though. He loved Shelby so very much, and if Linc lived through this crisis he knew he'd never have her.

However, if Linc died . . .

Christ! It was a no-win situation.

He glanced at his watch. Another three hours before they landed.

Lola decided not to wake Big Jay, even though she knew he'd go into a big sulk if she sneaked out by herself. Actually, she quite enjoyed the freedom of being out on her own, and it wasn't as if there were any crazed stalkers around this early in the morning, although in the past she'd experienced her share.

She jumped into her sporty electric blue Mercedes and set off.

Naturally, her trusty guard at the gate was asleep. Wonderful! What exactly was she paying him for? Certainly not to fall asleep on the job.

She honked her horn, activated the automatic gates, and sped out on the way to her mother's house.

"Never draw if the dealer is showing a picture card," Nick instructed.

"Why?" Cat questioned. "I might be feeling lucky."

"You can't play this game on the way you feel."

"I can do whatever I want."

"Oh yeah, I forgot—it's *you* I'm speaking to," he said, sitting down at a blackjack table. "Miss I'll Do It My Way or Not at All."

"You've given me the basics and I *get* it, okay?" she said, anxious to get started.

"Don't sit next to me and screw up *my* game," he warned.

"Would you prefer I went to another table?"

"Now you're talking."

"Screw you, Nick," she said, wrinkling her nose. "I could be a big asset."

"Or a big pain in the ass."

"You *jackoff.*"

"How come you know me so well?"

A cocktail waitress approached. "Mr. Logan, can I get you anything?" she gushed, ignoring Cat.

"Not right now, thanks."

"You're sure?"

"Yes, he's sure," Cat said.

"Are you making a movie in Vegas?" the waitress asked, fluttering her overly long, fake lashes.

The pit boss gave the waitress a steely glare, indicating that she should move on.

"Sorry, Mr. Logan," the pit boss said, coming over. "The girls are excited you're here."

"No worries," Nick replied. "I'm kinda used to it."

"We'll try and keep people away from you."

"While *he's* doing that," Cat said, "I'm finding my own table to play at."

"Be lucky," Nick said.

"I intend to," she answered, wandering off.

As soon as Cat left, a flat-faced woman slid onto the seat beside him. The woman glanced at him, then did a double take. "You're Nick Logan," she announced, as if she was telling him something he didn't already know.

"Right."

"I've seen all your movies."

"I've seen all yours," he retorted, straight-faced.

"I'm not an actress."

"Shame."

Puzzled, she turned away.

He winked at the dealer. "Let's get this show on track. I got itchy hands."

Tony Alvarez lived way up in the Hollywood Hills. Matt maneuvered the sleek Bentley through the winding streets, searching for the address he'd found in Lola's organizer.

When he located the right house, he drove past the gated entry a couple of times before parking farther up the street.

He sat in the parked car for a few moments, considering his next move. Eventually he jumped out of the Bentley and made his way back down the hill, checking out the tall hedges surrounding the property.

Nothing that he couldn't scale.

If there was one thing Matt excelled at, it was athletics.

CHAPTER

45

Tony had to piss so badly he could barely stand it. Maria and her blond girlfriend were still draped across him. Taking a surreptitious peek at his watch, he decided it was too early to wake them. Jeez! He felt like pissing all the way to the ceiling—although it occurred to him that maybe he should try holding it in. Nothing like a piss hard-on to start off the day.

A smile played around his lips. Two girls. Two delectable *young* girls. It had been *some* party.

He closed his eyes again, drifting back into a half sleep.

Was he really ready to give up Lola?

Yes, if she didn't get rid of that dumb prick husband of hers and make up her mind.

Lola Sanchez . . . they did have something special going.

Lola was exciting and unpredictable. Not to mention a body to die for . . .

Maria and her girlfriend paled in comparison. They were like delicious and not-too-filling starters, while Lola was the main course, sating his appetite in every way imaginable.

Yes, Lola was the woman for him. And it was about time he did something about it before starting his upcoming movie.

"Hi, Mama," Lola said, bursting into the kitchen of her mother's house.

"Lucia, dear," Claudine said, greeting her famous daughter with a warm hug. "You look so lovely without makeup."

"Are you saying that I look like a hag *with* it?" Lola said, circling the center island and stealing a crisp piece of bacon.

"Don't be foolish," Claudine said, busying

herself at the stove. "I am merely saying that *I* prefer you without it. Your skin is flawless."

"Inherited from you."

"Perhaps," Claudine said, with a pleased smile.

"You *know* you have gorgeous skin, Mama. It's the envy of all your girlfriends."

"What are you doing up at this time?" Claudine asked, slapping Lola's hand away as she went for another strip of bacon. "This is most unusual for you."

"I get up early all the time. Sometimes I'm in the gym by five A.M.—*especially* when I'm on a movie."

"Sit down at the table and stop trying to steal things before you eat," Claudine scolded. "Tea or coffee?"

"I love your cooking, Mama, I always have," Lola said, sitting down at the table.

"I know. That's the only reason you come here."

"No, it's not."

"Remember when you got so skinny at the start of your career? I was quite alarmed."

"Mama! I was *never* skinny. I lost the weight 'cause the camera puts on fifteen pounds," she explained. "You don't want a *fat* daughter up there on the screen wobbling away, do you?"

"You were always my baby," Claudine said with a fond sigh. "Always my little one."

"Really, Mama?" she said, quite touched. "I thought Selma was your favorite."

"I love all of you the same," Claudine said briskly. "Although there's something special about the youngest."

"Mama," Lola ventured, thinking this might be a good time to bring up Tony. "I've been doing a lot of thinking over these past few weeks."

"Yes, dear?"

"I know you probably won't approve of what I have to say, although I honestly think you want me to be happy."

"Of course I do, Lucia."

"I have a wonderful career," she continued. "Only sometimes a career isn't everything, and the truth is . . . Matt doesn't make me happy."

Claudine frowned. "Why not?"

"Because he's boring."

"All men are boring," Claudine replied.

"That's a ridiculous statement."

"You have to train men *not* to be. Look at

your papa," Claudine said, ladling pancakes onto a plate.

"Yes, *look* at him," Lola responded.

"What do you mean by *that?*" Claudine asked, her lips tightening.

"Well, Mama, it's no secret that Papa is always . . . he's . . ."

"What are you trying to say, Lucia?"

"Papa has other women and you know it," Lola blurted.

Angrily Claudine slapped two pancakes onto a plate, almost throwing the dish at her daughter.

"I'm sorry, Mama," Lola apologized. "It's true. *Everyone* knows."

"Eat," Claudine ordered.

"I am *not* staying with Matt."

Claudine stood by the table, hands on hips. "I suppose *your* idea of happiness is getting back together with that *drug* dealer?"

"Tony Alvarez is *not* a drug dealer," she said, so sick of having to defend him all the time. "He's a fine movie director. People look up to him. Ask Selma, *she* loved him."

"Yes," Claudine said, her lip curling. "And look where it got *her.*"

"What happened wasn't Tony's fault."

"Whose fault *was* it, Lucia?"

"Whatever, Mama, I refuse to fight with you. I wanted you to hear it from me. I thought perhaps you'd understand. I *am* going to divorce Matt and marry Tony. I'd like to do it with your blessing."

Claudine shook her head in a despairing fashion. "I can't tell you what to do," she sighed. "You know very well how I feel."

"Sorry, Mama."

"Yes," Claudine said ominously. "So am I."

"You ran out on us," Jonas said accusingly, catching Cat at the blackjack table, where she was winning big time, with a stack of blue chips in front of her—each worth twenty-five dollars.

"This game's way cool," she said enthusiastically. "I could play all day."

"Cash in," Jonas said.

"Why?"

"I'd like to talk to you."

She pushed her chips over to the dealer, who changed them into five-hundred-dollar tokens, which she threw in her purse. "I've got like three thousand dollars," she said, leaving the table. "How good is *that?*"

"Excellent," Jonas replied.

"Gambling is a major kick."

"Let's go get coffee," Jonas suggested, "before you turn into an addict."

"Sure. Where's Amy?"

"Over with Nick."

"How's *he* doing?"

"Winning."

They made their way through the crowded casino to the coffee shop. Cat got a double espresso and a jelly doughnut.

"I'm in heaven!" she exclaimed, taking a big bite. "So, c'mon, spill—what's all this about you and Merrill? Tell me everything."

"I took your advice," Jonas said. "Went to him and told him I thought I'd done a good job on *Caught,* and I'd like to continue being a producer on his next project. He agreed!"

"When did all this happen?"

"After you left the party. He's putting me on his next movie—*Joe Fabulous.* They're trying to get either Jim Carrey or Mike Myers to sign on. It's such a great thing for me, Cat, and it's all because of you."

"You would've done it one of these days," she said, taking another bite of her dough-nut.

"Not without your encouragement and support."

"Well . . . ," she said, teasing him. "You were a lousy executive assistant."

"Sure."

"Now you can be a lousy producer."

"Thanks a lot."

"You're welcome."

"How's everything with you and Nick?"

"You know what—we're just having a good time. I'm not looking on it as anything lasting."

"According to Amy, he's very into you. She says she hasn't seen him like this before."

"Look, I know he's had a million different girls. Believe me—I'm not taking it seriously," Cat said, squeezing his arm.

"If that's how you feel—"

"It is," she said, quickly changing the subject. "I'm so psyched for you, Jonas, and since this is such a special weekend, let's make sure we all have a blast, 'cause after this, it's all work, work, work!"

With a minimal amount of effort, Matt scaled the hedge around Tony Alvarez's property. Landing on the other side, he found himself within easy sprinting distance of the one-story Spanish-style house.

He crouched on the ground for a moment, getting his bearings. The sprinklers had recently gone off, and the grass was wet and spongy.

One deep breath, and he made a quick dash toward the house. Hopefully there were no TV cameras to capture his arrival; not everyone had the kind of security Lola insisted on.

Lola. His wife. The famous Lola Sanchez. Without Tony Alvarez around, maybe she'd revert to the girl he'd married. The girl who'd once loved *him.*

He'd spent the night wandering around Lola's house, chugging beer and trying to figure out how to right a situation that had gone horribly wrong.

Every time he'd come up with the same solution.

Remove Tony Alvarez from Lola's life. Remove the bastard, and she would be all his again.

Matt had grown up in a household where his parents had vied for his affection. His mom was a rich girl whose family had disowned her when she'd married his dad, a lowly beat cop. They'd met when his dad had given her a parking ticket. Shortly after that—much to her family's disgust—they'd fallen in love and gotten married.

Even though there wasn't much money in the Seel household, his mom had always wanted the best for him. She'd grown up with the best of everything, and she'd wanted him to have privileges too, so she'd insisted that he take tennis lessons, while his father had made sure he learned how to handle guns.

The battle began when he was extremely young. He was never sure which parent to please first.

He excelled at tennis and received a scholarship to a good school, which led to a career as a professional tennis player.

His father had considered it a sissy occupation, so to appease his dad he'd learned everything he could about guns. Every birthday, from the age of eighteen on, his dad had gifted him with a gun. He had quite a collection. Usually they were locked safely in a drawer at the house. Every weekend he took them out to clean them, exactly like his dad had taught him to do.

When he married Lola Sanchez, his father

was delighted, his mother was not. She considered Lola beneath him, not good enough for her son, even though Lola was a big movie star.

During his first separation from Lola, his mother had told him exactly what she thought of her sexy daughter-in-law. It wasn't pretty.

When Lola had taken him back, his father had said, "Hang in there, son. You belong with a beautiful woman"—a wink and a nudge—"and a sexy one too. Take no notice of your mom—it doesn't matter that Lola's not our kind."

What did *that* mean? He'd never quite understood.

Now he was skulking outside Tony Alvarez's house, and the education his dad had given him was finally about to pay off.

He had a Glock semiautomatic pistol stuck in the waistband of his pants, and a thirst to eliminate the man who stood between him and his gorgeous wife.

Matt Seel was on a mission.

"Bye, Mama," Lola said.

"You listen to me, Lucia, do not do anything foolish. Think carefully about everything we've talked about this morning. Oh, and give my love to Matt."

Lola shook her head. Wasn't Mama listening?

I'm divorcing Matt. I want Tony, and that's the way it is, so stop trying to manipulate me.

One of these days she was going to have to reveal the truth. "I can't have children," she'd say. Mama would be sad, but she'd understand. Or would she?

"You had *another* abortion, girl?" Claudine would shriek. "God is punishing you for your sins!"

No, she could never tell Mama the truth; it was safer to make up a story.

At least she had her nieces and nephews, on whom she lavished much love and affection. Next weekend she decided to plan a trip to Disneyland. Big Jay would organize guards and maybe they'd all go early before the place opened.

Yes, it would be fun. The children would love it, and so would she. Sometimes she had to let the little girl in her out to play.

After the verbal skirmish with Mama, she'd eaten one pancake too many, which meant she'd have to punish herself at the gym.

Lately she hadn't been taking care of herself. What with Selma in the hospital and *that* whole drama, she'd lost the drive to work out, eat right, and generally stay on top of things.

She had a sinking feeling that *New York State of Mind* would not turn out to be one of her better movies. Linc Blackwood was a mistake. He'd been a bad mistake when she was eighteen, and he was a bad mistake for the lead in her movie.

Plus she needed to play stronger roles— roles that meant something. The other night she'd watched Sophia Loren in an old movie on TV. *That's* the kind of role she should be playing, dramatic and sexy, a showcase for her acting talents. She had to play women with brains as well as a body. Why couldn't she score the kind of role Shelby Cheney played in *Rapture?* An Oscar-worthy role.

The sun was coming up, signaling another glorious California day. She hoped Matt was not going to return home and give her trouble. In case he did, she decided to alert Otto, although she was sure she'd have to endure one of Otto's lectures.

"I'm paying you," she often wanted to yell at her overpriced lawyer. "Don't argue. Do as I say."

Otto was a big-time lawyer, which meant that if she wanted to keep him on her side, she couldn't say shit, although sometimes she couldn't help herself.

Oh God! She'd have to tell Faye that she was dumping Matt again. *That* wouldn't go down well.

Wasn't it amazing? Here she was, this big superstar, and she had to answer to people she *paid.* It was a ridiculous situation.

Maybe she should fire everyone and surround herself with a new crew of people, who wouldn't *dare* criticize her.

What a great idea!

The blonde stirred, her long silky hair a gossamer cloak around her delicate shoulders. Maria snored lightly.

Tony's eyes suddenly snapped open. He felt a wave of doom, as if he'd just awakened from a particularly frightening nightmare.

Someone was in the bedroom.

Someone was standing at the foot of the bed pointing a gun at him.

All he could make out was the shadow of a man and the gun, the metal glinting in the dusky half-light creeping through the black-out blinds.

Tony struggled to sit up, attempting to shove the girls off him.

"What d'you want?" he said in a low, angry voice. "You want money—I got plenty. On top of the dresser. Take what you want an' get the fuck out."

Maria woke up. "Tonee," she cried out, not sure what was happening.

"Stay still," Tony warned. "Everythin's gonna be fine."

"I . . . don't . . . think . . . so," Matt said, feeling tough and in control.

Who had the power now? Not Tony Alvarez with his flashy demeanor and insulting mouth.

Not Tony Alvarez—wife stealer.

Oh no, not Tony Alvarez.

Not the fucking spic.

For once, Matt Seel was *totally* in charge.

CHAPTER
46

"I've been thinking," Nick said.

"Hang out the flags," Cat joked. "Mr. Logan's been thinking!"

Nick and Amy had joined Cat and Jonas in the coffee shop. Cat still had her three thousand dollars winnings, and Nick had won twenty-five grand. Neither Jonas nor Amy were into gambling.

"You wanna hear what I've been thinking, or not?" Nick said, devouring a plate of scrambled eggs.

"Not," Cat said, drinking espresso.

"Are you *ever* serious?" Nick asked, throwing her a look.

"Only when I'm working. Remember?"

"Cat has a quirky sense of humor, like me," Amy offered, holding hands with Jonas.

"That's great to know," Nick said. "But here's the deal—*I'm* trying to be serious here."

"Sorry," Cat said, reaching for a slice of his wheat toast. "Go ahead—be serious."

Before he could reply, two giggling teenage girls approached their table.

"Are you Nick Logan?" one of them asked.

"Course he is," the other one giggled, nudging her friend.

"Guilty as charged," Nick said, poker-faced.

"Can we get your autograph?"

"On what?" he said.

They turned to each other and completely broke up.

"Maybe on my tee shirt," one of the girls suggested, thrusting out her small breasts.

"Got a pen?" Nick asked, unfazed.

"Oh." The girl looked blankly around the table. "Does anyone have a pen?"

Amy reached into her purse and obliged. Nick spun the young girl around and scrawled his name on the back of her tee shirt.

"The girls at school will go like *nuts!*" she exclaimed. "You're the *bomb!*"

"You were *sooo* hot in *The Jack,*" the other girl gushed. "I like saw it like *four* times. I even cut class to see it."

"Thanks, girls."

"Do you know Ashton Kutcher?"

"Never met him."

"He's cute too. Can we take a picture with you?"

"Got a camera?"

"We'll get one from the gift shop."

"Do that, an' if I'm still here, you'll get your photo."

Giggling, the two nymphets ran off.

"Doesn't that drive you crazy?" Cat asked.

"What?" Nick asked, finishing his eggs.

"The attention."

"If I didn't have the attention, they wouldn't go see my movies. And we want them to see *our* movie, right?"

"Don't you miss being able to walk around and not be bothered?"

"It's a trade-off," he said. "I'm not wild about it, but I gotta put up with it."

"Oh *please,*" Amy interrupted. "You *love* it. Ever since you were a little boy, you *always* wanted to be noticed."

He grinned. "My married sister with the big mouth."

She grinned back. "My famous brother with the big—"

"Hey," he interrupted, motioning her to shut up. "Enough already."

"No need for modesty," Amy said mischievously. "I'm sure Cat has already noticed your enormous . . . ego."

They all laughed.

"So c'mon, what were you thinking when I interrupted you?" Cat asked.

"I was thinking that since we're only here for a day, how about taking a boat out on Lake Mead?"

"You're amazing," Cat said. "You drive all night, sleep for two minutes, win twenty-five thousand bucks, and *now* you're up for a boat trip."

"Why not? It's all in a day's fun."

"*I* think it's a fine idea," Amy said, joining in. "Come on, Jonas, we'll go to the front desk and find out about hiring a boat."

Jonas jumped up, and the two of them went off still holding hands.

"Ain't love grand?" Nick remarked.

"Seems like it," Cat agreed.

"He'll have a shit fit when he catches her act."

"Why?"

"She's tough."

"Like you?"

"I'm a pussycat."

"Sure."

"Hey—y'know what we should do?"

"Tell me," she said dryly. "I can't wait."

"Organize some kinda party."

"What *kind* of a party? There's only the four of us."

"I know people here. *C'mon,* blondie," he said persuasively. "We gotta throw them a wedding party."

Cat looked at him fondly. "You really are a total nutter."

He met her gaze with one of his own. "An' you love it, doncha?"

"Guess I must," she said, unable to keep the smile off her face.

And she realized as she said those words that she was becoming far too attached to him. While they were making the movie she'd been able to keep her distance; now it was a whole different vibe, and it was a dangerous one.

She had no desire to get hurt again, not after Jump.

Nick was nothing more than a diversion for a fun couple of days, and if she took it more seriously than that, then she had only herself to blame.

"You've been asleep practically the whole flight," Pete said, as Shelby stirred and opened her eyes. "We land in less than an hour."

"Sorry," she said, quite flustered. "Was I leaning all over you?"

"Don't worry about it," he said as he attempted to get some feeling back in his arm.

"Should we call the hospital?" she asked.

"No, it's better to wait until we get there. There's nothing you can do from the plane. You'll go straight to the hospital from the airport."

"I feel so helpless," she said, drinking from a bottle of water.

"I know the feeling."

"It's not as if I haven't tried so many times

to help Linc," she said, her eyes tinged with fatigue and worry. "I *begged* him to have therapy or get into rehab. He did it a couple of times for about five minutes, and that was it."

"Nobody ever said Linc was easy. He's a stubborn sonofabitch."

"You know about his childhood?"

"He talked about it a few times."

"It's the reason I put up with so much of his crap, because I *know* how difficult it is for him to get over what happened."

"I'm sure you helped him a lot."

"I've always tried to be there for him, Pete, but there comes a time when it's enough. Unfortunately I reached that point." She paused for a moment. "Oh, God, I *never* imagined something like this would happen."

"Shelby," Pete said gently, "you have to realize that Linc has moved on. He hasn't been calling you and begging you to come back, has he? He's got himself a new girl-friend."

"I know," she answered sadly. "But when I tell him about the baby, things can change. The last four years *I've* been the one who's protected him, Pete. He *needs* me."

"Is that what you want for the rest of your life? To be his guard? Watching everything he does, spying on him, seeing that he doesn't take a drink or does a drug? Is that how you intend to live? *Especially* after you have the baby."

"All I want is for him to get over this. Then I'll see."

"Can I get you anything? A real drink? Something to eat?"

"No," she said, shaking her head. "I want you to know that I'm happy you're with me, Pete."

"What was it they said in that old movie— just whistle and I'll be there."

"Thanks. It means a lot."

"Don't move or I'll blow your fucking brains out," Matt said. He'd heard those exact words on a cable TV show, and they seemed totally appropriate.

Very slowly and carefully, Tony was trying to get himself into a sitting position.

Maria, aware of what was going on, began whimpering softly. The other girl still slept.

Matt felt a surge of adrenaline. He had his rival exactly where he wanted him, and nothing and no one could stop him from blowing Tony Alvarez to kingdom come.

He had the power, and he was about to use it.

As he stared at his antagonist, he realized there were two girls in the bed. Two witnesses.

He hadn't thought about witnesses. Matt Seel was not a killer. He was an assassin of one person and one person only.

What if these girls recognized him? What if they identified him?

No. Impossible. It was dark. He had on his wool ski mask and cap. His face was totally hidden. One shot and he'd be out of there.

As these thoughts flew through his mind, he tightened his grip on his gun.

Everything was happening in slow motion for both men.

Tony's mind was alive with ideas of how to stop this crazy sonofabitch. He had his own gun under the pillow; his plan was to reach it and blow this cocksucker away. Unfortunately the girls were in his way.

Now the blonde woke up and began whimpering too. He wished they'd both shut the fuck up. Had to concentrate. Had to make this go away.

"Go in the bathroom," Matt commanded, jerking his gun at the two girls. "And stay in there. If you use the phone I'll kill you."

Another surge of power raced through his body. This being-in-charge shit was really something.

The girls didn't need asking twice; they jumped off the bed, making a wild dash for the bathroom.

It was exactly the opportunity Tony needed. As the girls moved, so did he, reaching for his MAC 10 automatic he kept under the pillow.

Matt caught the movement and fired his Glock.

He was too late to stop Tony from spraying a fusillade of bullets.

Both men were hit.

One of them fatally.

By the time Lola arrived home she had it all worked out. She would summon Big Jay to come upstairs and pack up Matt's things. Then she'd call Tony and tell him that they had to have an immediate get-together, where they'd discuss her marriage idea. She was sure he'd go for it. Why wouldn't he? They'd been engaged once before. This time no engagement; instead, a quickie marriage the moment her divorce was final.

After that was settled she'd start concentrating on her career. She'd call Faye and instruct her to put out an announcement that she was divorcing Matt Seel. If Faye didn't like it . . . too damn bad.

Big Jay greeted her at the gate with an expression of deep frustration. "Miss Lola, how many times I gotta ask you not to go places without me?" he complained. "You never know who's waitin' to follow you. There's always photographers hidin'. It ain't safe for you to go runnin' around on your own."

"Sorry," she answered casually. "I had to pop over to my mama's. You were asleep."

"Not good enough, Miss Lola," Big Jay scolded. "In future you gotta wake me."

"Yes, Jay," she answered obediently.

After dealing with Big Jay, she drove up the long driveway to her house.

There was no sign of her Bentley in the motor court. Damn! She loved that car.

She went straight to her dressing room,

changed into her workout clothes, then headed for the gym in the pool house. Usually she worked out with a trainer, but since getting back from New York she hadn't bothered to reinstate her workout time. Besides, sometimes she liked taking advantage of the solitude.

The gym was large and airy, filled with the latest equipment. It overlooked the swimming pool, a wall of bougainvillea, and a cluster of palm trees. Most of the exercise equipment she'd gotten for free, because the manufacturers all wanted Lola Sanchez working out on their machines.

She clicked on the TV and jumped on the Life Cycle. Half an hour of cardio, forty-five minutes on the Life Cycle. Gotta get rid of those pancakes!

She felt pretty good, considering; making decisions always filled her with energy.

After a while she buzzed Jenny on the intercom. "Arrange for a trip to Disneyland for me and all my nieces and nephews on Saturday. Alert Big Jay."

"Done," Jenny said.

Next she reached for her cell and called Isabelle. "I've decided to take all the kids to Disneyland on Saturday," she said. "Can you stop by the Gap and get them new outfits? My treat."

"Can *I* come?" Isabelle asked.

"I was thinking just me and the kids."

"You'll never manage all of them."

"Big Jay will be with me. I'll have him organize another couple of guards."

"But I'd *like* to come," Isabelle insisted, never one to miss out on a public outing with her attention-getting sister. Isabelle's dream was to have her picture in *People* alongside Lola.

Lola knew better than to argue; when it came to Isabelle it simply wasn't worth it. "Whatever you want," she said, resigning herself to her sister's company. "Have you spoken to Selma today?"

"I called the hospital," Isabelle replied. "She feels much better and can't wait to see you."

"I'll go over there later," she said, returning her attention to the TV.

The handsome Mr. Lauer was interviewing a politician on the *Today* show. He'd interviewed Lola a few times and she liked him a lot. He had an easygoing style, although he never let an interview subject get away with anything, which was quite re-freshing.

Humming softly to herself, she watched him do his thing until a breaking news story interrupted the program.

A dark-haired newscaster appeared on the TV screen, her face serious.

"Reports are coming through of a shoot-ing at the Hollywood Hills home of award-winning film director Tony Alvarez. Mr. Al-varez, onetime fiancé of movie star Lola Sanchez, was shot to death this morning in an apparent home invasion. We have no more details at this present time. We'll keep you updated."

Lola almost fell off the Life Cycle and im-mediately began running back toward the house.

"No!" she screamed. *"Nooo!* This can't be true!"

Coming up the driveway was her Bentley, Matt behind the wheel. The car was weav-ing from side to side; it looked as if he'd smashed the front in.

Crazed with shock and grief combined with fury, she yanked open the driver's door.

Matt fell out, drenched in blood.

She stared at him in horror. "Oh my *God!*"

she screamed. "You *bastard*—you killed Tony, didn't you? OH MY GOD!"

Word had spread that Shelby Cheney was on her way to New York. There were dozens of photographers and TV crews at the airport awaiting her arrival.

Shelby was silent as airline officials met her at the plane and shepherded her through the media crush. She'd already arranged with Pete that they should not be seen together, and he'd promised to call her at the hospital. The last thing she needed was a photo of her with Pete. It would infuriate Linc even more.

She was escorted out to a waiting limousine, where Linc's publicist, Norm, waited for her. Norm got in the limo with her.

"How is he?" she asked, full of concern.

Norm shook his head, his expression gloomy. "It doesn't look good, Shelby."

Silently she slumped in the seat, covering her eyes with her hands. "What happened, Norm? You have to tell me."

"The situation was out of control. Linc was hanging out with that model, Allegra. She was obviously a very negative influence."

"Where was he when he collapsed?"

"At an after-hours club. They called an ambulance, but by the time they got him to the hospital, he was in bad shape."

"And now?" she asked, holding back tears. "How's he doing now?"

"I told you, not good. His sister's at the hospital waiting for you."

"Will I be able to see him?"

"It's up to the doctors," Norm said, unable to look her in the eye. "I'm trying to control the press. They've turned it into a feeding frenzy. You can imagine."

"I'm sure," she said quietly.

"The driver's going to take us around to a back entrance. We'll sneak you in that way."

She nodded silently as the limo sped into the city.

"When we get out of the car, put on your sunglasses and move fast," Norm instructed. "I'm sorry we have to do it this way. I'm sure there'll be paparazzi staked out the back too, so be prepared. They know you're coming."

The price of fame. No more privacy. Everything was chronicled, it didn't matter how painful.

"We're here," Norm said, as the limo

finally pulled to a stop. "Head down and let's go."

She put on her dark glasses, pulled her jacket tightly around her, got out of the limo, and made a run for it, with Norm holding on to her arm.

Two cops were waiting to assist her as a pack of journalists and photographers surged forward, yelling for a comment.

"What do you have to say, Shelby?"

"Are you and Linc separated?"

"What do you think of Allegra?"

"Are you and Linc getting a divorce?"

She made it into the hospital with the help of Norm and the two burly cops. "You okay, ma'am?" one of them asked.

"Yes, thank you," she managed, although she wasn't okay at all. She felt numb and sick to her stomach.

"He's in intensive care," Norm said, hustling her into an elevator. "Connie is waiting in a private room."

Connie was sitting on a couch with her girlfriend, Suki. The two of them jumped up when Shelby entered.

Connie rushed over to her. "I'm sorry, Shelby," she muttered, her eyes red-rimmed and swollen. "I'm *so* sorry. I *know* how much you loved him."

"What . . . happened?" she asked, her throat dry with fear.

"It was peaceful. It really was."

"What was peaceful?" she heard herself scream.

"Linc passed away ten minutes ago."

Shelby felt her world spinning out of control.

And that's the last thing she remembered as she slumped to the floor in a deep faint.

CHAPTER
47

There were two funerals taking place in Hollywood on the same day—both big events, causing people to wonder which one they should attend.

Some people decided they should go to both, making it to the service of the first one and the reception of the second.

One funeral was a very serious affair.

The second was a celebration of a flamboyant life, and therefore, after the Catholic church ceremony, there was a huge party— a request plucked from the deceased's will.

Lola had buried her husband the day before. Matt Seel. Son of Pat and Martin Seel. Husband of Lola Sanchez. Murderer of Lola's lover.

She'd attended the discreet service reluctantly, because everyone had said that if she didn't show up it would reflect negatively on her.

Like she cared. Matt had murdered the love of her life, and she was empty inside. There would *never* be another man like Tony Alvarez. Never.

Her mother and sister had flanked her, making sure the photographers could not get too close. And there were many photographers jostling for position.

Matt's parents ignored her. They hated her. The feeling was mutual; she knew they'd never approved of her. Once Matt had confided that they'd told him he'd married the maid. Matt had thought it hysterically funny. She'd been mortified. Maybe it was then that she'd started to cool toward him.

After the service there was a reception at the Seels' house. Lola chose not to go. Instead she had Big Jay drive her home, locked herself in her bedroom, and sobbed for the man she'd loved, so brutally shot in the heart.

The last few days were surreal. First the news about Tony. Then Matt collapsing in her driveway with several deadly bullet wounds—he'd died on the way to the hospital. And finally Linc Blackwood passing away of a drug overdose in New York.

Christ! She'd known all three men, in the biblical sense. Had she bestowed some kind of horrible curse on them?

Her family rallied. Claudine even moved into her house to be with her for a while.

"It's not necessary, Mama," she'd said. But Claudine had insisted.

Now, as she attended Tony's funeral, her entire family accompanied her—including Selma, out of the hospital and making brilliant progress.

Tony had a lot of friends in the Latin community. Some of them nodded in her direction, others ignored her.

The press had been brutal—making it seem as if everything was her fault, *including* Linc's unfortunate demise. SHE DROVE HER COSTAR TO DRUGS, screamed one tabloid. FEMME FATALE, screamed another. HUSBAND

AND LOVER SHOT TO DEATH IN JEALOUS FEUD OVER SEXY LOLA, screamed a third.

She couldn't win. She'd lost the love of her life, and the newspapers were blaming her. How unfair was that?

Tony's widowed mother flew in from Cuba, where she'd settled with a new husband. The woman ignored Lola completely.

What is it with me and mothers? Lola thought. *I haven't done anything to them. All I did for Tony was to love him more than anyone.*

Maria was front and center. A heartbroken fiancée, a sweet little innocent caught in a horrible Hollywood scandal.

Lola considered it so unfair that in death Tony did not belong to her; he belonged to this young girl he'd barely known. A girl Lola was sure he'd not loved.

Two funerals in two days, and Faye was urging her to go to the third. "If you *don't* go to Linc Blackwood's funeral," Faye assured her, "the tabloids will pull you to pieces."

"They already have," Lola said quietly. "It's enough, Faye. I'm going home."

After their boat trip on Lake Mead and an outrageous wedding celebration party for

Amy and Jonas pulled together by Nick, they got in his Maserati and set off for L.A.

"This is the best time I've ever had with a girl," Nick said as he raced his car down the highway on their way back to L.A.

"Oh," Cat said jokingly. "So you've had better times with the boys, huh?"

He threw her a quizzical look. "Y'know, Cat, you're very defensive. That's usually *my* deal."

"Didn't mean to be," she said. "I gotta admit I had a great time, too."

"Glad to hear it."

"Here," she said, fishing in her purse. "I bought the new Norah Jones CD for our drive home."

"That's girls' music."

"No, it's not, it's *sexy* music. She's fantastic."

"*I'll* listen to Norah Jones if *you'll* listen to Fifty Cent."

"I can see I'm going to have to educate your music tastes," she said. "Aren't you into old music?"

"Like what?"

"Like classic soul, stuff like that."

"Who has time?"

"I suppose you don't watch old movies either?"

"Like I said, who has time?"

"Did you ever see *The Godfather* one and two? *Pulp Fiction? Scarface?*"

"*Godfather* one."

"Man! We have serious work to do."

"*How* old are you?" he asked, shooting her a look.

"You know how old I am. Nineteen. Why are you asking?"

" 'Cause every once in a while you sound like you're forty."

"I'm wise way beyond my years," she said, her face quite serious. "Besides, after I dropped out of school, movies and music became my passion."

"When's your birthday?"

"Next month."

"Does that mean you'll be legal?"

"Legal for *what?*"

"I dunno. You're so young."

"I bet you've had younger," she remarked, popping the Norah Jones CD into the player.

"Ah," he said with an evil laugh. "Already she knows me so well."

"So," she said casually, "when we get

back to L.A., you can drop me at my apartment, and I'll see you when I see you."

"It's like that, huh?"

"C'mon, Nick, we both know what this weekend was—casual fucking, right?"

"Wrong."

"Wrong?"

"Dunno about you, but I was thinkin' I'd like to make it more."

"Please!" she joked. "I'm a married woman."

"You're about to be a divorced woman," he reminded her. "And when you finish editing our movie, you're joining me on location."

"So I can watch you casually fucking your way through the entire female cast and crew?" she said lightly.

"Hey—I'm gonna behave myself. Whaddaya think of that?"

"I don't understand."

"Yes, you do," he said briskly. "You're a smart girl."

"Let me make sure I'm understanding you. Are you saying you want us to be exclusive?"

"You got it. Hey—if I can do it, you can too."

"But I thought—"

"I don't give a crap *what* you thought," he said, reaching over to take her hand. "We've got something special going, so let's not screw it up, huh?"

"Well . . . ," she said unsurely.

He glanced over at her. "Well?" he said, swerving the car over to the side of the road.

"Well . . . uh . . . okay."

They exchanged smiles. Things were looking very promising.

E P I L O G U E

"Y'know, I've been thinking," Nick said, sitting around in the kitchen of Cat's apartment in L.A.

"Oh, here we go again," she said. "Back five minutes from location, and already he's thinking."

"No, seriously, blondie, I've been thinking I should buy a house."

"Why?"

"'Cause we've been together a year and it's time we moved in together."

"We're practically living together as it is,"

she pointed out. "You always stay here when you're in L.A."

"I know, but it's *your* apartment."

"Okay, so *I'll* buy a house."

"No," he said. "*I* will."

"No," she corrected. "*I* will."

"Hey listen, just 'cause *Caught* is a big hit, there's no need to get carried away."

"I'll tell you what," she said agreeably. "We'll split the cost and buy a house together. Then if anyone gets bored, we can buy the other one out. How about *that?*"

"My girlfriend—such a practical little soul."

"Anyway, I've got a surprise."

"You're pregnant?"

"*Pul-eeze!* You'll have to wait ten years for that piece of news. Women shouldn't have kids until they're thirty!"

"I didn't need a fuckin' *speech.* What's your surprise?"

"I finished my new script, and Merrill is *desperate* to finance it. He's mumbling about casting Colin Farrell, only I told him it's you or nobody."

"Gee, I dunno if I can fit it into my busy schedule."

"You want to read it?"

"Of course I wanna read it. I gave you the inspiration, didn't I? The character's *me.*"

"Maybe . . . ," she said, grinning.

"Maybe my ass."

"You're impossible, Nick. You think *everything's* about you."

"So do you," he countered.

Cat had to admit that being with Nick made her extraordinarily happy. There was something about him that turned her on in every way. He was never predictable, never mean to her either, and he was always supportive.

"We'd better get ready," she said. "We've got a wedding to go to."

"Who am I gonna know?"

"You'll know everybody, Mr. Movie Star."

"I was thinking," he said.

"Not again," she groaned.

"This time I was thinking we should take a vacation before you get all caught up in your next project."

"Where did you have in mind?"

"Somewhere exotic—Bali, Tahiti." A long beat. "And oh yeah—maybe we should get married first."

"Maybe we *shouldn't,*" she said nervously. "I've done it once, that was enough."

"I've *never* done it, so perhaps I want to."

"Give it another year and we'll see."

"Man! You are the most difficult woman I've ever met."

"That's why you like me, Nick."

"That's why, is it?" he said, giving her one of his quizzical looks.

"Yes."

"If you say so."

"I do."

"Okay, blondie, whatever you say."

"Why are you agreeing with me?" she asked suspiciously.

" 'Cause I'm gonna drug you, and marry you while you're sleepin'."

"Cool. It'll make a great future plot."

"C'mere," he said affectionately. "It's time you discovered who's *really* the boss."

She fell into his arms and happily stayed there.

Nick was the perfect man for her.

How lucky was *that?*

The reviews of New York State of Mind were bad. Not as bad as Lola had expected, but still, they were pretty grim. And so they should be; it was not a very good movie.

After a period of mourning she'd flown to

New York for the press junket, but her heart wasn't in it.

On the plane to New York, she'd sat next to film director Russell Savage. Although he wasn't her usual type, she'd found him to be an extremely interesting man. They got to talking, and she'd asked him how he'd gotten such an amazing performance out of Shelby Cheney in *Rapture,* a performance so excellent that Shelby had been nominated for an Oscar. She hadn't won, but getting nominated was reward enough.

"Shelby needed a director she could trust," Russell had explained.

"That's exactly what *I* need," Lola had said. "I've got it in me, you know. I can do other things than be the girl with the great body and the sexy smile."

"You're probably underrated," Russell had commented. "Most beautiful actresses are."

"Maybe we should work together," she'd suggested.

"I'll keep you in mind," he'd said.

A week later she'd called him. She'd felt bold doing so, because she had not been out with anyone since the demise of Tony. Russell seemed different. He was mature, established, not the type of man she'd ever imagined being with. However, she'd had a strong feeling that if she spent enough time with him, he would surely see her potential.

He saw more than her potential—he saw a strong, spirited woman with plenty of ambition and quite a bit of talent. Russell Savage fell in love.

Soon they were an item, and when Lola introduced Russell to her family, they were impressed—especially Claudine, who sat her daughter down and told her that she should not let this one go.

Lola realized Mama was right. Russell Savage was a keeper, and not just because he could advance her career. He was a kind and caring and interesting man who adored her. That was enough. For now.

Today they were attending a wedding.

For the first time since Tony's death, Lola did not wear black.

Four-month-old Linc Blackwood Jr. was sitting on his grandma's lap. A gorgeous baby, he resembled his late father, except that he had his mother's brown eyes and full lips. It was a lethal combination.

"There's a good boy," Martha Cheney

crooned, bouncing him on her knee as they sat in the front row of a line of chairs arranged for guests at the outdoor wedding that was about to take place.

Inside the house, Shelby, clad in a white satin Vera Wang wedding gown, nervously hugged her father.

"Are you *sure* I'm doing the right thing?" she asked for the tenth time.

"It's not *me* who should answer that," George Cheney said. "It's you."

"I *am* doing the right thing," she said. "I know I am. Pete loves me, *and* he loves the baby. And y'know, Dad, somewhere up there Linc is watching us. He's probably livid that I'm marrying Pete, but life goes on, doesn't it? And he'll always have a place in my heart."

"Yes, sweetheart, life goes on."

"You called me sweetheart, Daddy. Linc was the only man who used to call me that. He *is* watching us today. He's sending me a message via you. So now I feel that I have his blessing."

"You *look* beautiful."

"Thanks, Dad," she said, taking a deep breath. "It's almost time. I see the wedding planner approaching us with that look on her face."

"*I'm* ready," George said.

"Did I tell you that you look very handsome?"

"Not as handsome as your bridegroom."

"Oh, you've seen him?"

"*I'm* allowed to, *you're* not."

"Dad!"

The ceremony was taking place at her new house, overlooking the ocean in Pacific Palisades. After Linc's death she'd sold their Beverly Hills home and moved. There were too many memories to deal with; she'd needed to move on.

This dreamy white house was a new beginning. A new beginning for her *and* Pete.

Pete had been very discreet. He'd left her alone for several months, told her he was there if she needed him, until eventually they'd gotten together, and from the moment they went out to dinner, three months after Linc's death, they'd never been apart.

He was there when she had the baby. He was there when she brought the baby home. They had not actually moved in together, but when he asked her to marry him, she knew without a doubt that it was the right thing to do.

As Shelby made her way down the flower-strewn aisle, there was a gasp of admiration from the guests. She looked a vision. So beautiful and so serene.

Pete could not believe how lucky he was to have her. They'd gone through a lot, but it was worth it.

They were married at sunset, with helicopters hovering overhead and paparazzi climbing trees outside.

"I love you, Pete," she whispered.

"You too, baby," he answered.

"And we'll never be apart," she promised.

"Never. This is it, Shelby. You're mine for keeps."

"And that's exactly the way I want it to be," she said softly. "You and me, forever together."

It was a Hollywood wedding, but Shelby knew for sure it was never going to be a Hollywood divorce.